W9-BTS-215

MONROE COUNTY GEORGE DOLEZAL BRANCH LIBRARY
3251 OVERSEAS HIGHWAY
MARATHON, FLORIDA 33050

514

MARA

# JAMES W. HALL

# HARD·AGROUND

**A Gift to the
MARATHON LIBRARY
From the Friends of the
Marathon Library**

MONROE COUNTY GEORGE DOLEZAL BRANCH LIBRARY
3251 OVERSEAS HIGHWAY
MARATHON, FLORIDA 33050

A Gift to the
MARATHON LIBRARY
From the Friends of the
Marathon Library

# JAMES W. HALL

# HARD·AGROUND

**Delacorte**
**Press**

MONROE COUNTY PUBLIC LIBRARY

Published by
Delacorte Press
Bantam Doubleday Dell Publishing Group, Inc.
666 Fifth Avenue
New York, New York 10103

Copyright © 1993 by James W. Hall

All rights reserved. No part of this book may be reproduced or transmitted in any form or by any means, electronic or mechanical, including photocopying, recording, or by any information storage and retrieval system, without the written permission of the Publisher, except where permitted by law.

The trademark Delacorte Press® is registered in the U.S. Patent and Trademark Office.

Library of Congress Cataloging in Publication Data

Hall, James W.,        1947–
    Hard aground / James W. Hall.
        p.      cm.
    ISBN 0-385-30797-7
    I. Title.
    PS3558.A369H37    1993
    813′.54—dc20                                        92-21638
                                                             CIP

Book design by Robin Arzt

Manufactured in the United States of America

Published simultaneously in Canada

January 1993

10   9   8   7   6   5   4   3   2   1

BVG

To Evelyn, the love of my life

And for Nat and Judith, valued friends,
who make me better than I am.

And a special thanks to Bob Carr and
Jan Fleischer-Weiner and Les Standiford
for their invaluable help.

Archaeology is a total study. It involves analyzing everything that remains from the past, with the aim of reconstructing that past as fully as possible. Although some people regard archaeology as synonymous with excavation, it is far more than that. Excavation is only one of many of its processes.

—Jane McIntosh, *The Practical Archaeologist*

# CHAPTER 1

"**F**OUR HUNDRED MILLION DOLLARS IN GOLD AND SILVER, coins and bars, emeralds, rubies, jewelry of every kind. Sunk somewhere within a few miles of the coastline of Miami, probably not more than an hour by boat from where we are standing today."

A greedy murmur passed through the audience.

"Bullshit," Hollings said, normal voice.

A few people in the row in front of him glanced his way. An old lady sitting beside him got up, changed seats.

Hollings was in the back row in the conference room of the Holiday Inn at Seventy-ninth and I-95. For the last twenty minutes he'd been scanning the audience, that bunch of retired morons, thinking to himself, shit, if he threw a grenade out into that bunch, say an M26, it sprayed its steel jacket for ten yards around, what with a 50 percent hit probability, Hollings figured he could take down sixty, maybe seventy, of these buttfaces at once. The rest of them, though, they'd probably just stay right where they were. That's how hypnotized they all were by Max Hunter.

Max Hunter, world famous treasure salvor. That's what it said on the poster Hollings had seen. How to discover and mine gold, how to locate Spanish ships hidden for centuries, how to read seventeenth-century maps and stake your claim to thousands, even millions, in jewels and booty that's just lying there waiting, with your name on it. All that hand-lettered in red, the poster taped to the barbershop window on Collins Avenue where Hollings got his flattop trimmed every Saturday.

Hollings shifted in his seat, glancing over at the exit, wondering why the hell he was there. He should be saving his money for his September rent payment, but no, he'd stood in line and paid his sixty-nine ninety-five, tax deductible, and now he was stuck. Wasting his Saturday afternoon watching that tall blond guy in an Italian suit and blond walrus mustache strut back and forth in front of the audience, two hundred and twenty-eight losers. Hollings had amused himself for a while by counting them all, and multiplying times sixty-nine ninety-five. Close to sixteen grand the buttwipe was walking away with.

Hollings tapped his foot, certain this whole thing was a royal con. And, as it was turning out, not even a very entertaining one. Hunter spent most of his time talking about some library in Spain where all the ship registries were stored. He'd been over there to this library, dug around till he found the right book; he'd got the list, all the things on the *Carmelita,* the ship he'd been talking about. Then Max Hunter went to some other library in England, looked up the newspaper for 1633, checked the weather reports for that month, saw what the other ships sailing about that time had to say about where the *Carmelita* went down, and when he'd done all that, he'd been able to start drawing a pretty accurate map about where this goddamn ship was. He'd been using this map for almost five years. He'd found this and that, a cannonball, some coins from the ship, but not the mother lode. So, he told them, anybody in that audience today could do the same thing, follow the clues, draw up their own map. Or better yet, for five hundred bucks, they could buy a copy of his, with all the places crossed off where he'd looked already.

Hollings listened, scanning the audience, trying to pick the exact spot for grenade number two. 'Cause he'd decided already, his first one was going up onto the stage, wipe out the walrus mustache, the Italian suit.

He waited around another twenty minutes till the question-

and-answer period, then he stood up. Max Hunter took a sip of water and nodded back at Hollings.

"What I want to know is," Hollings said, "if you're for real, whatta you want five hundred of my dollars for, when you could just go haul up all those doubloons and emeralds yourself?"

Everybody in the room rustled around in their chairs, turning to see who this was giving their hero some shit. And Max Hunter nodded, and smiled halfway, and said he was glad Hollings asked that particular question, in fact he'd been expecting somebody to ask it. Then he proceeded to go off into ten minutes of total bullshit about how he didn't mind having a little competition out there on the high seas, and about how competition actually improved mankind, made us all sharper, work harder. Not to mention the fact, Max Hunter said, smiling right at Hollings, he'd slipped a goddamn disc last year hauling up so many gold bars, now he needed to engage in lighter work. Everybody in the room chuckled, then craned around to shoot Hollings ugly, see-there looks.

After the question-and-answer, Hollings walked up to the stage to check out the exhibit. Some of the loot from wrecks Max Hunter had salvaged. A couple of armed guards stood on either end of the glass cases watching the people pass by. There were necklaces and rings, gold cups and little things you couldn't tell what they were, all in gold with sapphires and emeralds sprinkled over them. There were photographs of Max Hunter and his crew out on their barges and swimming underwater, one with Max straddling the barrel of a cannon that was pointing up out of the sand.

Near the end of the line they'd set up a little exhibit of how the blower worked, the thing Hunter had invented that fit on the back end of one of his ships. It shot a ton of air down at the sand and cleared the ocean floor so they could see what was hidden. Hollings had seen all this shit before. In magazines, and a book he read once.

The only thing of any interest in the exhibit was the small gold brick. It was sitting there behind a thick plastic wall, rigged up so you could stick your hand through a slot and grip the gold bar and pick it up a few inches to see how much it weighed. Hollings put his hand in there, stroked it, then lifted the thing. Set it down and lifted it again. Touching that gold did something funny to his heart, jacking it up a notch. Felt so good, he might've stayed there the rest of the afternoon if the people behind him hadn't started grumbling.

He was out in the parking lot opening his Datsun B-210, kicking himself in the butt for wasting that kind of money, when a big guy with lots of shiny black hair tapped him on the shoulder and put out his hand for a shake.

"Name's Alvarez," he said.

Hollings shook the guy's hand. It was cold and hard like squeezing that gold brick.

"What you said in there, it made a lot of sense."

Hollings said, "A goddamn waste of money is what that was. You, me, all those other assbrains in there, throwing our dollars at Max Hunter. And he didn't tell us shit."

Glancing around, Alvarez said quietly, "You want to go to a bar I know about, have a couple of cold ones, wash all this phony baloney out of our mouths?"

"Why would I want to do that?"

"I may have a proposition for you."

"Yeah?"

"I'm looking for somebody I can trust to help with some of the details on a project I'm working on."

Hollings said nothing, looking down into his Datsun, feeling the heat pouring out of it, stinking of mildew from the rotting carpet. Jesus Christ, what the hell was he doing out there in the hundred-degree sun talking to some guy stupid enough to pay sixty-nine ninety-five for some con-job lecture?

Alvarez said, "Last year or two, I been devoting my time, pretty much twenty-four hours a day, to tracking down this ship, this *Carmelita*."

"The four-hundred-million-dollar one?"

"That's right. At least four hundred mil."

"And?"

Alvarez said, "You got any military experience?"

Hollings leaned against his car and said, well, he had two tours in Nam. Did that count?

"I thought so," Alvarez said. "I looked at you, I thought to myself, yeah, there's a vet. There's a guy I could count on."

"You can stop horse-shitting me anytime now."

"I know where it is," Alvarez said. "That ship, I know where it went down, more or less."

"More or less?" Hollings said. "Which is it?"

Alvarez gave him a long, measuring look, then said, "Pretty fucking less."

Hollings could feel his heart begin to tread water in there.

"So you interested?" Alvarez said. "Wanna help?"

Help? Are you kidding, man? Help? He didn't say it out loud, but just having Alvarez come up to him, single him out, he was ready to follow the guy anywhere. It'd been that long since anybody had thought Hollings was special.

But what he said was, "So you know where this thing is? And you're going to split it with me? Just like that? Walk up to a guy in the parking lot and split it with him."

Alvarez said, "The absolute truth is, I don't know yet exactly where it is. But I know the guy that *does* know."

"Who, Max Hunter?"

"Naw. A guy I been following. He knows where it's sunk."

"You're kidding me."

Alvarez peered at Hollings for a couple of seconds and said, "I don't kid."

Hollings looked at him a little more carefully, catching an ugly glimmer in his eyes.

"So that's what you want me for," Hollings said, "to reason with this guy?"

Alvarez smiled. "That interest you? You have any talents in that direction? Reasoning with total knuckleheads. Inflicting measured amounts of pain."

Hollings looked off at the side door of the Holiday Inn. There was Max Hunter and a blond woman and one of the bodyguards.

All of them smiling and yakking away, probably deciding on ways to spend all the money they'd just ripped off.

Hollings said, "What's to keep you from reasoning with this guy yourself? You look big enough."

"I gotta keep my head down. I'm a known quantity around this town. I'm easily recognized."

"Well, that's one problem I don't have."

"There's considerable profit involved here," Alvarez said. Letting it hang there.

"I'd like to make a profit, yeah, sure," said Hollings. "But I'm at the time of life, when I do something, it's 'cause I want to, money or not. Money's only a minor part of the picture for me."

Hollings gave Alvarez a hard look, like There, that's who I am, take it or fucking leave it.

Alvarez said, "Whatta you, a thinker, some kind of philosopher or something?"

"I'm just saying, money isn't all that important to me. I'm interested in other things. Getting higher satisfactions."

Alvarez smiled, patted Hollings on the shoulder, kind of turned him around a little so they were facing the same direction.

"Well, shit, then you're like me," he said. "Been a little guy all your life, doing somebody else's work. Got no pull. You're sick of that shit now. And you're waiting around for the right thing to come along. So maybe you can pledge yourself to a greater purpose."

Hollings had heard that when jet pilots got up into the stratosphere or whatever the hell it was called, they couldn't breathe anymore, had to keep their air masks on or they'd die. You could get up so high there was no way to bail out. That's exactly how Hollings felt at that moment, hearing Alvarez say that thing about a higher purpose. Feeling like he was up there, up above the oxygen. Feeling all of a sudden woozy, his eyes fuzzing over. This guy, this complete stranger, standing out in a Holiday Inn parking lot, saying what were Hollings's own personal magic words, the words that took all the oxygen out of his air. He'd been looking for something, had been for a long time, a higher goddamn purpose.

"I'll think about it" is what Hollings said. "I'll give your proposition some thought."

Alvarez stared at him.

"Well, maybe I got the wrong guy here. Maybe I've made an error in human judgment with you."

Alvarez started to turn away, but Hollings quickly put a hand on the guy's big shoulder.

"That bar you mentioned," Hollings said. "It around here?"

Alvarez turned back around. The guy tilted his head to one side, twisted his mouth like he might've caught a whiff of something didn't agree with him.

"A couple of beers would be good," Hollings said. "We talk a little more, then we could have a toast to our new partnership."

"I didn't use that word, did I? Partnership?"

"That was my word."

"Yeah, well," Alvarez said, "I'm not exactly looking for partners. More like soldiers. A couple of people I can trust. A couple of people with special skills."

"Mercenaries," Hollings said. "Soldiers of fortune."

"Yeah, I like that. That's good. Soldiers of fortune."

He moved a half step closer to Hollings, lowered his voice.

"So tell me," he said. "You kill anybody in Nam? Take any scalps over there?"

Hollings took out his car keys, jingled them, looking at all the other guys getting in their cars, pulling out of the Holiday Inn parking lot. Like the end of the shift at the loser factory.

Hollings said, "You see how full that room was, all those morons, rows and rows of them turning out to hear Max Hunter?"

Alvarez waited, said nothing.

Hollings said, "I notched more gooks than all of that."

"You're shitting me now," Alvarez said. "Hundreds? You killed hundreds of gooks?"

"I killed so many," said Hollings, "they had to send me home early. I was to stay over there any longer, they'd run totally out of the little guys, have to call off the war."

Alvarez smiled with just his mouth. Clearly not believing Hollings, but not saying it out loud. Hollings guessed this guy had never been anything but top dog in his life. Pissed higher up on the tree than all the other dogs, got the pick of the bitches. Hell, that was all right with Hollings. He wasn't pit-bull material himself, but was comfortable enough being around tough guys. He could take orders fine and still keep his self-respect. Learned that in the military. Fact was, he kind of hated to admit it, he'd always been a follower of one kind or another, felt comfortable with that. Blending in, harmonizing, doing what he was told. Probably came from being the fifth of five boys.

Alvarez said, "You wouldn't happen to have anything against black people, would you? Like, are you racist or anything?"

Hollings said no, he wasn't racist. Not the least little bit, far as he knew.

"That's good," Alvarez said. "'Cause the person I got in mind, somebody you'd be working with, she's black."

"She?"

"Yeah, I'm supposed to meet her tomorrow, the next day. If I can convince her to come in, it'd be the two of you together."

"Me and a black woman. With you calling the shots."

"That's how it would go, yeah. I'm the general, you could be the colonel or whatever rank you want."

Hollings said. "So tell me, this guy who knows where the *Carmelita* is sunk, what's his name anyway?"

"Don't go getting ahead of things, man. We haven't even shook hands yet."

Hollings let a second or two go by, not wanting to seem too eager, pretending to deliberate on it. Then he put out his hand.

Alvarez cocked his head back a couple of inches and studied Hollings for a moment, making him wait now. Then very slowly, he reached out, put his hand in Hollings's, and squeezed the shit out of him.

"The guy in question," Alvarez said. "His name is Tyler. A real zero."

# CHAPTER 2

HAP TYLER WATCHED HER SLEEP ON THE TWIN BED IN the corner of the boathouse. As far as he could tell, Joyce Hardy always slept in that same position, flat on her back, hands at her side like she was about to be fired from a cannon. Her head stayed in the same dent in the pillow for eight hours, and she never disturbed the sheets. It'd scared Hap last week when he'd awakened next to her that first morning and she was lying in exactly the same position as when she fell asleep. Rigid as a mummy.

Joyce's clothes were arranged on the wooden chair beside the bed, jeans hung carefully over the back, the creases straight, her T-shirt positioned with the Nike logo showing, her panties folded into a rectangle on top of the T-shirt. Tennis shoes squared off beside the bed. The woman was seriously fastidious.

Making love with her was the same thing. Unfailingly efficient and methodical movements. Her orgasms: the same long gasp, same three shrieks, followed by a four-second shudder, a hard embrace. And then after an interval she would give him a peck, roll out of bed, go shower, wash her hair, brush her teeth.

But still, Joyce Hardy was smart and attractive, their conversation came easy, she laughed at his jokes, and he thought hers were funny, and it really didn't turn him off that she was such a neat freak. Hell, that might even be a good stabilizer against Hap's tendency toward total personal chaos.

She was just two years out of college and already one of three women partners in an advertising firm. He bet she was damn good at her job. Maybe someday he'd find out all about it, visit her office, meet her friends, her family. But first he had to tell her the truth about himself, see if there was any hope. He'd been wanting for a long time to make it to week two with a woman. Peel back a few more layers of intimacy, educate himself in the ways of the normal. Hap Tyler knew all about sex. What he wanted to know about now was the other thing.

All right, so Joyce Hardy didn't ignite the grand passion in him. Well, big deal. The truth was, Hap Tyler already had plenty enough fires raging inside. He could settle for something less than grand passion. Anyway, maybe grand passion was one of those things that came in week two or beyond. Something you had to work up to.

At sunrise this morning he'd been jerked awake by the insistent bleating of an osprey in the sea grape by shore. He'd eased out of bed, put on flip-flops, T-shirt, and baggy white shorts, his Miami Heat cap, and he'd tiptoed over to the far corner of the boathouse, the workshop area, and he'd plugged in the hot-knife and had begun to carve quietly on the fiberglass sailboard he'd started yesterday.

Hap Tyler had invented the electric hot-knife a couple of years before. It was shaped like a slingshot, a thick copper wire strung tight between its aluminum prongs. With two hundred and twenty volts running through the wire, the knife could slice through solid fiberglass laminate as if it were a slab of cheddar. Hap was using the knife to trim away a few inches of the sleek tail on the sailboard, giving it a blunt, squared-off look.

This was as close to a vocation as he had, customizing these blanks. So far, he'd made almost nineteen hundred dollars, selling his modified fiberglass boards to some of the hard-core windsurf guys who hung out on the Rickenbacker Causeway beach. Nineteen hundred bucks. A damn fortune for Hap.

"Hey, sailor."

Hap looked up. Joyce Hardy was sitting up on the edge of the bed. Naked, her stomach narrow and tight, breasts small and taut. A gymnast's build, though she wasn't an exercise person. It was one of those no-maintenance, good-gene bodies that she had no reason to be proud of, but was anyway.

She stood up, stretched out her arms to him, and he put the knife down and went over and kissed her. Held her for a moment afterward, and could feel himself thicken against her thigh. She hummed her readiness, shifted her leg so her quadriceps flexed against him. All it would take was his hand caressing her hip, or a nudge deeper into the embrace, any small acceptance on his part, and he knew she would pull away, quietly lie back on the bed, smile at him, and invite him down.

"Good morning," he said, and stepped back. "Sleep well?"

"Wonderful," she said. But her smile dwindled slightly.

He went back to the workbench and Joyce reached into the pocket of her T-shirt and took out a Salem. She smoothed the wrinkles back out of the shirt, realigned it on the chair, then picked up the Zippo lying on the bedside table and lit the cigarette. She took a long drag and let it out with a luxurious groan. She came over to take a look at what he was working on.

"I don't know, Hap."

"What don't you know?"

"I thought windsurfers liked pretty boards, snazzy, colorful. But yours are so boxy, so bland."

"Ugly and fast," Hap said. "That's what I do."

"You chop off their sexy curves. Doesn't that bother you?"

"Hey," he said. "This bland thing has an eighty percent hydrodynamic efficiency. When I'm done, it's going to be faster than any board out there. From light wind to gales, wave-jumping or slalom, it'll be out ahead of anybody."

"You should write ad copy, Hap."

He set the hot-knife down on the tool bench and opened the oak cabinet, took down his wood-burning set. He plugged the thing in a wall socket, waited a few seconds, then bent over the board and began digging deep gashes, from tail to nose, six parallel grooves two inches wide, an inch deep, that later he would fill with strips of

ceramic, carbon, and Kevlar. He bought them from a gun manufac-
turer up in Hialeah. Some guy who'd invented an all-plastic pistol
for beating airport X rays. Guns, next to sunburns, being Miami's
major export.

Those carbon-Kevlar strips would eliminate another six
pounds, a pound for each groove, and at the same time make the
board about twice as rigid. Bring its net weight down to twenty-eight
pounds without losing any flotation. It would have a volume of 210
liters. A weight-to-volume ratio of point sixteen. So a ten-year-old
kid could carry it, and a two-hundred pounder could get it up on
plane in a five-knot breeze.

Joyce came around the bench and stood behind him. She
lifted the hair that hung over his collar, breathed on his neck,
pressed her breasts against his back, and kissed the thin skin behind
his ear. The line Hap was drawing wavered.

"Well, it turns me on seeing my man so hard at work."

She waited for a moment for him to respond. But he held
himself back, and in a moment she let go of his hair, took another
drag on her Salem, exhaled it into his back, and began to wander
around the boathouse, checking out some of the other boards that
leaned against the walls.

She blew smoke up at the rafters, where it tangled in the
sprockets of light shining through the slits in the boathouse wall.
Little galaxies of dust spinning in each one.

She had two earrings in one ear, one in the other. Her blond
hair in a boyish cut with a part. Hap had worn his hair that way
twenty years ago, at eighteen. Joyce had green eyes. A small straight
nose. It was pretty face, with a flicker of irony in her eyes.

He'd met her at the Taurus bar, one of thirty trendy restaurant
bars within a mile of his house. Any night of the week, a thousand
stools filled and waiting. He could walk out at eight o'clock, walk
back in at eleven with a giggling female. You live *here,* on the water?
Sure do. All this land in the middle of Coconut Grove, it's yours?
Belongs to my brother and me, yeah. Wow! Ever hear of Commodore Randolph Tyler? he'd ask them. Well, yeah, I think so. How

about if I show you the boathouse he built a hundred years ago? It's down there, right on the shore.

Maybe it was the mischievous light in his eyes that attracted them. Or his eat-from-the-can approach to things. A certain air of reckless fun. He wasn't sure what made them break loose from their safe perches and swim home with him. But they did. Regularly.

"You ever heard of Radisson Acres?" he said to Joyce Hardy.

"Radisson Acres?"

Hap took a breath and gave her a long look. It wasn't too late. He could still go over to her, kiss those lips, one more time let his glands overrule his conscience.

"It's up close to Ocala," Hap said. "Rolling hills, lakes, a nine-hole golf course. Very nice place."

"I like Ocala," she said. "All the horses, white fences. It looks like Lexington."

"Yeah, well, you don't visit Radisson," he said. "You get sent there."

"Sent?"

"By court order," he said. "It was either there or Starke."

Joyce was just holding her Salem now, letting it burn.

"Starke, the prison?"

Hap nodded.

"I've had some lapses," he said. "Mental lapses."

"What're you saying?"

"I've gone nuts a few times. I mean, I could put it more politely, try to make it sound okay, but nuts is what most people call it."

"You're joking." She was trying to smile, but it was turning sour at the edges.

"Radisson wasn't all that bad, really. They had us play a lot of badminton, croquet. The staff spoke to us very politely. Wonderful enunciation, like we might not understand them if they slurred their words."

"Tell me you're kidding, Hap. Come on, stop."

"I'm saying, Joyce, I like you. I'd like for us to get to know each other better, so I thought I should tell you about it. Be straight with you."

"You're insane?"

"I wouldn't go that far. Just a little . . . I don't know, a little unpredictable. Like I got a screw loose. But just one, and just slightly loose."

"Unpredictable."

"I can be normal enough. And it's been a long while now since I was weird, but I thought I should tell you anyway."

"Weird how?"

"Just weird. I don't know how to describe it."

"Well, hell, everybody feels weird now and then. It's probably just a phase of some kind."

But he could tell she was trying to convince herself. And it wasn't working. Her eyes had begun to map the quickest route to the door. He considered for a second retracting it all, smiling at her, saying he was sorry, it was all a bad joke, slide back into bed, get to week number two that way.

"No, this is a different kind of weird," he said. "I might wake up in the night, or I could be walking around the grocery store, doing anything really, and there's a voice, it talks to me, tells me to do things. And I do them. I obey it. I think it's my grandfather's voice, the Commodore's. You might've read about me in the paper. I've made some headlines."

"No," she said. "Not that I recall."

She stubbed out her cigarette on the seashell she'd been using for an ashtray. She smiled painfully at him, with that funny squint she used when she didn't completely understand something. Craning forward, her eyes narrow like she was trying to peer through slits.

Hap looked away. The breeze was picking up, dust swirling faster in the wedges of light. He heard muffled thunder out to the west, a Miami August morning.

"I haven't done anything weird in a while," he said. "I might not ever again. I'm trying hard to be better."

She considered it a minute, looking at him blankly. Then she lifted her gaze to the dirty window, took a few breaths. Finally she brought her eyes back to him. They were sad, but hard. He knew what she was going to say. He'd heard twenty versions of it in the last few months, ever since he'd started telling them the truth.

"Thanks, Hap," she said. "I mean for telling me now, instead of later, when it might've gotten serious between us. That was thoughtful."

She looked at him for a few moments. Naked on the side of the bed. Her marvelous body. Goddamn, goddamn.

She said, "I'm sorry, sweetheart. I don't want to be mean or anything. But you know, if you got mental-health problems, it's just not what I'm looking for."

"Yeah," he said. "I understand."

"You're a sweet man. You really are. I appreciate your telling me. Some guys wouldn't."

"You're welcome."

When she'd dressed and was at the door, she stood there for a moment looking at him.

"You gonna kiss me good-bye?"

He went over to her and kissed her.

"You're not just trying to drive me away, are you? 'Cause if that's it, tell me. Maybe it was something I did. I scared you somehow. Came on too strong. I can do that."

He kissed her on the forehead.

"You didn't do anything. You're fine," he said. "I told you the truth. I hear a voice. I do what it says. It's been a while since I heard it, so I don't know, maybe it's over now. But there's no way to know for sure."

"I hope so," Joyce said. "For your sake."

Hap saw his older brother, Daniel, and Marguerite Rawlings coming down the lawn toward the boathouse. Both wearing shorts, T-shirts, and baseball hats. They were holding hands, but they seemed awkward doing it, like school kids on a field trip, required by the teacher to keep a grip on their buddy.

"Bye, Joyce."

She smiled, told him good-bye. Maybe she'd see him around.

"Yeah, maybe."

At the end of the dock, she had to squeeze by Daniel and Marguerite. They exchanged a quick hello and then Joyce kept on going toward the main house, where she'd parked her new Porsche. Daniel and Marguerite watched her go, then came out on the dock. Hap sat down on the bench outside the boathouse door.

"She had that look," Daniel said. "Like she won't be back."

Hap said yeah, yeah.

"We're not even a week into August," Daniel said. "And that's eleven ladies since June."

"You missed a couple, I think."

"What was wrong with this one?" Marguerite said.

"She folded her underwear."

"Well," Daniel said. "We can't have that now, can we?"

"Why don't you give me some shit, Daniel? Huh? Why don't you grind my ass a little?"

"At least this one was out of puberty," Marguerite said. She stood behind Daniel, looking at the bay, at some low-flying sandpipers skimming along in the same convoy with a couple of grebes. She watched them intently.

"We wanted to know if you were interested in going diving," Daniel said. "We'll stop at the Yacht Club and pick up the tanks. Have an early lunch, be back in by one, two o'clock."

"I got work to do."

"Marguerite packed a couple of extra sandwiches for you."

"Can't do it," said Hap. "But I'll take a rain check."

"We don't give rain checks," Marguerite said, still not looking at him. "Unless it's raining."

"It'd do you good, Hap. A little diving, we're going to explore a wreck I know about."

"Thanks anyway."

Daniel gave Hap a look that he meant to be half sympathetic, half prodding. Come on, kid brother, pick yourself up, dust off, and get back to it. Hap Tyler had been seeing that look all his life, and not just from Daniel either. He was sick of it, and pissed off at himself for bringing it out in people.

"I appreciate the offer," he said. "But I have a couple of boards I want to finish today."

After they'd puttered away in the *Boston Whaler,* Hap went back into the boathouse and sat down on the edge of the bed. Joyce Hardy's head print was still in the pillow. He picked it up, held it to his face. Coconut shampoo. A hint of vanilla. He'd read somewhere that when you smelled things you were actually coming into physical contact with the molecules of the thing itself, an invisible residue left behind.

Sound was simply air jiggling in the ear, and sight was only reflected light that flickered on the retina. But with odors, fragments of the goddamn thing itself trickled along the neural pathways. Maybe that's why it could hurt so much, catching a whiff of something that was gone for good, just those last few particles lingering.

Hap Tyler set the pillow down and went back to the workbench. If he stayed at it, kept his focus and didn't make any serious mistakes, he might have that board done by five this afternoon. So he made that his goal. Five o'clock. No mistakes, stay focused, get through the day. Just like ordinary people must do.

CHAPTER 3

In the week after he split with Joyce Hardy, Hap hatched a plan. Quit the bar scene cold turkey, put his jinxed love life on hold, sublimate like hell, redirect all those sexual juices into his board business. Turn them out faster and more economically, then market the hell out of the things. Yeah, Hap the businessman.

It was high time he got his ass out of that house, went out on his own, rented an apartment somewhere. And it was time he broke as many of the old habits as he could, wiped clean the brain stems. Started over, goddamn it. Acquired some new addictions, and chose them a little more shrewdly this time.

So he invited Daniel to an early breakfast Saturday at the Silver Sands on Key Biscayne. It was a funky fifties motel restaurant, big windows looking out at the beach, the sun easing out of the Atlantic, turning the clouds to jewel tones, pinks and blues. Across the dining room steaming trays of bacon, grits, eggs Benedict. The idea was, get Daniel relaxed, calm, his mouth full of good food, then Hap would make his pitch.

He'd gone over and over it all week, even had a notepad covered with scribbled numbers. Just where the money would go, what Hap could expect to clear his first year. Best case, worst case. Talk about the design of the board itself, show Daniel a couple of drawings, discuss buoyancy factors, speed-weight ratios. Prove he knew what the hell he was talking about.

But now, for the last half hour, Hap had succeeded in doing nothing more than stutter around, looking for a way to begin. Feeling more and more awkward as Daniel looked at him strangely. At this point Hap was about to scrap the whole goddamn thing. Finish breakfast, pay the bill, go on home the same failure he'd been when he arrived.

He should've realized it. Hap didn't even know how to chitchat with Daniel anymore. Lately, the ten-year spread between them seemed to have doubled, tripled. Christ, they'd never even been that close to begin with, not in the same generation. Didn't listen to the same music, watch the same movies, read the same books. Hap always thinking of Daniel as more of an uncle or a benign stepfather. On average, they didn't exchange more than five sentences a week. Days went by without Hap even bumping into Daniel around the house. What'd he been thinking! Ask Daniel for fifteen thousand dollars, Christ!

Hell, the last time he'd even been around Daniel for more than thirty seconds was a couple of weeks ago when Hap bumped into him and Marguerite in the kitchen late one night. They were having a brandy, and Hap stumbled in with an eighteen year old he'd met at CocoWalk. They hadn't exchanged names yet, though they'd been kissing down by the boathouse for an hour. He was on his way upstairs with her to show her the spectacular view of Biscayne Bay from his bedroom.

And the first thing out of Marguerite's mouth was, "Well, I see little brother's still splashing around in the kiddie pool."

"This the newspaper lady?" the young woman said. "One you warned me about?"

Hap said yeah, it was. The famous Marguerite Rawlings.

"I tried to read your column once," said the girl. "About saving the Del Monico Hotel, but it was too stupid. I couldn't finish it."

"Stupid, really?"

"Yeah, I been by the Del Monico. It's all run-down. Just a bunch of retired Jewish ladies sitting out on their aluminum chairs waiting to die. It smells bad too."

"Oh my, I didn't realize it smelled bad."

"It was a dumb article," the girl said, giving her hair a flounce, and suddenly looking a hell of a lot younger in the kitchen light than she had at the shadowy bar. She stood in front of Marguerite and said, "South Beach is hip now. It's new wave, live bands, bars, skaters in the street. Full of juice. They should put those old people in a van and drive them somewhere else. That's what I say. Knock that stinky place down and build a parking lot. There's not enough parking out there."

"God," Marguerite said. "What a great idea. How sensitive of you to think of it. How caring and humane."

"Hey, Daniel," said Hap, "could you curb your bulldog, please?"

Marguerite stood up, looked around like she was searching for something to bludgeon them with. The eighteen year old gave Hap a cold good night and stalked out the kitchen door and disappeared into the dark. Hap called Marguerite a goddamn pseudointellectual sarcastic bitch. She called him a cradle robber, and Daniel had to stand up, practically pull them apart.

After the scene was over, Hap went up to his room alone and lay in bed drinking rum from the bottle. A while later he heard his brother and Marguerite come upstairs and begin whispering in Daniel's bedroom. And still later he heard the quiet tap of Daniel's headboard against the adjoining wall. A languid rhythm, slower than Hap could manage with the women he brought home.

Now, that was really good. He didn't know his own brother well enough to have a decent conversation with him, but Hap knew how fast he made love to Marguerite Rawlings. Great.

Hap set his coffee cup down, wiped his mouth, cleared his throat, did a drum roll with his fingers against the tabletop.

He said, "Okay, Daniel, here's the deal. I want to start manufacturing sailboards. Fifteen thousand bucks should take me through a year. I need to hire a couple of part-time people, buy some hardware, mast tracks, custom daggerboards, the blanks themselves, a few tools, and there'll be some marketing costs. I got all the figures written down right here. I'm serious about this. It's something I can do. And I need to do it, to have a job, something more than the goddamn tours. It's my shot. My chance to get on my feet. I really want this, Daniel. A lot.''

Daniel cut his eyes to his plate, put down his fork. He straightened his place mat.

''Wow,'' he said. ''Now, there's a white-hot thunderbolt.''

''Fifteen thousand,'' said Hap. ''It'd be a loan.''

''Well, I was wondering. Breakfast, all this.'' Daniel waved his hand at the restaurant.

''So, what do you think?''

''Frankly, I think trying to start a new business is pretty hazardous at any time, but with the economy like it is right now, it'd be downright crazy.''

''Oh, yeah, right,'' Hap said. ''Crazy. I'd almost forgotten.''

''Now, come on. I didn't mean anything. It's just a word.''

''You're not even going to listen to my proposal. You know already, you can't loan me anything because I'm nuts, a goddamn lunatic. I might take the fifteen thousand and what, Daniel, what would an insane man do with fifteen grand? Let's see—''

''Stop it, Hap. I'm sorry. I used the wrong word.''

''Yeah, yeah, sure you did.''

Daniel picked up his fork again, began to cut a strip of bacon. And Hap tried to eat, too, get back some normalcy, but the hollandaise on Hap's eggs had congealed to a greenish glue, the prongs of the fork didn't even leave an impression. Hap put the fork down, had a sip of the bitter coffee. Set the cup in its saucer.

''Anyway,'' Hap said, ''it's been years, Daniel. Years.''

''Seventeen months.'' Daniel's gaze slid out to the beach, where a red-haired father and his red-haired son were fishing. Gulls swirled above them as the father baited his son's hook from a plastic bucket.

''Seventeen months?'' Hap said. ''What? You count them, keep a tally? Sixteen months without a major problem, seventeen.''

Daniel kept watching the father and son.

Okay, so yeah, maybe it was seventeen months ago that Hap had another episode, hearing the voice again, doing what it told him. Pretty damn bold of him, too, got in the paper and everything.

And one of those guys was in town writing a book about Miami. Flew in from New York City, an instant expert, spent five weekends down there researching his hip sociological study of the city, and Hap made it into the book. That's how expert the guy was, thinking Hap was some kind of important local figure.

Seventeen months ago. The Grande Biscayne episode. His brief war against Shorty Busser.

Back in the sixties Shorty had owned an outdoor raw-bar and marina in the Grove. Place was a hippie employment agency. Guys playing six-string out on the wood deck or in the kitchen frying up conch fritters, and the long-haired ladies hoofing beers. Fifteen years later Shorty sold the place for about ten million more than he paid for it. And in one quick real estate transaction, Shorty Busser went from a slightly seedy outsider to one of Miami's major civic leaders.

Shorty promptly aimed his attention at a little park in the center of Coconut Grove. The place was run-down, weedy, where the blue-collar crowd and glassy-eyed minstrals played softball and threw Frisbees on weekends. Shorty proposed tearing out the seesaws and building a forty-story condo, flashy shops downstairs, luxury apartments up. All of it neo-deco, architectonic. Lots of random cutout patches of reds and greens, tubular railings. A place where Shorty's new pals could feel comfortable.

The city commissioners listened politely to all the protests from the neighbors, then voted Shorty in. Some legal wrangling followed, and finally the whole thing wound up in some office in Tallahassee. Phone calls were made. The project was given the state's approval.

About that time Hap's voice woke him up late one night. It told him that this land that Shorty wanted was the place where Adam Munroe had constructed his first sawmill in 1877, where the planks were shaved that built the very house Hap lived in now. Hap must do something. He must have courage, and act.

So the night after Shorty Busser's workmen hauled in their construction trailer, Hap borrowed a friend's tow truck, plowed it through the chain link fence, and hauled that fucking trailer right back out. Dragged the thing to city hall, pulled it halfway up the front steps, then he doused it with kerosene and set fire to it. Then he drove downtown to Centrust Towers, where Shorty had his office, and broke in. Using some of his old military skills he sneaked past three security guys, and spent the next two hours wallpapering the place with the petitions signed by about ten thousand locals protesting the project. He emptied all the desks, the computer drawers, and dumped them out the forty-third-story window. A blizzard of paper. When he was done, the cops were waiting for him downstairs, guns drawn.

Hap got a two-year sentence for criminal mischief, suspended. Released into Daniel's custody with the understanding that he would be put under a psychiatrist's care.

The instant expert put him on page sixty-eight of his hip book about Miami. And right away, all the local environmental groups started calling Hap to see what he might have up his sleeve on their behalf. But the voice had quit talking to him by then, and he told all the groups to screw off. Leave him the hell alone.

Daniel set down his coffee cup.

"Look, Hap," he said quietly. "I'd like to help. I really would. But I'm afraid there's just no money. No fifteen thousand to lend you."

"Whatta you talking about? No money. What about the Commodore's trust fund?"

"That's been gone for years," he said. "Dad ran it dry. All there is is my salary—that, and what you're able to bring in, of course, with the tours."

He stared at Daniel for a moment, then picked up his knife and aimlessly cut his eggs Benedict in half, then into fourths, eighths. He shoved his plate aside, dropped the knife onto it.

"There's nothing?"

"There's debt, that's all there is. I could loan you maybe three, four thousand, Hap, my personal savings. But beyond that . . . No, I'm sorry."

Daniel had shaved his beard off earlier in the summer. He looked younger now, and thinner, even more handsome. He was wearing his hair shaggier than he had in a long time. Hap believed both things were due to Marguerite Rawlings's influence. She was a couple of years younger than Hap. More into the social scene than Daniel ever was. She was getting him to hobnob with the hundred people who ran the city. In less than a year she had taken Hap's shy, archaeologist brother and transformed him into a public figure. And Hap hated her for it.

Daniel was just under six foot, an inch taller than Hap, and ten pounds lighter. A four-letter athlete in high school, and now a distance runner. Forty-eight years old, the guy ran twenty-six miles in under three hours. Narrow face, a longish straight nose. Green Irish eyes from their mother, and the heavy beard and Slavic cheekbones of their father and grandfather. He was handsome in a gaunt and scholarly way. In Hollywood they would cast him as a dark-eyed Lawrence of Arabia, with those far off, sun-stunned eyes.

Nothing had ever been difficult for Daniel, not school, not women, not the mysteries of faith and belief. A man who was born with such an unnatural zeal and curiosity and optimism, he could have succeeded in almost anything. He could've been a governor, or a matinee idol.

"Look, Hap . . ." Daniel heaved a sigh, glanced around the restaurant. "I don't know if this is the time or place, but hell, you need to know some things. It's time you did."

Hap shook his head, looked out at the red-haired kid holding up what looked like a grunt. For a minute he considered standing up, getting the hell out of this restaurant, just leaving his brother sitting there.

Daniel said, "Have I ever explained to you the difference between salvage archaeology and normal archaeology?"

Hap pushed back his chair, rolled his eyes up to the ceiling and back down. Daniel smiled, made a bear-with-me wave.

"Salvage archaeology is used in instances where construction is about to occur. The land is about to be permanently altered, so we're allowed a few days to retrieve all we can from the site before it's lost to the bulldozer. Delicate procedures can't be followed. Time is critical. It's crude work, down and dirty."

"Christ, Daniel, and I thought I was the crazy one. I mean, what in the fuck're you talking about?"

Daniel waggled his hand again. Be patient.

"I'm sometimes forced, through the requirements of my job, to engage in salvage archaeology. But under normal circumstances, on a day-to-day basis, I believe it's far better to leave any truly valuable site undisturbed. Learn what we can from surface study, and hypothesis, but leave the site intact. Archaeologists have been guilty of as much destruction of historical sites as the bulldozers have. It's like studying a forest, or some living thing. If you wrench something that fragile from its natural home to put it under the laboratory microscope, you'll probably kill it. I'm even finding it harder and harder to justify museums, their undying hunger for new materials."

A dark swatch of sweat had begun to show on Daniel's shirtfront. He leaned forward, held his green eyes to Hap's as if he were trying to see behind Hap's eyes, to see if any of this had penetrated and was taking hold. Finally he sighed, looked down at his plate, and sat back in his chair.

Two old ladies holding hands walked by on the beach. They passed by a teenage couple who were trying to skip rocks into the surf. In the back of the restaurant the waitresses were smoking, one of the busboys flicked his dishrag at another busboy. Hap watched it all through a periscope, as his body slid into a cold gray sea of despair.

"Look, what I'm trying to say, Hap, what I'm trying to prepare you for is . . . well, there *is* money in our family. Of a sort."

Hap felt his heart stumble.

"For years now, certain assets have been under my stewardship. And for a long time now I've been wanting to share this with you. I mean, the responsibility of managing it. The decision-making part."

"Yeah, and why haven't you? Let me guess."

"Hap, it's not a simple thing. I could lay it all out right this second, and maybe that's what I should do. But I think it's important you understand a few basic values that relate to these assets first. Then you can decide how you want to handle things. If you come to believe that it's worth it to use some of these assets to start your business, then so be it."

Daniel peeled open a pat of butter and dropped it into the center of his grits, mushed it around with his fork. Looking up, then his eyes shifting off.

"Whatta we talking about here, Daniel, stocks, mutual funds? I mean, this is still pretty goddamn cryptic."

Daniel glanced out at the beach, then brought his eyes to Hap's. He licked his lips, leaned forward, his palms flat against the tablecloth.

"It's treasure, Hap. An incredible treasure."

Daniel held his eyes to Hap's.

"You're kidding."

"Hap, what I said about archaeology, it's crucial you understand that first. Because, believe me, it's very easy to destroy the thing you want most to preserve if you're not extremely cautious getting to it."

Daniel lowered his eyes, had a sip of his coffee, another one. He wiped his mouth. In the same blue work shirt, same scruffy khaki pants as always. His brother, Lawrence of Miami.

He looked up again, searched Hap's eyes for a few seconds, nodding his head slightly as if he might be having a private conference with some voice of his own.

"It's not that I don't trust you," Daniel said. "It's just that I've been alone with this secret for so long, it's hard for me just to blurt it out to you right here, like this."

"You're not kidding."

"No, I'm not."

Hap flicked a crumb of toast off the table, brushed away the rest. Hearing a high whine start up in his inner ear, the sound of his blood squealing through his constricted veins. He pushed his plate further to the side, set his napkin on top of it.

"Are you familiar, Hap, with the *Carmelita*? The Spanish ship? Have you ever heard of it?"

Hap made a face. What the hell!

Daniel said, "Treasure hunters have been searching for it for centuries. It was destroyed in a hurricane in 1633, shortly after it left Havana on its voyage back to Seville. That's known for certain. It was an *aviso* vessel, a dispatch boat. Most of the treasure ships were galleons, huge things that sailed in fleets and carried enormous cargoes, but the *avisos* sailed alone, and were much smaller. They carried no passengers, just a small crew, and the most valuable loads. The pick of the plunder."

"Dan? Hey. Hey." Hap waved his hand in front of his brother's face. "What is this shit?"

"I know where this ship is, Hap. The *Carmelita*."

"Get you boys anything?" The waitress with the ornate stack of white hair was holding a pot of coffee out to them.

"How about a little CPR?" Hap said, his hand against his heart.

"Those grits getting to you, huh?"

"The check," Daniel said. "That's all."

When she was gone, Daniel reached out and took hold of Hap's hand. Held it tight. Hap could smell a trace of his new Marguerite-inspired cologne.

"Hap, I know we haven't been close for a long time. Maybe we've never been as close as you would've liked. But I want you to know, I'm proud to have you as a brother. I love you. Very much. And I trust you completely to do the right thing."

Hap nodded. Words barged into his throat, stumbling there, piling up in a hard knot. He was silent. Out of practice being sincere. Hell, out of practice even *hearing* sincere.

Daniel gripped Hap's right hand in both of his. A numbing clasp. Ten feet away at the coffee stand, the waitress gave Hap a disapproving eyebrow lift. And there she'd thought they were a couple of nice boys. Wouldn't you know.

"For some time," he said, "I've been managing the treasure, making decisions. I've felt very isolated not telling you or anyone about it. And guilty too. Because, Hap, I've had to do things, shameful things, that run contrary to my deepest beliefs. But I felt I had to do them. For you, for both of us."

Hap adjusted himself in his chair, leaned forward.

"Hey, listen, I appreciate your honesty and everything. Really. But you think you could be a little more specific here?"

"Tomorrow," said Daniel. "First thing in the morning, I'll take you there, Hap, let you see it for yourself. I'll explain everything, how it all works, the particulars. But till then, just overnight, I want you to consider what I said. We don't want to wind up destroying the very thing we're trying to preserve."

"No," Hap said, looking out the window at the father and his son. "No, I suppose we don't want that."

# CHAPTER 4

ALL THAT SATURDAY AFTERNOON DANIEL TYLER WORKED at the Rawlings Mill site. With a trowel in his right hand, a whisk broom in the other, he sifted meticulously through the soil a hundred yards from the Miami River. He was on his knees in one of the trenches that marked off a seven-by-five rectangle of earth, excavating what used to be the basement of the Rawlings's house.

The light was dying now, at seven-thirty. By eight the mosquitoes that spawned in the stagnant stream nearby would cloud the air, and Daniel's work would be impossible. He'd decided that when he heard the first mosquito's whine, he'd pack up, go home, and tonight he would speak to Hap again. Reveal everything. It would be good to have him finally in on it. In fact, Daniel was irritated at himself for the way he'd blundered around at breakfast today. Blurting out half the truth, then holding the rest back. Once he'd gotten going, he should have told Hap everything.

Daniel stood up and carried the bucket of dirt to the worktable. He poured the soil across the filtering screen and then shook the screen from side to side. Nothing but rocks, a fleck of glass. A dark twisted piece of iron, perhaps a nail, some broken piece of a garden implement.

It had taken him most of the afternoon to work below the fill level, the foot-thick layer of debris and coral fragments dumped there a hundred years ago when the drainage canal was cut, the canal that was now known as the Miami River. At around five o'clock, with the rubble cleared away and the rich dirt exposed, he'd begun dusting his way down, layer by layer.

What remained of the true Miami River was a few feet away, hidden by weeds and Florida hollies. It was a dead creek, blocked up, moving nowhere anymore. A shapeless ditch filled with rain water and debris. Though a century earlier, the heavy flow running through that same gully had powered the mill on this site, the Rawlings Mill where coontie was ground into a starchy paste, something like damp flour. All the coontie was gone now from south Florida, in fact, almost everything from that time was gone. All those indigenous plants, paved over, extinguished by overuse, trampled by settlers, or strangled by exotic species the newcomers brought.

That stagnant water, the remnants of the original Miami River, was full of car tires now, styrofoam burger containers, cigarette packs, you name it. A couple of trailers sat in the woods nearby, old Cadillacs parked out front. People playing their radios loud all day while Daniel dug and sifted, or some days laid out more exploratory trenches across this deserted acre.

Where those old Goodyears were was about where the rapids of the river had once been, where the Everglades water had once spilled over the rocky Atlantic coastal ridge, the wall of rock that acted as a dam against the eastern edge of the Everglades.

A hundred years before, when they dynamited the rapids, it was as if they'd blown a hole in the dike, the dike that kept the millions of acres of pristine water from pouring into the bay, bringing along its dark silt. All of it gone now. Gone the mill and the coontie, gone the rapids, the local plants. Gone a huge chunk of the Everglades. All of it gone so that more dry land could be made habitable for wave after wave of new residents.

For thousands of years before the white man came, the only dry ground in southern Florida was the five-mile band of earth running along the coast. It was where the Tequestas lived. And every other tribe for ten thousand years since that land emerged from the sea. Just west of that coastal ridge where Daniel Tyler worked, all there had been for millennia was the Everglades, the vast domain of muck and mire, filled with alligators, herons, egrets, flamingos.

Without blowing the plug, draining a large portion of the river of grass, there would only be that five miles of dry land to occupy, land enough for merely a few thousand humans. It was pure stupidity, and uninformed pride, that made those first Yankees believe they could tame this territory. Despite the good weather, the southeastern tip of Florida was as inhospitable to human habitation as anyplace on earth. To establish a city on the edge of the Everglades was as idiotic as trying to build one on the peak of Mount Everest, or on the floor of the Grand Canyon.

Sure, it could be done. Yankee ingenuity would find a way to chop down the jungles, drain those millions of acres, so the trainloads of other fools could enjoy south Florida's perpetual summer. Oh yes, what a long list of disastrous achievements could be credited to one ingenious Yankee or another determined to prove he could accomplish the impossible, change the course of rivers and history.

Daniel Tyler knew there were two histories of Miami. There was the sunshine history, a pretty story that chamber of commerce types liked to recite, about Julia Tuttle, a tough widow from Cleveland who moved to Miami when there were less than a hundred settlers there. With her industrialist husband's money, she bought up six hundred acres of that mosquito-infested wilderness and began her campaign to bring a railroad into its heart.

In the sunny version, Julia Tuttle sent an orange blossom to Henry Flagler, the great railroad tycoon. The blossom was to prove to him that the freeze of 1895 hadn't harmed Miami, while it had devastated Palm Beach, where Flagler had terminated his railroad line and built his grand hotel. Julia Tuttle wanted to let him know that if he and his rich pals wanted to truly and finally escape the cruelties of winter, they would have to come a hundred miles further south. Into her town.

And though all along he had vowed he would not take his railroad a mile deeper into that state, Flagler was convinced by Julia Tuttle's orange blossom. Finally he ordered his legions to carve through that last hundred miles to the bottom of the peninsula, to invade the jungle frontier with his great steel rails.

A pretty story, orange blossoms, an ambitious woman seducing a great man. But Daniel Tyler knew the other version, the shadow history, which told a very different tale. The unofficial story that most didn't know, and those that did wanted to suppress. It was the chronicle of another woman, Ramona Rawlings, also a widow, also with a good sum of cash at her disposal.

Ramona had been living along the Miami River for seven years before Julia Tuttle arrived. And Ramona would have none of Julia's idea of progress. Tuttle could just, by god, take her grand designs, her vision of a great, shining city on the edge of the Everglades, somewhere else.

An abrasive speechifier, Ramona could talk down the boldest of the men. At town meetings she liked to illustrate her points by bringing along examples of the beautiful swamp creatures that would turn to dust if the Everglades were pumped dry. She was relentless and her speeches could rise to eloquence. She organized Daniel and Hap's grandfather and the Munroes and several other prominent families to stand alongside her. In short, she became an intolerable thorn in the sides of all the speculators, those giants of northeastern industry who came to see in Florida the potential for a vast vacationland for their fellow millionaires.

On a January night in 1898, Ramona Rawlings's house and mill were torched. Her charred body found inside the rubble, not far from where Daniel was working now. A bullet hole in her skull. Her six-year-old son, Anthony, survived only because he'd been sent away to visit relatives. And on that January night, in the shadow history, Miami became the city that murder built.

The *Metropolis,* the Miami paper that Flagler owned and controlled, called Ramona's murder a sign of the moral deterioration of the times. The sinful ways of the north beginning to defile their Eden. However, Ramona's case remained unsolved. The investigation was suspiciously brief. Everything Ramona owned was lost. Her land given over to her staunchest ally, Commodore Tyler, to hold in trust for Anthony. Her body buried on her land, in a gravesite long since forgotten.

Now, four generations later, Marguerite Rawlings had committed herself to rebuilding the mill, and to bring what was in those shadows into full light. Using the surviving blueprint, Marguerite intended to re-create her great-grandmother's homestead exactly as it had been, a perfect replica of an operating mill and pioneer dwelling. She'd sold the county school board on the idea as an educational museum celebrating one of Miami's foremost female settlers. In Miami, a city of ceaseless glitz and trendiness, a city that prided itself on its cake-frosting facades, its pastel neon, and trompe l'oeil, the Rawlings Mill and homestead would be one simple, authentic thing.

Marguerite had raised additional contributions from some of the wealthy ladies in the Miami Preservation League; she'd had the site designated as a historical landmark; and she'd cajoled the city's most prominent female architect into donating her services. Then she'd lined up woodworkers, electricians, a contractor who specialized in restorations, and through her newspaper columns she'd even bullied several county commissioners into publicly supporting the project.

But before any construction could begin, Ramona's grave had to be located. Marguerite insisted on it. She wasn't going to have the bulldozers that prepared the site accidentally violate her great-grandmother's remains. A horrifying image, Ramona's bones scattered by the blade of an earth mover.

So one morning a year ago Marguerite had turned up in Daniel's office. Since he was the county archaeologist, she wanted to know if he would consider volunteering his expertise on an occasional weekend to find Ramona's grave so that Marguerite's project could officially begin. He didn't answer her immediately, but gazed at this striking dark-haired woman. He'd known her since she was a girl of thirteen, but it had been a while since he'd seen her last. And after a long moment, he said, yes, yes of course, he would do whatever was required. Absolutely. Count him in.

At the time, it appeared to be a modest project in archaeological terms. But now after digging here almost every weekend for a year, Daniel still had half an acre left to explore and had found no sign of Ramona's grave. Most weekends when she wasn't meeting a deadline at the paper, Marguerite joined him at the site, kneeling alongside, sifting the loamy soil. And though it was frustrating to both of them that they had not yet located Ramona's remains, still, Daniel relished his time there. His official job was increasingly administrative, and now, with his hands in the dirt again, the old joy that had drawn him to archaeology in the first place had reawakened in him.

So there, in the weakening light, at seven-thirty when his trowel tip clinked against something an inch beneath the surface, he smiled, and as had happened so often lately, he felt his heart rise and shake itself awake.

With a couple of swipes of the whisk broom, Daniel cleared the object. He set down his tools, curled his finger into the sandy soil, hooking it under the nugget of bright metal. And with his breath staggering now, he pulled it up. For it was not a single nugget of metal after all. Lifting it out was like tugging a root from the soil. It broke a path a foot and a half long.

And my lord, what he had found. For in that instant, still covered with dirt and in the bad light, it was an object he knew, recognized its age, its style of workmanship. Its source. Indeed, Daniel Tyler was sure that he alone knew more about this particular piece of jewelry than any man alive. Dusting it with the whisk broom, he held it up to the last light of this day, the twelve golden jaguar heads, their eyes inlaid with jade.

Behind him, a car door slammed. Daniel didn't turn around to see who it might be, but dropped the necklace back into the dirt, quickly scooped soil over it. Tamped it down with the flat of the trowel, roughened the dirt with a swish of his hand, and busied himself by inspecting a wedge of blue glass he had discovered an hour before. As the footsteps approached, Daniel held up the shard as though it were of powerful interest, though it was nothing more than dime-store material, some fragment of bottle.

"You find anything exciting, Tyler?" A tinge of Cuban in his English.

Daniel looked over his shoulder at the stocky man with dark hair combed into an intricate pompadour. He wore sunglasses, a checked sport coat over a white shirt and dark pants. He was a big man, six feet at least, with the shadow of a heavy beard. Daniel was sure he had seen him before, but at the moment he couldn't recall where.

The man was smiling unpleasantly. Daniel started to stand, but the man raised a silver pistol casually into view and motioned him back down. This man with the insincere smile and the dark hair aimed the pistol at Daniel's chest.

"I prefer you like you were, kneeling in the dirt."

Daniel went back to his knees, moved his fingers carefully through the soil in front of him, searching for the trowel handle.

"You want my wallet, is that it?"

The man laughed, and stepped into the trench beside him. With the barrel of the pistol he prodded Daniel backward a couple of feet, and turned to the mound where Tyler had been working. He dug his fingers into the loose dirt.

Daniel measured the distance to the trowel. A second to get it, a second to turn and take a swipe at the man.

"Well, hello," the man said. "And what the fuck do we have here?"

He drew out a flake of pottery, crusted with charcoal.

"Oh, now there's a nice find," Daniel said. "From a jar, I would think, possibly for flour or sugar. The charcoal crust is most likely from the fire when this house burned down."

The man threw the piece back into the dirt in disgust.

"Okay, Tyler, dust yourself off, and let's go. It's time we got a few things thrashed out between us."

Daniel thought he might be dead.

But he didn't know. It wasn't something anyone had a lot of experience with. How could you be absolutely sure? But if this was it, what it felt like, then it wasn't so awful. A bit confusing perhaps, with time minced up and resorted, a jumble. A deck of minutes shuffling, reshuffling.

This much Daniel knew. He had been driven from the Rawlings site to the Sonesta Hotel on Key Biscayne. The man had not spoken to him during their trip. And Daniel had been silent as well.

What bothered him now, more than anything else, as he wandered about in time, not knowing for sure if he was alive or dead, was that the secrets he had held so long might now be lost for all time. Secrets about the history of this city, this region, the forces at work a hundred years ago that had directly resulted in this hotel, and the land under it, and every other hotel in this city, and every other building and house and road.

And what a terrible irony that today should be the day he would find the necklace. For that necklace was the key. The key to the fire at the Rawlings place, the death of Ramona, the dynamiting of the rapids, the railroad coming down another hundred miles from Palm Beach into Fort Dallas, that muddy trading post that was destined to be Miami. And most likely Fort Dallas would have stayed a trading post were it not for that railroad. Were it not for that necklace.

Without intending it, Daniel Tyler had been preparing himself all his life to know this enormous thing, and the final proof of it was coming to him at a moment when he was no longer certain if he was alive or dead.

Eventually the man with the unpleasant smile had taken Daniel into a hotel suite, a room with a view of the Atlantic, air-conditioned cool, shadowy light. Outside, the surf rose and fell like soothing static. The man directed Daniel to the bedroom, but he balked in the doorway. He waited till the man had moved close and had put a hand on his back to shove him inside, and Daniel spun, and fired an elbow backward as he came around.

But the man was too quick. He stepped back and Daniel's elbow cracked against the door frame. He recovered quickly and drew back his fist, but the man had the pistol aimed at his face. Very calmly, he instructed Daniel to go on inside the room and make himself comfortable, and when Daniel turned to obey, the man hammered him on the back of the head.

"Turn him over."

It was a woman's voice, high-pitched, strange. Perhaps disguised. Daniel was naked now. His clothes gone, though he didn't remember that part. Naked in this dark, timeless room, seeing these people as shadows, if they were people and not spirits of the next world.

"Turn him on his belly," she said.

And then he was on his stomach, watching them, the big man in the jacket and this woman in the dark he could not see, but he could see the hypodermic syringe. The glint of its needle as fluid squirted from it, readying it.

"All right, spread his legs," she said.

And with strong hands on his ankles, the man widened Daniel's legs. And he felt cool fingers prying between his legs, touching the folds of his private parts, felt the needle, its prick, felt now or then, or whenever it was, the plunge of fluid into his body. Felt himself rise out of his head, rise to the frayed edge of his rational self, time quickening and scattering like the explosion of a hundred stars.

Gasping, he lifted his head, tried to see her.

He could feel whatever drug they had given him beginning to work in his eyes, the way they unfastened from the room, began to sink away, the world taking on an unnatural shine. He remembered bucking as if he were being electrocuted. He remembered hovering for a moment, then sailing away through a bright constellation of light. Lying there on his belly, numb and heavy, watching the twinkle of his own inner lights, hearing himself grunt and growl and fight the drug.

"Where did it go down? How deep was the water, the loran coordinates, latitude, longitude, anything? How far offshore?"

"Ask him where he hid the fucking map to the place. There's got to be a fucking map."

"The *Carmelita*, the *Carmelita*, the *Carmelita*."

These voices came to him as if across a wide, haunted water, clear but distant. A voice he recognized, a friend or business associate, someone he had trusted, someone in his inner circle. But the drug was spinning things away from him, keeping everything, every memory, every thought, just out of his conscious grasp.

And suddenly the babble erupted from him, poured out of his mind, or, he couldn't tell, possibly it remained inside his head. Words, spoken or thought. There was no partition anymore, no way to know. Outside, inside. No such things.

He said, or perhaps he only thought it, that they should leave it all alone, not dig it up and destroy it, not even for a museum or science, better that the treasures were left where chance had buried them, hidden from our greed, our incompetence. Better that we remain ignorant, better that than learn some trivia by digging up the treasures and destroying what could be known by who will come later and have more skill. It was no fair trade to gain a small amount of knowledge or wealth now and lose forever the object itself. He had done this himself, he admitted it, he had committed the worst sin of his profession. Selling for his own benefit what belonged to all people. He regretted it, was ashamed, asked forgiveness of whoever might be listening, on this his apparent deathbed. Babbling all this, either inside his head or out loud.

Then a face was close to his, its breath of peppers and garlic. A pungent breeze from the living world.

"Where the fuck is it? Say it, you asshole, say the words. The location of it. Or you'll die."

Yes, then he was dead. Certain of it. Something final had happened to his body. Some last violent shrug. And that was all. For this dark was different. Softer and quiet and with great distances spreading outward in all directions. And he had always thought it would be lonely to be cut off from those he loved, those who nourished his life, that the loneliness would be the hardest part. But there was none of that. The dark was simply filled with more dark, and that dark was of a deeper darkness, a rich, pure dark. And the darkness was a comfort. A deep comfort. All that was necessary was being there, in it. No longer important to describe it. He felt his words leaving. Not needing them any longer. All the words departing like an immense flock of beautiful birds rising in unison into the sky. Leaving behind only a dark, enormous silence.

"You stupid bastard, you gave him too much."

"Six cc's," he said. "Exactly six cc's."

"Well, it must've been a couple of goddamn cc's too many."

Tyler had winced, stared up at her with his real eyes for a moment. Surprise and sadness there, a spark of rage. Then clenched them shut, and a sound had begun inside him, as if coming from his groin, rising up through him, resonating like the quiet rumble before an earthquake, until his lips peeled back, teeth exposed, face cramped and red, his cheeks buckling, as though he were letting go of a howl he'd held back his whole life, and at the moment when his heart must have lurched out of rhythm and seized up, the noose tightening at his neck, an explosion of light in his eyes, a strangled syllable had broken from his throat.

He had croaked it again and again. The same rough cry.

"The fucking jerk died on us," the man said, standing over the bed, watching the still body. "You understand any of that shit he said? Sounded like fucking nonsense to me. Giving us a goddamn lecture about archaeology, for christsakes."

"No," she said. "I didn't follow it."

"None of it? We go to all this trouble, I put myself at risk like this, and you fucking didn't understand any of it?"

"Just the last thing, the thing at the end."

"Yeah! What?"

"Hap," she said. "He was crying out 'Hap. Hap.' "

# CHAPTER 5

LEANING AGAINST THE PORCH RAILING OF THE MANGROVE house, Hap Tyler watched what looked like blue fire flickering on the surface of Biscayne Bay. A cloudless Sunday afternoon, brilliant light. The coconut palms down by the shore rattled in a twenty-knot breeze. A mile farther out a catamaran with a tall pink sail was tilted over on one hull, riding hard on a beam reach.

Best wind of the summer, and there Hap was, stuck with two grandmothers armed with cameras and notepads. He shifted against the railing and watched as a couple of stringy-haired teen-agers with matching black T-shirts walked around the corner of the house and joined them on the porch. The kids might have been girls or boys, or some combination. Both of them dangerously skinny, with dry, vacant eyes as if they had heavily overdosed on adolescence.

One of the grandmothers shuffled her feet, cleared her throat, and shot out her hand as though she were stabbing at a passing fly. Then she cocked her arm, her cuff drawing back to expose her large wristwatch. She brought her face close to it, shaking her head in dismay.

Oh, lord. Hap took a long breath. Another retired school-teacher. The woman hadn't tolerated tardiness for thirty years, and by god, she wasn't about to begin today.

"Two-thirty yet?" Hap said.

"Two-thirty-*six*," said the grandmother.

He took another quick look at the bay. Two windsurfers sizzling past. Damn. Double damn. He sighed and pushed himself upright.

"Good afternoon, folks." He nodded politely to each one, made eye contact. "I'm Hap, your tour guide. For the next thirty minutes or so we'll explore the Mangrove House, designed and built by one of Miami's first, and most important, pioneers, Commodore Randolph Tyler. But first before we begin, there's the little matter of three dollars apiece."

Since getting out of Radisson that first time, Hap had recited this speech twice a day, six days a week, twelve months a year. Even taking a few vacation days off now and then, and subtracting a few more for hurricanes and holidays and hangovers, Hap was up in the thousands.

He was way beyond being bored with the Commodore and the house and the history of the place. These days he simply collected the fee, put his mind in neutral as he spoke the words, and let his eyes stray out to the daydream water. But he continued it, for this was his penance, his proof to Daniel that he was sane and capable. That Daniel had been right to free him from Radisson.

"You got that wrong," the old woman said.

"Which?" Hap said as he was making change for the teenagers.

"Henry Morrison Flagler," she said. "He was the most important pioneer in Miami's history. Randolph Tyler was important, but number two at best."

"All right," said Hap. "I'm negotiable. Welcome to the Mangrove House, the home of the number two most important pioneer in Miami's history."

He smiled at the grandmother, but she was busy jotting something on her notepad. Lowering his grade already.

She had a point, though. Henry Flagler was the financial genius behind Standard Oil, the robber baron who boosted John D. Rockefeller to the highest plateau of wealth. In his spare time, as a hobby, he created Florida. Laid those first steel rails through the wilderness, constructed the original luxury hotels, and imported the first millionaires to fill them. The Johnny Appleseed of resort towns, planting them one after the other down the eastern coast of the state.

And wherever he went, he bought up the newspapers, the electric companies, the water utilities, so no one could muster any strong complaints when his men hacked away the wilderness. A hundred years ago they had done that in Miami, destroying the saw grass and scrub oak, the palmetto and loblolly pine, deep-dredging the Miami harbor, and started the long chain reaction that would transform the lush and rugged landscape into a paradise of pastel concrete. Yeah, Flagler was the yang to the Commodore's yin.

When the grandmother had finished her note, Hap said, "If you'll kindly follow me into the foyer . . ."

"What kind of wood is this?" She was glaring at the floorboards of the porch, tapping the toe of her heavy shoe against it.

"It's Pensacola pine," said Hap pleasantly. "Heart of pine. As is all the wood in Mangrove House."

"If it's pine, where did it get that red tint?"

Hap took a longer look at this woman. Her hair drawn back into a steel knot. Her eyes were shrewd, lips puckered as if she'd devoted the morning to chewing on wedges of lime.

"Well," she said. "Do you know why it's red, or don't you?"

"Yeah, why's it red?" one of the teenagers drawled. Always happy to grind an adult.

"Blood," said Hap.

"Ha," the schoolmarm scoffed.

"Blood?" said her companion.

"That's right," Hap said. "Pensacola pine's so hard that when the termites try to digest it, they piss blood."

The teenagers smiled uncertainly, but the schoolmarm and her sidekick, a gentler sort, frowned at each other, then took a half step away from Hap.

"We didn't come here to hear that kind of language," the teacher said.

"We did," said one of the teenagers. The other one grinned and they slapped high-fives.

Hap told the ladies if they weren't satisfied with the tour, he'd cheerfully refund their money. While the two of them consulted in whispers, Hap stared out at the bay. Empty now, except for a single windsurfer, this one leaning way back, trailing her blond hair in the water.

The teacher cleared her throat. Hap turned and smiled.

"All right, you can continue," she said. "But watch your mouth, boy."

Hap led the group inside the house and began his monologue, speeding it up as many RPM's as he thought he could get by with. He'd decided to give them the sanitized version. Have them in and out in twenty minutes, be on his sailboard by three-thirty.

He'd leave out the details about the Commodore's search for antidotes for his declining virility. All those raw alligator testicles he'd eaten, the beaks of flamingos he'd ground into powder and sprinkled on his food. This wasn't the crowd for that.

Hap led the group into the large dining room. He pulled down the window shades and clicked on the opaque projector that sat in the center of the dining table. While he played the stack of black-and-white photographs against the whitewashed wall, Hap told them the Commodore's story.

How in 1878 Randolph Tyler of Buffalo, New York, had brought his bride of one year to Miami on a belated honeymoon. Both of them were charmed by Florida. Unbothered by the mosquitoes, the reptiles, the heat, the Indians, the lack of social life or ordinary conveniences, they bathed in the sea, sailed on the shallow bay, loved it all. For weeks he and Rebecca Tyler stayed in the one primitive hotel and explored the area with delight.

"That's Rebecca," he said. "On the left, their first visit."

"She was beautiful," the gentle grandmother said.

"Yes, she was," he said, and went to the next photo.

Three years later, Hap told them, Rebecca and the Commodore made the voyage to Miami again, this time purchasing forty acres along the Biscayne Bay, paying two hundred dollars for what was now some of the most expensive real estate in America.

They settled on their Florida land, living first in a small boathouse the Commodore constructed and later in the two-story pine octagonal structure that he designed and built himself. Like the shoreline plant it was named for, the Mangrove House was a rugged if unlovely creature. Raised three feet above the ground on pitch pine posts that were anchored to the limestone ridge, the house had withstood several hurricanes and many floodings. After all that abuse, the walls were still plumb, the floors level, and there wasn't a trace of rot.

In a short time Randolph Tyler became one of the leading entrepreneurs in the region. He designed and built shallow draft sailboats, which was the source of his nickname, the Commodore. He started a sponge farm near Key Biscayne, a pineapple plantation, a cannery, a sawmill, and a barrel-manufacturing plant.

He was licensed as a salvage operator and he personally scavenged over thirty ships wrecked on the Florida reefs. He was a fine fisherman, an imaginative architect, and was possessed of a charismatic personality. Inspired by his youthful friendship with Henry Thoreau, the Commodore was also an ardent environmentalist. One of Miami's first antigrowth fanatics.

He was also a robust man who liked to stage boxing matches down by the shoreline, and as far as anyone could recall, he'd never been so much as knocked down. Through his many successful businesses the Commodore also became very rich, a friend of governors, bankers, tycoons of every stripe.

Hap turned off the projector and led the group upstairs, continuing the story as he went.

During the delivery of their first son, Matthew, Rebecca died. The Commodore was heartbroken. While his empire continued to flourish, he lived a life of abstinence and seclusion until his death of congestive heart failure at the age of ninety-five.

"Wrong again," the teacher said.

By then they were standing on the second-story landing, gazing up at the enormous transom the Commodore had designed to expel the heat. Hap nodded at the schoolteacher, inviting her to set him straight.

"The Commodore may have been heartbroken," she said, "but his last years were full of promiscuity."

"Let me guess," said Hap. "You used to teach history."

"The Commodore was an infamous Don Juan," the teacher said. "He had Seminole concubines, ladies of the night, every manner of wench. What you're quoting is the history book story. But I know the oral history, the truth. He was a dedicated lecher."

"She's a native," her mild friend said. "She grew up here."

"Didn't we all," said Hap.

"Whatever happened to Matthew?" the meek grandmother asked.

Hap gave the teacher another long look, then turned to the meek one.

"The Commodore's only son, Matthew Tyler, passed away in nineteen sixty-eight, after devoting most of his adult life to squandering the family wealth on numerous foolhardy business schemes. His wife, Louise, died in nineteen fifty-four, giving birth to her second son, just as Rebecca died giving birth to Matthew." He looked at the teacher again. "That agree with your oral history?"

"It's your tour," she said. "Tell whatever stories you want."

The teacher's voice grated, her eyes were gray ice, even her false teeth seemed to be set at an aggressive angle. But for some reason he was starting to like her. Maybe when the tour was done he'd throw his arm across her shoulder and give her a hug, the way boxers do at the end of a particularly bloody match.

The teenagers were leaning into Daniel's bedroom, mumbling. A red velvet rope marked off the passageway and they were pressing their hips against it. Just the sight of a bed had set their hormones humping.

"And where are the Commodore's two grandsons now?" the mild one said.

"One of the grandsons works for Dade County," said Hap. "He's the regional archaeologist."

"Can we go in this room?" one of the teenagers asked.

Hap shook his head.

"Off-limits," he said. "Fragile stuff in there."

"How about the other grandson?" the schoolmarm said.

Hap gave her an ominous look.

"Well?" she said.

"He's insane," Hap said quietly. "Institutionalized."

"Far out," one of the teenagers said.

"I never heard that," the teacher said.

"Criminally insane," said Hap.

The teenagers moved close, lured back from the sexual brink.

"Deeply deviant," said Hap.

Hap was standing with his back to the glass case of conchs and ancient starfish, the bay sparkling in his peripheral vision. A steady breeze pulled through the house, fluttering the lace curtains on the bedroom windows, humming up the stairwell, spiraling toward the transom, cooling the uncoolable air. Just as the Commodore had known it would. And just as the house did every day, every night, hissing with the spirit of the old man.

"What'd he do? The grandson?"

"Unspeakable things."

Hap looked out the French doors that opened onto the up-stairs porch. The palm fronds fluttering at the shoreline.

"He at Raiford, or where?"

"No, not at Raiford," said Hap.

"Where?" the schoolmarm said darkly.

"Why, right here," said Hap. "In this house."

One of the teenagers sang a few spooky notes.

"As punishment for his sins, he's required to lead tours around his family home. Answer moronic questions. The same ones again and again."

They were still for a moment, their eyes on Hap. The only noise was the wind sifting through the house.

"You're him," the schoolmarm said. "You're the grandson."

"Deeply deviant," Hap said. "Endless moronic questions."

The teacher took her friend's elbow and drew her to the top of the stairway.

"The Better Business Bureau is going to hear about this. Don't believe they won't. This is extremely inappropriate."

"She's right, you know," a man said, laboring up the stairs, nodding to the ladies as they hurried down. "I'd have to agree with her on that."

The man plucked at the front of his green madras shirt to get a little air inside it. He wore black pants sheened from wear and scuffed black shoes. He let go of his shirt and boosted himself up the stairs with one hand on the rail and the other pushing off his knee. He had a round, pasty face, and black hair parted an inch above one ear in an attempt to conceal his baldness. As he reached the landing, he let go of a weary sigh, then stared at the teenagers.

"Hey," he said. "Why aren't you two in school?"

"It's still summer vacation," one of them said. "Dork."

The man questioned Hap with a look, and Hap shrugged.

"It's the reason we're losing to the Japanese," the man said. "Letting you little turds wander around three months a year. It's why we can't build cars anymore. TV sets, nothing."

"We've just finished," Hap said to the man. "Last tour of the day. You're too late."

The madras man took a slow glance at the rooms he could see from the landing. He moved like big people often do, with a slow grace, an almost luxurious peacefulness. He had dragged his bulk to this place, and now goddamn it, he was going to drink this in.

Behind Hap, on a small maple table, the phone rang, and in a spasm of surprise Hap jerked the receiver to his ear and said hello.

A man's voice said, "We're finished fucking around."

"You got the wrong number."

"I don't think so, buttface."

Holding the receiver away from his ear, Hap watched the big man staring at a photograph of the Commodore.

"You hear me?" the voice on the phone said. There was wind-rush and honking in the background, a car phone. "You either hand it over, or I'll have my people sign their names in your flesh. And believe me, dogfuck, they got long names."

"I'll be expecting them," said Hap. "Why don't you come, too, we'll have a goddamn party."

Hap set the receiver in the cradle and shook his head. It wasn't the first of those he'd gotten. Not the same guy, but over the years there'd been others, dumb shits so stoned on their venom they were always misdialing. The Miami airwaves were apparently zinging with death threats.

"So?" the big man said, his back to Hap. "It true the Commodore ate raw alligator nuts? So he could keep his pecker up?"

"So they say."

The man shook his round head and turned around.

"Even for my pecker, I don't think I could do that. I'd do a lot of things for it, but not alligator nuts."

The man slipped a dime store notepad from his shirt pocket, paged through it. When he found the place he was looking for, he put a fat finger against what was written there.

"Hapfield Otis Tyler," he said. "That your correct name?"

Hap made an affirmative noise in his throat.

"Brother's name Daniel Oliver?"

Hap nodded. The teenagers had drawn close.

"Hey, kids," the man said, turning their way. "Why don't you take a hike, okay. Go sniff some Kitty Litter or whatever the hell you do to get high these days."

"You can't tell us what to do, you putz."

"Yeah, it's summer vacation. We can do what the fuck we want."

The man reached in his back pocket, withdrew a fat brown wallet and flipped it open. A silver badge and photo ID. Hap leaned in with the teenagers to see.

Detective Jordan Wills. Metro-Dade Homicide.

"Now," the cop said. "Did I hear somebody use the word *fuck* just a second ago? I mean, saying the word *fuck* to an on-duty police officer, you know, this is not a genius idea."

One of the kids stepped closer to Hap.

"We came for some water."

"Yeah, please," the other one said. "We got our five bucks."

Oh. He should've realized. They weren't here for the tour. They were water weirdos.

Twenty yards east of the house, the Devil's Punchbowl was hidden behind a stand of buttonwoods and fishtail ferns. A century ago it had been a sacred place of worship for the Tequestas. Before the Everglades was drained, fresh water had flowed from the limestone rock, but now it was only a dark shaft, a dying well that required a tin bucket on a long braided line to scoop up what was left.

Years ago there had been a brisk market for the water. Mainly Seminoles. All through Hap's youth, gaunt silent men had arrived in pickups from Immokalee and Ocala, stood around gravely as Matthew, and later Daniel, hauled up the water and poured it into their canteens.

But in the last few years, as the supply of old chiefs had dwindled, a new set of mystics began to appear at the well. Long-haired men and women, fresh in from the astral plane. Semicomatose rejects, the cerebrally hot-wired. They'd escaped from schiz wards across America, making the pilgrimage to Coconut Grove to hand over sweaty dollar bills for a little water.

Where the crazies learned of the well, Hap never knew. Maybe some divine radio beam that only the severely tripped-out could hear. However they discovered it, they came. Pulling up in battered VW's covered with the calligraphy of their cult. Men with wispy beards and smogged eyes, women with scrawled tattoos and purple makeup, people whose minds you couldn't kick-start with a poleax.

"We're all out of water," said Hap.

"We got the goddamn money. Show him, Gayle."

"I said we're out of water."

"Get out of here," Wills said. "Go on, scat."

He waved his arms at them, and they scattered down the stairs.

"Kitty Litter?" said Hap. "Do they do that now? Sniff it?"

"Not that I know of," the cop said. "But I'd be willing to bet those two'll be down on their knees snorting away within the hour."

He winked at Hap, then paced down the hallway a few feet, peered in the rooms, humming to himself.

"You know, my wife dragged me in here a couple of years ago.

All of a sudden one day, she caught some kind of culture virus, had to come to places like this, go to museums, art shows, you name it. Day I was here, it was you giving the tour, same as now. It was me and my wife and a bunch of Germans, and those people on that particular day were giving you a serious raft of shit. Calling you every kind of jerk. I don't remember what set them off, but seeing the old ladies today, it reminded me."

Hap straightened a picture on the wall beside him. The Commodore and Rebecca sitting on a coral boulder. The Commodore leaning back in that nineteenth-century pose of naturalness. Legs crossed, arms straight, with both hands clasping the knee of the crossing leg. Rebecca behind him with her hands on his shoulders.

The cop said, "So I take it that's your modus operandi, huh? Makes you kind of irritable, all these strangers invading your privacy twice a day. You resent having to depend on their money. So occasionally you gotta piss on them. That it?"

"Isn't there a law, practicing psychiatry without a license?"

"I read books," he said. "They give me ideas."

The cop did something with his eyes, an apologetic shrug. It looked like he'd had a lot of practice at it. No one appreciating his advice. He flipped the notepad closed, put it away.

"I'm afraid I got some bad news to relate to you, Tyler." He patted his bald head, moved a greasy strand of hair back into place. "Maybe we should sit down."

Hap didn't move.

"Okay," the cop said. "Well, I'm sorry to report to you that your brother Daniel Oliver suffered a fatal heart attack sometime Saturday night or early this morning. Coroner hasn't put an exact minute on it yet. But he will."

"Daniel?"

Hap had sagged against the glass showcase of conchs and starfish. He listened as Jordan Wills described how a maid had found the body this morning in a room at the Sonesta Hotel on Key Biscayne. Wrists and ankles tied up with a pair of stockings.

"See, at the moment this isn't exactly a police matter, and it won't be unless the coroner comes back with something not immediately apparent at the scene. But I thought, you and your brother being the Commodore's grandsons and all, it was a special case, and I should come by, break the news. Fact is, I happened to be one of them who thought your brother was doing good things."

"Good things," he said blankly.

"Yeah," the cop said. "Going one-on-one against the bulldozer and hard-hat crowd. Guys won't be happy till Florida's got the Great Wall of condos around it. Your brother had balls."

Hap didn't hear the rest of what Jordan Wills said. Instead he listened to the steady moan of the breeze that funneled out the transoms. Hearing only that noise, not the cop's voice, not the thud and skip of his heart. Just the wind flooding through the windows and doors, disorganized when it entered, but blended by the shape and order of the house. A low bass here, a chilling soprano there, the ghostly choir rising up the stairway, through the cracks in the floor, harmonized by the house. The Commodore's house, after all these years, still showing the wind what to do, and the wind, by god, doing it.

# CHAPTER 6

"YOU GONNA BE ALL RIGHT?"

Hap said yeah, sure, of course. But a woozy yellow steam was
rising behind his eyes, hazing them, and the floor had begun to
slide underneath him.

"Your tan's draining off," Wills said. "Maybe you need to lie
down."

Hap said he was okay, fine. Christ, it wasn't like he and his
brother were that close or anything. You know, not like normal
brothers. It was just hi, hello, like that, seeing each other coming
and going around the house, but not a lot in common, except, of
course, being brothers.

"You could give me the name of somebody else to do the ID.
That, or come in tomorrow when you get hold of yourself."

Hap said no, he'd do it now, get it out of the way, he just
needed to make a quick visit to the john, he'd be right back. Wills
said fine, he'd wait for him downstairs.

Hap went into the bathroom, shut the door. He turned on the
water, brushed his teeth, brushed them a second time, splashed
water on his face, and dried himself off. He closed his eyes tight and
tried to urge up a sob, force a tear, clenching his gut, bowing his
head. But nothing came.

He opened his eyes, put his hands on the lavatory and leaned
close to the glass. His coarse blond hair was cut shaggy, hung low

and uncombed across his forehead. Hazel eyes, dimples that had become permanently embedded, a spray of wrinkles around each eye, long lashes, dirty blond eyebrows.

He hardly ever looked at himself. A glimpse now and then in the dusky mirrors of midnight bars. At those times, he always looked young, a surfer boy, tan and lean, quick with a smile. His face washed clean of twenty years. He looked like a boy unacquainted with worry. Relaxed, ready for the night's fun.

But now, in this ruthless light, all the weariness showed. The accumulated pain. Thirty-eight years of nicks and scuff marks, each grim millimeter of sag. He saw the shadows beneath his eyes, the strain, a twitch at his mouth. Gravity's steady work aggravated now by this new catastrophe.

Hap closed his eyes, opened them again, but the image was still there. He took a couple of difficult breaths, broke away from the reflection, and headed back downstairs.

The cop was still standing in the breezeway between the house and the Commodore's study. He was tracing his finger along the carvings on the heavy oak plank that hung on the outside wall of the study. Cannons, triangular stacks of cannonballs, voluptuous mermaids. One of the Commodore's salvage operations. Near as Hap could tell, the plank had been part of the ship's transom.

"You know, Tyler, if it's any comfort to you," Jordan Wills said, touching one of the mermaids, running his finger down her long hair, "this sort of thing happens all the time. A guy thinks it might be fun, he has himself tied up, getting professional treatment, heart can't take the kinky excitement."

"Not Daniel. He wasn't into that sort of thing."

"You sure about that? I mean, if a guy is into serious hooker action, I don't think he'd go around broadcasting it."

"My brother wasn't the hooker type."

"But you said the two of you weren't close. How do you know for sure?"

Hap, staring past Wills out at the bay, kicking up good now, said. "I don't know for sure, goddamn it. At the moment I'm not sure of a fucking thing."

"I know the feeling," Wills said. "Know it all too well."

Glenn Hollings loved his GTA metal detector. Walking along the beach at Key Biscayne early Sunday afternoon, starting to get hot, swinging the GTA 1000 back and forth in a two-foot arc. He'd already dug up fourteen quarters, nine dimes, a dozen pennies, and three oddball coins, Costa Rican or Panamanian or some shit.

It wasn't much compared to four hundred million in Mexican gold and silver and emeralds. But in the week since he'd gone out for a drink with Alvarez, the guy hadn't gotten back to him. Hollings was a little depressed about it at first, swooping down from that excited high.

What he figured now was, Alvarez had been interviewing him, see if he was right for the job, and somehow Hollings had slipped up, said the wrong thing, and bang, it was over. His big chance. His come-from-behind finish. Gone.

Yesterday morning, Hollings had even looked in the Miami phone book under Tyler, imagining maybe he could still wriggle into this, invited or not. But there were two hundred and nine Tylers in Miami. So he just shut the book and gave up thinking about it. Then this morning he'd come out to Key Biscayne, the GTA started pinging, and he was just about back to okay again.

With the old-style metal detectors, you had earphones, but with these new ones, you got a couple of warning pings from the box, then on the little amber screen you saw the goddamn shape and size of the thing hidden down there, its exact depth, everything. The 1000 had twenty-four separate discrimination notches, a detection cursor, coin depth guide, errorless pinpointing. A slide-off battery pack to clip on your belt, a coiled cable that ran to it.

It had 2-D elliptical cross fire search coils, with smart sensors that could tell a pop top or bottle cap from a coin. With the knife-edge scan pattern Hollings could stand on top of a trash pile and discover every speck of treasure in it.

This week so far, he'd hit Haulover Beach for seventeen bucks and change, South Beach for twelve, and Hollywood Beach for a real score, nineteen seventy-five in coins and a twenty-dollar bill folded up around a fifty-cent piece.

There was a shitload of advantages to being a professional prospector. For one thing, with all the Europeans over here now, the beaches were thirty, forty percent topless. He could work on his tan, get a good dose of fresh air, be his own boss, and stare at different titties every day of the week. All that and the fun of picking up other people's lost money too.

Far as he could tell, there was only one hazard to this job. The assholes who trailed you down the beach and gave you shit. Last week at South Beach it'd been a crazy old woman, bag lady type, she'd hollered at him from the time he got out of his car and crossed Collins Avenue, and she stayed right on his trail all the way out to the beach. Pretending she knew him, saw his aura or some shit, tagging along, screaming at him, that she knew exactly what he'd done, and exactly what he was about to do. Evil man, evil man, she kept hollering. The lady wearing eight sweaters in the August heat and screaming at him he was evil, till a couple of young guys, Hispanics, joined along with her, and one of them finally stepped forward and stopped Hollings with a hand on his chest and asked him what the hell he'd done to this old lady to make her scream these things at him.

Hollings thought about it a second, then told the kid that this was his mother, and she'd been abusing him since he was two years old. And now that he was thirty-nine and on his own finally, she didn't know what to do with herself, so she followed him and kept trying to abuse him out in public. The Hispanics asked the woman if this was right, and she looked at them, looked at Hollings for a long time, and said yeah, yeah it was right. She was his mother, and she'd abused him, but he, by god, deserved it, 'cause look at him, how evil he was. One of the Hispanics pushed her down in the sand. And the other one called her some kind of Spanish name. Hollings spent the rest of the morning congratulating himself on getting himself out of that one.

Today it was Hispanics again. Five girl Hispanics. All of them wearing black ankle-high Reeboks and toreador pants, spandex tops, different colors. Big girls. Wasn't one of them under one-eighty. Looked like the two-ton basketball league had called off practice for the day. All of them walking down the beach together, coming toward him, eyeing him good, then when they got close to him, swerving over.

"Hey, that's my quarter," one of them said. This one wearing an athletic jacket, orange sleeves. *Marta* was stitched on the front of it.

Hollings took the quarter out of his egg strainer. Two nickels too. He dropped them into the net bag he wore on his belt, and looked up at her.

"I lost it right there, last week," she said. "Didn't I?" She turned to her hefty friends. They all nodded. One of them holding a wine bottle, two others with cans of Budweiser.

There he was, isolated out there, a mile from the nearest life-guard stand, an empty stretch of beach smack-dab between the sunbathers and the north end where the nudists hung out, and the homos.

Hollings reached in his bag, found a quarter and held it up.

"What's the date?" he said.

"What you mean, date?"

"The asshole wants a date with you, Marta."

"He wants to take you out and run his electric thing up and down your body, look for treasure."

"Fuck that," she said. "Gimme my quarter."

The four other girls were fanned out on either side of Marta. All of them staring at Hollings like they hadn't fed on any Anglo flesh in a while.

"If it's your quarter, then you'd know the date. I know all the dates on my quarters."

She turned and said some Spanish to her gang.

One of them said back, "The date, it's on the quarter, the year it was printed in. He's joking you."

Hollings turned his back on them and started sweeping the sand down toward the water. You never found much at the water's edge, but he was starting to think if things with these roller-derby queens kept escalating, he might have to swim out ten, twenty yards, keep the GTA over his head. Might as well mosey on down there now. He was fairly sure he'd be safe once he got out into water over his head. Just 'cause they looked like walruses didn't mean they could swim.

Then at the surf line he got a multiple coin signal on his screen, a major multiple, down six inches. From how it looked on the amber screen, it could be a roll of quarters. Ten dollars, enough to buy his lunch and gas over here. He moved the disk till he was right over the spot, then got down on his knees and started digging at the wet sand. Surf foam blew to the right of him, a sea gull stopped to watch.

Somebody put her foot on his back and pushed him over, and Hollings went flat on his stomach, the surf choosing that second to come in, wetting him front and back.

The girls were laughing.

Hollings sat up, turned around. Marta had picked up his GTA 1000 and was pressing the buttons. Changing all the settings Hollings had worked so hard putting in there. Hollings got to his feet just as she was raising his detector above her head. She hammered it down against the edge of a coral rock. He heard the radius stalk crack and the glass over the readout panel tinkle out. She dropped the broken GTA in the sand.

One of the girls had pulled out a little pearl-handled .22 and was aiming it at Hollings. Another one was showing him a big kitchen knife, its grip wrapped in adhesive. All of them with that look; mean smiles, come-hither, asshole, let's get it on.

Hollings moved up to Marta. He glanced down at the GTA. Maybe the warranty would cover getting smashed into a rock by a bunch of girl hoods, but he bet not.

"Here's your quarter," he said.

"Fucking-A," she said. "Fucking-A, it's my quarter. And everything else you got on you too."

"Including his underwear."

"Yeah, let's get his fucking clothes."

Something behind Hollings caught the girls' attention and they stared in unison. Marta didn't see it right off, but kept giving Hollings the evil eye as her gang started inching backward behind her. Finally one of them called out to her to look out, and she glanced over Hollings's shoulder, and her face went dead slack.

It was everything Hollings could do to keep from turning and looking, but he kept watching Marta, his hands ready to block anything she threw at him. Finally she leaned forward and sneered in Hollings's face, gave him an "up yours" hand jerk. She said something in Spanish that sounded like a voodoo curse, turned and lumbered off down the beach to catch up with the pack of walruses.

Glenn waited till she'd gotten ten yards away and he swung around, getting himself ready for the next attack. And there was Alvarez. In a white shirt and sunglasses, dark Bermudas, sandals. Thick hairy legs, and the hair on his head shining like hot asphalt. Looking bigger than Hollings had remembered him.

"Jesus Christ, you scared the shit out of me."

"What the hell were those girls doing to you?"

"It wasn't anything," Hollings said. "They were just bumming money from me."

Alvarez made a doubtful noise in his throat.

"That's not how it looked. How it looked was they were mugging your ass."

Hollings had a spooky feeling right then, like he should grab his GTA, make a run for it. The look in Alvarez's eyes wasn't right. Some kind of strange whirl of light.

"If I'm not mistaken, those are the Latin Madonnas," Alvarez said. "Famous for their drive-bys. But I gotta say, man, their mugging technique is a little suspect."

"The Latin Madonnas?" Hollings felt some give in his knees. "Jesus Christ, the joy-killers?"

"Hell, Hollings, you're lucky you're not dead meat right now. Of course, then on the other hand, if you were, we wouldn't be having this conversation, would we?"

Damn, there it was again. Another one those things that made sense, but didn't make sense. Hollings had been running into more and more of those lately.

Alvarez said, "So now that I saved your life, I guess you'll be indebted to me forever." Hands in the pockets of his Bermudas, looking pleased with himself.

Hollings unbuttoned his wet shirt, took it off, wrung it out, and put it back on. Feeling clammy and a little sick at the stomach all of a sudden. The whole time Alvarez was staring at him, giving him a shit-eating smile.

"What the hell're you doing here, Alvarez? How come you didn't get back to me like you said?"

"Well, Hollings, to be absolutely truthful with you, before I got you involved, I wanted to try a different approach on this thing. A creative idea I had."

"But it didn't work out."

"To put it mildly," Alvarez said.

"Yeah, and how'd you know where to find me? You clairvoyant or something?"

"I used to be a cop, remember?"

Alvarez had told him at the bar last week, having their drink after the Max Hunter lecture. Metro-Dade, narcotics. One of those cowboys, kicking in doors, shotguns blazing. It must've been why the Madonnas took off like that, recognizing the guy from his past life, one of the bad dudes in blue.

"So what's that mean?" said Hollings. "You been following me around?"

"Well, yeah, I been surveilling you a little. Not every minute. But I checked you out. Ran your credit history. Like that. It's my policy to know everything I can about the people I'm going to depend on. I mean, four hundred million dollars is a lot of folding money, Hollings. I'm not taking somebody in on a thing like that, I don't know nothing about them."

"And what'd you find out?"

"That you're a full-time loser."

Alvarez smiled.

Hollings shook his head a couple of times, trying to clear it.

"Yeah? So, I'm such a loser, whatta you doing here?"

" 'Cause you're just what I'm looking for."

"Fuck you, man."

"Tell me something, Hollings. If you'd had a gun with you a minute ago, would you've shot one of those girls? I'm curious."

"I don't kill women as a rule," Hollings said. "Least not on the public beach, eleven in the morning."

"But if it came down to it, it was either her or you, could you kill a woman, or not?"

"You got a particular woman in mind?"

"I might have."

"They broke my fucking GTA. So hell, yeah, I had a gun I would've winged at least one or two of them, payback. That metal detector cost six hundred goddamn dollars."

Alvarez smiled again. Big white teeth, straight.

"Hollings, my friend, we get this treasure ship up from where it is, you can buy the factory makes those pieces of shit, have them design one with your own name on it."

Hollings looked out at the ocean, a big pelican bobbing near shore seemed to be eyeing the two of them.

Alvarez asked him, was his schedule clear tomorrow morning?

" 'Cause I'm such a loser, now I get to be your partner."

"Not partner, Hollings. Remember that."

"Oh, yeah. One of your flunkies."

Alvarez looked off down the beach and said, "Myself, I would've killed at least one of those broads. Just on principle, 'cause they were so damn ugly."

"I don't have anything against ugly women," Hollings said. "It's the other kind you got to watch out for."

"That's good," said Alvarez. " 'Cause this other person I'm teaming you up with, she's a particularly ugly woman."

"So when're you going to tell me what exactly you expect me to do to this Tyler guy?"

Alvarez stooped down and picked up a hunk of seashell, stood back up, set his feet and sidearmed it at the pelican. Wide by a foot.

The big bird squawked and paddled its wings, lifted itself up and got the hell out of there.

"When it's time, Hollings, I'll tell you what you need to know."

Something squealed. A high-frequency shriek that made Hollings jump.

Alvarez reached into his back pocket, came out with a black plastic thing the size of a cigarette case. He flipped it open, pulled up an aerial, punched a button, and said, "Yes."

Alvarez turned his back, but Hollings could still make out a word here and there, and more than that, a change of tone. Ray Alvarez was talking on the phone to somebody that was making his pecker wilt. Damn, Hollings sure would like to get a look at that guy.

When Alvarez was done, he closed up the phone and slipped it back in his pocket.

"Isn't no end to the pecking order, is there, Alvarez?"

"Huh?"

Hollings didn't say anything.

"Come on," Alvarez said. "Time to go to work."

He turned and started striding toward the tall pines that bordered the parking lot.

Hollings hesitated, then he bent over and scooped up the broken GTA and hustled on after the guy. What the hell. So Ray Alvarez believed he was a loser. Shit, that didn't bother Hollings so much. Wasn't like Alvarez was the first person who'd made that observation.

# CHAPTER 7

**D**R. BACHAY, THE CORONER, WAS A BONY MAN WITH lacquered red hair and an incessant Howdy Doody smile. He stood beside the color video monitor in the family room of the city morgue, pointing with a long, thin finger at the victim's wrists and ankles. "We found no damage to the radius, the semiulnar, or the magnum. None of the attendant flexors had been strained."

Wills said to Hap, "His wrists weren't broken."

Daniel lay on a metal table two floors below, a towel draped across his waist. The family room was furnished with brightly uphol-stered chairs and a couch, a couple of seascape paintings, fresh gladiolus on a table in the corner, and a TV fastened to the wall. It was somebody's idea of a pleasant place, a civilized way to verify the dead. No rows of silver doors or sliding trays. But it wasn't working for Hap. He could taste the fumes from two floors below, the spicy burn of disinfectants and that numbing, colorless aroma of death.

"Which indicates," said the coroner, "what we see here is not true torture, but playacting. A bondage and discipline game."

"A game," said Hap.

The doctor wore yellow pants and a green polo shirt, on his way to the links. He asked the name of Daniel's physician.

"He didn't have one. He didn't like doctors. Neither do I."

"Count me in on that," Jordan Wills said.

Hap turned on the coroner.

"So what do you do now?"

"I go back to my office," Bachay said. "Get back to work."

Hap edged into the cross hairs of the coroner's smile.

"You know who Marguerite Rawlings is?"

The doctor tipped his head to the side and squinted at Wills. Who *is* this shitbird?

"The newspaper lady?" Wills said.

"Yeah, she's that, and also Daniel's girlfriend."

"Really?" said Wills. "Now, there's a handsome pair for you."

"I would think you'd want to question her."

Wills laid his hand on Hap's shoulder again, massaging the meat, and said, "Since the doc here says there's no foul play involved, it's now a low-priority situation, finding the sex partner, that is. Not really police business anymore per se."

"The bellman, people in the lobby," Hap said. "Somebody had to see them together. And you got the pubic hair. The stocking."

The coroner chuckled.

"Yeah, Detective Wills, why didn't you think of that? You could go over to the *Herald,* ask Miss Rawlings if she'd mind giving us a pubic hair sample. But then, I sure as hell wouldn't want to read the morning paper for a while after you did that. Get those newspaper people on the warpath about the coroner's office, or the homicide division. No sir, I think that would be highly unwise."

"You're kidding me." Hap said. "You're not going to at least talk to her?"

With his Florsheim, the coroner counted off a few seconds on the beige rug, giving Wills an impatient look.

"What about an autopsy?"

Wills said, "Not in death by natural causes. Just violent deaths, accidents, like that."

"Look, Tyler," the coroner said. "Your brother was thin, an athlete. So that probably makes you suspicious of the heart attack. But let me tell you something. I see men on my table every day of the week who show no outward signs of heart disease. And then I cut them open, there's enough plaque in some of their arteries to make a brick of cheese.

"Like it or not, apparently your brother simply wasn't up to the activities he was engaged in. The long and short of it is, he copulated himself to death. But believe me, Tyler, from a strictly medical perspective, I'd have to say there're worse ways to go. Lots of worse ways."

Hap leaned past the coroner and snapped off the TV monitor. He stepped up close to the Howdy Doody smile. Felt the clamor in his chest, a gray static in his head.

"You know, Bachay," he said. "They should keep you locked away in the basement with your goddamn corpses. 'Cause you fucking well don't have the skills to come up here aboveground and deal with living human beings."

With both hands he took a deep grip on the man's belt buckle and lifted hard. The crotch seam must have caught him just right, because Bachay had nothing to say, just a squirming groan. Hap held him up on his toes and watched his face turn from red to chalk. Wills clamped a heavy hand on Hap's shoulder and gave him a squeeze. Hap dumped the doctor against the TV.

"Okay, okay," Bachay said, struggling for breath. "Okay. Maybe an autopsy is a good idea. Yes, now that I think about it."

"So, Tyler." The cop fought off a smile and said, "You got to talk to them out in the front office, before you leave. Pick a funeral home, make the arrangements and all that. Okay?"

"Yeah, right."

"And listen," he said. "I'll talk to Marguerite Rawlings. Okay? Will that make you feel better?"

"Don't let her bully you," said Hap. " 'Cause she'll damn well try."

Back at the Mangrove House, Hap locked the gates on Main Highway, turned the sign over to CLOSED, walked down the narrow buggy path, an acre of hammock jungle on either side of the trail. He plodded into the house, fixed himself a large jug of iced tea, and went out to the stone storage shed at the edge of the woods and found a shovel and a pickax.

The small graveyard had been laid out by the western edge of the property. A steel picket fence surrounded it. Hap opened the gate and went inside. He paid his brief and silent respects to the Commodore, and to Rebecca, who lay next to the great man, and then to Louise, his mother, and finally to old Matthew, his father, the full-time fuck-up. He stood for a moment looking down at the remaining grassy area. Just big enough for Daniel and him. Their place in the dirt. Then he drove the point of the shovel into the ground, began to hack a rectangle out of the sod.

He was four feet down in the sandy soil before he hit the limestone ridge and needed the pickax. He'd drunk a half gallon of the tea, and sweated out two gallons. By the time he was chin deep in the grave the sun was setting, and his muscles were so far gone he wasn't sure he could drag himself out.

When he was finished, he trudged back to the house, drank water till he was breathless, then sat down in one of the porch rockers. He had no appetite. The daylight was deadened, his touch numbed. He sat there until it got dark. And then darker. He listened to the air sigh as it stumbled about, then found its way through the house. The goddamn Commodore's house.

When Hap was in elementary school, Daniel was already a teenager. In those years, he would sometimes let Hap tag along with him as he prowled the vine-tangled acres of hardwood hammocks along the shoreline of the Grove. Daniel, stooping continually to dig, probe with his trowel, sift the soil. Then carrying his flakes of pottery and other trinkets home in paper sacks.

And there were longer expeditions, both of them riding their bikes across the drowsy summertime town. Daniel would stand very still along the banks of the Miami River, silent, looking out. And when Hap asked him what he was doing, he said he was feeling the secret heartbeat of the place, how it used to be. Taking its sacred pulse.

Daniel's teenage room had been filled with arrowheads, shards of clay, ancient conch shells, bits of limestone with intricate patterns embedded in them. It smelled bad in there. Dank marine rot, and the mustiness of old books. A dark room with drawings and photos of the days when Miami had dirt streets and wooden buildings and all the men had beards to their waists.

When Daniel finally went away to Florida State to study anthropology, Hap was in junior high, the tricky world of girls opening before him. There Hap discovered that being Daniel Tyler's little brother was his strongest asset. Handsome Daniel. Athletic, smart, funny, and gentlemanly. His picture was in the glass case by the front door of the school. Holder of practically every athletic record in the school. Valedictorian, and the only student in school history to score a perfect sixteen hundred on college board exams. So, on the first day of each school year, when Hap's teachers read his name on the attendance sheet, they each paused and gave him a hopeful gaze. Are you *that* Tyler? Yes and no, Hap would say. But mostly no.

Try as he did to live up to it all, Hap was at best a *C* student, only a fair athlete, and had none of Daniel's easy charm. He came to believe that Daniel had inherited a full dose of the Commodore's charismatic blood. Which left Hap with only the pink froth that ran through Matthew's veins. The insipid, watered down, failure-prone strain of the Tyler family. And gradually a mist of doom settled over Hap, followed him everywhere, drove him into alliances with losers and jerks, misfits and ducktailed creeps.

He began to skip school. And on the rare days he attended, he would slouch in his seat and mock his teachers. He took up beer and cigarettes. Experimented with marijuana, tried some LSD. Let his hair fall over his shoulders. He stole a car, got caught. Then another one, and caught again. Found he had a knack for entertaining the hoods and punks, a daredevil boldness, a gift for the preposterous that promoted him to the court jester of his group.

Then two months shy of Hap's graduation, as Hap was lying in bed one night half-drunk on cheap bourbon, his father Matthew came in, bumbled around in the foyer, and made it halfway up the stairs before he crashed. Dead on the tenth step up those Pensacola pine stairs. Fifty years of cigarettes and disastrous business deals had finally bumped him off.

Daniel returned from Tallahassee for the funeral, and afterward sat Hap down to announce that he'd decided to drop out of graduate school and to return to Miami to maintain the Mangrove House, and to supervise the rest of Hap's childhood.

"I'm eighteen, for christsakes," Hap had said. "I only have two more months of high school."

"Exactly."

Eventually Daniel became Dade County's chief archaeologist, and for the next twenty years he battled some of the same kids who'd once been so in awe of him. Bankers now, real estate developers, having to lay their plans before the historical preservation commission to prove that their project was worthy enough to disturb a Tequesta village, a thousand-year-old burial mound.

Daniel developed a religious fervor for his job. He fought the builders in the newspaper, in court, in every forum he could find. And he won more than he lost, forcing several of them to build their downtown skyscrapers up on twelve-foot stilts, only their pilings permitted to desecrate the sacred pulse of the place. And he required others to radically redraw their plans, leave undefiled small pockets of strangler fig and gumbo limbo, silver palms and live oak where ten thousand years before men and women had plied the tip of that limestone peninsula, built their ceremonial fires, prayed to the stars, and waded out with their spears into the fish-thick waters of Biscayne Bay.

# CHAPTER 8

**H**AP LOOKED OUT AT THE BAY. IT WAS MONDAY MORNING, and he'd spent the night in that rocker drifting in and out of a fretful sleep. His back ached and there was an auger boring in one temple, on its way out the other side. Beyond aspirin. He drew a long breath, let it out, pushed himself up from the rocker, and went out to the railing. He stood there for a few minutes, watching the iron water, the hazy gray dawn. A single fishing boat near shore. Looked like it had run aground. Usual jerks, gouging long white wounds across the flats.

He walked down to the boathouse, paused at the shore and drank in the strong breeze for a while, feeling thick-headed and queasy, a boozeless hangover. In the boathouse, he hauled down one of his boards and took it outside. When he finished rigging it with a six-meter O'Brien, he stripped down to his Jockey shorts, and pushed off from the land.

A hundred feet out he settled back in the harness, and the sailboard rose up on plane, a wake boiling behind him. Ahead, gauzy roses and blues were dying out across Biscayne Bay, and the mirrored towers of Coconut Grove were filling with flat gold suns. The August air was swollen with ragweed, heady and thick.

Muscling the sail deeper against the wind, his flesh tingling, Hap brought his butt down to spank against the fast water. The bay lightly scalloped but still almost transparent. And as he flashed across patches of brain coral and sponge, beds of turtle grass, over his shoulder he glimpsed the silver flash of barracuda, and schools of pinfish flicking out of his path. A mile west of Rickenbacker Causeway, the rush of water across his bare feet, the air fresher than air ever was on land, he felt that reliable surge in his heart.

But the heaviness was still there, ten pounds of undigested gloom in his gut. Daniel dead, and now he, the Commodore's worthless grandson, the last of the red-hot Tylers, the ass end of a legend, left to carry on.

The Commodore, the Commodore, always the Commodore. Christ, Hap couldn't remember a time when the Commodore hadn't been the measuring stick for his life.

As a kid, Hap would be working on one of his hobbies and Matthew would show up beside him, watch for a moment as he ground a sander up and down the hull of a wooden skiff he was building. Boy, he'd say sadly, you should have seen your grandfather's shallow draft racing yachts. Now, there were boats. Designed them himself, and built every inch without the cheat of electric tools. My god, how the world had shrunk in its achievements. How shabby and limited were the possibilities of mankind in modern times.

Any goddamn thing Hap tried his hand at the Commodore had already been there and planted his flag, setting the standard so far beyond what Hap might reach, it was silly to try. His first few warbles on a harmonica, some preliminary slashes of paint against a canvas, even his singing in the shower got scoffing smiles from his father. God, boy, if you wanted to hear a man sing, a man with a voice that could charm the great fishes from the depths of the sea, could make the fine ladies weep and wail, a baritone so pure it could bring the dying back to life, you should have heard the Commodore.

Even when Hap graduated high school, Matthew dead, the goddamn Commodore was still there, overseeing every decision he made. It was what pushed Hap into the army at the peak of Vietnam. The Commodore had never been a soldier, probably never even heard of that tiny Asian country, so Hap figured maybe ten thousand miles away, doing something the Commodore had never dreamed of, Hap could be on his goddamn own for once.

And sure enough, he did feel free over there. Nobody once saying to Hap, Oh, so you're *that* Tyler, are you? Hap liked it all. Liked the jungle, the heat, the humidity, reminding him of Miami, how it might have been a hundred years earlier, requiring a machete to move about freely. And the combat wasn't so bad either. After a week, he was over it, the fear of dying. He didn't try to make any God bargains, didn't try to dodge the dangerous patrols, dig his trenches any deeper, didn't do anything particular to stay alive. He felt so comfortable, so into it, he was pretty sure no matter what he did, he wasn't going to get killed. He even found himself hoping the war would last forever.

That's where he first heard the voice. Coming to him one night in Nha Trang, as he was about to parachute from an HH-3E Jolly Green Giant helicopter into the jungles on the border of Cambodia to rescue a black box from a U-2 spy plane that had crashed. Forty guys going in to keep the precious codes out of the hands of the Soviets.

That night in the chopper Hap watched the guy's chute in front of him, heard the voice, in a deep commanding tone, telling him not to do this, to stay where he was. And Hap stopped. Two guys in front of him bailed out, then his turn, a push from behind, but he didn't move. The voice told him yes, yes. Then his commanding officer was yelling at him, and they were pushing him from behind, but they couldn't budge him. He wouldn't go down there.

His platoon was ambushed five minutes after they hit, and Hap rode back to Nha Trang with fifteen bodies, a dozen more wounded. The frantic medic and the lieutenant stared at Hap, kept saying, now that the voice was quiet, you knew, you knew.

That incident and another like it put him in the brig and finally got him shipped. A dishonorable. Sent home before his two years were up. And by then the voice had taken root. It would surface at unpredictable times. And Hap never disobeyed it. Not that he cared so much about avoiding danger, but because it became a habit. The voice spoke, he did what it said. He began to trust it, didn't like it, but it was so damn strong, so convincing, why not?

The shrink at Radisson Acres tried every therapy attack he knew. He tried to get Hap to repeat the exact words the voice used. And Hap had to keep telling the poor schmuck, it didn't use words. I know what it says, but there aren't words involved. What then? Images? No, Hap said. Not images. It's like thoughts, but not put in words.

Do you think it's the Commodore speaking to you? What're you, crazy? Hap said. The Commodore's dead. I never met the gentleman anyway, much less heard him talk. But it's your feeling of inferiority in the shadow of your grandfather that drives you to do these things, the shrink said. Makes you rebel, disobey direct orders. You're haunted by the old man, as well as by your brother. You want to earn your membership in the family by doing what the Commodore seems to be urging you to do, no matter how destructive it seems to be.

Hap said and how the hell do you know this isn't the voice of God I'm hearing? Huh? 'Cause if it's the voice of God, and you go fixing me so I don't hear it anymore, I'd probably have to sue your worthless ass. The shrink said well, is that what you think? The voice of God? And Hap said even if it wasn't God, and it was just the Commodore's voice, why in hell would he want to ignore it? How often you get the chance to hear a ghost talk? Plus, the goddamn guy hasn't been wrong yet.

After a half hour of sailing, with the sun full above the horizon, Hap unhooked the harness, pulled himself straight, and skimmed to within fifty yards of shore, then kicked up the daggerboard, and doing a sharp jibe, sailed back out a quick hundred yards, chasing a sea turtle part of the way.

He tried a windmill jibe, his back against the sail, arms extended, crucified on the boom, spinning the sail one-eighty inward against the wind, a couple of skip steps around the mast, hauling in, and there it was. Ending his jaunt with a flourish, some mild fanfare of muscle and balance. Something to give the arms a bit of heat when he landed.

At the shore, breathing hard, he stepped off the board, and sunk to his ankles in the seaweed and muck. He was sliding the board to land when he saw Marguerite Rawlings standing twenty feet away on the wooden dock. A strand of something hard and expensive glittered at her throat. The wind had starched her dark hair out behind her, and had set the spangles on her black dress into a shiver of light.

He slid the sailboard onto land, quickly unrigged the sail, and popped the mast loose.

Marguerite's black hair made her skin even whiter. Skin from the Ming dynasty, cream brought almost to a boil from some steady heat within. Her small breasts were flattened by her shimmering dress. Hardly any hips at all. But a face that belonged on the ceiling of a cathedral. A face to light candles to.

Hap wasn't sure why he disliked her so much. It felt almost chemical. A kind of deep allergic aggravation. Cell-level contempt. The sound of her voice, the way she moved, her eyes. All of it grated. All of it seemed arrogant, presumptuous. As if she considered herself some exiled princess forced to suffer out among the serfs.

Marguerite wrote an ongoing series of articles for the *Herald:* "The Way We Were." Hap considered her a nostalgia monger, each week focusing on another antique gas station or billboard or coral wall that was about to pass into oblivion. She spearheaded campaigns to save oak trees and swimming pools and ancient sidewalks. If it was old, it was automatically her domain. A few years back she'd been awarded some prize, not the Pulitzer, but close, for a group of essays she'd written about the art deco district in South Beach. Some people gave her credit for reviving that end of the beach. Bringing back all the chic bars, the glamorous decadence of the twenties.

But not Hap. To him the woman was nothing more than a cheap sentimentalist. One of those sappy fantasizers who took their eyes out of focus when they imagined the past. The kind who believed that the possibility of true happiness died out a hundred years ago. A good long while before air-conditioning, mosquito repellent, and indoor plumbing.

Hap Tyler stood for a moment at the shoreline and watched the wind twist Marguerite's hair into dark brambles. And goddamn, he hated to admit it, but a prickly heat was working his blood. She irritated him more than any woman he'd ever known, but look at her. Look at that dress.

"Why didn't you call me, Hap? Tell me what happened."

"It didn't occur."

"You can be a real shit. You know that? A grade A prick."

"I try."

"You sicced Detective Wills on me, too, didn't you?"

"I may have mentioned your name. It seemed relevant."

Hap fixed his eyes on hers defiantly, but she shook him off, glancing out at the bay. She moved with a jerky hesitation as if she might turn and lunge from the dock any second now and try to strangle him.

"I was watching you," she said, her eyes still out on the water. "I was watching you sailing, and I couldn't believe it. Daniel dead, and you're out there playing around."

"I don't have to explain anything to you."

He stooped to finish unrigging the boom from the mast. He spread the sail out flat on the grass to dry, squatted down and untied each knot carefully. Not looking at her, watching the short focus of his work.

When he was finished unlashing the sail, he glanced up at her again, and she'd moved a step closer to him, to the edge of the dock. In the slack breeze her hair ruffled on her shoulders, thick bangs fell into place an inch above her eyes.

With a lull in the wind, he could hear a mower working the Peacock Mansion's six acres next door, and a high-winding dirt bike out on Main Highway, the lunatic scream of a parrot off in the oaks, insects snapping in the tall grass at the shore. He inhaled that blend of swamp gas and the faint sugar of rotting jasmine that always hovered this time of summer.

Out on the bay a sleek white heron was coasting low, and a sixty-foot Hatteras was in the channel, its chrome railings firing silver lasers at the shore. A clear, beautiful day. Everything going on as usual, high spirits everywhere. No flags at half-mast, no black armbands. And the one goddamn person in the world Hap Tyler might share his grief with angered him so much he could barely breathe when she was this close.

"Come on," he said. "We need to talk."

Without looking back, Hap started up for the house. Behind him, out over the shallows, the laughing gulls screamed.

Hap left Marguerite on the porch and went upstairs, took a hasty shower, put on a clean polo shirt, gray shorts, his good boat shoes. When he came back downstairs, Marguerite was sitting in an oak rocker on the front porch. The bay was empty now. He sat down in the rocker next to hers. After a few moments Marguerite cut her eyes to him, gave him an irritated look. And Hap realized he'd been staring at her fancy dress. He glanced away, out at a squadron of pelicans gliding low across the shallows.

"I was at a rock concert, if that's what you're wondering." She touched the fabric at her hip.

Hap was quiet.

"Daniel and I had a date. He was supposed to meet me at the Arena last night. Aretha Franklin. He didn't show. I left at intermission. When I got home Detective Wills was waiting for me. Thanks to you."

She had put on a pair of dark glasses, black square frames, very black lenses.

"When Wills left, I couldn't sleep. I drove around till it got light, then I came here."

"You screwed my brother to death, didn't you? Just left him there in the hotel room and walked away."

She stopped rocking, brought the chair all the way forward.

"Jesus, you *are* crazy, aren't you?"

"It fits," he said. "You were afraid. It could've been a career breaker. 'Sex games turn deadly.' You ran, that's what happened."

"What're you talking about, sex games?"

Hap watched a hornet circle her head a couple of times. It coasted in for a landing on the back of her right arm. He watched it take a few hesitant steps through the sprinkle of dark hair, moving toward her wrist, then suddenly it launched off into the breeze again.

"As if you didn't already know."

She swiveled around in the rocker to face him, gripping hard to the arms. Her lips moved as if she were searching for the right curse.

"The Sonesta," Hap said. "Tied to the bed frame with fishnet stockings. That ring a bell?"

She stared at him, took a few short breaths. Doing a fair imitation of shock. Then she found her breathing rhythm, and lowered her head. Her eyes behind the dark glasses were impossible to see.

"Don't lie to me, Hap. Don't screw around, okay?"

"Fishnet stockings," he said. "Tied to the bed frame. That's the way it was."

She took another quick look at him, then turned her head and stared out at the bay for a long moment. It seemed to Hap she might be auditioning for some melodrama, playing the devastated lover, trying now to blend that with the falsely accused.

"Wills didn't tell me," she mumbled. "Any of that."

"Well, I guess being the next of kin has some advantages."

She took off her dark glasses and stung him with a look. Her eyes were intensely gray. Slightly too large for her narrow face. But they were eyes you kept coming back to, the kind that would draw your attention across a packed stadium. Probably could set off smoke alarms if she stared at them too long.

This morning they were inflamed. Hay fever eyes. She showed them to him like badges of her grief. But hell, Hap suspected she'd rubbed them that way before coming over. Taken her knuckles and ground them against her dry eyes to make a mask of suffering she could hide behind. He didn't trust her, never had. It was all he could do at the moment to keep from reaching out, grabbing her from her chair, and strangling a confession from her.

Now the hornet was back, on her knee this time. Taking a bead on the dark tunnel between her legs. She saw it, and watched it for a moment as it tracked up her slim inner thigh, hesitating in the shadow of her dress. But before it took another step she finger-flicked it to the floor and crushed it with her shoe. A hard-core Miami girl, used to doing battle with insects.

"I don't believe a word of this crap," she said. "Maybe our relationship wasn't perfect, but I do not believe Daniel Tyler was in bed with somebody else."

"Yeah? Then what? Somebody trying to set you up?"

"Maybe."

"Somebody murdered my brother," Hap said. "Just to get Marguerite Rawlings in trouble? Come on now, you're a smart lady, you can do better than that."

Hap watched a gull hover out at the shoreline, tipping its wings, holding steady against the wind, studying the shallows. The breeze had chafed the water to a milky lime. The gull hung there a moment or two more watching for shadows, then let the wind carry it backward a few feet, tilted its wings, and plunged.

"What a fucking laugh," he said. "You were with him, things got out of hand. He had a heart attack, you freaked and hightailed it."

She scowled at him, a web of veins showing at her temple, keeping a royal-blue beat. Her skin was smooth and clear, showed none of the sun damage of most Florida natives. Her lips were parted, and she was breathing unevenly.

He didn't know her moods or how to read them. Her eyes at that moment might not even be seeing him. She might be about to laugh or to break into a sob. Or to lean close and scream curses in his face. He didn't know, and he didn't care to learn.

But still, there was something about her, some obscure power he couldn't name. Like the forces they say are out in deep space. Stronger than gravity. Even though no one can see them or measure them, the scientists know the things are there because they're slowly twisting the heavens out of their natural alignments. He felt that, whatever it was, something invisible tugging at his gut.

"Someone was tailing Daniel," she said.

"What?"

"Someone had been stalking him for the last couple of weeks. He told me, a white car, dark tinted windows. He tried to point it out to me a couple of times, but I never actually saw the car."

She stared up at a passing gull.

"You tell that crap to Wills?"

"No."

"Yeah, and why not?"

"I don't know."

"You didn't tell him 'cause it isn't true. And you knew he'd catch you lying. That's why."

"It *is* true. Someone was following him. At least he thought so."

"Sure they were. And I suppose you know why."

"I may have an idea."

"Yeah?"

"Not everybody liked him," she said quietly. "Not everybody thought he was on the right side of things. He annoyed some powerful people in this town."

"Christ," he said. "You're paddling as fast as you can up a river of bullshit. Just trying to save your own ass."

"Do you own a gun, Hap?"

He glared at her but said nothing.

"Something's going on," she said, "and I'd suggest you either buy yourself a pistol and keep it nearby, or else stay inside with your head down."

She put her dark glasses back on, stabbed them into place. She rose, and without giving him another look, walked down from the porch and across the lawn to her twenty-year-old Corvette. She got in, revved it slightly, and drove off. Hap watched her dust lingering for a moment.

Hell, the truth was, Hap had had a lot of practice keeping his head down. He'd been keeping it down ever since getting back from Radisson. Eight and a half months at that asylum, Hap becoming more dazed and withdrawn every day. And then Daniel had shown up unannounced, and had signed whatever papers he had to, taken the responsibility. Brought Hap back to the Commodore's house, and never once had treated Hap like a disgrace or a wild man, or anything less than his brother.

Okay, so he hadn't been close to Daniel, hadn't been his good buddy. Big deal. The fact was, Daniel had rescued him, saved him from a lifetime of croquet and numbing drugs. And just two days ago he'd been on the verge of admitting Hap into some inner sanctum of family secrets. The least Hap could do, the goddamn very least thing, was to take some time from his busy schedule, risk waking up his voice, and find out exactly what the hell was going on.

CHAPTER 9

THE GRANDFATHER CLOCK IN THE PARLOR CHIMED NINE. Marguerite had been gone for half an hour, and Hap was in Daniel's room tearing open drawers, digging through his underwear and socks, his running shorts and laundered shirts, slamming the drawers closed, pulling down books from his shelves, riffling the pages, searching for something, he wasn't sure what, a letter, a diary, a note from Marguerite, some glimmer of threat from her or anybody.

As he was pawing through a shoe box full of arrowheads and smooth round stones, a childhood collection, a raspy noise like a tugboat horn with a loose connection sounded behind the house. He marched out onto the balcony and leaned over the railing. In the grassy lot below, a Rolls-Royce Silver Cloud was parked, a metallic green paint job.

A man in dark sunglasses climbed out from the driver's door and glanced around. A little over six feet with a dark complexion, he wore a yellow long-sleeve Guayabera and white pants. His thick black hair was shellacked into place.

He leaned back into the car and held the horn down again.

Hap called out to him and the man nodded and ambled over to the porch.

"You Hap Tyler?" he called up.

"I am."

"Come on down, I need to talk to you."

Hap met the man in the shade of an avocado tree.

"Name's Ray. Ray Alvarez. And I'm here to pick you up."

Something about the guy tickled Hap's memory. He was bulky, and most of it looked like muscle weight. A meat eater with fat fingers and a couple of large gold rings on each hand. There was thick black hair at his cuffs, more at the throat of his shirt. He needed a shave, probably always needed one.

His black hair was swept back elaborately. Those white pants way too tight. He had a square chin, a deep crease in it. Strong cheekbones, and heavy eyebrows. Hand the guy a gem-studded guitar and he could impersonate Elvis. A Cuban Elvis. But his blue eyes were too cold for love songs. No, this guy looked like he'd seen a ton of bad shit. And some of it, he'd enjoyed immensely.

"Somebody wants to talk to you," Alvarez said.

"Yeah, and who would that be?"

"She says she's an old friend of your family."

"This old friend have a name?"

The guy was looking him up and down, shaking his head.

"Those the best clothes you got?" he said.

Hap looked down at his shirt and shorts.

"I don't know." The man smiled. "Maybe they'll let you in." He sniffed at the thought of it. "Things are slipping over there."

"I'm not going anywhere," Hap said. "So don't worry about it."

"She says to tell you she has some information you might find important concerning your brother's recent death."

Ray Alvarez muscled the big car out the long, narrow drive, and out onto Main Highway, into that shadowy tunnel of banyans with stringy roots dangling over the roadway. Past the Taurus Restaurant, the sidewalk cafés where waiters were hosing off the sidewalks, putting out the tables. Bread trucks unloading, the early-bird tourists starting to show up already, gawky Europeans and Japanese in their stiff sandals, bright Hawaiian clothes.

New shops were wedged in every free corner of the Grove. No

more funky gas stations or grocery stores, no more funky anything. You couldn't find a sandwich for a mile around for less than ten dollars. The waiters made better wages than most of their customers, and acted like it. The bums begged in three languages. There were some shops in the ritzy-titzy mall that hired security guards to run metal detectors across the bodies of anyone they didn't know by name. All in all, the place was becoming as bad as the rest of Miami. These days you were considered a bohemian if your German car was more than two years old.

Alvarez turned the Rolls right at the corner at Main and Grand in the center of the Grove, then down the slope past Peacock Park and the Dinner Key marina, and he swung abruptly into the left lane and into the valet parking area for the Grande Biscayne Condominiums. Its name etched into the shiny brass veneer. Palms in cement pots beneath the green striped canopy, trim young men in red uniforms holding open the doors of hundred-thousand-dollar cars.

"She's in the penthouse," Alvarez said as Hap was getting out. "Give this to the elevator guy."

He handed Hap a blank business card with an indecipherable scrawl on it, somebody's lousy signature. Hap said thanks.

Alvarez winked as he closed Hap's door.

"Watch out," he said. "This lady's going to blow your mind."

A maid who spoke no English met him at the door and led him to the wide balcony, and made motions that he should wait there. He moved up to the red tubular railing and looked out. The penthouse seemed to occupy half the top floor, the balcony wrapping around three sides of the building. The city was spread before him, north, south, and east, and if he leaned out, a sliver of west. The vast grid of streets that was Miami, the Commodore's nightmare coming true.

Hap had never seen the city from this height. Oh, maybe for a second or two landing or departing in a jet, but never to stand and study it, to have it hold still. From the thirty-ninth floor, the banks and office buildings downtown were a jumble of wind-smoothed headstones, Key Biscayne a green comma curling into the flash of the bay. Hap held to the railing. He wasn't sure if the building was swaying in the breeze or if his knees were going. Probably the knees.

The city seemed thick with trees and grass, the new condos along the bay all color and whimsy, and everywhere the green flicker of water. The earth was just far enough away, that enchanted distance, where all signs of noise, violence, and filth vanished. The twist of the river leading out to the bay, and beyond Miami Beach and Key Biscayne, the Atlantic swept endlessly to the east. To the north the Biltmore Hotel rose amid red and white tile roofs and the green mazes of golf courses. All of it lush and orderly. The same beautiful illusion that the astronauts always sent back. All you had to do was get far enough away from the planet, it became blue and serene. And of course, what it took to get that far away was cash, a lot of cash.

Hap stepped into the living room. For a moment he watched the dust swirl in the bright bars of sunlight that angled through the mauve verticals. Probably a better class of dust up here on the thirty-ninth floor than what he was used to. He went over to a wall of book shelves, ran his eyes down the leather spines. Biographies. Mary, Queen of Scots; Gandhi; military giants, Patton, Rommel. A shelf of presidents, another of Indian chiefs, *Iroquois King, Prince of the Tuscaroras*. A daydreamer's library.

He was just turning away when someone clapped him hard on the back.

"Mr. Tyler, Mr. Tyler. So good of you to come."

A smiling woman stepped back from him and extended her hand, and gave him a solid squeeze. A second before she told Hap her name, he recognized her. She didn't say Senator Rawlings, Vice-Presidential-candidate-in-waiting Rawlings, or mother of Marguerite, but he knew who she was anyway. Garnetta Rawlings.

"You like my view?" she said.

"Breathtaking."

Her hair was hidden under an intricately knotted silver scarf. On a leather thong hanging around her neck there was a small gold bell, making the faintest tinkle as she moved about. Her floor-length purple caftan was covered with coin-sized mirrors and glass jewels. And stitched in gold to the cuffs and lapels of the robe was some sort of hieroglyphic writing. It was a sorceress's housedress, something an outlandish grandmother on Miami Beach might wear to market.

"You like it?" the senator asked. She touched a sleeve.

"It's very . . ." Hap looked around the living room in search of a euphemism.

"Bizarre," the senator said. "That's the word you're after, I believe."

She smiled again. There was a British coolness about her, a brusque let's-get-on-with-it energy. Like a woman who'd just come down from climbing Everest, saying, yes, by Jove, I believe there's time before tea to wrestle some tigers.

She was in her mid-sixties, her blue eyes quick and piercing, a wisp of white hair showing at her neck. Dozens of sunspots stained her forehead. Things metastasizing into worse things.

"Your chauffeur said you had something to tell me."

"Yes," she said, and looked off for a moment toward her balcony. "I was shocked and saddened by Daniel's death. Please accept my deepest condolences."

He thanked her, but said nothing more.

She turned and motioned him to follow her across the living room. White leather furniture, a gray tile floor, glass tables. On the far wall were several oil paintings of pyramids, the Mexican or South American kind, Aztec, Incas, ruins that loomed from jungle mists. Temples with eerie lights rising behind them.

"Mr. Tyler, I know you're grieving just now, and believe me, I am too. But it's important we act quickly if we're to resolve this ourselves. Keep it out of litigation. And the papers."

Hap watched her standing in the middle of the room. Her face was pinched with concern as she glanced about at her paintings, but there was something in her voice that bothered him. Ringing a half note off sincere. And the way her eyes kept roaming the distances seemed a bit theatrical.

"Hap . . . can I call you that?"

He nodded.

"Hap," she said. "As you may know, at the time of Daniel's death, he and I were engaged in a business transaction. I had given him a large sum of money, but he hadn't yet given me what I paid for."

Hap was silent, holding firm to his poker face.

"You *do* know what I'm talking about then?"

"I have no idea."

She looked skeptically at him for a moment, then said, "Come in here, maybe it will help jog your memory."

He followed her into a shadowy room twice the size of the living area. Recessed bulbs focused soft lights on twenty or so glass cases stationed at three-foot intervals around the room. A small, very private museum.

Hap moved to the closest case. On a swatch of red velvet a gold frog squatted, a pendant. It was an inch long, rubies for eyes, its toes coiled into circles, and it seemed a bit battered around the backbone.

As he continued to roam the room, Garnetta hovered nearby.

More gold jewelry, some jade, some ceramic figures of reclining men, Indian priests, intricately carved animal figures of ivory or shell. In a corner of the room stood a five-foot stela, a stone relief of an Indian emperor. The room had the stale, airless quality of some museum exhibits.

She stepped up to a case somewhat taller than the others. In it there was a black-and-white Polaroid cocked up on a wooden stand. The photo showed a small gold mask held in the pinch of someone's thumb and first finger. It was an awkward shot, as if someone had held the mask at arm's length while positioning the camera in the other hand. The mask's face was twisted into an exaggerated grimace. A flat, wrinkled piece of work no bigger than a jar label.

"This is the object I paid your brother for." There was a strain in her voice, a small war being fought between her civility and her outrage in the nerve-endings of her vocal cords.

"This is Mayan?"

"Yes, young man, it's most certainly Mayan, early postclassic period. Much of it from Tikal, one of the great cities of the eleventh century."

"The Maya," he said. "They're the ones with the quarry, they threw virgins into it to keep their gods happy?"

She crossed her arms beneath her breasts.

"Yes, that's right."

He said, "The same ones, they cut hearts out, ran them up the pyramids as offering, if the heart stopped beating before the runner got to the top, he had to go back, cut out another one. Those the people we're talking about?"

She stiffened slightly, but smiled.

"Very good, Mr. Tyler. And the ball games, do you know about them as well?"

"Played for days," he said, "big walled-in field, trying to get a little ball through a tiny hoop. Like basketball and lacrosse combined. Could take them a week sometimes before anybody even made a goal, playing round the clock. The losing team got their heads chopped off, or was it their hearts cut out?"

"You're a student of anthropology then."

"I'm not a student of anything. Daniel read a lot of history, some of it slopped over, that's all."

"Why so contemptuous?"

Hap looked silently at the photo of the painful mask.

"Is it because you find it inconsistent, Hap, for a highly civilized society to be brutal? A society whose achievements in mathematics and astronomy and architecture were centuries ahead of their counterparts in Europe, a society that created some of the world's great works of art. Beautiful and brutal. Do you find this so incompatible?" She came a step closer to him, brought her nose close to his.

"Are we more civilized?" she said. "Is that what you think?"

Hap said nothing. He knew the sound of a trap being set.

"Let me ask you a different question, Hap." She squinted up at him. "Do you believe it's possible that people were once more developed than they are now?"

"Well," he said. "I know I was."

She smiled indulgently.

"I mean people in general," she said. "The human species. More religious. More spiritually enlightened."

"Maybe more superstitious," he said.

She made another smile, crisp, but empty.

"As you said, Hap, in the world of the Maya, death was carefully ritualized. It served a greater purpose. Human blood was the glue that held that great culture together. A unifying reverence for death and sacrifice. Death, yes, but not the random and meaningless slaughter of our age.

"It was through that ritual sacrifice, public mutilations and bloodletting that the rulers were able to lead that vast and complex society. Blood was the mortar for their greatest achievements. And as for us, Hap, what can we say? What does our punishment accomplish? Have we Americans even a fraction of the social harmony that these brutal people enjoyed? Absolutely not. Absolutely not."

She moved among the glass cases, looking into each one. Her shoulders back, the robe, a purple billow around her.

This was a woman who'd built her political career on bureaucracy bashing. Her campaign gimmick was to disappear for a week, usually into some branch of the grim network of public assistance. She would pretend to be a patient in a nursing home, a tenant in a housing project, or a temporary in a food stamp office. When she got back in front of the cameras, played her hidden-camera videos, the scenes were shocking. It was all as bad as everyone had imagined. The systems didn't work. They bred laziness and despair. The only answer, went Garnetta's refrain, was to dismantle those Great Society dinosaurs. Demolish the welfare state, and replace it with scratch-and-claw capitalism.

It seemed like everyone in the public sector should have had her picture on their walls, be on the lookout for her, but no one ever recognized her till it was too late. She always got the goods, witnessed firsthand the scams, the abuse, the degrading brutality that the system wreaked on those it was meant to serve. It was always a major event when she resurfaced.

Hap, looking again at the gold frog with the ruby eyes, said, "Listen, Senator, I appreciate the anthropology lesson. It's very stimulating. But the truth is, I'm having a lot of trouble picturing my brother selling you things like this, things that belong in a museum, a public one."

She moved to his side, took his arm in hers, and in a precise whisper said, "I paid him eighty-six thousand five hundred dollars for the gold mask."

He pulled away from her grasp.

"You got to be kidding."

"Hap Tyler," she said, a hand rising to touch her bare throat, "everything in this room, all of what you see before you, came from your brother. I've been buying his merchandise for twenty years." She moved in front of the photograph of the gold mask, took a long look at it. "In point of fact," she said, "I wrote Daniel a check last week, and he was to have handed over the mask today. That was our usual arrangement."

"Twenty years? I don't believe it."

"I'd gone to a lecture," she said. "At the public library downtown. Daniel Tyler was showing slides of recent archaeological finds in Mexico. And discussing current theories of the fall of the Mayan Empire. Volcanoes, I believe, ideas long since discredited. Anyway, when the lecture was over, I introduced myself to him and told him I shared his fascination with this culture.

"And then, it was just a week later he phoned me, said he wanted to meet privately. He claimed it was urgent. So I invited him to my home in Coral Gables, and at that meeting your brother, Daniel, offered to sell me that gold frog, the one you're looking at. I remember exactly what I paid him, five thousand dollars."

She gazed with him at the frog. Hap pulled away and looked at her. Her eyes filmy, mouth relaxed, head lifted. As if she were drifting into some fuzzy reverie, transported to another place. Hap wasn't sure, of course, but it seemed she might be looking out across some vast parade ground, her legions, her priests, her slaves arrayed before her, as she surveyed them all from the peak of one of those pyramids.

"Okay, Senator," Hap said. "So where in hell did Daniel supposedly get hold of this stuff?"

She took a long, even breath and returned to the moment. Her eyes refocused, and she turned and gave him another indulgent smile. This one reminded him of his old shrink. Hap saying to the guy, well, have you figured it out yet, why I'm crazy? And his shrink would smile like the senator. You poor sad fuck, if I knew the answer to that, you think I'd be asking you all these questions?

"I would prefer having that mask, Hap," the senator said. "But if you would rather give me something else, a substitute, I'd consider that as well."

"A substitute? And what would that be?"

"Another one of these," she said, and motioned to the display cases. "Something else that might fit alongside the others."

"I'm supposed to know where Daniel got these things?"

"Don't you?"

"Oh, sure," he said. "I'll just go swim down to the treasure ship, pick you out another one. How 'bout this afternoon?"

Her eyes snapped to his, and for a moment she worked them, reading him, or trying to. Hap smiled at her, his innocent smile, the one he'd perfected at Radisson Acres. And in a second or two she swallowed, smoothed her emotions back into place. Her expression regained its crafty alertness. A smile appeared. A vote-getter of a smile. Once again she was Senator Garnetta Rawlings, the champion of the little guy. That other woman, Garnetta, her royal empress, had completely disappeared.

"You know all about it, don't you, Hap? You know."

"Not yet," he said. "But I'm beginning to get the picture."

# CHAPTER 10

O N HIS WAY BACK DOWN FROM THE PENTHOUSE, THE elevator operator stared at Hap for a few floors.

"Don't I know you?" he said finally.

"Anything's possible."

The guy hunched his shoulders and asked Hap what the fuck his name was. Hap told him.

"Yeah, I thought so," the guy said. "You're the asshole."

The kid's mouth warped into a scowl. The red scar that ran along the edge of his sideburns burned red, then slowly died to white. The guy was a couple of inches taller than Hap, but forty, fifty pounds heavier. A shotput physique. After considering it a moment more, the kid stopped his car between the twentieth and twenty-first floors.

"I had low bid for the tile work on this whole goddamn place."

"So?"

"So you pulled your dumb fucking stunt, threw all those papers out the window, set them back two months with the bidding, I couldn't hold out that long. Went out of fucking business. Got reduced to this. This goddamn box."

"Sorry," Hap said.

But the guy wasn't looking for an apology. He glared at Hap for a short drumroll, then his eyes boiled over, and he lurched forward and jammed Hap to the wall, pressed his shoulder into

Hap's throat and gave him three uppercuts that relocated Hap's liver four inches to the north.

They stood a foot apart for a moment, the guy breathing hard, trying to think up some other humiliation. Hap figured, shit, he probably *did* have three liver punches coming. He'd screwed up this guy's career plans, taken steak off his table, and probably a few other tables too. Three bodyshots were about right. But anything more than that, no, that put him into cruel and unusual territory, and he'd have to defend himself.

"You're an asshole," the guy said. "Aren't you?"

Hap said nothing.

"Go on, say it."

Hap shrugged and said it. "You're an asshole."

"Man, now you're fucking dead meat," the tile guy said. "Dead, swollen carcass."

Hap devoted the rest of the ride down to swallowing an adequate breath. And when the doors opened onto the lobby, the kid grabbed hold of the scruff of Hap's polo shirt until one of the security men came over. They conferred in Spanish, but Hap understood enough to know that his sexuality was being called into serious doubt, as well as his relationships with household pets.

The concierge joined them, and another security man hustled up as well. The whole team. All of them standing around Hap, letting him see the force this place could marshal if necessary.

One of the security men took an armlock on him, but the elevator guy stepped in.

"He's mine," the guy said. "He insulted me."

"Okay," the concierge said. "But not in front of the tenants."

The kid took over for the security guard, shoved Hap forward and cranked his arm higher.

On the way through the front doors, Hap asked the guy if there was a name for the hold he was using. The guy cursed him, and Hap said he'd be happy to recommend a better way, you know, less effort, same result. One old commando to another. A thumb hooked deep behind a strand of tendons in the upper arm. Got to know the entry point, though, or you could break your thumb.

"Piss off," the tile layer said. "You fucking moron."

Hap wasn't the best fighter in his marine unit. Just didn't have the blood lust necessary for it. And since getting back from Southeast Asia, he'd tried to let whatever killing skills he'd acquired drain out of his body. To take a long, slow soak in the hot tub of America, anesthetize his body with sun and rum, go soft and dopey as everyone else.

But now, not out of anger, only as an experiment to see what was still there in the deep channels of muscle memory, Hap swiveled and dropped to a sudden crouch, twisting free of the guy's grip. Then he came up quickly and shot his stiffened fingers into the man's Adam's apple. The tile layer was staggered but still operable. So Hap moved back a half step and snapped a sidekick into the guy's solar plexus. It knocked the guy backward, made him stumble over his own feet, fall hard on his back, groaning and breathless. He looked up at Hap, then scooted backward beneath the running board of a Pierce Arrow.

Just as Hap expected, there was a lot of rust. Back in his Nha Trang days, it would have only taken that first shot to put the guy down.

Walking away, Hap tapped on the hood of the Pierce Arrow. It was fiberglass, just a replica from a kit. Could have a VW engine or a Maserati hiding under there. You never knew. Tile layers, Pierces, only way to find out what was under the hood was to mash the pedal down.

By the time Hap had walked the mile up South Bayshore to the Coconut Grove Bank, his liver had settled back into a cavity very close to its original one, and he could take four or five steps in a row without his breath burning his throat. But he'd pulled a muscle in his back firing that kick. And the joints in his leg were dry and stiff, his knee making a grating noise every other step.

He was on his way into the bank when it came to him. The thing that had seemed so damn familiar about the senator's chauffeur. It was his voice. Yeah, of course. The guy's voice sounded a whole hell of a lot like the voice on the car phone yesterday. The guy threatening to send his goons over to write their signatures in Hap's flesh.

He found the bank manager, Mike Romero, having lunch in the conference room. Back in the Grove's heyday, Romero had occasionally jammed with Jimi Hendrix, Ike and Tina, and some of the never-bes passing through the hard rock coffeehouses. He had a belly now, and he touched it secretively every so often like he might be remembering how it was to hold the old steel string against himself.

Romero managed to tear himself away from his peanut butter sandwich long enough to check Daniel's bank balance. And there it was. Eighty-six five deposited last Monday, twelfth of August.

"The check's cleared already," he said. "You want, I can just transfer this to your account now. I mean, technically I should wait, I guess, let the lawyers take a look at things first, probate and all that, but you might be needing it for something. And what I say is, we should fuck the lawyers, any chance we get."

"Yeah," said Hap. "Transfer the funds, why not. There's this and that to pay. The funeral home among other things. And, hey, by the way. Did Daniel have a safe-deposit box with you?"

Romero brushed his stomach again, strumming a chord against his straining buttons.

"Yeah, I think he had a couple."

"Can I look? Or should we call a lawyer, ask if it's okay?"

Hap sat in the privacy room and leafed through the contents of the first safe-deposit box. Birth certificates, Daniel's, Hap's, and their parents', some family snapshots, nothing he hadn't seen before. No will, no insurance policy.

Hap put it aside and drew out a handful of photographs, nineteenth-century sepia and blur. Commodore Randolph Tyler in stiff awkward poses, supervising the construction of the Mangrove House. The workers, all island blacks and Indians. The Commodore in various sailing vessels, bleak days and bright ones. The Commodore standing on the front steps of the Mangrove House, his hand on his son, Matthew's, shoulder. Matthew looking strained and nervous. And there were a couple of oval portraits of Rebecca, and one of Louise. The dead mothers.

The last photograph was larger than the rest, and had a worn and wrinkled surface. In it a tall, thin woman in a white blouse and Seminole skirt stood next to the great paddle wheel of a mill. Beside her was a young boy, ten or eleven, wearing a crisp white shirt and knickers. The river that drove the mill was only a few feet to their right, churning over the rocks.

Hap held the photograph out to catch the best light in the dim room. He was having a momentary case of dizziness as he looked at this woman, this tall, dark-haired beauty. She and Marguerite Rawlings were twins. The same thick black hair. Hair you could disappear into, spend a month, come out a happy man. Even those eyes were the same. They seemed to burn beyond the century that contained her.

Somehow, the Rawlings men who passed on Ramona's blood had kept her preserved inside them. A perfect duplicate, some recessive gene, some stray coil of DNA, staying intact for a century until finally it flowered again in Marguerite.

In the second tray Hap found a bundle of documents held together by a thick rubber band. Legal papers. He stripped off the band and dumped them on the table in front of him. Several dozen of them. All with accordion pages that opened up to some kind of handwritten certificate. The ink was blurry, and it was composed in the tortured hieroglyphs of nineteenth-century penmanship. At first it looked like stock in some long-defunct company, legal mumbo jumbo that only Daniel with his historical fascinations would bother preserving. But after a few moments' study Hap untangled the flowery script. Deeds. Titles to land. Probably property the Commodore had once owned. Those vast tracts the early pioneers were so fond of, now endlessly subdivided.

At the bottom of the packets was a single yellowed page, crisp with age. A squiggly line ran down its center like someone's aimless doodle. Hap was about to put it aside when he noticed the five-pointed star drawn just to the side of the twisty line. Hap turned it over, and on the back the page was dated 1881, the year the great man had settled in Miami. In the Commodore's jittery scrawl there was a single sentence. "A gift to him who knows its use, a curse to him who doesn't."

Christ. He closed his eyes, sat back in the chair. He listened to the grumble of traffic out on Main Highway, the phones ringing in the distance of the bank. A woman was coughing in a privacy booth nearby. And Hap Tyler was holding what looked a lot like a goddamn treasure map. As simple as they come. The sawtooth coastline, its coves, its inlets, sounds, and bays. It was as if someone had drawn their pencil point down the ragged edge of a maple leaf. And then there was that star, its quick five lines marking a spot very close to shore.

Hap had navigated the local waters all his life, spent hours studying the charts, but for the life of him he couldn't identify the location of that star. Couldn't place that configuration of squiggles. The perspective was hard to judge. Was the scribbled line five miles of coast, or fifty? And of course, the shoreline must have shifted some since 1881. But in any case, he had it in his hand, and if it *was* what it looked like, a map of the coastline, it should be easy enough to match that jagged line to a navigation chart. And then drop his anchor above the place where Daniel had been retrieving Mayan artifacts for years.

That is, if he could stand up. If the blood would return from wherever it had fled and circulate the oxygen again, and feed his muscles and help him unlock his body from this chair.

In a few minutes, when he'd recovered, he pushed himself to his feet and walked back into the safe-deposit vault, and asked the young lady in charge of the room for a sheet of onionskin paper, a pen, and a mailing envelope. He returned to the privacy room, made a careful tracing of the map, put it in the envelope, replaced the original in the safe-deposit box.

On his way out, he thanked Romero for transferring the funds. Mike stood up from the employee dining table and wiped peanut butter off his hands. Those hands used to fly so fast across the strings that even Jimi Hendrix had stopped playing and watched him work. Hap had been in the audience that evening. Back a few centuries ago, when Coconut Grove consisted of fifty guys with guitars and sandals and straight-haired girlfriends with leather miniskirts and tambourines. Everybody trying to scream in Janis Joplin's aching voice or go as gravelly as Mick. Back when you could cross any street in the Grove without looking, and when finally if a car did come along, it'd be somebody you knew. Back when all the stomachs were hard, all the drugs safe, all the diseases curable, when gravity and General Motors ruled the universe, back when Daniel sat out on the front porch rocker every night, a book propped in his lap, a lantern on the table beside him with a zillion bugs orbiting the thing. Back when everyone still had a sense of humor and a twinkle in his eye, even Hap. Despite his overshadowing grandfather, his worthless father. Even Hap Tyler had a twinkle for a while there.

Before he'd gotten ten feet onto the property at the Mangrove House, Hap could tell something was wrong. He was halfway across the back acre before he figured it out. It was his bedroom window. The shades were down. In all the years he'd lived there, he hadn't lowered them once. He'd forgotten they were even there.

He stood a few yards from the house and watched a couple of squirrels chasing each other up and down the trunk of an oak tree near the Devil's Punchbowl. Then he pulled out his shirttail, stuck the envelope in the waistband of his shorts, and tucked the shirt back in.

He exhaled, gathered a couple of breaths, went quietly up the front stairway, and swung open the heavy door. For a moment he stood at the foot of the staircase and listened. Only the perpetual mower at the Munroe estate. He waited a moment more, then began to climb, taking the path closest to the wall to avoid the two small creaks. At the top of the stairs he halted by his door. It was closed, and he never left it that way. He listened again, heard nothing, then carefully turned the knob and was in the room in one motion.

A black woman about Hap's height with her hair in cornrows

was bent over his gray Chesterfield, slashing one of the seat cushions. The other two cushions were lying at her feet, already disemboweled. She wore a loose-fitting black T-shirt and black jeans and white jogging shoes. Lots of bracelets and throat jewelry. Her T-shirt said MIAMI NICE.

"Whoops," she said.

"What the hell!"

"Well now, listen, honey. I'm just about done here. Finish this last one here, and I'm out of your way."

Hap looked around at the wreckage.

She tossed the white stuffing into the air, emptied the cushion and let it drop. Hap took a step toward her, then halted. There was a silver pistol wedged in the waistband of her jeans. The envelope suddenly felt conspicuous beneath his shirt.

"The senator send you over here?"

"Senator? Now what senator would that be?"

Hap was silent.

"Naw," she said. "I'm more of your independent-operator type."

The woman showed him her smile, and two gold-capped teeth.

"And you must be the famous Hapfield Tyler."

Hap said yeah, yeah he was. She widened her smile an inch.

"I been hoping to get the opportunity to speak to you, Hapfield. Something I wanted to ask. 'Cause see, I heard your name, and I was all of a sudden curious about what kind of asshole would give a baby a bullshit name like that."

The woman kept on smiling.

"See, what I thought when I heard it was, it's gotta be some Mississippi cracker idea. Some dumb Johnny Reb wanting to sound all Old South and uppity class. I bet that's it. Snooty name like that, gotta be a poor sharecropper got himself confused with the man in the big house. Tell me, that's it, right?"

Hap cut a glance at his desk three steps away, at the brass bookend, a red-eyed bass jumping for a fly. The thing weighed at least five pounds. He'd used it once or twice for a hammer.

"Hey, now," the woman said, following Hap's gaze. "Don't

let's have us no truculence, okay? Just because I point out you got a bullshit name, and you caught me doing surgery on your furniture, it don't automatically require you to get your head shot full of lead, you see what I'm saying?''

She'd withdrawn the pistol and had her finger in the trigger guard, dangling it.

"You know what, Hapfield? I been in here for a good while looking around awful careful, every damn place I could pry into, and I didn't find shit. But I want you to understand, I haven't given up. No, I'm like that pit bull sinks his teeth in your leg—you can kill that damn dog, its jaw's still clamped tight. Got to get a chain saw, cut yourself loose. That pit bull's me, lover. And I'm on your leg.

"I mean, hell, if it was up to me, I'd sit you down right this second, take this .38 and reason with your ass, get it all done in one quick session. But you know, that ain't on the menu today. Those aren't my instructions. So I guess we'll just have to put off that merriment for another afternoon now, won't we?''

She went over to Hap's wall mirror, fiddled with a couple of the braids, holding that .38 down by her right leg, like she was inviting him to try to jump her, give her a reason to do what she wanted to do. Her eyes in the mirror blinked slowly and shifted to Hap's.

"Well, enough of this shit. We got us some miles to go before we sleep, huh.''

She winked, and turned to go.

Maybe it was something Hap did, some small shift of his feet. Some unnatural, eye-catching move of his hands, shielding the envelope. She stopped. Came back in the room with a curious smile. Glancing from his eyes to his shirtfront and back.

"Now, what're we doing? We being tricky, are we?'' She raised the pistol and said, "Let me ask you a personal question, Hapfield. You ever been personally involved in a strip search?''

He took a slow breath, gauged the distance between them, two yards. He probably could make half of that before she shot him in the chest. He stayed put.

"Well, as for me,'' she said. "It just so happens I'm an expert in the technique of the North American strip search. And being the kind of person I am, generous and all that, I'm willing to share my extensive knowledge with you. Let's start with the fucking shirt.''

She motioned with the pistol, and Hap pulled his shirt loose and tugged it over his head.

She hummed with pleasure.

"Well, well. Now, you got yourself one of them hard bodies, Hapfield. Nice stomach, good shoulders, getting a little flab at the edges, but still, all in all, not bad, been working out. And what would that be there? That motherfucking paper in your belt.''

He pulled it out.

"Let's say you drop it on the floor and kick it over here. How would that be?''

He did that, and then she told him to step back another step and he did that too.

With the pistol on him, she scooped up the envelope and pulled the sheet out of it.

"Now, Hapfield, my man. Why don't you move your pale wrinkled ass right back up against that wall. Give this old gal a little safety zone, here, so I can study this thing.''

When he'd moved back, she looked it over for a long moment, then glanced up at Hap. Back at the page, and back at Hap.

"This what I think it is?''

Hap tried to keep his face neutral, but she seemed to see an answer there. She smiled, then rolled her eyes up, pantomiming ecstasy.

"Whooee, I believe I just done won the Florida lottery.''

"You've just won a shitload of trouble is what you've done.''

She chuckled at him, thumbed the hammer back.

"But let me tell you this,'' she said, her eyes full of quirky light. "I ain't one of those people wins the lottery, then says to the TV reporters, no sir, I'm not going to let this jackpot change my life. Going to work same as always tomorrow. Shit, no. Not this girl. If this scrap of paper's what it looks like, honey, this bitch ain't ever going back to work. No sir. Not me. Not ever.''

# CHAPTER 11

AFTER SHE LEFT THE MANGROVE HOUSE, MARGUERITE drove back to her bungalow on Asturia Avenue in Coral Gables. The family home, where she'd grown up, hers now. A twenties stucco, with red-tile roof, two tiny bedrooms, one bath. Original windows, plumbing, wiring. Only some kitchen appliances updated. No bars on the windows, no alarm system. Let the burglars come in, they'd find nothing of value.

In a daze Marguerite Rawlings showered, blow-dried her hair, applied her makeup with painstaking care. Used too much blush, rubbed it off, got it right finally. A quiet gray-green eyeshadow. She put on a pair of linen slacks, navy, and a sleeveless cream jersey, a string of pearls. Trying to do the ordinary things, a mantra of normalcy, maybe deceive her brainwaves, smooth them back into their usual rolling swells.

She took three aspirin, made a pot of coffee, but her hand jittered too much to drink it. She poured it down the sink, toasted a slice of wheat bread, buttered it carefully, studied it for a minute, then put a dab of orange marmalade on it. Standing at the sink, she listened for a moment to her neighbor's TV, a game show coming through the hedge, bells ringing, the audience whooping it up. She picked up her toast, carried it across the kitchen, and dropped it in the trash.

At eleven she was at the yellow clapboard house in Liberty City.

The home of Miami's first black medical doctor. She parked behind a red BMW 731 that was nosed up behind Millicent Benitez's Chevy Nova. The vanity license plate on the BMW said SHORTY. No need for further explanation in this town. There was one, and only one, Shorty Busser.

Last week it had been Marguerite's idea to have the meeting here. But now she wasn't so sure. In this light, on this muggy morning, the house looked wretched, not worth saving. The front porch was warped, a few of the pine planks had been ripped up and a Florida holly had sprouted through the opening. Only a vague memory of paint on the walls. The carcass of some rodent was decaying on the steps. Windows long ago broken out, the whole structure slumped toward the east.

The neighborhood air had an acrid bite, the dizzy vapors of fiberglass and powerful solvents wafting out of the two-story hangar that occupied the rest of the block on Sixth Avenue.

Shorty Busser had recently purchased that yellow clapboard house from the city of Miami, and was preparing to demolish it, and use the empty lot as a storage area for the speedboat hulls he manufactured inside that hangar. Comanche Racing Boats, Shorty's latest hobby. Building supersonic toys for his buddies.

Marguerite had protested every step of Shorty's plan. Weeks of battle, and several of her columns dedicated to the issue. Finally last Wednesday the city commission had listened to the arguments of Millicent Benitez, the preservation league's attorney, and then to Shorty. No team of experts for him, no pin-striped attorneys, just humble Shorty Busser arguing that the economic impact of his boat-building operation clearly outweighed the minor historical significance of the house of Miami's first black physician, Dr. Mercury Theobald Bloodworth.

Several of the commission members had great fun repeating Dr. Bloodworth's name. Over and over they enunciated it, hitting every syllable of his middle name. This man who arrived in Miami about the same time as Ramona, lived to be eighty, but who had left little trace of himself in the historical record aside from some smallish newspaper articles about his single-handed battle against a cholera epidemic among the early black pioneers. He'd saved hundreds of lives, maybe thousands, the core of the black community. But no one quite remembered him. And as soon as they finished having fun with his name, the commissioners voted unanimously to let their great, good friend Shorty Busser knock down Dr. Bloodworth's house. On the way out of the hearing that day, Marguerite had told Shorty that he could either meet her in the house this morning or suffer the consequences. She had, however, no clear idea of what those consequences might be.

When Marguerite entered the front door of the clapboard house, Millicent Benitez and Shorty Busser were standing in the living room, facing away from each other. Millie was wearing a tailored black-and-white suit, a white high-necked blouse with a black bow tie. Much too hot for August. Much too formal for Miami. Not to mention twenty years out of style.

She was only five feet tall, probably weighed less than ninety pounds. Looked like she could fit between the bars of a jail cell. She was only twenty-three, but she wore her hair, did her makeup, and dressed like Beaver's mom. Severe suits. Horn-rimmed white glasses. All in all, a geek, but a lovable one. And the only lawyer Marguerite could find who would donate ten hours a week to the preservation league.

She came over to Marguerite and took her hand, murmured a word of sympathy, and leaned forward to press her cheek to Marguerite's. When she stepped back, she nodded toward Shorty and gave a quick eye roll of distaste.

He was a thick man, five five. A couple of inches shorter than Marguerite, but probably outweighed her by a hundred pounds. He wore a pair of neon green bicycle pants and a tight white T-shirt. Showing how seriously he took this meeting by dressing up. His white hair had been permed recently and it coiled tightly about his head like a silvery halo of radioactivity.

The man had spent his life conquering bigger and smarter men, and it had given him a robust flush and a smile that could flick between benevolent and murderous in a second. His eyes were pool-water blue. Deceptively mild, because when he needed to, he could harden them, keep them staring unflinching into his opponent's eyes while he cut out their vital organs.

Shorty stepped forward, extending his hand, and Marguerite gave him a perfunctory shake.

"Good to see you, Margie. How've you been?"

"There've been better days."

"Oh, yes," he said. "I saw it in the paper. Horrible tragedy. I have to say, I always respected that man, even though we were usually on opposite sides of the table."

"Sure, Shorty. I know how much you admired him."

His smile decayed a fraction, then revived.

Marguerite glanced around the living room. Some gang insignia was painted on one wall. In the corner someone had recently built a fire and it had coated the walls and ceiling with soot. There were whiskey bottles and a broken chair in the adjoining room. What looked like a spray of bullet holes in the west wall. People had died in this room. And lately. The floor creaked ominously as Marguerite took an uncertain step.

Millie nudged her arm and motioned toward a window at the back of the house. Just outside, a skinny black man in a madras shirt was looking in at them. He had a dreamy smile and a scattering of broken teeth.

"I think he lives here," Millie said. "Shorty chased him out when we arrived."

The man smiled hopefully at Marguerite.

"That's what this house does," Shorty said. "Attracts vagrants, winos, the criminal element."

"Well, we better get started," Millie said. "I have a twelve-thirty I can't be late for."

"Far as I can see, we've really got nothing to talk about," Shorty said. "I mean, I came here today out of courtesy. But my legal people tell me the house is free and clear. The commission expressed itself. The property's mine to do with as I see fit. I mean, sure, you can find a way to prolong this if you want to spend your money like that, but you won't win. So look, why don't we just shake hands and get on back to our exciting lives."

Marguerite glanced out at the old black man. He nodded at her again, smiling, bobbing his head slightly. At her disposal.

"Tell me something, would you, Shorty?" She broke away from the man and turned on Busser. "In your exalted opinion, is there anything in this town worth saving? I mean, is there anything you wouldn't bulldoze if it was in your way?"

"All right, look, Margie. I know I don't have to do anything at all. But listen, I'm prepared to build a small monument to your Dr. Bloodworth. Granite, marble, you name it. Hell, I'll build it out of uranium if that's what you want. Engrave whatever little speech you want on it. Put it right out there by the sidewalk as a memorial. People walking by could see it, read it, whatever. Now, how would that be?"

"How incredibly generous of you."

"Oh, now, come on, Margie. Don't make me out to be a monster. I got nothing against the principle of preservation. Not per se. Just when it conflicts with business, with growth."

"With cash flow," Marguerite said.

"Right. There you go. Now you're getting it." Shorty ambled over to the front window, looked out, then turned around and swept his gaze around the room. "I mean, honey, be realistic. Look at this hovel. It's a crash pad for lowlifes like that fellow outside. Why in the world are we devoting our energies fussing over this old shack? I just don't see it."

"But the Deering Estate, say, or Vizcaya," she said. "You'd agree, those places are worth saving."

"That's no comparison," Shorty said. "Those are mansions, showplaces. We'll never see anything like them built again. A hundred rooms, gardens. No, I'm a thousand percent behind saving those places."

"Good for business," Marguerite said. "Tourists go there, take pictures, spend an afternoon looking at how the rich people used to live. Rich white people."

"Oh," he said. "Now I'm a racist."

"That might be part of it. Yeah."

"But Margie, see, that just doesn't wash. 'Cause look, what I'm doing by knocking this house down is, I'm doing good for these people down here. I'm bringing jobs to this neighborhood. Jobs that wouldn't be here if you had your way and just turned this house into some kind of educational museum, put plaques all over the wall. What I do is, I bring money into Liberty City, hard currency, every day of the week. And what would you bring, Marguerite? What would you bring here?"

She glanced down at the floor, out the back window where the two-story hangar loomed. The man had found a seat on a stump in the backyard. Smoking a cigarette out there.

"Heroes," she said.

"Heroes?"

"That's all I want, help them remember one of their people. One of their best. Return a little bit of what they've lost."

Marguerite heard the squeal of brakes outside.

"Oh, yeah." Shorty chuckled. "That's how you see it, is it? All they need down in this part of town to change from a crack-infested ghetto to a functioning, prosperous community is a good history lesson. That your take on things, is it?" He shook his head, looked at her for a minute and said, "Honey, where'd you pick up a corny bullshit idea like that, in some college class? Sitting around shooting the breeze with some Ph.D. about utopias and Walden goddamn Pond?"

"What the hell is she doing here?"

At the front window Marguerite stared out at the Rolls-Royce that was double-parked next to Shorty's BMW. Her mother getting out of the driver's door. Chauffering herself this morning.

"I asked the senator if she might drop by," Shorty said. "Thought it might be useful to have somebody who could reason with you. Help you see the light."

"We're going to court, Mr. Busser," Marguerite said, turning on the man. "I'm having Millie file a class-action suit on behalf of the citizens of Liberty City and Overtown to protect a building of historical significance to them and their community. And today we'll be filing an injunction with Judge Marcus to prevent you from demolishing this building until the time when our suit is resolved. We're going to run you ragged, as long as we can."

Busser shifted his eyes to Millie. He slid them up and down her with amusement, as if he might be searching her suit for a loose thread, something to unravel her with.

"Well, I see we're all here," Garnetta said, coming into the room. Wearing a white blazer, pink blouse, with a gray skirt. Her campaign clothes. Conservative, forgettable. Don't give them anything they can latch on to, criticize later.

For a moment or two her mother paced around the room, touching the old walls, running her hand along a window ledge. She didn't look at the three of them, or speak a word of greeting, but kept her focus on the house, this latest preoccupation of the daughter she pretended not to understand.

Finally Garnetta made an exasperated sigh and came to a halt in front of them.

"So?" she said to Shorty. Her eyes still hadn't passed over Marguerite. "Have we made any progress?"

"I've been getting a lesson in civic responsibility," he said. "I'll have to fill you in on it. Very illuminating."

"I believe I've heard it already," she said. "A few dozen times."

She glanced at Millicent, made another huff of disapproval.

Garnetta said, "Have you reached some kind of settlement then? Can we get on to other matters?"

"Your daughter is threatening more legal action," Shorty said. He ran his hand over the rump of his bike pants, the slick fabric. Seemed to Marguerite he'd puffed himself up a few pounds per square inch when Garnetta had come into the room. Get his ego out to proper size to deal with a U.S. senator.

"Ten thousand dollars," Garnetta said.

"I'm sorry?" Marguerite squinted at her mother.

Garnetta examined the back of her right hand, her manicure.

She said, "I'm prepared to donate ten thousand dollars to the preservation league if we can reach a settlement with Mr. Busser in this case. It would be a win-win situation. You get some much-needed money for your organization, I get some positive press, a tax write-off, Shorty gets back to work. Everybody gains. Ten thousand dollars, that's my offer."

"Christ," Millie said. "We could hire somebody part-time."

"Thanks," Marguerite said. "But no deal."

"Twenty thousand," she said. "Last offer."

Millicent sucked in a breath.

"No, Mother. Not ten, not twenty. Not anything."

Garnetta's face fluttered through various reactions, discarding each one in a millisecond, a twitch of lips, a jiggle of light in her eyes. Nothing holding. Then finally, yes, there it was. A sad, hurt smile taking over. But back there, behind her dark brown eyes, the cleverness, the contempt, simmered.

"All right. If that's how you want it. I certainly can't force you to take the money."

Millie motioned to Marguerite, and she followed her over to the corner of the room. In a whisper Millie informed her that if they filed their suit, at best it would mean a delay in the destruction of the doctor's house by a week or two. Shorty would win, sooner or later, no way around it. Take the damn cash.

Marguerite glanced over at her mother and Shorty. They'd turned away and were engaged in earnest conversation. She glanced again at the old man outside. He was standing now beside the stump, examining the last inch of his cigarette, watching its smoke curl.

Marguerite spoke close to Millie's ear.

"If we can't win, why in the hell is she offering that kind of money?"

"Because of Shorty," Millie whispered. "I heard downtown this week, they're talking about him for the new congressional seat. She's probably trying to keep him away from any negative press. Keep him out of court as much as possible."

"Christ. That woman."

"Take it, Marguerite. Take the twenty. We could do a lot of good with that kind of money."

Marguerite closed her eyes, bowed her head briefly, and

turned away from Millie and walked back over to her mother. Garnetta still with that condescending smile.

"We'll see you in court, Mr. Busser."

Marguerite looked into her mother's eyes.

"Aw, come on, honey," Shorty said.

"You could make it a hundred thousand, I wouldn't touch it." Still staring at her mother. But Garnetta was looking off at the far wall. Keeping herself above the fray.

"All this, honey," said Shorty, "for Mercury Theobald Bloodworth? Turn down twenty thousand dollars to save his house?"

"Nothing you'd understand, Shorty. He was an altruist."

"Marguerite," Garnetta snapped. "You have no right to talk that way about Mr. Busser. That man has given more of himself to this community than you'll ever know."

"I'm sure Shorty has done a lot of things to this community nobody'll ever know."

"And what's that supposed to mean?" Shorty poked Marguerite in the arm.

She looked down at his hand and he lowered it.

"Marguerite," her mother said, talking to that far wall. "You're determined to oppose me in any way you can. That's what this is all about, isn't it?"

"It has nothing to do with you, Mother. I don't even know why you're here."

"Of course it has to do with me. Everything you do has to do with me."

"What!"

"Your life, Marguerite, your mission in life is to oppose me in every way you can imagine. To denounce me. You know it as well as I do. You don't think of me as your mother, you consider me the enemy. You delight in finding new ways to antagonize me."

Marguerite turned her back on Shorty, stepping in closer to her mother, into the range of her lush aroma, that scent of Camay she'd used all her life instead of perfume. Her mother's secret aroma. The cloying, flowery smell of bathtime hanging to her all day.

Marguerite said, "Don't overrate yourself, Senator. I'm not against you. I'm not against anything. I'm *for* things. For *saving* things, preserving them, not destroying them. Can you try to understand that, please? For once, to get it into your mind what I believe in, what I want to accomplish."

"You're such a child, Marguerite. Such an unrealistic, immature child. I just keep waiting for you to grow up. To see how the world really is."

Her mother touched the collar of her silk blouse, still staring off into the middle distance. She said, "Things can't stay the way they were. They simply can't. It's impossible. The past is dead. Everything moves ahead, and you have to learn to move forward with it."

Her voice was shifting up through the oratorical gears. A woman addressing the masses without benefit of amplifiers. She slid her eyes to the left then the right, dodging Marguerite.

"All right, tell us, Mother. Why can't we keep things how they used to be? A few things anyway. The good things."

"Good, bad," Garnetta said, "things change. New replaces old. You either evolve in this world, or you . . ." She shook her head as if banishing the thought.

"What? Or you what?"

"You either change," Garnetta said, bringing her eyes at last to her daughter's, "or you die, Marguerite. You die."

"Like Ramona," she said, "like Dad? They wouldn't change, so they had to die. Or like Daniel?"

"All right," her mother said. "That's enough. I won't listen to that kind of talk."

Marguerite glanced over at Busser and Millicent. Shorty peered uneasily at Garnetta, Millie staring at Marguerite.

Her mother looked tired now. Worn down from this unusual exercise, having a conversation with her daughter. Making minor eye contact. Marguerite shook her head, blew out a long breath, and walked outside.

In a moment or two Millie joined her. On the sidewalk, next to her car, Millie said, "I've ordered the abstracts like you wanted, on the Mill site and the adjoining land. They'll be in soon. Today, tomorrow.''

"Thanks.''

"You okay?''

"I'm okay.''

"If it's any comfort to you, I have problems with my mother too. Almost everybody I know has some kind of mother problem. Mothers are complicated.''

"Mothers, fathers, lovers. Everybody's complicated.''

"Yeah,'' she said. "I guess that's right.''

"I'll talk to you later, Millie. Okay? Thanks for stopping by.''

"I agree now,'' Millie said, "I agree we shouldn't take the money. No matter how useful it would be, it would always seem . . . I don't know.''

"Tainted,'' said Marguerite.

"Yeah,'' Millie said. "That's the word. Tainted.''

The old man in the madras shirt was swiping a wad of newspaper across the windshield of her Corvette, smiling brightly at her as he smeared the glass. Marguerite dug into her purse and handed the man the only bill she could find. A twenty. He took it from her, looked at it for a moment, and backed away, nodding and smiling. When he was a few yards away, he turned and broke into a run.

CHAPTER 12

WHEN HOLLINGS AND MARTINA ARRIVED AT ALVAREZ'S house that afternoon way the hell out west in Kendall, every house in the neighborhood looking like every other one, imitation Spanish, red tile roof, same damn trees in every yard, Hollings had the same thought he'd had a thousand times before in Miami. Where in fuck's name did all these people get all this goddamn money? Row after row of houses that cost more money than would run through Hollings's hands in a lifetime.

Martina and Hollings had been together all morning, and in that time they hadn't spoken more than a dozen sentences to each other. Hollings saying eleven of the twelve.

Eight this morning the woman had picked Hollings up in her pink '57 Chevy, Hollings standing on the corner near his apartment just like Alvarez had told him to. He got in the car, said hello, put out his hand, and she looked over at him for a second, then put the car in gear and started driving.

She had driven them over to Coconut Grove, parked the car on Main Highway in front of some French restaurant, and she just sat there without saying a fucking word, not answering his questions, not even looking over at him, till this green Rolls came driving out of a driveway across the road. That was about nine.

Right away Martina got out, said stay here, dickbrain, and left Hollings sitting there while she crossed the street and went down

Tyler's long, wooded driveway. Hollings wasn't sure what the fuck
he was supposed to be doing. Watch the car? Keep the motor running? Christ, Alvarez hadn't told him diddly. Just that this woman
was going to pick him up, and for Hollings not to say anything that
might piss her off, her being so almighty important to the project.

Hollings didn't know, maybe Alvarez had a sex thing going
with this woman, and that's why he'd brought her in on it. He took
another look at her as they were getting out of the car, walking up
the front walkway of Alvarez's house. The woman had a high ugly
factor, but shit, who could tell with Alvarez?

Driving over here, Hollings asked her about her name. Martina, like the tennis broad? No, like Reverend King, buttbreath, she
said. She was dressed in white jeans and a black T-shirt that said
MIAMI NICE. And she was definitely overfond of gold. With a couple
dozen bracelets on her arms and at least that many necklaces and
bangles and gold ropes around her throat. Hell, if the woman fell
down, they'd have to call a crane to get her upright again.

Lady also had two gold-covered front teeth, one with a half-
moon cut out of it, the one next to it with a skull and crossbones.
She wore her hair in long cornrows, each little pigtail clipped at the
end with another brad of gold. Hollings hadn't ever liked the style,
not even when Bo Derek wore hers that way in some movie he saw.
The hairdo looked like hundreds of weird snakes dripping off her
scalp, like that woman in the Bible story or wherever it was, you look
at her, you die. But shit, with hair like that, who would *want* to look
at her?

Martina knocked on the door, and Alvarez pulled it open, nodded, and led them through the house into the family room. Martina
plopped down on a couch and started playing with the silver .38.
Alvarez walked over to a wall mirror, looked at himself for a second
or two, then took out a comb.

"You find anything?"

Martina said no, not a goddamn thing.

"Hey, Alvarez, get her to tell you, would you, what the fuck she
was doing in there so long. She won't talk to me." Hollings stood
next to the couch, looking down at the woman. She was lying there,

playing with that .38 like she'd never had a pistol in her hands before. Aiming it around Alvarez's family room. Fixing it on the TV set that was babbling away, then some light fixture, the painting on the wall, the doorknob.

Hollings said, "She was in there close to two hours. Tyler comes waltzing home, what'd you do, Martina, find some collard greens in the refrigerator, sit down and share 'em with the guy?"

Martina, aiming the .38 at water stains on the ceiling, said, "Let's don't get racist now, Hollings."

"Did Tyler get a look at you?" Alvarez asked.

"No, the guy never saw me. It's cool, okay?"

"All right, so lay off her, Hollings," Alvarez said. Still standing at the mirror, combing his thick black hair.

Hollings said, "I don't like this, man. I don't like working with some felon off the street."

Hollings glared at her, but Martina just licked her lips and gave him a lewd smile.

"I got respect for her," Alvarez said. "You will, too, you give her half a chance. Lady's the best B and E artist I ever run across. Gets in a room quicker than a guy with a passkey. Martina can't find something of value in there, it isn't there."

Alvarez kept combing his thick black hair, stroking it like it was his dick.

"Whatta we need with a goddamn B and E expert? I thought you told me we were just going to get the guy alone, try to talk to him. Slap him around a little if we had to. I didn't hear anything about this penny-ante bullshit, burglarizing his house."

Martina kept giving Hollings that smile, lots of teeth.

"Martina's a good woman," said Alvarez. "So just drop it."

Bang, case closed. No more discussion. Christ, the Cuban must've learned his negotiation skills straight from Fidel. The two of you didn't come to a meeting of the minds, you either met his mind, or you walked.

The man got fired from Metro police for something or other. That's what he told Hollings, but not what it was. One thing was for damn sure, if he got thrown off the Miami police, it meant he'd done something an average John Q. Citizen would be behind bars for, twenty to life.

Now Alvarez's job was driving a Rolls-Royce for a lady politician. Telling Hollings he got that job from working security detail for the senator for years whenever she came to town. She'd even started requesting him. So when he was thrown off the force he went to her, asked if there was something he could do for her, and she gave him her car to drive. As jobs went, Alvarez said, it didn't require much of him, the lady being out of town three quarters of the time.

"Since I didn't find nothing in the man's house," Martina said, "now I say we use a flashlight on him."

"What?" Hollings staring at the woman.

"Put his dick in a flashlight." Martina aimed the Colt up at the ceiling.

Christ, give an African a gun, they can't let go of it. Like handing a redneck a toothpick. She's just got to keep fiddling with it.

Martina said, "I saw it in a Charlie Bronson movie. Stick his dick in a flashlight, turn it on. Those little batteries, they don't look like much, but you ever felt the jolt you can get out of them? Run a little current through his Johnson, he'd give up his mother in a second."

Alvarez said, "Personally, I always wanted to put somebody's hand in a toaster, push down the lever. I had that idea in my head for twenty years. Don't ask me why. A big toaster, with slots for bagels, you know, in case the guy's hands are fat."

Martina aimed at the overhead light, shut her left eye.

"Flashlight would do the trick," she said. "A couple of blinks, this asshole be telling us whatever we ask him."

Hollings snapped off the TV, some show for housewives, teaching them how to wipe dust off furniture. Jesus.

He said, "Listen to you guys. Flashlights, for christsakes?"

"It worked for Charlie Bronson," Martina said. "I think it's worth a try, whatta you think, big Ray?"

Alvarez slid his long black comb into his back pocket. Guy got his rocks off in the mirror, now he wouldn't need to comb it again for at least half an hour.

"Well, we pretty much knew Tyler wouldn't be that dumb," Alvarez said. "Keep a map or some shit around the house. But you got to go through the steps, one, two, three. You got to be organized and logical if you're going to get what you want."

"Then tell me, Alvarez, how come we aren't over there right now, staking the place out?" Hollings said. "Tyler could go off, we'd never know. Sitting here in this opulent house."

"Uh-oh, there's another one," Martina said. *"Opulent."*

"Means high priced, excessive," Alvarez said. "Right, Hollings?"

Hollings nodded.

"I used *truculence* already today," Martina said. "I made it part of my permanent vocabulary."

"Keep hanging around Hollings, you'll qualify for a college degree."

"That right, Hollings? You a college boy?"

"A semester. Junior college."

"That's where you picked up those words though, huh? *Truculence, opulent,* all that shit?"

Hollings didn't say anything, watching Martina fiddle with that pistol.

"You know, it's a proven fact," she said. "The bigger your vocabulary, the longer you're gonna live. Better than eating carrots and broccoli for keeping a person alive is what I heard."

"Bullshit."

"No, it's true, Hollings. I saw a TV show on it. More words you know, longer you live. Ever since I saw that I been collecting new words. That's how come I hadn't minded you shooting off your mouth all day long. 'Cause I could tell right off, hanging around you, I'm gonna learn a whole shitload of new words, it's gonna help me live longer."

"Jesus Christ. What a crock of shit."

Martina said, "But let me tell you something, Hollings. Once I finished picking somebody's brains, vacuumed everything useful out of them, I don't put up with none of their bullshit anymore. You hear what I'm saying to you?"

"Hey, Ray," Hollings said, standing in front of the TV, doing his best not to look at Martina's smile, those dark lazy eyes. "Tell me, Alvarez, how come we're not staking Tyler's place out?"

Alvarez moved up beside the couch. He reached out for the pistol Martina was playing with. Martina looked at his hand, looked down at the pistol. Shrugged and handed it over.

Alvarez said, "See, Hollings, what it is, you got to understand human nature. I mean, the three of us, in one form or the other, we're people of the street, got the savvy that goes with that. But this Tyler, he's what, a fucking tour guide? He don't know from violence. He reads about violence in a book, it gives him a nosebleed. So see, this guy, right now he doesn't know what hit him. He's sitting there in his room. Waiting to work up nerve to go outside."

"Yeah, and when'll that be?"

"By the time he gets his guts together, one of us will be watching his every move."

"Yeah, you're so sure, are you?"

"Listen to me, man," Alvarez said. " 'Cause I got expertise in this area, the human behavior of straight citizens. I know how they think. So don't worry. This guy, sooner or later, he's going to lead us to the *Carmelita*. It just isn't going to happen tonight, you can bet on that."

"Man," Martina said. "You people so smart, I'm going to have to start paying fucking tuition."

"We got to remember," Hollings said, moving out to the middle of the room, staring back and forth between Alvarez and Martina, getting their attention. "We can't let it get lost in all this joking around. We got a noble calling here. A higher purpose. We're trying to uncover a thing, it's been lying around waiting for centuries. It's a piece of history, man. We find this ship, we get our pictures in the history book, our names, everything. This is the biggest fucking treasure ship of all time. Isn't that right, Alvarez?"

"Bigger than the *Atocha,* more than the *Santa Margarita,*" Alvarez said. "It's like Fort Knox down on the ocean floor somewhere, more loaded down with gold and emeralds than any ship ever sailed. Yeah."

Hollings waited a minute, see if Martina was going to say anything smartass. Then Hollings said, "A higher purpose." Like at the Masonic lodge. You stand up after dinner, put on your hoodoo robes, say the words, give some kind of secret salute to the chief muckety-muck.

"Go on, say it." Alvarez giving Martina a look Hollings couldn't read.

The woman smiled back, an I-seen-everything-now smile.

"I wasn't joking," Martina said. "I want to put that man's willy in a flashlight."

"Say it," Hollings said.

Martina propped herself up against the pillow. Still smiling, jerking her thumb at Hollings.

"Where'd you dig up this dickbrain, Alvarez?"

"Hollings is a man of deep thoughts," he said. "He's motivated by the sublime things in life. So go on, say it, make him happy. I got places to go."

"Christ. What horseshit."

"This isn't about money," Hollings said. "This isn't a greed thing. If all we wanted was money, we could go rob a bank or something. This is about doing something of importance for once in our fucking lives. Right, Alvarez?"

"A higher purpose," Alvarez said quietly, nodding at Martina.

"Yeah, yeah, okay," Martina said. "A higher purpose." But the broad grinned as she repeated the words one more time.

Jordan Wills wasn't in the office when Hap called, so he described the situation to the man who answered, left his name and number. He called Romero at the bank, but Mike was sorry, the place was closed for the day, and as a matter of fact, at that very moment a band of Federal regulators were doing their number on the bank's books. Not even an old friend with an emergency could get in after hours today. The best Romero could offer was for Hap to tap on the front door a few minutes before nine tomorrow.

So Hap spent a couple of hours straightening up. Putting books back, sweeping up broken glass, setting the furniture upright. With hammer and nails he pounded some of the pine panels back into place. Made a botch of the work, but was so swept up in the frenzy, it didn't matter. He just kept moving randomly from room to room, a dull roar in his head like TV snow.

Books were scattered across the bedroom, as if she'd gone methodically along each shelf, tossing them over her shoulder. Hundreds of them sprawled open on the floor, like a flock of birds buckshot from the sky. First editions, sailing adventures, children's stories with simple line drawings. An 1890 *Huckleberry Finn,* a long-ago birthday gift from Daniel.

Hap's bureau was rifled, the wooden drawers thrown into a pile. His mattress gashed open. On the front wall a few of the pine panels had been pried away, exposing the studs, the wiring and copper water lines. Broken lamps, overturned chairs. In the bathroom the lid of the toilet was on the floor, cracked in half. The medicine cabinet had been ripped from the wall and slung into the bathtub. The woman, not just searching, but going above and beyond, making a statement.

Next door, Daniel's room was even worse. Charlie Manson and his girls might have been festering in there for a month. There was a whirlwind of papers and file folders. And more books flung everywhere. He found several of them floating in the bathtub. The lady had left the water running and a cascade was pouring over the lip of the tub and snaking a couple of feet across the floor to make a pool in the corner. At least a dozen books had sunk to the bottom. A couple of Daniel's cordovans in there, too, and several gold and silver pocket watches.

Hap shut off the tap, pulled the plug, and plucked one of the watches from the water. It was Daniel's Elgin, the jewel of his collection. Hap pulled the winding knob and it popped open. Inside the lid Daniel had glued a photograph, black and white.

Their mother, Louise, was pulling aside a lacy poinciana branch plush with blooms, smiling flirtatiously at the cameraman, the dazzle of Biscayne Bay behind her. At the edge of the frame were the limestone rocks of the Devil's Punchbowl.

Probably only a year or two married, this girl in the first heat of love, giving her young man a sensuous grin. She wore a simple collarless blouse, and a hibiscus blossom behind one ear, on a brilliant cloudless Miami day fifty years ago. Hap's young mother full of happy mischief.

He touched the corner of the damp photo. The hot bath water had puckered the paper, and it had already begun to wrinkle, his mother's face turning to soft yellow pulp against his fingertip.

By six most of his outrage had boiled away, and he was spirit-weary, exhausted beyond anything he could remember. He walked aimlessly down to the boathouse, stood for a moment and looked at his unfinished sailboards, at his tools.

For a while he watched a spider repairing a corner of its radiant web, stretched over the edge of the west window. The creature scuttled out and back, caught in its own sinister geometry. In a moment or two it had finished its reweaving, and it crabbed along a gleaming track to a corner of the web. There it seemed to fall into a doze, no doubt exhausted by its labors.

Then a flitter among his tools drew Hap's eye. It was a small brown lizard hiding beside a claw hammer. The lizard darted to the wall and began a slow, spastic journey up the boards by the window. Hap watched as it hesitated beside a jutting nail head. An inch, another inch. The spider seemed to be looking at Hap, distracted from its watchful defense by this human head.

As Hap drew back, the lizard struck. Took the spider in one spectacular gulp. Then turned and retreated down the plank wall, the crooked legs of the spider dangling like strings from its mouth. Back on the workbench, the lizard stared straight ahead as it performed its gastric miracle.

The little fucker did five or six quick push-ups. Then holding still, it inflated its throat, made a scarlet bubble. Its silent song of victory. A meal to remember. He'd caught the cunning spider, the arachnid menace. All its intricate planning and industry gone in a blink, a flick of lizard tongue.

Hap looked out at the bay. Its surface was gray glass. When the water was that placid it was hard to imagine the swirls of blood and bone beneath it, all those fish slashing into each other. A daily thing, hunted, hunting. Where the tricks of your species were the only tricks you were ever going to have. Luck and accident your only hope.

Hap glanced around the boathouse, at the twin bed where he had slept with dozens of women. He looked at all those unfinished boards. Nothing had come of any of it. If the great lizard, or the great barracuda, came for Hap Tyler today, every trace of him would be gone in that same instant. He'd constructed nothing, left absolutely no sign of his existence behind. Not even a flimsy web. He hadn't half tried. He'd been pissing it away. Time, energy. Everything. He was the Tyler who left nothing. The Tyler who was never there.

His marine-issue M1911A1 Colt .45 was still in the leather holster, still in the middle drawer of the workbench where he'd left it years ago. He took it out. Two and a half pounds of blast and recoil. He unsnapped the holster, drew out the pistol. He checked the slide, popped the magazine. Unloaded. The cleaning gear was stowed in a leather pouch in the same drawer. He untied the string, emptied the pouch, and set the brush, the oil, and rags on the workbench. He spent the next twenty minutes polishing the pistol inside and out until it was immaculate. When he was done he opened the box of shells in the middle drawer, loaded the pistol, and slipped it back into the holster.

He carried it up to the main house, went upstairs to Daniel's room, and lay on the remains of his mattress, holding the pistol tight to his stomach. He stared at the ceiling. His eyes wandered from one wall to the other and back, charting different routes across the maze of broken plaster.

He watched the silhouette of a cabbage palm flutter on the glass pane of the Commodore's portrait. Daniel had hung the painting across from his bed so that when he laid his head on his pillow the Commodore looked squarely at him. Hanging there like Christ on a crucifix, the hallowed image of the Commodore scowled endlessly at his grandson, as if daring him to live up to the myth.

Hap raised the pistol. He sighted at the old gentleman. Let a few moments accumulate as he positioned the sight squarely on the bridge of the great man's nose. Then he fired. And he fired again. Three more times until all that was left of the photograph was the upper right quadrant of the Commodore's forehead, and a tuft of white hair.

Hap laid the warm pistol beside him on the bedspread. A sea breeze jangled the venetian blinds in the parlor downstairs, and there was the familiar gurgle in the plumbing somewhere in the house, the distant rumble of a racing boat a few miles out in the bay. He listened as the breeze funneled through the house.

# CHAPTER 13

"W̲E̲ CAN'T PRINT THIS," BERNIE SAID.

Marguerite stood in the doorway of his office. Bernard Saterfield, her boss, assistant managing editor. Thirty-nine years old, the guy collected comic books, had a couple of covers framed on his wall, *Superman* and an early *Conan the Barbarian*. Some of his artless attempts at cartoons thumbtacked around the office, a collection of dimestore rubber figures cluttered his windowsill. Bernie, short, chunky, curly black hair, glasses always fogged with fingerprints. The guy was bogged down in puberty, and making a career out of it.

For the last hour, in a manic burst at her computer, Marguerite had typed up just a fraction of what she knew about Shorty Busser's relationship with her mother. Without notes, she'd clicked out seven pages of bribes, payoffs, kickbacks. Dirt she'd been collecting for years without even being aware of it. Growing up in her household, overhearing these things all her life. Wondering about them, but staying quiet. Now that was over. She'd been silent too damn long.

"Hey, listen, Marguerite. I understand. You're upset. Your boyfriend passes away, you know, in an awkward situation. I'm sorry. Everybody around here is sorry. It was a surprise you even came to work today. I mean, you should take a few days off, pick up the column fresh next week. Go down to the Keys, eat some good food, dance a little. I can arrange that. Won't even cost you vacation time."

"Dance, Bernie? Eat some good food?"

She was trying to keep the rage out of her voice. Bernie was like one of those night animals, shy and easily spooked. But get him cornered, start to move in on him, he'd bare his fangs, turn savage.

Bernie Saterfield rocked his red leather chair back, put his sandals up on the desk. He dug something out of his left ear and surreptitiously flicked it toward the window, toward his collection of rubber alligators and muscled, caped superheroes. Today he was wearing a black long-sleeve shirt, beige pants, a wild jungle print tie. Tropical preppie.

"Let's just forget I saw this, okay, Marguerite? Can we do that? Chalk it up to a minor indiscretion under stress?"

He tore the pages in half, dumped them in his waste can.

"You can rip it up, Bernie, but it's still true. Every word."

"I'm not saying it isn't true. I'm saying it's unsupported."

"Unsupported."

"Marguerite, this isn't your bailiwick. Your skills aren't investigative. You're our history person, Marguerite. Our remembrance-of-things-past lady. You do that great. But this, this is a lot of unsupported, undocumented horseshit."

"Unsupported?" she said. "That's what's bothering you? What's making you so pale?"

Bernie shook his head, gave her a disappointed look. Before he could say the smartass thing growing in his mouth, she said, "I mean, I know there are lots of people in this building, any mention of Shorty Busser or my mother makes them nervous. But I didn't think you were one of those, Bernie. Not you."

He leaned forward, rested his forearms on his desk.

"Hey, what can I tell you, Marguerite? I can't go with this, I'm sorry. Anyway, whatever happened to the Sears Tower thing? Sears donates the building for an art center, it turns out, it's gonna cost thirteen mil to bring it up to standard. Taxpayers have to swallow that. Is it worth it? Tell us, Marguerite. Is that Sears place historically worth thirteen mil? Now that's your bailiwick, Marguerite. Tear into that."

Marguerite stepped inside the office and shut the door firmly behind her.

"Tell me something, Bernie. Be honest with me, okay? Just let me know if the paper has a hands-off policy where Shorty and my mother are concerned. 'Cause that's how it looks from down where I stand. Could you tell me that, please?"

She edged toward his desk and he sat back. His Adam's apple bobbed like he was trying to swallow a wad of Double Bubble. He squinted at her, twisted a loop of his curly hair around his finger, pulled it out straight and let it spring back.

"So," he said. "That all you wanted to see me about?"

"All right, let's try this," she said. "What if I fill out the details here? Full-blown story. I give you names, dates. I think it might interest our readers. 'Local developer has U.S. senator in his pocket. Busser gets inside information on numerous federal bids.' "

Bernie shook his head sadly.

"I'm apparently not getting through to you," he said. "Marguerite, I'm saying the phone could ring right now, it's the Pulitzer people giving me guarantees on the big prize for your piece, I still wouldn't say yes. No way am I gonna authorize this kind of attack on Busser and Senator Rawlings. Not without rock-solid confirmation of every single fact. Documents, corroborating witnesses, the whole nine yards. You following me here?"

"I witnessed these things myself, Bernie."

"That's not good enough. That's shit. Meaningless. You should know that. You're a journalist, or have you forgotten?"

He tapped his ring against his desktop. His famous Harvard class ring. Maybe if she got on her knees and kissed it, maybe then he'd relent.

"You know I can't get documentation for this. These conversations, I was the only other witness."

"Most of the things in this article, hell, you were a teenage girl,

Marguerite. You really think people are interested in things from twenty years ago?"

"Yes, I do. I think a lot of people are."

"No documentation, no go."

She picked up Spider-Man, blue and red, with a red formfitting face mask. She held him toward the window that looked out on Biscayne Boulevard toward downtown. Bernie hadn't boosted circulation enough yet for a water view.

"See all that, Spider-Man." She held it close to the glass. Keeping her voice calm, she said, "That's Miami. The famous Miami. Take a good look, kiddo, 'cause someday all that will still be theirs. The ten crooks who run this town."

"That all you had, Marguerite? 'Cause you know, if it is, I have a staff meeting, five minutes ago."

Someone tapped on the glass door of his office. Bernie gave them a just-a-minute wave. Features editor, two of the sports guys, all the junior Bernies assembling for their afternoon jock-talk. How good are the Canes gonna be this year? This new quarterback, is his arm as good as old what's-his-name?

"There is one more thing."

"Make it a quickie," he said. "Troops are waiting."

"Okay. Just a small remembrance of things past."

He groaned, rocked back in his chair.

"I know you're busy, Bernie, but I feel a need to unburden. Like you're always saying, we can come to you, tell you what's on our minds. Your door is always open."

"It has to be now, Marguerite? This minute?"

"Yeah," she said. "I'm afraid it does. It has to be now."

"All right, all right. Go on. Go ahead."

"Did you realize, Bernie, my father was a congressman?"

He said yeah, he was aware of that. Restraining himself, sighing in an indulgent way. Making it plain that he was going easy on her because maybe she was stretched a little tight over Daniel's death. But at the same time letting her know with his eyes that she was using up valuable points here.

"When my daddy was alive, you were still playing in your sandbox in Cleveland," Marguerite said. "So you probably didn't know Tony Rawlings's reputation. My father, the New Dealer. Dedicated himself to the old folks. Nursing homes, retirement benefits, social security. Pretty boring by today's standards. Not the sexy issues. But people loved him. They loved him, old, young. Everybody loved him.

"And I remember how he used to come home after a long day out there, fighting for the old people, and sit his daughter on his knee. And he'd tell me stories about how it was in Miami when he was a kid, and before that when his father was a kid. His father, Anthony, son of Ramona."

Bernie rocked forward. He ticked his eyes back and forth between Marguerite and his phone. Probably thinking of calling the white suits. Tell them to reserve her room.

"I'm telling you this, Bernie, because I think you should understand what the history of this town means to me. Because it's not just some specialization I picked out of the air. It's personal with me, Bernie. Very personal."

Bernie rocked back in his chair, and began to tug absently at a coil of black hair. He was staring at Marguerite's hands. At Spider-Man. She glanced down at the rubber figure and sighed. She'd ripped the little guy's head clean off.

Trying to keep her voice quiet, she said, "And I'm telling you all this, Bernie, 'cause I want you to know how Shorty Busser fits into this town. Who he is in the larger context. Because, see, what I believe is, Shorty Busser is just the latest incarnation of the same breed of crook that's been setting up shop in Miami for the last hundred years.

"It was a guy like Shorty that tried to shut Ramona up when she argued against draining the Everglades. And when she wouldn't stop talking, it was another guy like Shorty who held the pistol to her head, murdered her, then torched her house. It was a man like Busser who sat behind some newspaper desk back then and wrote about how awful it was that Ramona was killed. But hey, since the unfortunate thing had happened, let's make the best of it. Build,

build, build, come on down, folks, the weather's fine. Water's warm, fish are jumping."

Bernie's phone rang, and he looked at it for a moment, then picked it up and said, "We're busy," and set it back down.

He blew out an exasperated breath, his eyes dulled over. Not used to being lectured to, especially not by a woman. It was overloading the poor guy's circuits, tripping all his breakers.

"Just a couple more things, Bernie. I'm almost done."

"Hey, why stop now," he said. "Let's get it all out. Purge, purge."

"Okay, here's a scene for you, Bernie. Picture this, if you will. It's the afternoon my daddy had his heart attack. My mother's there, I'm there, in the Gables house where I live now. And when the heart attack happens, my mother gets very calm, very purposeful. She steps over the congressman's body, goes to the phone, not rushing, real detached. And I'm crying, getting hysterical in the hallway, looking down at my father's face changing colors. And who did Garnetta call, Bernie? Did she call the hospital, our doctor, emergency rescue? No, Bernie, she phoned my father's campaign manager. And what she said was, her eyes on mine the whole time, she said, 'Okay, Charles, it's happened. Now get me a goddamn speech writer over here fast.' "

Marguerite paused, let that float there for a moment. She got up off the arm of the chair, went back over to the window.

"My mother," she said, looking out at the clutter of skyscrapers ten blocks away. "Ever since that day I've tried to hate her. I know my mental health would be better if I could. If I could just get a real hot flame of anger going. I think about that day, and how she was. I think about her politics, what total garbage it is. All that pull-yourself-up-by-your-bootstraps crap. If Garnetta Rawlings could do it, then, by god, so should everyone else.

"Because after all, she was the daughter of a Georgia chicken farmer. She test-scored her way into law school. Soon as she could, she got out of that backward state, crossed the Florida line, and opened a practice. And then, hell, you got to respect that. A woman succeeding as much as she has. She worked hard. She was smart.

She had savvy. She was determined to better herself. You gotta give her that. You can't hate her for trying so hard. You can't hate her for latching on to Tony Rawlings. The man was clearly headed somewhere she wanted to go. You can't hate her for any of that. I sure can't. I can't hate the woman."

Marguerite went over to his office door, looked out at the guys waiting there, and they all came to attention.

"Well, I appreciate it," Bernie said, "confiding in me this way. I really appreciate it. It's been very educational."

"I'm not quite finished. Another minute is all. Okay? Got time for one more minute?"

"All right, look, is there a point here? Are you getting to something in particular, or we going to meander some more?"

"Okay. You want a point? Here's a point then. That night they murdered Ramona, and the days right after when nobody much cared about finding her killer, well, that's where it all started."

"What started, Marguerite?"

"The boom town morality, Bernie. You know how it goes. It's like hey, come on, everybody, let's keep the good times rolling. Forget about who might have to be sacrificed.

"That's Shorty Busser's morality. My mother's. They pray to the same idols, Bernie. The gods of windfall profits, that's all that matters. Just keep the good times rolling. Shut up the naysayers, drive them out of town. If they won't go, then, hell, shoot them and dump their bodies wherever it's convenient.

"The point, Bernie, the point is, that's what happened to Daniel Tyler. Daniel stood up against it, like Ramona did, and a few others have in the last hundred years. And I think they killed him for it, Bernie. I think they murdered him for the same reason they murdered Ramona, because he was making the scoundrels' lives difficult, keeping somebody away from the gravy train. He was stopping Shorty Busser, or somebody just like him, from getting a few million dollars richer."

Bernie Saterfield leaned back in his chair and made a big, leisurely deal out of clearing his throat and stretching his arms.

"That's it? That's the big conclusion to this? That someone killed Daniel Tyler?"

"Yes."

"Marguerite, I don't want to argue with you. Especially today, something this painful. But it was a heart attack, hon. It was a pure and simple heart attack. Nobody murdered him. I think you should get that straight in your mind. There was no evidence of foul play whatsoever. As much as you'd like to believe it, the facts just don't support what you're saying."

Marguerite dropped Spider-Man's broken body on the windowsill.

She said, "Don't believe everything you read in your goddamn newspaper. They killed him. And now, what I'm going to do, I'm putting you on notice. Very politely, but very firmly, I'm telling you I'm not going to be your quiet little history lady anymore. I've had it with that. I'm going after them. Every one. Shorty Busser, my mother, whoever else I find.

"Starting today, I'm writing down what I know, and let me tell you, that's a hell of a lot, Bernie. You don't grow up in the family I grew up in and not learn a lot of firsthand dirt. People have been saying things in front of me for as long as I can remember, things they thought they could get away with because I was Garnetta's sweet little daughter, I was harmless. Believe me, Bernie, I'm going to be putting these articles on your desk, today, tomorrow, every day from now on till I've worn you down. And don't worry, I'll get the corroboration. I will, I'll get it somehow. However I have to."

She turned her back on Bernie Saterfield and very slowly she marched out of his office. The Bernie clones parted for her. She looked off at her cubicle on the other side of the newsroom. It seemed about ten miles away and moving farther from her every step she took. But she could make it. She knew she could. Because after all, she was a Rawlings. Daughter of Tony, great-granddaughter of Ramona.

CHAPTER 14

HOLLINGS WANTED TO CALL A TAXI TO GET BACK HOME, but Alvarez said no, no. Go with Martina, she'll take you home, won't you, Martina? She shrugged, like sure, why not. Alvarez going yeah, yeah, go on, Hollings, get to know the lady, you'll like her, she grows on you. Yeah, Martina said, smiling that gold smile, like genital warts.

Now it was just after rush hour, and they were in her pink '57 Chevy driving slow up Biscayne Boulevard. Every other red light they stopped at Martina looks around and says, "I been in that one too." Meaning houses, apartments, hotel rooms. And not to deliver pizza either.

At a light in Miami Shores, Martina looked over at a two-story Spanish style, going, "That one, I got a TV, a nice Glock nine millimeter, three VCR's, the guy must've been ripping off an electronics store or some shit. Thieving prick. Still in the boxes, these things go retail for two-eighty, I get maybe forty if I'm lucky. I could go to the flea market, place like that, get eighty to a hundred. But then you got to sit out there in the sun with all these weirdos selling Hula Hoops and all that."

"I'm not interested in this bullshit," Hollings said.

But the truth was, he was interested as hell. Wanting to hear all about it, fill in some blank spots in his education. Mostly it'd been a pretty moral life for Hollings, never in jail, never in trouble in the marines, nothing except at high school getting paddled a few times for mouthing off. As a result, he felt sometimes like a priss, and got this itch of inferiority around punks and delinquents who talked about their arrest records like some guys did about all the women they'd laid. Hollings had nothing much to say on either account.

The GI bill had put Hollings through a semester at Miami-Dade. After that he'd just worked nights at a 7-Eleven on South Beach, spent his days sleeping, reading an occasional book. He preferred adventure novels, James Bond stuff with exotic guns and pretty women. All those great names for the women. And he read *Treasure Magazine*, which he pilfered every month from the store, cover to cover. Lately Hollings had started thinking maybe he was a little peculiar, liking to read books like he did. Compared to Martina and most of the other jerks he ran into these days, reading anything at all made him a stark raving intellectual.

Hollings said to her, "I could give a big shit about which places you robbed."

Martina slowed and said, "That one, right there, in back, behind that apartment building. Place had jalousie windows, I reach through, open the door, just walked in, the lady's in the shower, she had this little dog, one of those things with fur in its eyes, a Scottie or whatever, nipping after me the whole time, the lady, singing in the shower. She stops, yells at her dog, 'Roscoe, Roscoe, hush that!'

"All I got, an electric toothbrush and a set of vibrators. Eleven of them, all different. Big as bats, some of them. This woman, in the shower screeching away, sounding like she might've had the twelfth vibrator in there with her. And you know what I found out later? There's a market for those damn things. Not as good as handguns, but people pay hard cash for used vibrators. You believe that? I sold all but one of them, kept the smallest one for myself. 'Cause see, I think a girl shouldn't stretch herself out so much she can't enjoy a little guy when he comes along."

Touching her chin to her shoulder, smiling toward Hollings.

"Jesus," Hollings said. "You're too fucking weird."

"You better believe it, honey dumpling."

Both of them were quiet, driving up Biscayne, passing the Mafia restaurants of North Miami, the porno bookstores, discount drugstores, and places renting pissant movies. Then there were the Jewish delis and seafood joints, getting filled up now with the cheapo early birders, stayed that way for hours. And for blocks around, the air stunk of fried shrimp.

This was close to the neighborhood where Hollings grew up. Back then all of it was white working people. You didn't have your rich, you didn't have your poor. Just Archie Bunkers, Ralph Kramdens. Plaster guys, bakers, bus drivers, an electrician here and there.

Now look at it. Sleazy and getting sleazier. Hookers wrestling the bums for the bus bench seats. Broken glass and old mattresses and clothes blowing around in the middle of the street. Man, it was ground zero out there. Dead center where the Greedy Eighties exploded. People walking around dazed, looking up at the sky like they were waiting for some of that loot they'd been promised to finally start trickling down.

Two blocks east of the boulevard, over on the intracoastal, just that close by, the condos were tall and glossy. Assholes over there having their lobster thermidor, sipping their two-hundred-dollar Scotch, and the people over here, shit, they were having wet dreams about Rice-A-Roni.

"And there!" Martina aimed her chin at the front gates of the Jockey Club. Place hired ex-cops as security guards, big guys jacked up on steroids. Most of them had been fired from the Miami police force because they were too twisted.

"You lying turd," said Hollings. "You never got in there. They'd see you coming, let the Dobermans loose."

"I goddamn *worked* at that place, man. I made beds in there. And when I wasn't busting my ass with the linen, I was pilfering some of the biggest diamonds I've ever come across. A few months there, man, I was living the good life, I'm telling you, Jack."

"You lying turd."

"My domicile isn't far from here. Want to see it?"

"Hell, no. Just take me to goddamn South Beach, man, and quit this driving around shit."

"I'll show it to you. Maybe we'll have us some fun too."

She turned west off Biscayne onto a Hundred and twenty-fifth, went five blocks, turned north. A neighborhood of sixty-, seventy-five-thousand-dollar concrete block houses. Not great, but a white area, and better than he'd thought Martina could afford. Lady like her was probably hell on property values.

Martina swung the car into a driveway, got out and walked up to the front porch, fitting a key to the double doors. Hollings stayed put for a minute, then with Martina waving and yelling at him to come on in, it's safe, my dog likes white trash okay, Hollings got out and followed her inside.

"Whatta you think?"

Hollings looked around and saw a neon Miller beer sign lit up over the little bar in the den, an electric organ in the living room, lots of cheap plants, philodendrons and shit, a plaid living room set, all with that scratchy material—it looked okay, but it made you sweat sitting on it. And photographs on the wall. Lots of them. All of white people.

"Aw, shit."

"Don't worry," Martina said. "These damn people work till seven, eight o'clock every night. Husband and wife, no kids, they're busting their asses so hard, I thought it'd be interesting, come in here, see what they were working so hard to buy."

She had the chrome automatic wedged into her front pocket.

"You're making me a fucking felony accomplice."

Martina surveying the room from one spot, picking her line of attack, said, "Think of it, you know, like a fair trade for all those words you're teaching me. I'm teaching you something."

Hollings couldn't get himself turned toward the door. His legs were empty. Standing in the living room of some strangers' house, five in the afternoon, picturing it, the door breaking open, huge dude, guns in both hands, saying, you motherfuckers are dead meat.

Sure, Hollings had done his time on night patrols in the jungles along the Mekong River, all over Cuu Long Province, point man, guy that steps into it first, but this was a whole 'nother thing.

This was stealing from some half-assed working couple in the middle of the day. This was pathetic, not to mention illegal.

"Tell me something." Martina was going through the drawers of the china cabinet. "This higher purpose bullshit. You're kidding, right? You ain't that dumb, are you?"

"The hell I'm not."

Hollings was dizzy. Having a conversation in this room, while Martina was cramming silver spoons in her pants pocket.

"Bullshit. You're like me, I can tell that. You want to find that ship, haul up the treasure, turn around and sell it to the highest bidder. That's all it is with you."

"You wouldn't understand," said Hollings. "I could put it in real little easy words, you still wouldn't get it."

Martina stood up, clinking more spoons into her pocket.

She eyed him up and down, checking him out slow and careful like she was about to make a bid on him at auction.

"I'd like to know what makes you twitch, white boy. I never feel comfortable with a man till I find out what it takes to make him shoot his load."

Things were loosening in Hollings's gut. Sweat coming cold to his back.

"You and me," she said. "We got more in common together than with that Cuban. I mean, this guy isn't even a native-born American. Plus he's an ex-cop, and all of them are fucked. Don't you think?"

When Hollings didn't reply, Martina turned away and went deeper into the house.

"Now where the hell you going?" Hollings managed to say.

"I gotta get one more thing is all."

She came back in a couple of minutes and held up an over-size book.

"He said it'd be here, and sure as shit, here it is." Martina, smiling, waved the book at him.

"Who said that? Alvarez?"

Martina nodded as she glanced through the book.

"Whose house is this, Martina? Who lives here?"

Concentrating on the book, she said, "Some slick-looking dude with a fat blond wife, is all I know. And goddamn, does he have bad handwriting."

Hollings shook his head, looked around again at the place. Moved in on the photographs. And aw, shit. Look who it was in all the photos. Fucking Max Hunter, the King Kong of treasure salvors. In his skimpy swimsuit standing on decks of ships he'd used over the years to haul up, Hollings counted them, Christ, seven different treasure ships.

The man should've been richer than Billy Graham. What in hell's name was he doing living in a sixty-thousand-dollar cement block house, with a neon beer sign in his living room. And running sixty-nine ninety-five speeches at the Holiday Inn?

"Guy has himself some serious tax problems," Martina said.

Hollings swung around to stare at her, this mind invader.

Martina said, "According to Alvarez, the man failed to report a few million here and there, and he had to sell his opulent house, move in here." She smiled at him. "I use it right? *Opulent?*"

Hollings said, "Alvarez told you to come over here, steal shit from Max Hunter?"

"He suggested I might."

"He told you to do something, forgot to mention it to me?"

"Looks that way."

Hollings sat down on the edge of the scratchy sofa and Martina held out the book to him.

"You're the college boy. Whatta you make of this?"

Hollings took it, looked it over for a minute.

"For one fucking thing, it isn't bad handwriting, it's goddamn Spanish," he said. "And for another, the pages got like worm holes in them."

Hollings took a longer look, being careful with the crumbly pages. Then he sat back, his head sagged. He squeezed the bridge of his nose and groaned, put the book on the couch beside him.

"Christ Almighty son of a bitch. I'm getting out of here," he said. But he couldn't move.

"What is it, Hollings?"

"It's the goddamn ship's registry. From the *Carmelita.*"

"Registry? So what the hell's that?"

"He stole it from that fucking library, there in Spain. Seville or someplace. Max Hunter stole this fucking book."

"He stole a book? So what?"

"It's the thing he was talking about in his lecture, the registry from, I think it's the House of Trade or some shit, four hundred years old, where the records they kept back then are all stored. This thing, I can't read this writing, but I think what it says, it describes the stuff, whatever was in the ships, the galleons that came back loaded down with loot. The shit the conquistadors stole from the Indians. The book says how much gold, how much silver, emeralds, like that, was in each ship that particular month. Everything listed nice and neat."

"Wait a minute, wait a minute," she said. "If this goddamn ship sank, where'd the book come from?"

"The conquistadors, they sent a couple of other copies back on different boats just to make sure."

"Oh." Martina shifted the spoons around in her pocket, took her pistol out, like she was getting comfortable for a long stay. "So what good's that? You know everything that's in the boat, but you still don't know where the hell to find it."

"I don't know," Hollings said. "But if Alvarez wants it bad enough he's willing to break into some guy's house, it must be important."

"Not so important," Martina said, "he'd risk his own ass."

Max Hunter must have seen Martina's Chevy out front and come very quietly in the back door, and he must have stood there a minute deciding what to do. Then apparently he picked up the shotgun he'd stashed out in the pantry just for this kind of thing. He must've cocked it real careful, then eased in through the narrow hallway.

He must've had the idea that Hollings and Martina were a couple of crack-head nitwits looking to steal his TV set, idiots he could just scare away by waving the shotgun. Because that's what he did, stepped into the living room and swung the thing at them and made some kind of karate scream or something, which as it turned out was the wrong thing to do, because it gave Martina half a second to turn and fire her pistol four times, hit him in the chest and throat and face, leaving the man no time to do anything except get off one good blast at his own ceiling as he was going down onto the green shag rug.

# CHAPTER 15

SOMETHING INCREDIBLE HAD HAPPENED, MILLIE BENITEZ told Marguerite on the phone, and she should get over to Millie's office right away. Marguerite said no, she was too busy just now, though the truth was all she was doing was watching the cursor blink in the middle of her computer screen. Come on, Millie said. Get over here now. This is big.

So at six o'clock Monday evening, feeling drained, and embarrassed and angry about her scene with Bernie, she walked into Millie's law office in Coconut Grove, upstairs over the Oak Feed Shop, a health food store on the corner of Grand and Main. Except for Millie's diplomas and some computer equipment, the office was bare. Drab grayish-white walls, a couple of chairs you might expect in a cheap funeral parlor.

On the corner of Millicent's huge desk was the scale model display of the Rawlings Mill and pioneer homestead. The architect had reduced the acre of land to a twenty by twenty pad of foam. Next to the mill were three miniature oak trees made from twigs with clumps of green moss sitting atop them. A woman and a child cut out of posterboard stood just outside the doorway of the mill, while nearby a brown plastic dog barked at the paddle wheel. The buildings were made of balsa and pebble board. The wood shingles on the roof were small squares of construction paper. The Miami

River ran along the edge of the property, a plastic sheet of acetate, shiny blue, and rippled to imitate the rapids.

Millicent Benitez sat down at her desk.

"I stumbled onto something this afternoon while I was finishing up the legal history of the mill site," she said. "Titles, deeds, abstracts."

"Okay, I'm listening."

"Roots of title," she said. "That's where it all starts."

Marguerite nodded as though she understood.

Millie said, "According to the Marketable Record Title Act of 1963, you only have to start thirty years back and search backward till you locate a clear root of title."

Marguerite sighed impatiently, and Millie suggested maybe she should sit down, this could take a few minutes to make clear. So she sat, folded her hands carefully in her lap, tried to ignore the ache inside her. Now that the numbing shock of Daniel's death had worn off, she was starting to feel the first stabbing howls of pain.

"Okay, okay." Millie's fingers tapped on the table, a fast military drumroll. Her Cuban-coffeed hyperactivity was cranked up to an even higher notch than usual. "What I found out, Marguerite, is that you may own some other land. More than just that one acre. You may own the land adjacent to it too."

"What land is that?"

"Forty acres," she said, light breaking in her eyes. A widening smile. "You could own forty acres along both sides of the river, from the mill on downstream almost to the mouth."

"What?"

Millie repeated it.

"That's Miami, Millie. Downtown Miami."

"Right," she said. "Exactly. That's why I called you over."

Her phone rang once, twice, a third time, Millie looking down at it. Then she shrugged her apology at Marguerite and picked it up, and began to speak in Spanish.

Millie graduated fourth in her class at the University of Miami. But she wasn't enough of a game player to work in the bigger firms. She'd turned down offers all over the city, and now operated out of this cheerless office above the health food store. An office without a window, with sitars and zithers coming through the floor, the smell of alfalfa sprouts and wheatberries.

"Okay," Millie said as she put the phone down. "So you want the long of it, or the short of it?"

"Millie, I'm sorry. But I'm not in a kidding-around mood today. I'm a little worn down. A little frazzled, okay?"

"I'm not joking. I wouldn't kid about something like this. This is big, Marguerite. This is very big."

Overhead one of the fluorescent lights spit and fluttered, and they both stared up at it.

Millie cleared her throat and said, "Okay, you know how real estate works. You buy a piece of property, first you check to see the title is clear, free from liens, other claims. So you hire me, and I find the first clear muniment of title, which is known as the root of title. The law says I have to start looking at a point thirty years ago. When I go far enough back and find a clear title, then I check forward. It's to keep someone from buying property in good faith, then have it taken from them because there was a claim against the property from a gazillion years ago. Because see, all claims against property are void unless they appear in the root of title or subsequent to it."

Marguerite felt strangely aloof, a cool balm wandering her veins. She glanced again at the replica of the mill. The mother and the child in the doorway. A boulder, some shrubs. The river, a glossy blue snake slithering the length of the acre.

Millie said, "The land in question consists of two hundred and fifty feet of shoreline along both sides of the river, from Twenty-seventh Avenue east to the bay. Hotels, high rises, convention center. U.S. Customs. The Hyatt. And not just the land, but the improvements thereon, which of course means the high rises and hotels, the buildings themselves."

Millie was making an ink doodle on the yellow legal pad in front of her. Probably solving the space-time continuum in a moment's free time.

"How it works is this. Since your great-grandmother died intestate, and since her only surviving heir was a minor child and therefore could not legally receive inheritance, the sheriff of Fort Dallas and the circuit judge from Key West apparently got together and made an informal agreement to allow Commodore Tyler to act as the estate's personal representative. At least that's what we call it today. I'm not sure what they called it back then. But anyway, it was his duty to set up a trust fund in the name of the heir. It wouldn't happen that way today, so informally, but this was the nineteenth century, and there were only about a thousand people living here then, so it was all very loose, free-form.

"Anyway, so the Commodore took control of the land. He got permission from the court and purchased the land from Anthony. He paid twenty-eight thousand dollars into a trust fund, which was set aside for the boy. The one acre where the homestead was, the acre you still own, was also placed in trust. The title for the rest of the property passed to the Commodore. Twenty-eight thousand dollars, from what I can tell, was a very generous amount. The Commodore was probably making, like a charitable donation.

"So if the Commodore sold the land there would be at that point a clear root of title. And you'd be out of the picture, because the succession of ownership after that is all legal. Once the Commodore sells it, you no longer have a right to challenge title."

Marguerite leaned forward, tucked the hair behind her ears. Focused on Millie. Trying to hear this, trying to still the rising shriek in her bloodstream.

"But this is where things get interesting. Because the Commodore didn't sell the land."

"He didn't?"

"Well, not all of it. See, of the eighty acres in Ramona Rawlings's estate, the Commodore sold half of it within a few years of taking possession. He didn't make back what he paid for it. He paid the twenty-eight thousand for the whole eighty, then turned around and sold forty acres for only five thousand."

"And the other forty?"

She smiled.

"Well, I ordered the abstracts for those parcels like you wanted, just to draw up an ownership map, something for the exhibit. The original eighty-acre tract is broken down into literally hundreds of abstracts now, because the land's been so subdivided since then. When they came in, I thought it was some kind of mistake, because half of them were very thin. You know, it was odd, because in a hundred years just one fifty by a hundred lot can change hands so often you almost need a wheelbarrow to move that one abstract around."

"Why very thin?"

"Can't you guess?"

"Come on, Millie. No games, okay? Just tell me."

"Because forty of those acres were never sold. All that land was leased. Ninety-nine-year leases. Forty acres of downtown Miami all leased, subleased, and sub-subleased. And the original lessor is the same in all cases. Biscayne Enterprises."

"Who's that?"

"Well, I wondered that too. So right after I called you, I faxed the Division of Corporations in Tallahassee for a status report, you know, the names of the officers, the resident agent and all that. They haven't gotten back yet, but I think we can assume the corporation is owned by the Commodore's heirs. Daniel, and now, the other one."

"Hap."

"Yeah, but anyway, let me explain," Millie said. "The terms of these leases are very strange. Like whoever wrote them knew nothing about the law. For one thing, the lease rates on all those properties are fixed with no provision for them to change."

"And what's that mean?"

"It means the original leases are all locked in at nineteenth-century rates. Less than a hundred dollars a month total for all that land. Checks made out to Coconut Grove Bank, which deposits the funds in a Biscayne Enterprises account and draws against that account for banking services. Not much profit there. I mean, the banking services necessary to keep the account active could easily eat up more than that hundred dollars a month."

"And why in the world would anybody charge so little?"

"Maybe the Commodore wasn't much of a businessman. Or

maybe the lawyer he hired to draw up the leases wasn't very smart. Or I guess it's possible they couldn't imagine what that real estate might be worth at the end of ninety-nine years."

"You're telling me, all those buildings, all those businesses downtown, they're paying next to nothing for their property?"

"No, no. Not at all. It's just that the original-lease holder, Daniel, and now Hap, isn't getting the fruits of the higher market value. See, the sub-sub-subleases are in line with today's values. Individual leaseholders along the chain of lessors are making a killing. It's just that none of the money is being passed back to Biscayne Enterprises. That's just the way the original leases read."

Marguerite looked again at the replica of the mill, then at Millie's diplomas, the gray carpet. She listened to the tinkle of xylophone music coming from downstairs. Feeling a little sleepy now, a warm pleasant steam seemed to be filling the room.

"It's neat, isn't it," Millie said. "How it all works."

Marguerite blinked the mist away and studied this young woman for a moment. You'd think with the kind of IQ she had, the drive, the tire-squealing eagerness, that she would've devoted herself to something with a little more nobility. A heart surgeon, an astrophysicist. Marguerite had asked her something like that once, and Millie had stared at Marguerite, totally baffled. No one had ever told her a lawyer joke before. No one had warned her how wretched and disreputable the field had become.

"Okay, Millie," she said. Taking a breath, finding another position in that chair. "I'm with you so far, but how in god's name does all this add up to me owning this land?"

"Okay. If the original transferal of Ramona Rawlings's property to the Commodore was illegal for some reason, and that can be proved, then that original transferal of the land to the Commodore can be challenged. If we can prove that an illegal act was commited to effect that transferal, then the ownership of the land would revert back to the original line of descent. You."

"Me?"

"Yeah."

They waited for a jet to pass overhead, its tremor blending with the one growing in Marguerite's belly.

When it was gone, she said, "How was the transfer illegal? I mean, it all comes down to that, right? They gave the Commodore the land, this judge and sheriff, right? That's legal, right?"

"Well, what I'm telling you is, if that initial transferal was made subject to a felony, or any kind of fraud, that would mean Randolph Tyler came by the land illegally, even if he was completely unaware of the felony or fraud."

"You have some particular fraud in mind?"

"Ramona Rawlings was murdered, right?"

"Yeah."

"So if we could show that any of the parties who participated in the decision to dispose of her land had guilty knowledge of her murder, or were in any way complicitous, then they are accessories after the fact. That means you could legally challenge Biscayne Enterprise's ownership of the land. And if you won that, then the ninety-nine-year leases would pass back to the original owner's family. You."

"So I'd own worthless ninety-nine-year leases." Marguerite smiled. Leaned back in her chair. "I'd have to pay the bank a service fee so I could be the nominal owner of all that land."

"Well," said Millie. "You'd have to for a month anyway."

"What?"

"The wonderful thing about ninety-nine-year leases is, when the ninety-nine years are up, the original lessor still owns the property. Renewal of the leases would be completely your option."

Marguerite swallowed. She was dry-mouthed and it felt like she'd begun to sink into her chair.

"They're almost up, aren't they?"

"They're in their final ninety days," Millie said. "We've got that long to make a case, then if it turns out like I think it will, you'll own your great-grandmother's land again. You'll own a very healthy chunk of Miami."

Marguerite had begun to perspire. Her field of vision was yellowing at the edges like a page of newsprint slowly catching fire. Her heart was knocking.

"You okay, Marguerite?"

She blinked, got a swallow of air, and nodded. She made herself breathe. Staring at the miniature people, the dog barking. Ramona, her son Anthony. The boy who became her grandfather, the boy who survived.

"Could anybody else know about this?" Marguerite said.

"Well, yes," Millie said. "I'm pretty sure the lawyers for the Hyatt and Barnett Bank, or those other businesses, have checked out who's at the root of the lease chain. They must've read the original lease, and know it renews automatically. The magic day comes, their leases just roll over for another century. But what the lawyers have no way of knowing is that someone might mount a challenge to the original leaseholder. They thought they were safe, but they're not. The whole structure of their ownership is built on an illegal foundation."

"I would own the buildings too?"

"Yeah," Millie said. "The property, and the improvements thereon. That means the buildings."

"Jesus, Millie. This is amazing. Utterly incredible."

"You're happy?"

"Happy?" she said. "Maybe in a week, when I recover, I'll be happy. Right now I'm just trying to breathe, keep from sliding out of this chair."

Millie picked up her pen and began doodling again. Loops and squiggles, crossing out one drawing, beginning another. Wired, wired.

"What kind of proof would you need? Of a hundred-year-old felony?"

"The way it works," Millie said, watching her hand scribbling, "we don't actually have to prove anybody was guilty of murder in the usual way, beyond a reasonable doubt. What I'm talking about is a civil action. All you have to prove is that there was a murder and that from a preponderance of the evidence such and such a person seems to be guilty. Then if that person was instrumental in the sale of the property, the leases are void and revert to the original line of family ownership."

"Prove a murder from a hundred years ago?"

"We'd focus on the Commodore, because he obviously gained the most from her death. Plus, he set the terms of the leases suspiciously low. I would argue that he got worried, and maybe he was afraid somebody would claim he'd stolen her land, so he backed off, didn't want to seem to profit too much from it."

"That's it? That's how it goes? You stand up and argue some hypothetical scenario? Just make things up?"

"That's how the law works."

"No facts, just arguments."

"Well," Millie said, "we do need Ramona's remains, physical proof that a murder did occur, historical records won't do it. I'm afraid that's crucial. You locate the body, and I think the rest will fall into place. We sue Hap Tyler, the land is yours."

"Sue Hap?"

"That's the way it works. His lawyer tries to prove the Commodore was innocent so that Hap keeps the land. I try to prove he's guilty. I'm sure when the lawyers for the Hyatt and those other businesses downtown get wind of what we are trying to do, they'll offer Hap the best legal assistance around."

"You could do that, Millie? Prove something like that?"

"Believe me, it's a lot easier to have a jury find a man guilty who's been dead for a hundred years than a living man standing in front of them. It won't be easy. There're a lot of ifs, some big ifs. But if you find Ramona's body, and if the Dade County medical examiner says it's murder, I think I could do it. Yeah, I think I could."

"Millie, I hate to bring this up, but the truth, the real fact is, Randolph Tyler was Ramona's ally. They were fighting together against the railroad, the drainage canals, all of that."

Millicent thought about it for a second or two, more loops and swirls on her legal pad.

"If they bring it up at all, we'll just argue that the Commodore's greed won out over his idealism. That's something most juries can believe. All it is anyway is a debate, my cleverness against the other side's cleverness. It all happened so long ago, the truth is irrelevant. It's all just a matter of making a coherent presentation of the few facts that are there.''

Millie was focused on her drawing, her hand moving like a seismograph in an eight point two.

Marguerite smiled at her, this woman from another planet. A place where truth didn't exist, only superior cleverness. Marguerite listened to the flutes and zithers coming from the health food store. The aroma of baking bread. Everything now with keener vibrations.

"What would you do with it anyway?" Millie, head down, said. "The land, I mean, if it was yours? I mean, if you wanted to, you could have me renegotiate all the leases, and you'd be rich. Rich rich rich.''

There was no way to know for sure, no mirrors in the office, but Marguerite felt her face had turned wild, as if she were some aborigine who'd just stumbled into this office after a lifetime in the jungle. Millie, her first civilized human being.

"I'm not sure what I'd do," Marguerite said. "I never thought about it.''

"Well, you should. You should start right away.''

"No, I take that back. I do know. I know exactly what I'd do.''

"Yeah.''

"I'd tear those damn buildings down. Every one of them, the Hyatt, Barnett Bank, Convention Center. I'd change the course of the river back to the way it was, plant mangroves along its banks. I'd let the vegetation run loose. I'd put it all back how it was. Just exactly. That's what I'd do. Yeah, of course.''

"You're joking.''

"No, exactly how it was. The river, everything. I could make it right again.''

"They'd never let you do that.''

"If it's my land, I could do it. How're they going to stop me? Tear down the buildings, make it all green. How it was.''

Marguerite rose from the chair and began to pace the office, feeling clumsy now. As if she'd just migrated into this body, didn't know yet how to operate it. Feeling an uncomfortably long distance from her own feet.

"There could be a couple of hitches," Millie said.

Marguerite looked at her, came to a halt.

"For one, the land would actually belong to your mother, not you, if we can prove this."

"Oh, yeah," she said. "That's right, it would, wouldn't it?"

"That could be a problem, huh? I mean, you two don't see eye-to-eye."

"It could be a problem," Marguerite said. "Or maybe not."

She leaned over and looked again at the mill site. Ramona, Anthony. The barking dog. Those three oak trees. The flowery heart of the city where its first sin was committed, a sin against her family, against her. The shadowed, fertile garden where the serpent had won its first convert. For so long that acre had lived inside Marguerite, more myth than reality. Now, in the daylight, sitting on Millie's desk on a twenty by twenty pad of foam, it was as if flesh had grown on the bones of her dream.

"My mother," Marguerite said, "has a few things to hide."

Millie glanced up. A tentative smile, with some worry in it.

"What're you saying? Blackmail your mother?"

"All I need is some documentation, Millie. Some hard evidence. Prove what she's been doing all these years. The illegal stuff. That would take her out of the picture, huh? If she were in jail?"

"Jail!" She looked at Marguerite. "You'd do that? Your own mother, send her to jail?"

"If that's where she deserves to be."

"God, Marguerite. I know you don't like her, but jail?"

"What's the other hitch, Millie?"

"Well," she said, looking down at her scribbling. "I was thinking. It sure would make things easier in court if you could arrange it all beforehand with Hap."

"Arrange what?"

"Like a settlement. Make it to his benefit not to fight the suit."

"What? Have him stand back and let us argue that his grandfather conspired to steal Ramona's land? Was in on her murder?"

147

"Look," Millie said. "He gets nothing from the leases as things stand now. But if you could promise to cut him in on it somehow, things would be a lot easier. What's he have to lose?"

"The good name of his ancestors."

"Does that matter to him?"

"I don't know. It should. But I'm not sure."

Millicent Benitez thought about it for a minute, staring down at her pad.

"It wouldn't hurt," she said at last. "Just to talk to him, see if maybe he'd cooperate. We could win without him. But it would be easier if he was on your side. You could ask him, right?"

"The only thing in the world Hap Tyler cares about is where he's going to put his penis next."

"Well, then," Millie said. Giving Marguerite a suggestive smile. "That could make it even easier. Persuade him like that."

"You've got to be kidding."

"Well, he's cute, isn't he? Blond, tall."

"No damn way, Millie. Not even for Miami. Not even to own the whole goddamn city."

# CHAPTER 16

Hap came awake, breathless, gripping hard to the sheets. He cranked himself upright, brushed away the fine threads of dream. Something about the Commodore, a Mayan sacrificial quarry, diving down through the watery murk to a pile of gold.

Just before he'd woke, he'd heard what sounded like the whisper of wind through the Mangrove House. Inside his dream, he'd strained to hear it, that quiet whoosh of air. But it wasn't wind at all. And slowly it occurred to him that what he was hearing was the faint first breath of the voice. The goddamn voice, coming to him while he was at the bottom of the quarry, his finger reaching out to touch the stack of gold bars, the voice murmuring to Hap to wake up. He was in danger. Whispering inside his dream. Grave danger. Wake up. Wake up.

And when he opened his eyes, rigid and sweating, there was the crunch of a car rolling down the drive. Hap rose, gripped the .45, and waking by degrees as he went, he stumbled out of the room, down the stairs, and out onto the porch. He hustled along the jasmine hedge, staying low, then squatted behind the dense lantana that formed a low hedge to the east of the house.

He drew back the slide, racked a round. The car came to a stop twenty feet away in the private driveway, next to his own MG. He listened as the motor knocked for a few seconds after the ignition was turned off. The door opened, and Hap held aside a few branches of the bush with the .45. A large man wearing dark slacks and a shoulder harness over his light shirt got out of the car, his back to Hap. It was a white Ford. A plain white Ford with dark tinted windows like the one Marguerite claimed was tailing Daniel.

The voice hissed in his head like the sizzle of a live wire. Danger, danger.

Hap shifted his feet, then took a couple of duckwalk steps to the end of the hedge. The man slipped a blue sport coat on, adjusted it, and started toward the house.

Hopping out from behind the hedge, Hap came to his full height, both hands holding the Colt on the man. Picking a spot between his wide shoulder blades, no quiver in his hand, absolutely dead still. The same quiet focus he'd known during the grim joy of battle.

"Hands up," Hap said. "Don't even wiggle your fat ass."

The man stopped.

"Raise your fucking hands now. Now. Do it!"

The man hoisted them quickly above his shoulders. And Hap stepped forward keeping his aim steady on the center of the man's back. He was ten feet behind the guy. Half of him there, half of him inside himself listening for the voice, for its command.

"Now turn the hell around, and keep your hands up."

Warily, the man turned around. It was Detective Wills.

"Shit," said Hap. "I don't know what's happening to me."

"Well, till you find out, you mind pointing that goddamn howitzer some other direction, please?"

*"Papaver somniferum,"* Wills said. Holding his dime store notepad out so Hap could read it in the yellow glow from the bug lights. They were out on the front porch. Wills had thought it might be cooler out there. *"Papaver somniferum,"* he said again, as if he liked the feel of it in his mouth.

Wills took a long look at the bay. The last light of the day seemed to be trapped inside the water, turning it a dull silver. To the south the sky was already dark. Wills mopped his face again with the white handkerchief he'd been using the last few minutes.

It was about seven-thirty, in the mid-nineties, no breeze, humidity a couple of degrees higher than the temperature, squeezing every grain of oxygen out of the air. Evening like this, the fish could swim right up onto the land, keep swimming, they wouldn't know the difference.

"What's this, triazolam?" said Hap, pointing at the pad.

"Triazolam," he said. "That's Halcion. Valium's little brother. Fairly common prescription item."

"And the *Papaver*?"

"Just your garden-variety opium." Wiping at the sweat on his neck. "Put the two together, who knows? Bachay never saw it before, this particular combination."

"And this?" Hap tapped the third word in the list.

"That's my scribble," he said. "It's something else again."

"What?"

"Scopolamine," he said.

Hap sat on the railing facing the cop.

"A natural derivative. It's in the belladonna family. I mean, even I heard of belladonna." He fanned himself with the handkerchief. Looking down at his notepad, he said, "Works by paralyzing the parasympathetic nervous system. Blocks the action of the nerve endings. Same time it does that it's stimulating the central nervous system. Produces disorientation, can cause a heartbeat so loud, it can be audible several feet away."

Hap looked down at Wills's pad, at his loopy penmanship.

"I don't get it," he said. "Sleeping pills, opium, and this thing."

"Hell, don't ask me to explain any of this. You want to discuss the autopsy results, you better talk to Bachay."

"So somebody forced Daniel to swallow these drugs?"

"Subcutaneous injection is how it looks," he said. "They haven't found the track yet. Still looking. But somebody stuck your brother with a needle and shot him up with it." He took back the notepad and slid it into his pocket. Even little motions like that making him sweat. "I see you had the grave dug."

Hap looked out at the small graveyard, a heron perched on the Commodore's headstone. The white bird glowing in the last light.

"Well, anyway," Wills said. "Once Doctor Bachay got his Jockey shorts out of his crack, he started humping full speed for a change. The guy ran all the blood tests himself, did all the lab work. In Bachay's defense, I have to say, normal procedure is, a body comes in, if it's got all the signs of a heart attack, and there's nothing at the scene to make you think otherwise, you do the basic lube and oil change on it, get to the next one. That's how it works. But I guess it's a good thing you did what you did. Making your personal appeal to Bachay like that."

Both of them looked off at the bay. Monday night, off-season. The fish could rest easy. Nobody chumming, nobody trolling. The water was so still you could throw a rock out there, the ripples would wash ashore tomorrow in Bimini.

"One other thing he found," Wills said.

Hap sighed.

"Your brother was tied up *after* he died."

"What?"

"The doc is speculating, and I kind of subscribe to this theory myself, whoever gave him his injection might've wanted the scene to look like your brother was involved in some kind of kinky sex thing." Wills shrugged. "To make us think just what we did at first, it was a hooker or a girlfriend, instead of whatever it was."

"I don't get it. What difference does that make?"

"Oh, it makes a difference," Wills said. "The way it is now, the stocking thing seems more like an afterthought. Like whoever it was might not've been planning on killing him. They just shot him up for whatever reason they had, and when he died, the person stood around and thought this up. According to the lab guys these stockings had never been worn."

Hap looked out at the bay again. He was bottoming out. His rush had crashed ashore. Now as he watched the water going black, he was feeling weary at the bone.

Hap said, "You get my message? About my intruder."

"It's why I'm here," Wills said. "The techies should be arriving

in the next little while, dust for prints, the whole shebang. So what
were they looking for? You know?''

''A gold mask.''

''Gold mask?''

Hap told him about the senator, her Mayan collection, the
eighty-six five, the black woman with the gold teeth. But not about
the *Carmelita,* any of that.

''Hard to believe,'' Wills said, ''somebody'd go to these lengths
for some little gold trinket.''

''Maybe they thought they'd find a lot of them, not just that
one.''

''What makes you think that?''

Hap was silent, looked away, but felt Wills watching him.

Wills mopped his face and said, ''So you got this mask lying
around anywhere?''

''Not that I know of.''

''Maybe your intruder found it.''

''She said she didn't, if we can trust that.''

Wills patted the handkerchief on his cheek, checking Hap over
with his cop eyes. Sadness, skepticism.

Wills said, ''Your brother have any hidey-holes, places he
might've put this thing?''

''Don't think so.''

The cop glanced back at the house.

''When the tech nerds get here, I'll have them look around,
see if they can spot any sliding walls, trap doors, hidden cave open-
ings, that sort of thing. They love that, tapping on walls.''

''There *is* a root cellar,'' said Hap. ''A door in the floor, under
the kitchen table.''

''Worth a look, I guess.''

''You have any idea what it was like for Daniel?'' said Hap. ''A
mixture of drugs like that?''

Wills mopped his throat, leaned over and wrung out the handkerchief on the porch and then laid it on top of his head, a damp
mantilla. He looked at Hap, weighing how to say it.

''I asked the doc the same thing.''

"And."

"Well, it might hit different people different ways. And of course, the combination of drugs being so weird, it's hard to say exactly."

"Go on, Wills. I can take it."

Wills took a glance at him, then looked back out at the bay.

"Probably a period of euphoria," he said. "Imaginary freedom from anxiety. Kind of a dreamy feeling. Maybe enhanced memory, flashbacks, pleasant though. That phase probably lasted five to ten minutes."

"Then?"

"Then the turbo comes on, the scopolamine starts kicking his pineal gland all around the room, gives him a hyper-rush. He gets nervous, sweaty, dry mouth, could be he yammers for a while. Followed by complete respiratory paralysis, myocardial infarction."

Hap stared at the plank porch. Taking his time breathing, having to concentrate on the act a little more than usual.

"So this mix," Hap said, "it was clearly a lethal dose?"

"Hard to say. The fact is, it's possible it could've been used as a stimulant to the sexual activity, something new going on out there in Sexual Tomorrowland, and somebody miscalculated, though Bachay hasn't heard of it before. Or maybe the one and only purpose of using it was to kill him. That's how I'm proceeding on it at the moment, as a possible homicide."

"What? She screws him, and she kills him?"

"Praying mantises made it popular," said Wills. "And black widows."

Hap looked impassively at the cop.

Wills said, "Though, you know, I always wondered what evolutionary purpose that serves, female biting off the head of the male that just screwed her."

Wills squeezed a few drops of sweat from the handkerchief.

"Maybe what it is," he said, "the males know what's about to happen, it just makes them hump that much harder, shoot that last load as far as they can. If I knew I was about to get my head bit off, it'd probably have that effect on me."

"I don't like that story, Wills. Girl screws boy, using strange concoction, boy dies, girl flees. There's no gold mask in that story. Doesn't explain my house being ransacked."

"Okay, all right." Wills tapped his pen idly against the railing. He said, "Okay, so let's try another version. Same facts, new story. Let's allege Daniel Tyler had this gold mask. He's gotten it from source unknown, but someone knew about it, knew he had it, and wanted to get it from him, they gave him a drug, hoping that under its influence he would reveal the location of this gold mask. That's the yammering part, the scopolamine. Same drug the Third Reich used, I understand. But the drug accidentally kills him, the person panics, ties him up with fishnet stockings to confuse the issue, and beats it."

"That sounds better."

"More elegant," Wills said. "Elegant but still simple. Speaks to all the points we know so far."

"Daniel have any bruises?"

"No, nothing unusual, no contusions, lacerations."

"So he wasn't dragged into that room. He went willingly."

"Not necessarily," said Wills. "That's one of the many convenient uses of the small-caliber handgun. It gets people to do things they might otherwise not do, without leaving bruises."

Hap nodded.

"I'll show you the cellar."

He stood up, and Wills followed him into the kitchen. Hap found a flashlight in the pantry and handed it to him. As the big man was squeezing down into the root cellar, the phone rang. Hap jogged out to the front hallway to take it. Mike Romero from the bank.

"I just thought of something," he said. "I got home, had a drink of apple juice, and it came to me."

"Yeah?"

"You haven't written any checks on your eighty-six five yet, have you?"

"What's up, Mike?"

"Your taxes."

"What?"

"County real estate taxes," Romero said. "Daniel always came in this time of year, deposited a lump sum of cash to pay taxes. Most people do it through escrow, a little every month with the mortgage, but he liked to do it this way. Put in the whole chunk a month or two before they're due, just enough to cover them."

"Eighty-six five for taxes? That much?"

"Hey," Romero said. "You're on the bay, right, and you got, how much, ten acres over there?"

"Nine and a half."

He could hear the whir of Mike's calculator.

"Well, at current millage rates, your bill this year would come to, let's see, about eighty-five nine and change. Highest tax rate in the county."

"Jesus, so much?"

"I'm surprised you didn't know about it, man."

Hap considered it a moment.

"I've had some mental health problems," he said. "Didn't you know?"

"Yeah," Romero said. "I guess I heard."

"Big brother was probably protecting me from real-world shit like that. Sheltering me. Afraid it'd drive me crazy again."

"Well, hell, a tax bill like that would sure drive me crazy, I'm telling you that."

Looking off down the hallway, out the front door at the slope of lawn and the dark glitter of the bay, Hap said, "Mike, is there any way you could tell how much the taxes were on this property exactly twenty years ago?"

Mike was silent for a moment, then said, "Yeah, I think I could do that. You'll have to hold on a minute. I gotta see if I can find some old files. Shit like that isn't on the computer."

"Go on, I'll wait."

He kept his eyes out on the dark lawn, watching some lights winking on the bay. Two fast boats and one slow one passed by before Mike came back on.

"You there?"

"Let me guess," Hap said. "Twenty years ago, the taxes on this property were roughly five thousand dollars."

"Four thousand nine hundred and sixty-eight."

"Or in other words, one gold frog with ruby eyes."

"What?"

"Thanks, Mike. I appreciate your help. Thanks a lot."

He set the phone in the cradle.

When he came back into the kitchen, Wills was hunched over in a chair, resting, his elbows on his knees, staring down into the dark hole. He glanced up at Hap.

"Being down in that root cellar, how cool it is, it's enough to make me wish I was a root."

"Maybe in your next life."

"Stays as hot as this, that shouldn't be much longer."

Hap kneeled beside the opening and peered into the dark.

"Don't waste your time," said Wills. "Only masks down there are the ones the palmetto bugs are wearing. Matter of fact, Hap, you might call your Orkin man, you know, make a significant dent in the worldwide population of winged roaches in one spray."

He asked Hap if there was any water around, cold, with ice.

Hap poured him a glass, broke some ice from a tray.

"Don't you want me to come downtown and look at mug shots, find this woman? I think I could recognize her. We had a memorable encounter."

"How's tonight look?"

Hap gave him the water and he drank it in a gulp.

"I've got something planned for later," said Hap. "Tomorrow morning would be better."

"It's your call, but the sooner, the fresher."

"Tomorrow then," Hap said. "In the morning."

"You know, I got a theory about basements," Wills said, staring down into the dark hole, the smell of it, dank and fertile. "Wanna hear it?"

Hap shrugged.

"Reason Florida's got all the problems it does, it's because there aren't any basements." Looking at Hap, see if he was following this so far. Hap nodded.

" 'Cause see, you grow up in Florida, all you know about is the ground floor, and that's usually hard, terrazzo or some shit. Hard as marble. You never get any sense of being planted in the place where you're from. Hurricane comes along, it could blow everything away. Or bulldozers, they arrive one morning, bang, by five o'clock, land's all cleared, trees all pushed over, everything scraped clean. Nothing really anchored very deep, not plants, not the people, nothing. So the residents wind up not giving a shit. Not having enough at stake. Not planted."

"You sit around at night think all this stuff up?"

"Take your grandfather," he said. "He went to the trouble to dig this root cellar. He may not have known it, but it wasn't just to keep things cool, it was to have himself a foothold, a foxhole, a place he could go, burrow inside the earth, not just be sitting on top of it."

Hap watched this man staring into the dark square hole. A man who'd read too many books to be truly happy in any profession, much less the one he'd chosen.

"Hate to spoil your theory, Wills," Hap said. "But the Commodore didn't have anything dug. The house sits on top of a solution hole, a depression in the bedrock. He built it here so it would be off the ground in case of floods, and so he could draw the cooler air up through the house."

"Amounts to the same thing," Wills said. "It's still a basement. Just a natural one."

"Wills," Hap said. "You going to question Senator Rawlings?"

The cop thought about that one. Made him sweat some more working it around in his head. Long strands of his hair had pulled away from his bald spot and were hanging down over his ear.

"The woman sends her chauffeur over, takes me to her place, she gives me a song and dance about this gold mask, and I come home and the place is ransacked. She's the logical one to ask some questions, wouldn't you say?"

"No future in it," Wills said. He reached up to his head, felt around for a moment, then put the strands of hair back into place. "Unless you found the senator actually standing over a dead body with a red-hot .38 in her hand, forget it. And anyway, why would she send somebody over to do your place, then let you come home before the guy was through?"

"People screw up."

"Not her. Not Garnetta Rawlings."

"Yeah," Hap said. "It *is* hard to picture."

"I always liked her husband, you know. Congressman Rawlings. Now, there was a true gentleman. Wore white suits all the time, one of those flattop straw hats. Walked with a cane, knew every cop on the force by name. He was a gentle spirit, that man. Not like her. She's a tough one. Likes to get eyeball-to-eyeball with people, make 'em back down. She's hard to like."

"Maybe it's the fact she's a woman, Wills. You just don't like tough women. If she were a man, it wouldn't bother you."

Wills thought about it for a second.

"Naw," he said. "It's something else about her. Not how tough she is. It's something deeper than that. Meanness. Or something like that."

"Yeah," said Hap. "Her eyes're always a few degrees cooler than her smile."

"Right, that's it," Wills said. He stood up, dusting his hands off on his pants. "But then, of course, there isn't any law against smiling funny. Not yet at least."

"Maybe you should talk to her, Wills."

"I'll think about it," he said. "I'll give it some serious consideration."

# CHAPTER 17

As HAP PARKED HIS RUSTED-OUT MG OUTSIDE LARRY Victor's taxidermy shop along the Miami River, all up and down the street the hazy yellow streetlights flickered. Like everything else in this part of town, they were on the fritz.

When he stepped into the shop, Larry looked up, said hello, then turned his attention back to the white marlin laid out on his butcher table. Larry was six three, but hunched over like he usually was, he probably only measured five eleven or so. Very skinny, with long red hair he wore in a ponytail. T-shirt, gym shorts, flip-flops.

The marlin he was cleaning was over two hundred pounds. He'd split it open, and was dropping its guts into the big silver can by his side, water from one of the faucets running over the fish and into the gutters around the edge of the table.

The shop was full of stuffed cats and dogs, road-kills Larry had discovered. A few hawks, a couple of owls and herons. Also a small grizzly, some turkey buzzards, and a wild hog. There was one wall devoted to fish he and Hap had caught, all the reef ones, a good-sized cubera snapper, wahoo, pompano, small sharks. It was a dark place and smelled like formaldehyde and sour meat.

There wasn't a creature in the store that didn't look like it could still take a good swat at you, or flick its tail fin and disappear around a ledge of coral. And over the last few years he'd developed a real talent for portraying his animals in their last second, just as they realized they were doomed, Larry getting that look into their faces. The Peterbilt bearing down on them, the hook firmly in their jaw, they knew it was over, but by god they were going to make a fight of it.

Maybe that was the last look Larry had seen in his parents' eyes just before they'd been murdered twenty years ago by the drug cowboys. Small-time dealers, his parents made some kind of territorial error. Larry never found out what. At fifteen he'd witnessed their execution. He'd been outside on the lawn playing pitch with his dad, his mother looking on. One second it's all suburban sweetness, the next second his parents' bodies were bucking and dancing on the grass.

Or maybe his father and mother hadn't been courageous at all, and it was this look that Larry hungered for. Either way, his animals had expressions that were more poignant and heroic than most of the human faces Hap had run across.

Larry looked up again from his work.

"I saw it in the paper about Daniel. You doing okay?"

He scooped out the marlin's eyes with a small sharpened teaspoon, dropped them into the bucket.

"So-so," said Hap. "Just so-so."

Hap stepped over to the wall of fish, touched one of them, a schoolhouse snapper. He moved casually around the shop, then came to a stop near the birds. Red-shouldered hawk, falcon, a blue heron. All of them on perches above the raccoon.

The red-shouldered hawk's wings were spread, landing or taking off. Somewhere a rifle had been raised, the sights poised. The hawk could hear the hammer cock, a quiet noise like snapping a twig. That bird knew it was dead. All that in its face.

"You still have that oil you extracted, Larry?"

Larry looked up at him, a serious expression.

"Which? The skunk oil?"

"Yeah."

"The hell you want with that?"

"I had an idea."

"Better be a good one, man. Took me ten years to accumulate that stuff, one anal sac at a time."

"I want to break into a place," Hap said. "Thought this might be of help."

Larry stared at him, half admiring, half not so sure.

"All right. But you bring back what you don't use, okay?"

Hap said yeah, sure, okay.

"Promise me, man. Bring back whatever's left. I'm sentimental about that shit."

"I will, I will."

"Hey, man." Larry studied Hap's eyes. "You been hearing your goddamn voice again? That what this is all about?"

"Coming in strong," Hap said. "Loud and clear."

Martina parked the Bel Aire in a vacant lot two doors down from the taxidermy shop. The river right in front of them, one of those Haitian freighters docked there, on its deck a twenty-foot high pile of stolen bikes, mattresses, plastic buckets. Tyler had been in the taxidermy place for about five minutes.

Hollings's stomach was twisted into a hard lump from playing that scene with Max Hunter over and over in his head. He wanted to go home, have a couple of stiff ones. Maybe six stiff ones. Fall in bed and try to sleep his way past this.

Since they'd left Max Hunter's, Hollings had done everything but plead with Martina to take him home. But she just kept driving, never saying a word. Taking them from Max Hunter's house, back across town to Tyler's place in Coconut Grove. Hollings about to get out and flag down a taxi, when there was Tyler, pulling out in his MG, so Martina'd U-turned on Main Highway, and fell in behind the MG, and wound up over here.

This neighborhood was nothing but warehouses, busted bottles in the street, upside-down cars in vacant lots, deserted gas stations, everything gutted, blown out. Roofs caved in, walls crumbling, stop signs bent double, weeds taking over the sidewalks. And zombies in ragged clothes drifting in the shadows. It was the fucking Night of the Living Dead out there.

Of course, Hollings could always climb out here, except shit, he wasn't crazy enough to try to walk through this part of town without full battle gear. Ten-thirty at night, by now all the mole people had come up and were feeling their way through the dark with their switchblades.

Hollings cranked his tinted window down for a better view. Two buildings down from them was a small frame shack where Hap Tyler stood waiting under the porch light, talking to some tall skinny guy.

Hollings squinted into the darkness, saying, "Well, old Alvarez sure had it wrong, huh? Fucking Tyler wasn't too scared to leave his house after all."

"That goddamn Alvarez. Who died and made him King Tut?"

"Taxidermy," Hollings said. He shivered out loud. "Christ, dead animals always give me the willies."

"Hollings," Martina said, her eyes on Tyler and the store. "When this is all over and you got some extra money, you should look into some kind of a manhood implant. Something to bring your pecker up to speed."

"Yeah, tell me about it, cornrow."

Martina turned her head toward him, inch at a time, bringing those lazy eyes around. A Mona Lisa smile appearing on her wide mouth, Mona with a machete under her dress.

"He's getting away," Hollings said. "Come on, stay with him."

Martina kept smiling at him a second or two more, then slid the shifter into first, popped the clutch hard, and made her Goodyears burn.

She stayed a good way behind Tyler south on Twenty-seventh Avenue, having to run a couple of lights to keep him in sight. A couple of miles farther south, at the intersection of Coral Way and Twenty-seventh, a few blocks from Miracle Mile, they were stopped six cars back of the MG and with no word of warning, Martina opened her door and stepped out into the street.

"The fuck you doing now?"

"Old friend of mine lives a few blocks from here," she said. "I been meaning to stop in, say hi. Seems like a good time."

Hollings jerked a look back to the light. Still red. One of those long ones. Turned back to Martina.

"So what am I supposed to do?"

She closed the door, and leaned in the window.

"Keep following him, sugar," she said. "I'll catch up with you later on tonight. I'll get my friend to loan me her car."

"Catch up, how? You don't know where the fuck this guy's gonna lead me." The light changed, cars starting to move in front of the Chevy. Hollings scooted over behind the wheel.

"I'll meet you at Tyler's house later on tonight. Guy's bound to go home eventually. Don't you think?"

Horns honked behind him. Almost midnight, and the fuckers were still in a hurry to get somewhere.

"Whereabouts at Tyler's place?"

Martina shook her head, gave him that gold smile.

"All right," she said. "He's got this stone well or some shit like that. I saw it off to the east of the house, next to the woods. I'll meet you right there, whenever I get done. You just follow along. Meet me next to that well. Then we'll camp out there in the dark, watch the house, tell ghost stories. Scare the shit out of each other."

"Jesus Christ! You keep changing the plans. I don't like it one goddamn bit."

Hollings slammed the Chevy into gear and sped on after Tyler. The guy was way the hell on up the street, stopped at the next light already.

In the lobby of the Grande Biscayne Condominiums, Hap sat down in the first chair he came to. Leather wingback, a thick glass bowl of cashews in front of him, a copy of *Town and Country*. He watched a woman in a black cocktail dress moving among the chairs, serving drinks.

A stiff-necked man in a formal Hawaiian shirt and white pants had spotted Hap and come out from behind the concierge's counter. Same guy from this morning, recognizing Hap, and walking over to speak to the two guards who hung out near the entrance door.

A new shift of security. These two looked like they'd spent the afternoon biting the tops off vitamin bottles, washing them down with growth hormone. They nodded at the concierge, and swung their eyes to Hap. The concierge started over alone.

Hap reached out for a handful of cashews, popped some, and took an interest in the piano player, a redheaded woman who was tinkling out Chopin, holding her chin up as if she were waiting for her tiara to descend from heaven.

The guy in the jungle shirt kept coming, nodding at all his well-dressed, well-groomed tenants, greeting them by name. Looked like he'd trained for his job at mortuary school. Putting on a bereaved smile as he approached.

"You came back," he said, keeping a safe distance from Hap, his hands behind his back.

"A martini, please," Hap said. "Very dry with a twist."

The concierge looked up at one of the chandeliers, counted a few of its pendants, then brought his dreary gaze back to Hap.

"Sir, I would urge you to spare yourself any more embarrassment. Or physical abuse."

He gave his heels a soft click, like a vault door locking shut in Hap's face. Then he tipped his head, bent at the waist in a half-bow, and swept his arm toward the entrance, saying quietly, "And get the hell out of my building."

"Whatever you say," Hap said, giving the guy a wink. "Don't want to cause any trouble."

He'd only come inside to see if there might be an easier way of doing this. Not waste Larry's juice. But no, there wasn't. His hunch was that the senator had sent the black woman with the cornrows after the gold mask, and she'd found it somewhere in the Mangrove House, and had brought it over here, and it was up there now, propped up on its pedestal.

As he was heading out, the elevator doors parted and the tile layer who had reorganized Hap's internal organs this morning stepped out into the lobby. Working a hell of a long shift to keep the steaks on his table. He spotted Hap and gave him a menacing glare.

Outside, rounding the south corner of the building, Hap could hear the air-conditioning units rumbling like a half dozen Indy cars revved up at the starting line. He walked down a steep concrete ramp that led toward the noise. An underground parking garage for the maintenance trucks and employees' vehicles. Had to keep those jalopies out of sight around all that splendor, couldn't have the real world intruding on the guests.

He followed the rumble across the garage, came to a glassed-in cubicle in one corner of the parking garage. MAINTENANCE was stenciled on the door. When Hap tapped on the glass, a man in an orange jumpsuit rose from behind the desk inside the small room and came to the door.

"Help you?"

"You Al?" Hap said.

"Al? There ain't any Al here."

The man was in his seventies, white hair, stocky with washed-out blue eyes behind very thick lenses. A halo of bourbon hovered around him.

"Shit," Hap said, "it must be that damn Terecita again. Our receptionist. Always getting names wrong, addresses, everything."

The man looked dully at Hap.

"When we hired her, she claimed she was bilingual, but now I'm wondering if that doesn't just mean she's illiterate in two languages instead of one."

"So what can I do for you?" The man glanced back into the office. Probably having separation anxiety, getting out of range of his Jim Beam.

"Hap Daniels, with Jefferson Air-Conditioning. I'm here for the fluorocarbon check. Terecita set it up with Al, or whatever the hell his name is."

"Mickey Long works days, I work nights. And my name ain't Al."

The man leaned back in his office, took down a clipboard and squinted at it. Brought it closer to his face, maneuvered it for a little better light.

"I don't remember nobody saying nothing about air-conditioning work. And what the hell're fluorocarbons, anyway?"

"You know, the gasses that are eating holes in the ozone layer. Freon, shit like that."

"Oh, freon."

Hap was quiet, watching the guy squinting at the clipboard.

"Almost midnight, they send you out on something like that?"

"It's easier to spot at night," Hap said, going with it. This other guy, Hap Daniels, rising up inside him, this blue collar workaday gentleman. Hap hearing himself say, "Don't ask me why nights are better. I don't understand it myself."

"Where's your tools?"

Hap held up the shampoo bottle of skunk juice. Shook it for effect. The old man leaned forward and peered at the bottle.

"Doesn't require tools," Hap said. "Just a squirt or two of this stuff knocks out the problem like that."

"Fluorocarbons?"

"It's serious business," Hap said. "I'm no scientist or anything, but this shit is bad. We lose that ozone layer, the sun's just going to eat our asses alive."

"What'd you say your name was?" The man smacked his lips, swallowed. Thirsty guy.

"Hap Daniels, Jefferson Air-Conditioning. You want me take a look at that sheet, see if I'm on there?"

The man gave Hap an uneasy glance. He licked his lips, then held out the clipboard.

Hap ran his finger down the list of workmen, and said, "Yeah, here it is. They spelled my name wrong. Guess that's what threw you."

Hap held it out to the guy, pointed at a name. Harvey Winters Plumbing Service.

The man leaned forward, frowned at the page, and said, "Getting so bad, I can't make out my own handwriting, eyes clouding up like they been doing." He took the clipboard from Hap and scribbled something on it and put it back on the wall.

"I get much blinder, gonna have to buy me a goddamn German shepherd to get me around."

"Way things been going," Hap said, "there's not all that much worth seeing anymore anyway. Ruining all the good stuff."

The old guy nodded.

"Down that hall," he said. "Third door on your left."

Hap walked down the hallway, pushed open the heavy gray door and stepped into the roar of compressors and exhaust fans. Before him was an impossible maze of tubing and coils, and aluminum shielding. He let the door close, shrugged and headed into it.

There were eight units, each one the size of a Volkswagen. It took him twenty minutes, and in the bad light he barked his knuckles trying knobs that didn't turn. Scalded his forearm, sliced a finger, but finally he located what seemed like the filter trays. A small clip held the mesh screens in place. Pop the clip and the filters slid out of their slots on ball bearings.

He lifted the clear plastic shampoo bottle, sloshed it. A viscous honey-colored fluid. Larry had told him, one anal sac from one skunk could contaminate five city blocks. In this bottle, Larry'd accumulated close to thirty sacs.

Hap opened the tube of the menthol VapoRub he'd picked up at a 7-Eleven on the way over, dabbed some on his finger, and filled his nostrils with the cool jelly.

He waited behind a ligustrum hedge across from valet parking. Ten minutes, twenty. Beginning to think he'd chosen the wrong filters to spray the stuff into.

It was thirty minutes later when the front door finally banged open. The first ones out were three women in frilly party dresses. Coughing, fanning their faces. Then the pianist collided with them from the rear, pushed past, and ran out into the drive.

Hap waded through the hedge and sprinted across the parking lot. At the door he squeezed past more residents stumbling out. The lobby was in chaos. A woman in a robe and pink slippers was screaming, the concierge had covered his mouth with a handkerchief and was occupied with the screamer, trying to budge her away from the stairway where more occupants staggered down. Hap didn't see the security guys anywhere, probably bailed out the back door to barf in the alley. Dozens of people emerged from the bar and hurried for the exits, a couple of them laughing hilariously.

Hap went over to the elevators. He stood and watched the numbers count down until the bell rang and the doors parted. Another choking load of guests hurried past. When the tile layer stepped out, gagging, Hap moved up behind him, seized his cheap haircut. He banged his forehead into the stucco wall beside the elevator doors, and again for emphasis.

When he let him go, the guy turned his dazed eyes toward Hap, taking short gasps. Hap swiveled him around again, pinned his cheek against the wall. Pressing his forearm to the base of the guy's neck, Hap tore the keys from the clip on his belt. He stepped into the elevator, pulled the elevator guy inside. Hap fit the key to the slot and turned it and the car began to rise. The guy had a queasy color, probably beginning to regret his supper choice. The VapoRub was working all right, but Hap could still taste the stench, feel an uneasy gurgle in his own stomach.

When the elevator came to a stop, the doors opened onto the foyer of the penthouse.

"Which one?" Hap jingled the key chain in the elevator guy's face. The kid chose one.

Hap fit the key to the lock on the penthouse door and was turning it just as the door swung open and Marguerite Rawlings, in faded jeans and a blue tennis shirt, stumbled out past him. In her hand was a file folder.

She glanced at Hap, did a double take, then turned and stood for a moment, looking back into the apartment as if it were on fire. Confused, touching a hand to her throat.

She coughed, then her eyes let go, and she sagged back against the door frame. She coughed harder, and pressed both hands against her stomach, swallowing back the nausea. She looked at Hap, eyes dizzy.

"You did this?"

Hap smiled his confession.

"Your mother here?"

She shook her head no.

He pulled off his belt, turned the tile layer around and lashed his hands behind his back. Marguerite swallowed once or twice, and eased down onto the floor. Her eyes unfocused, her skin a seasick green.

"You won't give us any trouble, will you, leather nuts?"

The kid shook his head. Marguerite set the file folder on the floor beside her, and looked around at the tile as though she might be choosing a spot to vomit.

"Okay, I'll be right back."

He pushed open the door and went straight for the Mayan room. It only took a moment to see the mask wasn't there. The photograph of it was still propped up on a small wooden stand. Shit, damn, hell. Shit. Double shit. He walked around the room again, studied the jewelry and vases. Everything just as it had been this morning. Shit, shit, shit.

On his way through the living room he halted, looked at her paintings, her books, her furniture. He had to keep searching. Even if it meant being caught, he had to go on. He'd come this far, caused all this fuss. The gold mask was here somewhere, it had to be.

There were three bedrooms, all of them off the main hall. The first was the senator's study. A polished slab of teak that was awash with papers and file folders faced the doorway. One of the drawers was open, several files pulled halfway out. He tucked them back in place and shut the drawer.

The senator's black swivel chair put her back to the window and that glittering view of the bay. On one wall there were a couple of photos of her, official publicity shots, soft focus and diffused light that smoothed the wrinkles from her face, tightened her wattles, air-brushed away her character.

The next was her bedroom. As Spartan and efficient as a Holiday Inn. Only a hint here and there of the woman's presence, the two small bottles of perfume on her dresser, the wineglass on her bedside table with a spoonful of red still in it. A couple of framed prints on the walls, a Gauguin and a Matisse.

A makeup kit sat on her bathroom counter. The medicine cabinet was empty, the drawers as well. A few items on the countertop, but the senator appeared to be traveling so much she didn't bother to unpack. He dug through her kit. Nothing the least bit unusual.

On the walls of the guest bedroom there were framed posters, color photos of the French countryside, a sunrise over some ocean. A double bed, covered in a putty-gray comforter. The dresser drawers were empty. Nothing under the bed.

In the guest bath, he began opening drawers in the vanity. Long past expecting to find anything, but caught up now in the same manic frenzy he'd felt this afternoon when he'd tried to straighten up the Mangrove House.

Nail files, cotton balls, Band-Aids, extra toothpaste, brushes, a plumber's helper, old WaterPik. Motel soap bars, bobby pins, rubber bands. He pawed through it all, found nothing, and shoved the last drawer closed.

As he reached his hand out for the medicine cabinet, a distant siren sounded, and another began behind it. With a jumpy heart, he opened the mirrored door. More miniature bottles of shampoo, conditioner, a sewing kit.

He was about to shut the cabinet when a glint of metal on the top shelf caught his eye. Even before he reached up for it, his gut began to shrivel. A sphincter tightened. He reached out, moved aside a blue bottle, and pulled out a small package. The plastic wrapper was torn open. With light-fingered care he held it out to the light.

A packet of four hypodermic syringes. One of them missing.

He studied them for a moment, their awful angularity, their unsettling combination of soft plastic and steel. It was like holding up a nest of scorpions.

He reached up, took down the blue vial, a bottle the size of his thumb. It couldn't hold more than a couple of teaspoons. No label or markings. Hap unscrewed the cap, and there was a rubber seal stretched over the mouth of the bottle, a single pinprick in its center.

He bent down and tore off a wad of toilet paper, twisted it into a finger-shape, and poked it into his right nostril. He cleaned away enough of the VapoRub to get a sniff, and drew in a strong hit of the bitter nutty flavor. Medicinal, with a corrosive undercurrent.

Quickly, he wrapped the bottle in tissue, put it in the pocket of his shorts. He slid the pack of needles in the other pocket. Breathing hard, he stood before her sink and listened to the sirens down below. In that harsh fluorescence, he stared at his image in the mirror. Wild eyes, waxy skin, his forehead crisscrossed with grooves like some kind of fleshy griddle. An insane grimace twitched at his mouth.

This wasn't any Hap Tyler he knew. This was a caricature, a garish Halloween mask. Somebody coming to the door dressed as the maniac grandson of Commodore Tyler. And Hap had opened the door and now stood confronting this plastic face, a grotesque replica of himself looking back at him with weird, drunken eyes moving behind the gargoyle mask.

# CHAPTER 18

Marguerite stood beside the MG and watched as more TV trucks crowded into the lot of the Grande Biscayne. She was playing with the collar of her tennis shirt. Still seemed stunned and queasy.

The TV crews fanned out, searching the throng for eyewitnesses. With only half an hour before the evening newscasts there was a frantic pace. Hap counted seven police cruisers, all with their blue lights spinning. Shy of his record of sixteen for the episode at Centrust Towers, but still, seven was a good turnout. Must have been a slow night on the mean streets.

He saw Dick Vasquez, the night-beat reporter for the sleazy independent station. The guy got down from his van and rolled up his sleeves. An assistant misted his face with phony sweat, and then his cameraman lit the TV lights and started filming. Vasquez hunched down as if a gun battle were in progress behind him, and he began to babble away. Normally the guy liked to kneel on the pavement next to the damp blood from a shootout, dab his finger in it and hold it up for the camera. Nothing to dab tonight. Not yet anyway.

"Jesus Christ, Hap." Marguerite stood next to the rear fender, hands on hips, her hair lifted by the breeze. "What the hell were you trying to do?"

"What I want to know is why *you* were up there, rummaging around in your mother's apartment."

The color was coming back to her face, but Marguerite said nothing, looking out at the crowd.

"You were snooping, weren't you? Same as I was."

"Hey, look. It's my mother's condo. I can come and go there anytime I want."

"Then she knew you were there? Is that what you're saying?"

Marguerite closed her mouth, looked away from him.

"I guess you didn't realize in all the excitement," he said, "you forgot to close her file drawer, the one you were digging through."

She jerked her gaze up at the building.

"Don't worry," he said. "I closed it, put it back to normal. So what'd you take?" He nodded at the file in her hand.

She sighed in frustration and held out the file folder. Hap took it, opened it, a single sheet inside. Marguerite Rawlings's birth certificate.

"Middle name Ramona, huh? Born in Miami, Florida. Eight pounds four ounces. Chubby little thing."

Hap handed it back to her.

"What're you doing with this?"

"I think I'm entitled to have my own birth certificate."

"Don't tell me you snuck into your mother's apartment to get *that*."

She crossed her arms, her lips tight, eyes furious.

"You went in there looking for something else, didn't you? But I interrupted you and all you got was this."

Hap saw the two security guys come out the front door. They were moving with the uneasy walk of men who'd been at sea for a week. Behind them the concierge in the Hawaiian shirt waved out at the crowd, and the two goons moved ahead and began to prowl.

"So, want to get a drink? Find a bar with a TV, see how this thing turns out?"

"Screw you, Hap. Just screw you."

"Well, if you really want to know why I broke in there," he said, "I was thinking about my dead brother. Remember him?"

"You bastard," she said. She dropped her arms, looked ready to slap him.

Hap turned back to watch the pandemonium at the front of the building. One of the security guys was peering in their direction.

"Let me ask you something," he said. "I been wanting to know this for some time now."

She gave no sign she'd heard him.

He turned to her. Drew a step closer.

"Did you love him? Daniel."

She dropped her head and closed her eyes for a moment, then slowly opened them. She took a slow, calming breath. And brought her eyes up to his, glaring.

"Hap, you're so fucked-up, it's unbelievable."

"You didn't, did you? It never looked right. So stiff. So formal."

"What do you know, Hap? You and your Lolitas."

"The two of you," he said. "It wasn't about love. You just had the same fixation. Both of you dancing the same hundred-years-ago waltz, that's all it was, I bet. A mind game. In love with the by-gone days. All that dopey bullshit.

"I never thought you two looked right together. It wasn't just the age difference. Never any nuzzling, any of that. You touched, but never any real warmth."

"Jesus Christ." Marguerite shook her head in disgust, turned from him, but as she started away, Hap put his hand on her shoulder, held her.

"Look, sweet one, we need to have a private conversation. And we need to do it now. Come on, you're going with me."

She stared at his hand till he removed it. Then turned her eyes to him, her face flushed, her mouth crimped as if she were about to strangle on some curse.

"All right, then," Hap said. "Maybe my old buddy Dick Vasquez can get you to talk. In fact, I bet I can get us both on TV tonight."

Hap took a couple of steps in Dick's direction and Marguerite barked for him to stop right there. Hap looked back at her, then called out, "Hey, Dick! Dick Vasquez. Over here."

"Goddamn you, Hap." Marguerite opened the passenger door and climbed inside. "All right. Come on, damn it. Come on."

Somebody in his crew spoke close to Dick's ear and pointed toward Hap's MG. Dick waved his arm for his cameraman to follow, and began to trot their way.

Hap opened the car door and got in. He fired it up, put it in gear. He leaned over and turned on the radio, took a second or two fiddling with the knob, pretending to look for a station.

Marguerite slapped the dashboard.

"Go on, damn it. Go!"

He smiled innocently at her, let out the clutch, and accelerated out of the parking lot.

When they were out on Bayshore, heading north, he said, "You know, I always heard tomato juice is the only thing can get this stink off your skin. Got to soak in it for a good long time. But these clothes, I think they're goners."

Christ, that Chevy Bel Aire was a ham-fisted piece of machinery. For one thing, hell, it didn't have power-steering, so Hollings had to grunt and curse it around every corner. For another thing, he had to lag two blocks behind Tyler just to keep from being heard. The Chevy had lakepipes, chrome exhausts running below the side panels. Loud-ass mufflers. Damn, just idling, the Chevy was probably rattling dentures four stories up.

Hollings would fucking well like to know what was going on. All those people running out of the Grande Biscayne, the fire trucks and cop cars coming, but no flames anywhere, then smelling something terrible floating out of the building, something five days dead. Tyler in on it somehow, coming and going like a sneak.

Then when Tyler hustled out of the condo there's a woman with him. Lady dressed in jeans and a tennis shirt, long black hair. Damn good-looking lady. Playmate of the Month material, though she seemed a little light on knockers. Christ, if Hollings ever got this Tyler guy alone, he'd have to get the name of his aftershave.

He stayed back of the MG north on Bayshore until it turned into Brickell, passed all the glass banks, the yuppie high-rise condos, over the Miami River bridge into downtown. Past the Hyatt, then a left on Flagler, going west. Winding back toward the same bombed-out neighborhood as before. Tyler a braver man than Hollings, driving through this part of town with his top down. Stopping at lights exposed like that, a shadow could ease up, press a knife to your throat, take whatever you had.

Hollings pulled into the same vacant lot as before, watched Tyler stop his MG in front of the taxidermy shop. Hollings leaned back, shook out his sore arms. That Haitian freighter was gone now, on a midnight crossing back home with all those hot bicycles. Hollings thinking, yeah, it was only right a bunch of spoiled Cuban kids should have to donate something to their black brothers in Haiti.

Man, he had to laugh sometimes, watching the Miami news. Everybody always talking about how mean and awful it was to be racist, but then every other day some skinny illiterate Cuban comes floating up the Gulf Stream in an inner-tube rubber raft. The Coast Guard runs out, devotes a couple thousand dollars of high-test gasoline and man-hours to picking up the skinny Cuban and bringing him ashore, and there he is in front of the TV cameras, a hero, all his fat cousins standing around behind him cheering and smiling. The pig roasting and black beans bubbling somewhere in the background. It could be the same day, same newscast, the Coast Guard catches a boatload of skinny illiterate Haitians coming from a lot farther away in a leaky shrimp boat. But goddamn if it wasn't one completely different story. Nobody cheering or smiling. The Coast Guard brings them all aboard the shiny cutter and turns the hell around and steams their poor black asses right back to Haiti. Hasta la vista, Creole. Learn some Spanish and lose the pigmentation, we might invite you back, Jacques.

Hollings watched a tall skinny guy come to the door of the taxidermy shop, Tyler handed him something, looked like a bottle of some kind. Shook hands. The skinny guy held his nose, waving at Tyler as he backed the MG up, turned around, and headed off.

\* \* \*

After dropping off the remains of the skunk juice, Hap stopped at a drive-through Farm Store, bought a six-pack of Miller, and two cases of tomato juice, a case of V-8. Their complete stock. As they were pulling away, the young woman in the tube top who sold it to them coughed and fanned her hand in front of her nose.

Marguerite had relaxed a little, wasn't cursing him every five minutes anymore. He wasn't sure. She was either seething or resigned, maybe both. Her arms crossed tight across her chest, not looking at him. Jaw clamped. Face into the wind. He looked over at her again, could tell she knew he was staring, but kept her eyes from him, face forward, the wind snarling her hair.

Hap made an impulsive left off Bayshore and drove out the Rickenbacker toward Key Biscayne, pulled off at Windsurf Beach and parked. Dark clouds sailed past the moon. A ten-knot breeze had put a white fringe on the charcoal sea. He pulled up the emergency brake, and reached into the back for the six-pack.

"Beer?"

She glared straight ahead.

"I thought we could stop, chat awhile. You might like to tell me about it. Unburden yourself."

Hap popped the beer, took a pull.

"About what, Hap?" In an iron voice.

"Scopolamine, *Papaver somniferum.*"

"Now what the hell're you talking about?"

"You know, Marguerite. The drugs you and your mother used."

She turned her head, gave him a savage look and opened the door, got out.

"I don't believe this," she said. "My mother? Drugs!"

"The drugs you used to kill Daniel."

"God help me. I'm out here alone with a raving lunatic."

She stalked down to the shoreline, stood there, hands on hips, staring at the rippling silver.

Hap stayed put, sipped on his beer.

Twenty yards to the east there was another car parked under the coconut palms. A thirty-year-old Chevy. In any other town in

America that car would've been rusting in a junkyard. But in Miami the immigrants recycled them. Old Chevies, old buildings, old neighborhoods. The Cubans, Haitians, they'd located the abandoned, discarded things, got them cheap and moved into them, and given them a fresh coat. With their hot food and music, their colors, brighter than this town had seen before, the immigrants had jacked up the city's pulse, given it an infusion of zest.

But everywhere you heard complaints. The Cubans didn't blend in, the Haitians didn't melt in the great bubbling pot. Well, shit, as far as Hap was concerned, who could blame them for not wanting to disappear into the homogenized, colorless gruel they saw around them. They'd kept their tang, by god, the rhythms and aromas of their homelands. Ginger and garlic and cinnamon breezes blew down Calle Ocho and Biscayne Boulevard.

But there was something tragic about all that cultural pride. Because give them a generation, let TV and the schools do their leveling work, and he was pretty sure the Haitians and the Cubans would finally blend in and disappear, and Miami would once again be as bland and innocuous as the rest of America.

Beside the old Chevy, in a flare of moonlight, he saw a man and woman lying next to each other on a blanket. They were wearing bathing suits, working on their moontans.

Hap sipped his beer and watched Marguerite walk slowly back from the shore. She came up to the passenger door and looked across at him.

"Tell me something, Hap? Are you having another breakdown? Is that what this is? You going around the bend again?"

The moon had put an ivory rinse on her hair. She balled her hands and crossed her arms again across her chest. Her face was in shadow, but Hap thought he could feel the stab of her gaze.

"Yeah," he said. "I'm so far around the bend, I can see a few things I couldn't see before."

He had another slug of the Miller.

"All right, goddamn it," she said. "Just take me back to my car. The news people are gone by now."

"I'll take you back, sure. But before we go, why don't you tell me about this." He pulled the packet of syringes from his shorts and held it up. She leaned over the door to see.

Hap said, "Your mother have allergies by any chance? Or maybe she shoots up collagen, something like that, injects it into her wrinkles, staying young. I'm sure if you tried, you could think something up for me. Be creative, go ahead."

He pulled the knob for the headlights, got out of the car and came around into the flood of light, holding the package of needles out in front of him into the light.

She moved close, craned forward.

He said, "I put a little pressure on the medical examiner, and he finally did an autopsy. What they found was that Daniel died of a drug injection. It's what induced the heart attack. Scopolamine, *Papaver somniferum.* An injection, you know, with a needle, like this one I found in your mother's medicine cabinet."

"You idiot."

"In her medicine cabinet, Marguerite. In her goddamn bathroom medicine cabinet."

The guy on the blanket had switched on his car radio. A salsa station to block out this Anglo argument. Steamy music, steamy night. The skinny guy got out of the car, lay down again beside his sweetheart. The glow of a joint passed between them.

"Tell me something, Hap. What is it you're so mad about? What would make you break into my mother's apartment, try to dig up evidence?"

He had another sip, watched the breeze filtering through the palms.

"You think maybe it's possible," she said, "you were so goddamn used to having a hundred and ten percent of Daniel's attention, being his precious, fragile little brother, always coddled and fussed over, it pissed you off when I came along? Could that be it? You didn't want to share him with anybody. And now you'll do anything to see me hurt. Go after my family to try to get some kind of sick, pathetic revenge."

She stepped around to the front of the car, back into the blaze of lights.

Very casual, he said, "So you gonna tell me about it?"

"I've got nothing more to say to you."

"All right, then. Here's how I see it," Hap said. "Here's my take on things."

"Oh, this ought to be rich."

"The two of you, you and your mother," said Hap, "you were in this together. Trying to find out where the gold was. Daughter dates the guy, sleeps with him. But that doesn't work out. He never slips up and tells you. So the senator gets involved. You two decide to give the guy a little injection of truth serum. You get him in bed, get him very relaxed, then you stick him with the needle, start asking him some questions. Where's the gold hidden? But it screws up. Daniel's heart can't take this particular drug.

"He's lying there, then suddenly he's dead. Mother turns to daughter. U.S. Senator, newspaper reporter, upstanding citizens. What're they going to do? Only thing they can do. Get the hell out of there. Take the rest of the drug with them. They save it, because who knows, they might need to shoot somebody else with it. Somebody who might also know where the rest of the Mayan gold is. Somebody like me, maybe."

Marguerite stared at him through the windshield for a long moment, shaking her head in disbelief.

"And about your little escapade tonight. That guilty look you had when you came out of her place. Well, maybe things are disintegrating between you two. Maybe you're starting to worry she's about to ambush you, put the whole thing off on you. So you went up there to get something on her to protect your ass. How's that? That cover everything? That have the ring of truth?"

She let out a long, harsh groan.

"What total, complete horseshit. My mother and I working together, plotting? Some kind of bizarre conspiracy. You're nuts, Hap. Totally, unequivocally delusional."

He said nothing. And damn it, looking at her, her eyes steady and unfazed, he had to admit that what he'd said, dangling there now in the warm night air, it sounded ludicrous. Like one of those things you harbor in some quiet passage of your mind, some private bias you conceal, feasting on it so long that it solidifies, and eventually seems indisputable, rock-hard belief. But the first time you put air to it, give it voice, the whole mountainous construction sounds so preposterous, so embarrassingly dumb, it completely evaporates.

"All right," he said. "Okay, then let's hear your story. You can start with an explanation for these." He held up the syringes. "I'm listening."

"They're my father's. Those were his needles."

"Oh, come on, Marguerite. That's lame."

"It's the truth, goddamn it."

"What? You're going to tell me he was a heroin addict or something?"

"Insulin," she said, her voice remote. "He was diabetic. There were needles lying around the house all the time when I was growing up."

"So why the hell are they still there? Your father's been dead for years."

"I assume Mother kept them."

"I'm supposed to believe your mother kept your dead father's needles around the apartment, years after he died?"

"I don't give a shit what you believe, Hap."

"Diabetic, my ass. I'm going to give these needles to Dick Vasquez, see what the news people make of them."

Across the beach, the salsa was finished, and a breakneck Spanish DJ began. Hap took a breath, trying to sort this out. He glanced over at the two of them on the blanket. Embracing, writhing near the Chevy's open door.

When he looked back, Marguerite was standing a foot from him, her hand cocked back. He shot an arm up to block her punch, but it was sand. Sand in his eyes. He staggered back, tried to wipe away the grit with his left hand while he kept the packet of syringes from her. She grabbed his arm, tore at his wrist.

He swung a blind forearm at her, made contact, but nothing significant. She clawed at his arm, and he spun away from her. With his back to her, he wiped furiously at his eyes, but she jumped onto his back, got her thin forearm under his chin, mashed hard against his throat. Before he could pry it loose, she'd locked it into the crook of her other arm. A police stranglehold, a neat little lever, one hand behind his head pushing it forward against the lock of her forearm. Throttling the air from him. Something she'd probably picked up at rape prevention class.

"Give them to me, goddamn it. You're not getting away with this."

He whirled but couldn't break her loose. He elbowed at her ribs, but she had his head pressed so far forward that sparks began to glitter at the edge of his vision. He was losing his strength fast.

In what seemed like his final hope before passing out, he threw himself backward, a free-fall with all his weight coming down on top of her. But somehow at the last second she twisted away, so he hit flush on his tailbone against a root or branch or ridge of stones. A warm numbness poured down both legs. He couldn't even groan.

She tore the packet from his hand and scrambled onto his chest, a bony knee against his throat. Dimly, he could make out the Latin guy standing behind her watching this spectacular moment. This Anglo beauty pinning her boyfriend in the sand. Hap had neither air nor blood in his body. Muscles gone.

Hap made a noise, a grunt or growl that came from behind his sternum. He couldn't lift his legs. The light was dimming and returning, someone playing with the rheostat.

She kept her knee against his throat.

The Latin guy was standing over her now. Reaching a hand out to poke her in the back, timidly, as if he were afraid she might be electrified. Hap gathered himself, dragged a breath down his throat, timed his move with the guy's hand coming close to Marguerite's back. Until he was there, a touch.

"Hey, lady," the guy said. "Whatta you doin'?"

And when she jerked her head around to see, Hap bucked upward and twisted and rolled to his right. She was on him in a second, an alley-cat frenzy, on his chest before he could get to his feet. The Latin guy now a full participant, followed her over, and tried to push her off him. Marguerite slashed at him with the packet of needles and the guy jumped back.

Hap drew a croaking voice up from his gut. Told the guy to piss off. Mind his own business. The guy stood there for a moment, wavering. Marguerite again with one knee on Hap's chest, the other at his throat.

"You like that shit?" the guy said. "Woman treat you like that? Man, and they call *me* fucked up."

He and his girlfriend stalked off toward the swirl of salsa.

Marguerite had sand on her cheek, a raw spot on her forehead. She was panting, her eyes fierce.

"Goddamn you, Hap. And I was actually going to try to reason with you. Give you a chance to spare yourself a difficult legal situation. Then you go and pull this shit, and you know what? Now I think, well, just screw being civilized. I'm taking you to court and my lawyer's going to grind up your ass and hand it to you in a Baggie. And I'm not going to give it a second thought. Not one second thought."

He grunted. And from twenty years before at Fort Benning, from that hellish, exhausting six weeks of boot camp, he summoned a roundhouse punch, and threw it all the way from August in Georgia into Marguerite's shoulder. She shrieked, and went sprawling in the sand. Hap came to his knees, gasping. As she tried to stand, holding her shoulder, Hap took a painful breath and lunged forward, got her by the ankle. Pulled her down, climbed on top of her.

She wasn't strong. Her only advantage had been the lucky blow to his spine. She tried to wrestle him off her, but had no chance at all. He pinned her on her back, pulled himself astraddle her, his butt on her stomach, pinning her wrists beside her shoulders.

He shook the packet from her hand. She snarled and twisted one hand free, reached up and gripped his hair, lifted herself, pulling him down to her, his own growl matching hers, and she might have been opening her mouth to bite at his nose, gnaw his flesh, curse him to hell, but he lowered his head quickly and blocked her mouth with his.

And when their teeth clicked, their mouths began to struggle for advantage. Lips, tongues. He tasted blood, his or hers. And as their growls died to groans, that was the last of it, the end of Hap's recent season of torment. That feeling Marguerite had stirred in him for the last several months, the ache in his chest that Hap Tyler had convinced himself was hatred.

In the sand, beside the dark water, the salsa quiet, the wind rose and clattered in the palm fronds. A wash of moonlight, then dark. Rolling left and right. Struggling. Their clothes opening, unbuttoning, the zip and tear of cloth, his hands fumbled against hers. They strained, still battling, but joined now, fighting this other thing together.

Flesh on flesh, he pinned her, sand everywhere, and she pinned him. The crunch of sand in his mouth, the burn of her lips on his, hips grinding. The sting of her, the fit of her. The warm crush of her naked body as she wriggled on top of him and he rose to meet her. Their growls quieting.

It lasted till all the clouds had blown from the sky, till the moon was hidden behind a stand of silent palms. Till neither of them had the breath to move.

# CHAPTER 19

"Don't think this changes anything," she said as they drove across the long span of Rickenbacker Causeway. She turned her head, looked out her side of the car across the dark shimmer of bay at the skyline of downtown Miami. The bright crayon lights.

"You want me to take you home then, to your house?"

"Is that what you do, Hap? This the routine? Have your fun, then dump them off at home, get rid of them quick?"

It was a couple of hours before dawn. A humid night. No breeze, not enough air to get a good breath, even with the top down, the air vent pointed in his face. And now there was a scalding wire binding Hap's chest, the full expansion of his lungs. As he drove, he could feel the packet of syringes jiggle in his pocket, tap against his thigh. And in the other pocket the blue vial. Every tap seemed to tighten the wire at his chest.

Hap said, "Usually they aren't so mad afterward. Usually there's a certain glow."

"Oh, I'm glowing," she said. "Just not that way."

"I see that."

After they'd made love, they'd pulled their clothes back into place. She sat in the passenger seat while Hap leaned against the hood, watched the dark water, having a slow beer. He offered her some, but she kept her eyes straight ahead, wouldn't reply. Finally he climbed silently into the car.

"So you don't want me to take you to your house?"

Hap glanced over at her. She was still staring out her side, her hair knotting in the wind. He slowed for a red light, waited for a moment, then drove through it, made a hard left, accelerated up Bayshore, past the old mansions up on their coral bluffs, the shadowy parks. Darkness roared in his ears.

"Even being with a lunatic," he said. "It's better than being by yourself. Huh?"

She didn't say anything, but he could tell from a small movement of her head that she was listening.

"I could keep this up," he said. "Have both sides of this conversation, tell you how you're feeling. Respond to it. I mean, you don't have to talk if you don't want to. I can just chatter away for both of us, all night if I have to."

She swiveled forward in her seat and watched the road.

"You're probably good at that," she said. "I bet it's a necessary skill with your teenyboppers."

"Damn, Marguerite. Where'd you pick that up? That hair-trigger meanness? All those snappy comebacks. At the newspaper office, holding your own with the guys?"

As they passed by Vizcaya, the Planetarium, she looked over at him. A grudging thaw in her eyes.

"I learned most of it from men, yeah."

"But the truth is, you don't hate me as much as you're pretending, do you? I mean, it bothers you, what happened out there, what you're feeling now. It worries you a little. The physical brother. The nut. The one without the IQ, the lecher. It worries you. A guy you can't just mind-fuck. Like Daniel."

"Daniel and I," she said, "did more than mind-fuck."

Before she could settle again into a sulk, he said, "So where *does* this put us?"

"There isn't any *us*," she said. "You must not've been listening, Hap. This doesn't change a goddamn thing. That was an aberration back there. Freaking out, grabbing whatever's close by and holding on to it. Nothing more.''

"I don't want to argue," he said. "I mean, god knows, I always disliked you at least as much as you disliked me, but now I don't know. It occurs to me, we just may have the basis of an interesting relationship here. Think about it, Marguerite. Our neuroses seem to match up pretty good. Same pattern of arrested development. Preoccupied with ghosts. Emotional growth stunted by people we never even knew.''

She looked over at him. A long, sizing stare. Then said, "Before you get too far along here, Hap, you should remember, the men in my life seem to die awfully young.''

He downshifted up the long hill into the center of the Grove.

"Well, I'm touched," he said. "You're actually worried about me.''

He turned left onto Main Highway, drove slowly through the western edge of the Grove, and finally through the tunnel of low-hanging banyans, turning in at the Mangrove House.

Hap parked the MG near the house, got out, and lugged one of the cases of tomato juice upstairs. Marguerite followed him silently into the house, up the stairs. She watched him put the case inside the upstairs bathroom. Go back for more. Three trips.

When he'd set down the last case, he unhooked the velvet rope that blocked the doorway to his parents' room, stepped inside and switched on the light. Still in disarray from the black woman's search. He hauled the mattress back onto the bed, the same deep feather mattress where Hap had been conceived.

Above the bed there was a needlepoint his mother, Louise, had stitched, Home Sweet Home, with a fair replica of the Mangrove House. Except for that, Hap's father had purged her from the house, taking down all the photographs of her, her other needlepoints, her bright, awkward oil paintings. It was probably the old man's attempt to strip-mine his grief. But it hadn't worked. Her absence only seemed to echo more harshly from the naked walls.

Marguerite came into the room, gave Hap a wide berth, and sat on the edge of the bed. She glanced about the room, her hair disheveled, her tennis shirt rumpled and hanging out of her jeans.

She stared at him as he stooped to gather some spools of his mother's thread, scattered across the floor. He dumped them into her sewing kit. Rain pattered on the tin roof, then stopped. A breeze trembled at the curtains, and the air freshened a few degrees. With a fingertip, she traced the perimeter of one of the quilt patches, a random piece stitched to another, swatches from the shirts, dresses, and pants of a family that had dwindled down to this one last member.

He looked over at her and she adjusted the hair on her shoulder, lifting it, releasing it. She frowned at him, giving him a prying look, a small cant to her head, as if from that special angle she could see past all his defenses, glimpse his private self.

Out on the lawn a cat wailed. That time of night when they gathered and paired off. There was a hot swelling in Hap's throat, felt like a fish bone was lodged there, the blood gathering around this foreign object, pulsing in the tightened passageway. Hap, half strangling, not sure whether to cough it out or swallow. Looking at Marguerite Rawlings in this harsh light, mussed up as she was, she didn't look as good as usual. At this moment, she was only gorgeous.

"I assume you don't want to sleep in Daniel's room or mine. So you can stay in here," he said. His voice husky. "You know where the bathroom is. Let me know when you're finished."

Her expression kept making small fluctuations, her eyes moving up and down some moody scale. Like the fickle light changing out on the water, showing you its depths, then hiding them.

She stood up and came over to him.

"Why'd you do that, Hap? Pull that stunt at the condo?"

"Because of your mother," he said.

"What's my mother have to do with it?"

"She'd bought another Mayan trinket from Daniel, but he died before he could deliver it to her. She brought me up to her condo to see if maybe I had the trinket. And while I was there this happened." He waved at the room. "So I figured she'd sent somebody over here to get it. I wanted to see for myself."

"And was it there?"

"No."

She shook her head in wonder.

"You're a piece of work, Hap. You know that?"

She gave him a weary smile. Finished fighting for a while. Worn out.

"Yeah," he said. "Yeah, I guess I am."

She came forward, stood just inches from him. He braced himself for whatever it would be this time. More wrestling, more love. Breathing unevenly, she reached out and gripped him just above the elbows, held him away from her at arm's length. She examined him for a moment as if he were a canvas she was painting and she was a bit bewildered at what was emerging there.

"You're nothing like Daniel, are you?"

"I always wanted to be," he said. "But no, if you're looking for a duplicate, it isn't me."

She let go of him.

For a moment, he thought he would try to kiss her again, something to smudge that bruised look off her face. But he debated it too long, and felt the moment grow cold, then tip the other way. He let go of a long breath.

"Listen," he said. "We need to get this thing straight. The syringes. Those needles."

"I told you the truth," she said. Waiting, a frank stare. "There's nothing else to say."

"All right then. All right. Let's say you're innocent. Then who killed him? What's going on?"

She hesitated for a moment. Bent her head over, squeezed her eyes shut, as though fending off some jab of inner pain.

When she opened them again, she stared at Hap, and it seemed her eyes had cleared. As if this were the first time she'd actually seen him, the first time she'd let him have a good honest look at her. And the truth was, she wasn't tough. She wasn't so bitter and dead certain. A tragic light shone in her gray eyes, a candle flame wavering at the end of a darkened hallway. She was fumbling her way forward, guided by only that uncertain glimmer. Just like Hap. Probably just like everybody who was worth a damn.

"I'm not sure," she said. "But maybe it's like what you said before." She took a difficult breath, let it out. "That story you told, only minus the mother-daughter conspiracy thing."

"What? Just the mother? Working alone?"

"I don't know. I haven't figured it all out."

Her face was scuffed from their struggle, and had a high color. Her lips chapped and swollen. She seemed to be pulling herself together, consciously reassembling her composure.

"But I believe she's capable of it, Hap. Capable of evil."

"Evil!"

"I've sensed it for a long time without giving it a name. How she treated my father, how she treated me. How frigid she can be, how empty. That imperious, self-important way she has."

"Cold-hearted, corrupt? I mean, hell, Marguerite, every politician is that way to some degree or another."

"No, Hap, not corrupt. The word is evil. Capable of anything. Remorseless."

She stepped back, touched either side of the door frame as her large gray eyes tracked around the room. A beautiful woman. Elegant, tenacious.

For a quick moment, Hap revisited that photo of Ramona Rawlings standing alongside the rapids, her long dress, her stalwart gaze. A woman of strength. A pioneer who had endured that primitive place and time, and had triumphed over almost all of it. A woman staring down a long passageway of time through these same large gray eyes.

She lowered her gaze to the floor, let go a weary sigh, ready for a week of solid sleep.

"You were right," she said. "I *was* in her condo going through her things. I was trying to find documents, evidence she's been selling favors, taking kickbacks, whatever I could find. I mean, I know she's rotten. She's been doing illegal things, but I need the documents if I'm going to expose her. Bring her down."

"And?"

"Nothing. I didn't find anything. Just that birth certificate."

Hap looked behind him at the bed. Saw the depression she'd left in the quilt and let himself down into it.

"Well, while we're confessing."

"Yes?"

"What you said out there on the beach, your analysis of me. I guess it's partly true. I felt jealous of you, hell, I felt jealous of you *and* Daniel. I'd lie there in my bed some nights, listen to you two making love, and I wanted to be Daniel making love to you. And goddamn it, I wanted to be you too. I wanted to know him the way you knew him."

She nodded, her cheeks flushing.

"We're a pair, aren't we?"

"So now tell me the truth. Did you love him?"

She winced and looked away.

"Did you?"

"I loved him as much as I could."

"As much as you could?"

"Yeah," she said. "Considering he was a stand-in."

"Really?" he said. A doubtful grin. "For me?"

She looked his way and smiled uneasily.

"No, not you, Hap."

"Well, who?"

"Think Oedipus. Think Freud."

He stood up, went over to the dresser. He straightened the white crochet his mother had made. Took a moment more arranging the metal pillboxes, the photos.

"My Freud's a little rusty," he said, his back to her. "Help me here."

"Well," she said. "What you said earlier, how formal Daniel and I looked together. That's true. He was so courtly, always so old-fashioned about things. We were close, but not really close. There was the age difference, twelve years. But it was more than that. I mean, I think I loved him because of who he reminded me of, not who he was. Older man, very successful. A man with a vision, a charismatic personality. A man so enthralled with the past, he always seemed a little lost in the present."

Hap touched the lid of one of the pillboxes.

"You're saying you have a case of unrequited Daddy-love, and Daniel was helping you through it?"

"Close enough," she said.

"Well, I'm sorry to hear that." He turned around, all the fun gone out of him now. "Because as we've already established, I'm nothing like Daniel. That's not a service I can render."

"Maybe that's not a service I want anymore," she said.

Marguerite let go of the door, gave him a long, speculative look, and turned and went out into the hall.

Hap listened as she closed the bathroom door, ran some water. He heard the rip of the silver adhesive sealers, the slosh of juice into the tub. Hap walked to the window, put his hands against the windowsill, and leaned out to see into the night. A starless, empty sky. No moon, nothing. Infinity taking the night off.

Jesus Christ. He'd spent his entire adult life splashing around in the shallow bay, one sexual frolic after another. But always the sandy bottom was a flutter-kick away. Even a mile from shore, it was easy to walk back to safety, back to land anytime he wanted. But now, suddenly, with Marguerite, he felt like he was out in the real sea, treading water miles above the dark canyons and plateaus of the ocean floor. And he was completely unprepared. Unfit to be out there where the big fish lived, the dangerous ones, where swimming was an act of consequence.

Man, Hollings had a terminal hard-on. He was so goddamn horny right then he would've screwed the crack of dawn. Got that way from watching Tyler and the black-haired girl doing it on the beach, a couple of animals, clawing at each other, slapping, punching. Never seen anything like that before. Made him so hot, standing in the bushes twenty, thirty yards off, he'd started touching himself through his pants. Sliding his hand up and down. Like at a porno movie, and split screen, too, 'cause twenty yards away off to the east, another couple was going at it on a blanket. Christ, he didn't know which pair to watch, finally settling on Tyler and the black-haired lady, hissing and spitting right there in front of him.

Now he was standing around in the woods just to the east of the two-story house where Tyler lived. Mosquitoes having a banquet on his neck and cheeks and arms. Hollings in a dark green short-sleeved shirt with blue jeans and black loafers, no socks. The fuckers were working on his ankles, too, and even pricking him through the goddamn shirt. It felt like they were marching back and forth on his flattop.

Shit, what he wouldn't give for a can of bug spray right now, some Off! or something. If somebody was to lay a naked woman out in front of him and set a can of Off! beside her and told him he could only have just one or the other, he'd have to take the Off!

But then on the other hand, now that he thought about it a little more, maybe not. Maybe, if it was the right naked lady, say the one with the black hair and the tennis shirt, he'd be willing to put up with the mosquitoes. Otherwise, just an average woman, it was the Off!

The two of them had been in the house ten, fifteen minutes, and he'd probably already lost a pint of blood standing out there. Lights on upstairs. He could see some shadows moving around, but otherwise it was quiet. Probably up there having another go at each other, this time on a mattress.

Hollings leaned out from behind the tree where he'd been standing and hissed Martina's name a couple of times into the dark. No answer.

Damn, for the last ten minutes he'd been wandering around in the woods, looking for the rocks where they were supposed to meet, but he hadn't come across them. Hollings believed he was east of the house like she'd said. And now he wasn't sure what he was supposed to do. Drive Martina's car back to his place on the beach? Go check in with Alvarez? Stay out there all night in case these two decided to go off and lead him to the sunken ship? But then, shit, how the hell was he going to follow them if they got in a boat? Like, if they walked down to the dock down there and started up their boat and just took off.

They did that, then all his suffering out here with the mosquitoes was for nothing. He might just miss out completely. Of course, he could walk right into the house, surprise the two of them, use the pistol Martina had left in the Chevy to scare the truth out of them. That'd be good. Walk in on them in the middle of something hot and wet, maybe get a look at the black-haired woman naked under some hundred-watt bulbs. Make her get out of bed, stand up, turn around.

But no, that wasn't such a great idea. He might go in there, hold the pistol to their heads, and still not find out where the *Carmelita* was. The guy might resist, might be a fighter, might have a gun himself. Might've even spotted Hollings following him and was lying low in there waiting for him. You heard about shit like that on the TV news. Fucking Miami crazies, setting up booby traps in their houses, just hoping somebody'd try to break in so they could test the fucking thing out.

Maybe the smart thing was to walk on down to the boathouse there, find Tyler's boat, disable it some way so if they did get a wild hair to go off and haul up their treasure, they'd have to wait till Hollings was prepared with a boat of his own. Yeah. That seemed right. Plus, it had the advantage of getting him out of these fucking woods with all those vampires whining in his ears.

He was stepping out of the trees, picking his route down to the boathouse, when something scattered the leaves at his feet. He made a sharp yip, stumbled backward. Goddamn.

A few yards away, a cat yowled, another cat answered it. Cats, Christ. Now he was thinking maybe he should go back to where he'd left the car tucked in the woods a few hundred yards from the house. Maybe he should get that gun before he proceeded any farther. But no. That was another bad idea. Jumpy as he was, he'd probably wind up shooting one of the goddamn cats or a raccoon or something. Give himself away out there.

He crept along the edge of the woods, went ten, twenty yards, then off to his left he spotted something. Rocks. White craggy rocks lit up in the moonlight. He loud-whispered Martina's name again as he started edging over there.

He was maybe ten yards away, still swimming in mosquitoes, when he saw something else white. Not rocks. From that distance, it looked like legs to him. Like legs in white pants, lying on the ground.

Christ, Martina had beat him over here and was taking a quick nap. So what he thought was, he'd sneak on over there, get right on top of her, get his face into hers and scare the bejesus out of her. Yeah, that'd be funny, see that ugly woman jump.

When Hap pushed open the bathroom door, Marguerite was in the tub, up to her shoulders in tomato juice, the swell of her breasts at the surface, the rest of her body hidden. The juice moved around her as sluggish as lava.

He looked across out the open window at the starless sky. He could feel the voice inside himself. Quiet now after urging him through the skunk juice episode. Quiet, but still there, getting ready to speak again, give him more commands. Hap thought he could hear it, its first tentative hisses.

"You want something," she said, "or you just looking?"

She scooted to the back of the tub, her breasts rising up from the juice. She patted the surface of the tomato juice, washed her hand through it. She cocked her head to one side.

"There room in there?"

"There might be. You could try."

Hap unzipped his shorts, eased them off. He peeled out of his polo shirt. Stood there in his Jockey shorts.

"What're you, shy all of a sudden? Or you think maybe I have a syringe hidden in here, going to stick you with it, see what you know."

"I'll risk it."

Hap found a hurricane candle in the medicine chest, lit it, took a moment to drip some wax onto the edge of the lavatory. He set the candle in place and turned off the overhead light.

"So, do the nymphets go for that? They swoon?"

"It's romantic," he said. "A newspaperwoman like yourself, cynical, hardened to the finer sentiments, you think it's silly, but

I'm a simple sort. Guys like me, candlelight adds a certain something. A fairy dust. Enchantment."

She smiled. Her eyes very tired, but smiling through it. This thing happening between them, neither of them sure of it, but still, not fighting it anymore. Not backing away.

Outside, a couple of the Munroe cats wailed in the holly trees fifty yards to the east. Then there were more cats, a nation of cats braying, screaming their seductions in the pines. The wild ones from the Munroe woods, the domesticated ones from wealthy neighborhoods nearby. Homeless cats. Cats and more cats pouring in for their nightly tail-switching Woodstock.

Hap peeled out of his underwear, then hesitated for a moment until she reached out a slow hand for him. He stepped forward and she brought him to life.

"No comparisons, okay?"

"There are none," she said.

"And what does that mean?"

"You're you, he was somebody else," she said. "Men do comparisons. We're not much into that."

Outside, the cats had suddenly grown still.

"And not so rough this time," he said, and smiled halfway.

"You know, it's funny, Hap. My lawyer, she recommended I seduce you."

"What?"

She laughed to herself, then raised her eyes and gave him part of the smile.

"I need to tell you about it," she said. "It involves you."

"Does it have to be now?"

"No," she said. "I suppose it can wait."

He settled into the tub, facing her, arranging their legs, his outside hers. She scooted forward, inched her face toward him. He reached out, held her face, and as they kissed, he began a long disappearance. Going somewhere where there was neither light nor air, nothing left behind but their lips shaping, reshaping. Tongues touching. Her hand slid between his legs, explored him, discovered hollows and sinews and tendons, tender places the others hadn't found. And he let go of her face, kissing still, scooted forward, deeper into her, his hand finding her, finding the tangle of hair, the luxurious florets of flesh, her sleek legs. Her hand going deeper, fingers nosing.

She groaned, and in a while Hap leaned back, found a comfortable position between the faucet and handles, and Marguerite Rawlings rose up from the juice, dripping red, and squatted over him, took hold and guided herself carefully down his length. Settling snug, butt to hip, his hands molding her waist, the spread of hips, while their eyes held comfortably. Hers, large and gray, watched him as their bodies played up and down this soundless scale, hitting a new octave, then another, stretching the range of that familiar instrument.

She rose and came back down. Rose again and this time lowered herself, slow, excruciating, a sound coming from her throat, a croon that climbed in pitch on each downward inch. Behind her, on the tile wall, their candle-shadows fluttered, those other selves capering, the black ghosts who were always there.

That's when the scream came. A terrible bellow from somewhere out in the yard. Marguerite surged away from him, pressing herself against the back of the tub. The howl came again, this time more tortured. Like the voice of one of those wounded soldiers in the helicopter that night over Cambodia, one of Hap's buddies howling desperately for morphine, or for death.

# CHAPTER 20

H AP TOLD MARGUERITE TO WAIT THERE, HE'D SEE WHAT it was. He toweled off swiftly, wiped away the stickiness from the juice, pulled on his shorts, stepped into his shoes. He ran to his room, got the .45 off his bed, rushed downstairs, out through the kitchen. Lights off at the back of the house. Stood there in the dark listening to the hush.

As he edged down the back steps he heard a car engine start. Sounded like it was out in the front drive. He headed off at a run and as he reached the end of the grassy lawn, he saw a set of tail-lights up ahead, thirty, forty yards. They bumped down the long, rocky drive headed out to Main Highway. An older model, Chevy, Ford.

He chased the car, gaining a few yards, a few more, then veered left through the woods, a shortcut. He came out ten yards from the stone entrance pillars, panting, and held up the .45 and waited till the headlights swung around the last turn and shined in his face.

The car came to a sudden stop. The engine revved and Hap set his feet. The driver coasted forward a few feet, stopped. A few feet more. Hap shifted the pistol, found a better grip. Then the driver revved the engine, higher, then higher still. The horn honked, became one long, continuous blare, the lights blazed to bright, and the car lurched forward, gathered speed so fast that all Hap could manage was a dive into a bed of ferns beside the drive, and even then the fender thumped him hard on the right shin. The .45 fell in the ferns, and by the time he'd gotten it again, the car was hurtling out the last ten feet of drive.

Hap scrambled to his knees, focused on the license plate, but the dust obscured it. The car hit the asphalt of Main Highway, swerved east toward the Grove and was gone. It was a Chevy, late-fifties model. Or maybe a Buick. Hell, he wasn't even sure of that, things happening so fast.

He limped back down the trail, still hearing the echo of the scream. He was halfway down the drive when Marguerite shouted his name. Shouted for him to come quick. He broke into a stiff-legged sprint.

As he raced around the edge of the house, she yelled his name again. She'd switched on the floodlights, and the Mangrove House was bathed in white light.

As she called out again, Hap vaulted the porch railing, stumbled to a halt with the pistol out, aiming it at the two people there, and in the half-second before he fired, he recognized them, and caught himself.

The woman wore an ankle-length Indian print skirt, a peace medallion dangling on a macramé necklace against her vast pregnant belly. The guy had on a black velour vest loose against his bony chest. Shiny maroon bell-bottoms and tire-tread sandals. Both of them with the Jesus hair, the five-watt eyes. They were water people. Devil's Punchbowlers. Fresh in from Evansville or Biloxi, steered by the divining rods they used instead of brains, they'd wound up on the Commodore's front porch at four in the morning with one microscopic thought crowding their minds.

Marguerite was in the doorway, a towel wrapped around her, holding up the heavy brass fish in her right hand. Going to clobber these morons if need be.

"It's okay," he told her. "It's nothing."

"You're new here," the guy said.

"Yeah," said Hap. "I only been here thirty-eight years."

"For the baby," the woman said, patting her huge belly. "The holy fluid." Using the blotto shorthand reserved for fellow zombies.

"We spring from the amniotic, and return to the amniotic," the guy said, squinting at the .45 as if it was who he was bargaining with.

"One of you idiots scream a minute ago?"

"No sir," the woman said, "but we sure enough heard it."

"You see a guy running away, a guy get in the car?"

"Not to get a good look at him, no sir."

Hap asked Marguerite if she was okay, and she nodded.

The woman moaned and swayed, holding her enormous belly.

"Okay, get out of here," Hap said, "you loons. Leave us alone."

The woman, cumbersome and stiff, tottered briefly, then let herself painfully down to the pine floor. She folded her legs and settled her enormous butt, and Hap could see she was making herself immovable. She had the bland and bloated expression of the perpetually pregnant. A face gone generic. Hap would probably have to hire a tow truck to get her out of there.

He glanced over at Marguerite. The two wackos had softened her face, given her the closest thing to a full-fledged smile he'd seen there. She turned away, let the screen door slap behind her, and as she went back up the stairs, he thought he heard her chuckle.

The gaunt man cut in front of Hap.

"Mama Rachel won't get up without some of that god water," he said. "And look out, pardner, she's close to her time."

The two of them performed some kind of mystical blather as Hap stood in the halo of his flashlight and drew up the bucket of stagnant water. Papa Ron shut his eyes and began to chant the names of the months. And she, staring up at the dark sky, chimed in with days of the week.

Each of them held out a plastic gallon jug they'd retrieved from their truck, and as they ran through their calendar routine, they swayed in a dazed druid tango. Hap watched them until he'd hauled the bucket near the brim, then turned back to his work.

The water had grown greener and darker since he'd been here last, and it smelled now of sulfur, and something else, a rancid gas of some kind, as though the bowels of the earth were withering with gangrene.

But the two lunatics didn't seem to mind. While they swayed and chanted, Hap used the tin funnel that lay on the rock near the well, filled both of their jugs. When he was done, the man held out a bill.

"Here's your holy payment."

Hap took the bill, but it felt odd, so he shined the flashlight on the thing. He'd seen more realistic twenties in Monopoly games. These two had used some nickel-a-copy Xerox machine to run off the bill, trimmed the edges with pinking shears. Hadn't even spent an extra nickel to copy the backside.

They watched him uneasily as he examined the paper.

Finally Hap sighed and slid it into the pocket of his shorts.

"May you be blessed by the great god amniotic," the woman said. "May your descendants populate the hemisphere."

"And may your sperm always swim fast and straight," her brainless mate said.

The woman started off, her man behind her. Two yards later they stopped and stared down into the ferns. The woman clasped her arms around her large belly and swayed and moaned, and the man turned to Hap and said, "Mister, you got yourself a problem over here."

Hap shined the flashlight into the ferns, edged around the limestone outcropping. Tennis shoes stuck out of the green ferns at an awkward angle. A pair of white pants, the person lying on their stomach. The two water weirdos shuffled away into the dark, mumbling.

"Hey, wait!" Hap called after them. "Whatta you know about this?" But they kept on going.

He kneeled down by the ferns, shined the light up higher on the form. A black T-shirt. He prodded the body in the hip, but there was no response. After a minute, gathering himself, he put down his light, gripped the body by the shoulder and turned it over. The shoulder was cold.

It was the black MIAMI NICE T-shirt she'd worn this morning. He groped for the flashlight, got it, and shined the light, looking for her face. He leaned forward, angled the beam down on the body, and then he saw it, the ragged cut, the slime at her throat. Twists of gray gristle leaked from it. A few thousand carpenter ants had discovered the body and were swarming around the dark porridge that spilled into the grass. Where the cornrows should have been, the gold teeth, the smart-ass smile, there was nothing. The woman had been decapitated. The head was gone.

He stood up, shined the shaky light into the ferns, searching for it. But after a few minutes he was glad enough he couldn't find it. He aimed the light back on the body, stooped close for another look. Insects boiled at her neck. A mist of gnats hovered nearby. Hap stared for a moment longer. Then flicked off the flashlight. He straightened up, walked very carefully back to the Devil's Punchbowl before he staggered, and caught himself against the limestone shelf, and lost his lunch, and the meal before that.

"Calm down, Glenn."

"Calm down? Calm the fuck down? Hey, Alvarez, don't fucking tell me to calm down. Her goddamn head was cut off."

"Either calm yourself down," said Alvarez, "or *I'll* calm you down."

Hollings went over and sat on the couch, fidgeted with the ashtray on Alvarez's coffee table. Bounced his legs up and down.

Alvarez in a yellow robe began to read Max Hunter's crumbly book. Standing up in the family room of his house out in Kendall, way the hell west of the turnpike. Till a few years ago all it was out there was alligators and mosquitoes and standing water, now it was Alvarez and Hernandez, Juan and Gisela, and still a shitload of mosquitoes.

Hollings had surprised himself finding the place again after only being there once earlier in the day. Every house looking alike, every street, but he guessed it was just another of the things adrenaline could do for you, give your memory a boost.

Hollings, sitting across from him, watching him turn pages, said, "Hey, Alvarez. Hey."

He turned more pages. Guy was a fast reader, had to give him that. Flipping through it, till he found what he wanted, then bearing down. A minute or two more and he clapped the book closed and tossed it onto the couch beside Hollings. Four-hundred-year-old book, the guy treated it like it was yesterday's newspaper.

Hollings said, "Now you're gonna tell me, huh, why you had us steal that thing? Put us in that kind of dangerous situation, when you could've just gone up to Hunter, asked him whatever you wanted to know. He would've told you probably."

"Max Hunter was a nothing."

"Guy discovered seven galleons," Hollings said. "I don't call that a nothing."

"Yeah, but put all those seven together, you wouldn't have half what's in the *Carmelita*."

Alvarez made a face Hollings couldn't read. Could be he was sneering, or maybe fighting back a laugh, his mouth twisted into an ugly grin.

"So, Glenn, finish telling me your story. The events of this evening." His tone polite, respectful. But Hollings was hearing it different now. A way of manipulating, that was all. Alvarez, patient, polite, and fake, said, "You found Martina, then what?"

Hollings rubbed his neck. Everything all tightened up. Needed one of those Saigon massages. She starts with the cock and works up.

Hollings sighed, said, "Then nothing. I came here. Fast as I could drive."

Positioning himself in front of the gold-flecked mirror, Alvarez took out his comb, looked at himself, and began to work on his hair. Using a shiny silver comb this time, like the jerk had one for every occasion. Alvarez giving his scalp a handjob.

Hollings had decided, it wasn't that Alvarez was vain, had to admire himself all the time, it was something else, something about getting every hair just right. Guy was probably one of those anal retentives. Had to arrange his peas on his fork before he could eat them, five peas per fork, chewed everything twenty-three bites or some shit like that.

"Did Tyler come out of the house before you got away?"

"What the hell difference does that make?"

"Did Tyler come out of the house before you got away?" Alvarez turned and held his comb out in front of him, and stared at it thoughtfully. "I want to hear it all, and I want to hear it correctly."

Hollings considered it for a minute. The guy must think he was running an interrogation again, like the old days. Every detail in the right order, all neat and anal retentive consistent for the report. It was shit like that, a witness saying it one way then changing it to the other, it was the kind of thing that kept all the guilty sleaze weasels out of jail. You had a hair out of place, it wasn't a legal bust. Yeah, so Alvarez combed his hair. Combed it and combed it.

"No," Hollings said. "I got away before he came outside."

"Good."

There was the quiet click of the family room door opening, and Hollings came to his feet.

A kid, ten or so, stuck his face into the crack. He was wearing Superman pajamas, his hair all everywhere. The kid said something in Spanish and Alvarez answered him in Spanish, and the boy came into the room and sat down in the corner under a lamp and opened a book.

"You may go on with your story," Alvarez said.

"In front of him?"

"He doesn't speak English."

Hollings sat back down and watched the kid read for a minute. Yeah, shit, there it was. A ten year old, his father talked like a native-born American, the kid doesn't understand word one of English. But then, hell, in this town, it made sense. If you only knew one language, you were better off with Spanish. You could starve to death you didn't know a little of it at least. At Hollings's local liquor store, there was a sign at one of the registers, ENGLISH SPOKEN IS AT THIS LOCATION.

Hollings moved over next to Alvarez and said, "I got away and came here, end of story."

"Did you kill Martina?"

"What?"

"You heard me."

"Fuck no, I didn't kill her. I didn't kill anybody."

"When you saw the body, did you make a noise? Something Tyler could hear, know that someone was out there?"

"I might've."

"Yes or no?"

"Jesus Christ. Yes! Yes, I yelled. I was scared, so I yelled. What fucking difference does it make?"

Alvarez didn't answer back. Just stood there, comb, comb, comb.

Hollings shook his head sadly. Finding out things about Alvarez he should've seen coming. The man spent his life in a violence-prone profession, what did Hollings think, he was working with the nuns?

The kid said something to Alvarez, asking a quiet question, and Alvarez answered politely.

Hollings said, "So who you think it was did Martina?"

"Our enemies," Alvarez said. "You didn't think we were the only ones looking for the *Carmelita,* did you?"

Hollings watched the kid for a minute, sitting there under the lamp reading a kids' book, like it was the normal thing around the Alvarez house, four in the morning, father has a friend over to talk about murder and mayhem, son reads a book in the corner.

"I wanna know what's going on, Ray. I wanna know what the fuck's happening here you haven't been telling me about."

"Don't use this language around the boy."

Hollings opened his mouth to protest. If the kid didn't know English, what the fuck did it matter how Hollings talked? But then he felt all the words catch in his throat, tangle up there. Wanting to argue, but knowing it was useless. How he used to feel in boot camp, and later in the barracks in Nam, the guys ragging his ass for no reason. He closed his mouth. He waited, watching the kid read till the blockage cleared.

He coughed, and said, "Okay, now listen, man. I thought we were going to work on this *Carmelita* thing, find the ship, make the history books. But then suddenly I got this partner, and you start ordering her to do things, not checking it with me first if it's okay. And it turns out the bitch is psycho, unruly and unpredictable. Then to top it off, she gets her goddamn head chopped off. I mean, we're into some serious shit here."

"If you continue to speak this way in front of the boy, you will have to leave my house."

Hollings walked over beside Alvarez, looked into the gold-flecked mirror with him, meeting his steady gaze.

Alvarez said, "Are you sure the woman you saw was Martina?"

Hollings stared at Alvarez's mirrored eyes.

"It was a black girl. Same clothes, same body. Christ, I'm supposed to take her fingerprints or something?"

"It's just as well."

"What?"

"We didn't need her anymore."

"Hey, Alvarez." Hollings gripped the man's arm. "That's it? Lady you recruited, she gets decapitated, you blow it off?"

Alvarez looked down at Hollings's hand on his arm. Hollings sighed and let go. The guy smiled at Hollings and with his fingernail he played a scale on the teeth of his comb. Up and back.

"This is too much for me. I mean, the woman's head was fucking sawed off. You hear what I'm saying?"

Alvarez turned to Hollings and smiled. Teeth all straight and clean, an empty smile, holding it for a long time, then said, "Glenn, what we're doing, what we're looking for, it's more important than a single life."

Hollings had a shiver, seeing Martina again, her corpse lying there, stringy white things coming from the neck. A big dark bird standing beside the body taking pecks at the fluid. Even Hollings's scream hadn't scared the fucking bird away.

Hollings drew in a couple of breaths, watched the kid turn a

page. He was waiting to get a little blood back into circulation before he tried walking out of there.

"I don't know about this anymore," he said quietly.

Alvarez moved close. Brought his broad Cuban face right up to
Hollings. Everything tightened up, jaw, mouth, forehead. His eyes
becoming hard little buttons.

In a grim whisper he said, "Listen to me, you moron. Did you
forget? We're doing something here, something so important, it
doesn't matter we got to bend the law now and then. Heroes, man,
they don't always play straight ahead by the rules. They get it done
any way they can. Do whatever it takes, Glenn. They got a higher
purpose. That's permission, man, permission direct from God to
take whatever extreme measures are deemed necessary. Permission
from on high."

Hollings was breathing hard. Caught between the two things.
That corpse and the magic words. Pecker-shrinking fear versus flying up into the stratosphere. He glanced around the room, feeling
the sweat trickle out of his armpits, begin a long, cold ride down his
rib cage.

"You drop out now, Glenn, there is no coming back later."
Alvarez edged close again, Hollings smelling his green-pepper
breath. "Because, Glenn, my friend, I know where the *Carmelita* is
now. It is here, in the registry. I have the key. I know where it has
been hiding all these years. Jewels, gold, silver, all of it. Do you want
a piece of that, or do you want to be a nothing for the rest of your
life?"

Hollings felt something begin to tumble inside him, something
heavy falling a long way down. He'd felt the same way some nights
on patrol, hearing the jungle shift and creak around him in the
dark. His head saying, go ahead, take your best shot, I'm not scared
of you slanty-eyed buttwipes. And at the same time his heart was
trying to parachute out his asshole.

"What do you want me to do?" he said quietly.

Alvarez reached into the pocket of his yellow robe, doing it
slow, holding on to Hollings's eyes as his hand went in, stayed for a
second, then started coming out. Hollings going uh-oh, here we go.

Gonna shoot me in front of his kid, scar him for life. But what he came out with was a gold thing, a necklace it looked like. Holding it out for Hollings to inspect. Cat heads with green eyes, a dozen of them strung together. Looked like skulls with pointy ears.

"So?" said Hollings.

"It comes from the *Carmelita*," said Alvarez. "It's listed here in this book from Max Hunter. *Collar jaguar de oro.* So valuable it's listed separately. One of the items aboard the ship. A necklace of golden jaguars. Something the high priest wore. Gave him extra magical power."

Hollings stared at the thing.

"So if you know where the ship is, what do you need me for? Get your snorkel and flippers and go pull it all up yourself."

"I'm showing you this, Glenn, to explain to you. Although I know where the ship is, if Tyler is frightened, let's say, he calls the papers, the TV, reveals the location to the public before we can get to it, we are fucked. We could lose everything."

Hollings shook his head.

"Oh, now I get it. Now it's coming to me."

Alvarez slipped the necklace into the pocket of his robe.

Hollings said, "All along, that's all you wanted me for. To put the sting on Tyler. It's why you hooked up with me in the first place, isn't it? Martina does the B and E, I do the murdering, you sit back here, pull the strings, take zero risks, rake in all the loot."

Hollings stared at Alvarez's blank face a couple more seconds, see if anything started feeling better in his gut.

"Naw," said Hollings. "Forget it. Count me out. The body count's up too high already."

"A loser, Glenn. All you'll ever be is a loser."

Moving next to his son, Alvarez kept staring into Hollings's eyes, holding him there, challenging him. The boy looked up at his daddy, and Alvarez reached out and smoothed the kid's hair into place, very gentle, brushing his kid's hair while his eyes were still locked on to Hollings.

"Fuck it," Hollings said. "Maybe a loser is all I was supposed to be. Maybe that's enough for me."

# CHAPTER 21

"I T'S JUST AS WELL," SENATOR RAWLINGS SAID. IN A yellow robe, a match to Alvarez's. She had the jaguar necklace around her throat, her hand reaching up to touch it now and then. "I don't know what you saw in this Hollings person in the first place."

"I liked him," Alvarez said. "I liked him because I could say to him, Hollings, go stand on that rooftop over there, flap your arms real hard, see how far you can fly. And he'd do it. I liked him 'cause of that. Every operation needs a Hollings."

Alvarez was on the couch, paging through his kid's book. Ricky back in bed now. The senator, standing by the door to the kitchen, started to fiddle with the belt on her robe. Tipping her head to one side, trying to get sexy in her necklace. Poor old woman, couldn't see how ridiculous she was, how much she turned Alvarez off.

"What's wrong, Ray? Too tired?" Her belt open now, hands on the lapels of her robe, wriggling for him, grandma stripper come to entertain at the retirement home. "Young man like you, all worn out?"

"I can still smell you."

She held the robe still. Then closed it a little.

"I took a shower," she said. "I was in there for an hour."

"I can still smell the skunk on you. It's disgusting."

"Damn." She tightened the belt on her robe. Pressed her nose to her shoulder and sniffed.

"Why'd you go in there anyway? I told you not to."

"To make sure the collection was intact, Ray. I had to check."

"You should've stayed outside, sent one of the security guys to do it. You wouldn't stink so bad."

"Ray, don't start with me. I'm not in the mood for your macho hormonal thing. I won't be bossed, least of all by you."

Voice all stiff now. Like he liked her, bitchy Anglo broad. Sixty-something years old, but still had some kick in her. Nothing like his ex-wife, the Puerto Rican twenty-two year old with the orange hair that ran off with the Jamaican Marijuaneros.

Man, now that was a nightmare woman. Alvarez had to chase her down there to Jamaica. His honor dictated. Tracked her to some Rasta restaurant outside Ocho Rios. Walked in, the jukebox playing reggae, all of them around a table drinking rum and smoking those big fat cigars of grass, and right away, he raised his Remington and cock-fire-eject, he shotgunned all of them, his stoned Jamaican-loving wife, her boyfriend, four of these other heroes in their tall leather hats. Got caught in the middle of his work by about a dozen local militia who'd seen him come to town and followed him over there, oh boy. They stood on his back, pressed him facedown on the floor of the restaurant, blood running past his nose out into the gutters. His wife's blood, her boyfriend's. Nobody reading anybody their fucking rights, no sir, not down in old Ocho Rios town.

Lost his goddamn Dade County job over it too. The authorities down there easing off on him because of his affiliation with the law, and some phone calls the Metro chief made on his behalf. The chief managed to keep it all quiet, out of the papers, but still, shit, Alvarez lost his pension, ten years seniority, health benefits.

"Tell me something, Ray," the senator said. "Who was this woman Hollings was so upset about? Martina."

"Beats the shit out of me."

"Ray?"

"Hey, remember, I was with you all night," he said. "Some

black girl gets killed, how am I supposed to know anything about it? I was driving the Rolls. Mark's Place, then to South Beach for a drink with some of your right-wing friends, then back to your smelly condo. I don't know what that goddamn Hollings was so worked up over."

"You're not telling me the truth, are you, Ray?"

"No," he said. "But what do you care? You got what you were after now. It gets dark tomorrow night, we have everything set, we go over there, dig up the gold. We're rich. It's all over. We have it. Whatta you care about some dead black woman?"

The senator padded barefoot around the family room, glanced in the mirror, touched her hair.

"Isn't it amazing, Ray," she said. "All these years, I've been paying Daniel Tyler a fortune for things that were buried on my own land. That sneaking bastard."

He said, "That land's just been sitting there, huh. How come you never did anything with it? Built something on it, an apartment house or something?"

"You've been there, Ray. Is there a lot of activity in that neighborhood? You think that would be a wise real estate investment, do you?"

She smiled, came over to the couch, getting the look again, ready for action, making her lips bigger, her eyes latching to his.

"If it weren't for you, Ray, we'd never have known. You're so smart sometimes. So clever."

"I am," he said. "I'm smart."

"You figured it out, all on your own."

"It was a hunch, a cop hunch."

"You're my big smart boy, aren't you, Ray?"

Alvarez paged through the kid's book, keeping his eyes away from the old woman.

He said, "Minute I walked up to Tyler Saturday, I knew something was fishy. Guy had a hard-on about something, that was obvious. I looked in the dirt right then, but like I told you, wasn't anything there but a piece of broken glass. Then, after he died on us, I kept thinking about that, wondering what it was had him going like that. It stayed with me. So I went back there, dug around in the dirt, and this is what you're wearing now. First of many. Just lying there, waiting for us.''

''I love your hunches, Ray.''

''Way I figure it is, the ship was running from the hurricane, looking for some bay or harbor to tie up. It sailed into the mouth of the river. The storm hit, the surge drove it upriver, and what with all the flooding and shit, it just kept on riding and riding inland until it came to rest right there.''

''Against the rapids,'' Senator Rawlings said. ''The Rawlings mill was built just above the rapids. If a ship had been driven like that upstream, it would've piled into those rocks. Amazing, isn't it. And certainly incredibly lucky for us. Right on my own land.''

''Way it works though,'' Alvarez said, ''doesn't matter you own the land. The state gets wind of it, they could come in, clamp down on it, try to claim it, historical protection and all that public domain bullshit.''

''I know the law, Ray. Don't forget who I am.''

''I couldn't do that,'' he said. ''You'd never fucking let me.''

Alvarez put the picture book aside, stood up. He moved around the coffee table, headed over to the mirror. He touched the comb in his robe pocket, considered taking it out. But no. He could do that later.

''It was a good hunch, Ray.'' Stiff again now. Pissed.

''You like the way I hunch, don't you, Senator?'' Alvarez changing directions, moving toward her, making a wicked smile.

''I love the way you do everything, Ray. I love the smell you give off. The stink of the streets.''

''Though tonight,'' he said, ''you're the one stinks.''

The senator stayed put where she was. He kept coming toward her. She lifted her head, softened the way she was standing. He got right up to her and she stepped forward against him, pressed her face into the opening of his robe, into his chest. Turning her head to speak to him in her sixty-year-old sexy voice, trying to butter him up with it. But still he could smell her, like bad eggs, swamp gas. The skunk stench hovered all around her. But the weird thing was, he was starting to adjust to it, to think it was sexy in some fucked-up way.

"I keep meaning to ask you," said Alvarez. "Whatever happened to your husband? How'd he die?"

"A heart attack," she said quietly, nuzzling his chest hair.

"You didn't shoot him by any chance, did you? Or maybe stick him with a needle when he wasn't looking?"

"Ray."

"A heart attack, huh?"

"He couldn't take the pace. He was weak, Ray. A weak man. He had no aspirations, no desire to move to the top."

"Yeah, well, I don't have those problems. The higher I get, the better I like the view. And I haven't come across the pace yet I couldn't take."

She snuggled against him. Alvarez grimaced, but held on.

"I love that speech you made to Hollings," she said. "That higher purpose nonsense. Good god, the Boy Scout was looking around for a flag to salute."

"But I do believe it," Alvarez said, his chin touching the top of her head. "A higher purpose. It's what keeps me going, what keeps me motivated."

"Right," she said. "Sure you believe it."

"Money," he said. "Cash, money, American dollars. There isn't any higher fucking purpose I know of."

"Ray," she said. "You were so utterly convincing. I was standing there thinking, that man lies well enough, he could be a first-rate politician."

Alvarez looked down at the senator's silvery hair. At the part he could see down to her scalp, her yellowy roots. The lady got so distracted by things, so wrapped up in her Maya bullshit, she'd been forgetting her beauty shop appointments. Alvarez hated this, a woman who neglected her hair. It was a sign of other things, bad hygiene in general.

"You don't have any morals, do you, Senator? You're worse than me, do any fucking thing to get what you want."

Against his chest she said, "Some people are chosen, Ray. I'm one of those. I *make* morals, I don't follow them."

"I like that. You make morals. That's good."

She said, "Morals are for the masses, the little people, to keep them from too much independent thinking."

"We get that treasure tomorrow," Alvarez said. "You don't have to worry about the masses anymore. Don't have to keep flying off to Washington. I mean, you call in, quit your job, just sit around the rest of your life, play with your gold toys and jewelry."

"Oh, no," she said. "I wouldn't do that. I like my work."

"I know what you like. You like grinding people."

"Yes, and I like the view from there. How far you can see from Capitol Hill."

She nibbled the skin near his right nipple. Alvarez tensed, but hung in there.

He said, "So you could probably use a guy like me up there, huh? An arm-twister type. Maybe you could groom me for something legit. Introduce me around." He had worked his hand inside her robe, was touching her breasts. Sad things, all the air leaked out of them. She made a humming noise, could've meant she agreed, or it could've meant she was putting him off. She snuggled in closer to him.

He pressed his lips to the part in her hair, the yellow roots. It was revolting. The smell, the bad hygiene. But he kissed her again.

Hap said, "I'm telling you, Wills, that was her, the woman I caught ransacking the house. Black woman, gold teeth, cornrows. Wearing those same white jeans, same black T-shirt. Miami Nice."

"Well, we'll know for sure in an hour or two," he said. "Let Bachay have a good look at the body. See if the fingerprints match up with the ones the techies lifted here yesterday."

They were in Hap's bedroom. He'd showered, changed into hiking shorts and a T-shirt, an old pair of Keds, moving around gingerly as if his head were a glass filled to the brim. The moment he had found the headless corpse, a headache had begun stabbing at the back of his eyes. That was three hours and half a dozen Advil ago. The clock on his bureau said ten after seven. Out the front window he could see the dawn setting fire to the cumulus east of Key Biscayne.

"How do you figure this, Wills? She burglarized my house, then later the same day she's dead on my lawn."

Wills said, "Too early to figure anything."

"So what about the fingerprints from yesterday? Your guys put a name to them yet?"

"Oh, yeah. They came up with a well-known name. Fingerprint guy claims he recognized the prints without even going to the computer match."

"Well, who is it?"

"This particular perpetrator, you put the name in the computer, you can go out and have a five-course meal, see a movie, go dancing, have a couple of Irish coffees, walk on the beach, come back to the station house, you still gotta be prepared to sit around another hour before it's done printing out all the shit this felon's pulled."

Hap could smell the bacon downstairs, the coffee. And fresh bread. Marguerite had gone out to the store, come back and cooked up a feast for the police officers who were still hanging around. Everybody pretty much making themselves at home. Maybe Hap could start renting out rooms. He was damn sure going to need to do something like that. With an eighty-six thousand dollar tax bill coming due every year.

"So what's this perpetrator's name?"

"Martin Phelps."

"Martin?"

"Yeah, Martin Phelps. Guy's wanted in connection with four separate murder investigations, three dozen burglaries, a rape, a kidnaping, trafficking in stolen goods, car theft, and a half dozen armed robberies. A bank, a liquor store, gas station, adult bookstore. About the only thing this guy's said no to is drugs."

Some of the policemen were laughing down there. Marguerite probably entertaining them with newspaper gossip. The inside dirt.

Which judges were taking payoffs this week, which weren't. The going rate for acquittals.

Wills said, "Two years ago Martin Phelps escaped from Southwest Regional Detention, then pretty much dropped out of sight. Till now."

"So you're telling me this guy, this notorious felon, was in my house, too, along with the woman I saw?"

Hap sat down at his desk. Finally the Advil was starting to unravel the snarl of pain.

"No, that's not what I'm telling you at all."

"Well?"

"Take a look at this, tell me what you see."

Wills dropped a glossy photograph on the desk in front of him. Hap held it up toward the window. Looked up at Wills.

"Imagine the guy's smiling," Wills said, "you can see his gold teeth. Imagine cornrows."

Hap blinked, rubbed his eyes into focus.

"But with breasts," said Hap. "My version had breasts."

"They can do that, of course," Wills said. "Silicone, any size and shape you could want. You get your hormone shots, lie still for the knife, you got yourself a new lease on life. See the world from both sides."

Hap studied the photograph some more.

"Well, is it her?" Wills said.

"Jesus Christ."

"Well?"

"She sure wasn't the best-looking woman I ever saw." Hap handed the photo back to Wills. "Yeah, this's her."

"Never ceases to amaze me," said Wills. "The lengths these idiots will travel to change their appearance, and then wind up staying in the same damn town where they committed all their other stupid goddamn crimes."

"It's not likely anybody'd go through all that, operations and everything, to hide from the law. More likely the guy just wanted to be a woman."

Wills chuckled.

"So tell me, Hap. Why would anybody in their right mind want to be a woman?"

"Yeah, and why would anyone in their right mind want to be a goddamn man?"

Marguerite called up the stairs to ask Wills if he was staying for breakfast. He stepped out into the hall and shouted down that yes, given the smells making their way upstairs, he thought he would. Hap got up, went to the bathroom, and while he was downing another Advil, Wills came back into the bedroom, started running his finger across the spines of Hap's books. He took one or two down, flipped them over, scanned a few pages. Hap watched from the bathroom, holding the Advil bottle as Wills browsed his closet, then checked out the ashtray full of change on his dresser, picked up a pair of Hap's sunglasses, tried them on.

"Something in particular, Lieutenant, you're looking for?"

"No, no." Wills smiled, turning the mirror lenses on him. "Just trying to get to know you better. Maybe get an idea what's crawling around in your head."

He took the sunglasses off, put them back on the dresser.

"You know, Tyler, how I understand police work is, it's my job to get into all the players' heads. Sympathize with them, see things from their point of view long enough so I can get an idea of the dynamics of any given situation. When I've done that, getting into the Big Why of things, thinking like the players think, I'm well on my way to seeing who did what to whom."

"So you go around, put on people's sunglasses? That does it for you?"

Wills rubbed his cheek like he was checking his shave.

He said, "Now, I think I got a fix on this Phelps guy. He's maybe a few millimeters out of whack, got a history of mixing murder with what amounts to some awful piddling thievery. But basically, I know where he comes from, and I can picture how he came by his world view. Even his sex change thing. I got a rough idea about that. But you, Tyler, you know, you confuse me."

"I'm honored."

"I read about you in the paper," Wills said, "a while back, the

Grande Biscayne thing, setting fire to the construction trailer. But then, I keep looking at you, and I have an awful hard time fitting all these pieces together."

"Hey, what can I say? I'm nuts. This is how we are."

"I got a son," Wills said. "He's fifteen, hangs out there at Rickenbacker with the windsurfers. I mentioned your name, you know, what case I'm working on at the moment, and Jackie started doing goddamn backflips. Panting like a dog, promised me he'd get all *A*'s the rest of his life, and sign up for the priesthood if I'd ask you something."

"I don't give out the name of my shrink."

Wills smiled civilly, and Hap sat down on the edge of the mattress, inhaled the bacon smells. He could hear Marguerite down there chatting to the uniformed guys. The clink of silverware and glasses. Decapitation giving everybody a huge appetite.

Wills said, "My boy'd give anything to have one of your boards. I mean, I'd heard him talking about them before, but I didn't pay any attention. But he tells me you manufacture them."

"I've made two or three is all."

"Well, he's seen one, I guess. How much you get for them?"

"I don't have any for sale at the moment."

"No?"

"What does this have to do with anything, Wills?"

"Well, see, Jackie wanted me to ask you, should he hold off buying a secondhand board he's been looking at? You know, like are you going to get off your ass anytime soon and make any more of these, or should he go shop elsewhere?"

"Fuck you."

"I mean, it's a valid question," Wills said. "I think it strikes to the heart of this situation. See, my point is, I can understand what makes Phelps tick. He's on a steady arc. It's a very fucked-up arc, but it's consistent. You though, you're here, you're there. You do these tours around your grandaddy's house, you're from an old solid citizen family, but you burn trailers, you spend most of the rest of your time riding around on a windsurfer, and as a hobby you empty hotels with skunk oil."

Hap smiled.

"Yeah, I know about that, Happy. You're back in the papers, though they didn't call you by name. But I figured it out. Talked to a guy down in maintenance there, told me the alias you used. Man, now that was dumb, using your own name."

"I needed to get in there," he said. "You want to know why?"

"Oh, I'm sure there's a very good explanation for it, something probably only a trained psychologist would understand. But see, I'm not interested in practical jokes. What I want to understand is, where's the center here? Who the hell is Hap Tyler anyway? Which one of these guys is he? 'Cause I don't know that I can help much till I'm on more solid ground with that."

When the phone began to ring, Hap rose, gave Wills an indifferent shrug.

"Maybe I'm just a colorful guy."

"Colorful?" said Wills. "Man, you're the whole goddamn color chart."

Hap trudged to the hall, got it on the fourth ring.

"Hap Tyler?"

He said yes. Didn't recognize the voice.

"This is Michael Overbeck, Crandon's Jewelry."

Hap said yes again.

"I'm sorry to have to call you like this. But then, well, I thought even at a time of sorrow it was important that we talked."

One more time Hap said yes.

"A woman came into the store last Friday. I didn't wait on her, so that's how it happened."

Hap glanced out the front window. The bay empty. No wind in the palms out there, but a small breeze still moving through the house. Always that, the steady updraft.

"She had the receipt," Overbeck said. "So Peggy didn't question it. Your brother's receipt. For the gold mask."

"A gold mask," Hap said.

"Yes," he said. "Why I called, I wanted to see if this woman was picking up the mask for you. When I saw that Daniel had, you know, had passed away, I checked on the mask, and learned from Peggy what had happened, and well, it bothered me. So that's why I called. Was she picking the mask up for you?''

"The woman," said Hap. "What did she look like?''

"A black woman. Peggy remembered her as being very, very unusual-looking, but polite. Yes, quite polite.''

"Why were you keeping this mask?''

"Oh, we weren't keeping it. We were cleaning it. It was something of an annual affair for us. I always handled it personally for Daniel. Every year he brought something else in, another surprise. And I cleaned it up for him.''

"The black woman must've found the claim check," said Hap, "when she was burglarizing the house.''

He thought he heard Overbeck gulp.

"Well, we had no way of knowing that, of course. But I'm terribly sorry.''

"I know.''

"I can't tell you how upset I am—all of us are. Naturally we are deeply embarrassed by this episode. But the woman did have the proper claim slip. And I don't think Peggy technically, I mean, legally did anything wrong handing the article over.''

"Don't worry, Overbeck. No one's going to sue anyone here.''

"I can't tell you," he said, "how sorry I am. It was such a lovely piece. Of course, I'll be happy to cooperate with the police if you think that's necessary.''

Hap thanked Overbeck, put the phone down.

"Bad news?'' said Wills.

"I'm starting to think," Hap said, "if it's news at all, it's gotta be bad.''

HOLLINGS SLEPT AS LATE AS HE FUCKING WELL FELT like. Noplace to go, nothing to do. Waking once or twice in the early morning, remembering his conversation with Alvarez last night, resigning his commission in the army of treasure hunters, then turning over in the bed and digging back into sleep, feeling empty and depressed as shit. Sleep the rest of his life away maybe. A fuck-up, a nothing.

Who'd he been trying to fool anyway? He'd never been worth a shit in school in any subject, much less history. Couldn't remember dates, never got it straight which king beheaded which wife, who the hell the Romans were and why they were so almighty important. None of it had ever had squat to do with Hollings or anybody he'd ever known. Then he goes to one Max Hunter lecture, and suddenly he's pretending to be some kind of expert on the *Carmelita*. Man, what he should do, he should just send the GTA 1000 back to the factory, pay whatever it cost to fix the thing, and get back to his real calling. Loose change and naked titties.

As Hollings woke for good, the light coming hard through his torn red curtains, he could hear water running somewhere in the house. He turned over, picked up the electric clock. Eleven.

When he'd gotten home last night, he hadn't turned on any water. In fact, he was damn well sure of it. He lay still and listened to it. Probably a broken pipe, the floors ankle deep in water. Something else to call his landlord about, and another goddamn reason to stay in bed.

In a minute or two the water shut off with a jerk and tremble of pipes, then a motor switched on. Hollings had to think for a minute before he figured out what that was. Yeah, the damn washing machine was going. Hollings coming out of sleep a little faster now.

He lay there. Okay, so maybe there'd been a thunderstorm last night and lightning had spiked through the wires and flipped the thing on. Hollings wasn't any electrical ace, but still, that didn't seem likely. Lying there, scratching his balls through his pajamas, looking at the ceiling and listening to the machine chugging away in the little utility room off the kitchen. The thing wasn't but twenty feet away. And while he was working on it in his head, trying to picture how electricity surging through the wires could've flipped the thing on, he heard the sharp screech of the washing machine lid opening.

Shit. That gave Hollings some major lift and thrust, and he kicked up out of bed, slid open the drawer in his bedside table, drew out his .45 and flicked off the safety. He dropped to a crouch, brought the sights up as he swiveled.

Priming himself, he stared at the open door, at the wall opposite it, the narrow hallway. He turned and grabbed up the pillow from his bed, edged to the door, listening but hearing nothing out there but the wash cycle getting under way. He lifted the pillow and waved it out into the hallway, into the line of fire from the living room. Nothing.

He tossed the pillow back onto the bed and brought the .45 up to the edge of the doorjamb, pressed the side of the cold barrel to his cheek. Steadying himself, he took a breath, gripped the pistol double-handed, cocked his elbows, stilled the jitter in his hand, then hopped forward into the hall, leveling the weapon at the long, empty space.

Hollings puckered his lips and blew out a breath, eyes flitting from the end of the corridor to the closed bathroom door halfway down the hall. He inched forward, listening to the chug of the washer. The house was carpeted with a nubby red polyester rug.

The walls were covered with dark walnut paneling, the quarter-inch fake shit. Some previous renter had scratched nutso slogans into the veneer. Stuff about TV Bible hucksters. How Oral Roberts got his name, what Jim Bakker was baking these days. Things like that. Hollings had started to sand it off, but then decided, what the hell, it was good to have a reminder that some people out there were more fucked-up than he was.

Pistol extended, Hollings took a breath, then hopped into the kitchen. The remains of his Big Mac, fries, and shake from a couple of days ago sitting on the table, the sparrows flitting around in the bird feeder out the one window. A couple of cockroaches not paying any attention to him as they explored the baseboards.

And now the washer was out of balance, banging against the wall of the utility room. Hollings having to hold himself back, wanting to rush in there, fix the fucker before it threw a belt. But wanting to try to think this through first, figure who might have a key, who would think they could just walk in, do a load.

Last person had a key was Brenda Gross, six months ago. Lady was sixty-nine years old and worked as a crossing guard at the elementary school over off Prairie. A full thirty years older than Hollings, but she turned him on somehow. With her long white hair, thick glasses, and how she liked to scream Spanish when she was coming. Though the woman was Jewish as far as Hollings could tell, she'd go oy, oy, *Dios mio, Dios mio*. And then when her orgasm hit her full blast it'd be, *madre, madre, sangre cristo*.

He finally had to throw her out, she talked so much. During sex and the rest of the time too. Though he had to say, he'd liked it at first, all her talking, 'cause it took his mind off his own troubles. Yimmering and yammering. Then one day at breakfast he looked over at her with her mouth full of oatmeal, a little trickle of it coming out the corner while she went on and on about something in the news, poking her finger at the news story, and he reached over, took hold of a handful of her hair, and yanked it hard as he could.

Brenda's eyes watered up, and she looked like he'd lifted her stylus and her record was still spinning but no noise was coming out anymore. She got up, put on her crossing-guard uniform, left and never came back. No, it wasn't Brenda washing her clothes.

The longer he stood there outside the utility room thinking about it, the more pissed off he got. Pissed that someone had broken in, and pissed that he didn't have a goddamn friend in the world who it might be. Pulling up the waistband on his pajamas, Hollings set his face, and stepped forward into the doorway of the utility room.

Nobody there. The machine thunking harder now, making a hell of a racket. Hollings flipped up the lid and shut it off.

With his butt to the machine, eyes on the doorway, he reached behind him into the washer and felt around till he found a big knot of wet clothes off to one side. He jostled them, dragged up something heavy and wet. Took his eyes off the door long enough to see a pair of black jeans from somebody fairly big. He let them slosh onto the concrete floor.

He reached into the machine again and this time took hold of the mother lode. Felt like the whole wash had got balled up inside a T-shirt. Ten pounds of wet glop. Hollings cursed quietly and hauled the knot of soaking clothes out, and dropped it on the floor at his feet.

He looked down. And holy mother of Jesus, if he wasn't staring into the face of a black woman. The severed head wrapped in a blue T-shirt, the eyes peering out the neck opening. One eye open, one closed. A death wink.

At that same moment, the toilet flushed in the hall bathroom across from the utility room. He stumbled backward. Caught himself. Hollings's heart misfiring. And he brought the pistol up and focused it on the door just in time as it swung open.

Martina stepped into the hall, wearing a red bra and red panties. She was working on her teeth with a length of dental floss. Humming something to herself.

Hollings danced away, holding the pistol on her.

Jesus Mother of Mary and all the little lambs.

Smiling at the pistol, at Hollings, Martina said, ''I just stacked some serious real estate in your toilet. I'd watch out, give it a week or two, let the air settle before I walked in there.''

"What the fuck?''

"Hey, dude,'' Martina said with a big grin. "What's wrong? You even whiter than normal.''

Hollings was backing down the hallway toward the kitchen, the pistol still centered on Martina's chest. Martina coming toward him, but cautiously.

Hollings throat was stuck shut, voice locked away down there.

"That head, case you were wondering, it belongs to a lady name of Deshawna Racine Barkley. I thought it'd be kind of funny, you finding it that way. Give us something to laugh at together.''

Hollings made a croak. Aiming the pistol at Martina, he felt like he was gripping the thing hard enough it should've gone off. His fingers starting to hurt.

"I guess it hasn't struck you funny yet,'' said Martina. "But maybe it'll be one of those things, a time-release joke. We're sitting around next week, we start looking back on it, talking about it, a head in the Kenmore washing machine, you know, it might just hit you then, and you can't stop laughing. I had that happen couple of times.''

Hollings made another noise, his throat beginning to open, but still it wasn't anything you could call a word yet. Nothing even remotely like what he wanted to say to this black woman standing in his kitchen smiling at him.

"I mean, you got a sense of humor, right, Hollings? You laugh now and then, don't you?''

Martina walked around the kitchen opening and closing cabinets, drawers. Humming, not seeming very concerned about the .45 Hollings was still pointing.

"See, that head in there,'' Martina said. "That's a crucial part of our new game plan. A whole new idea I had for how you and me are gonna get rich.'' Martina swung her head around, doing a fast survey of the grubby kitchen.

She said, "And I'm talking rich rich. Money enough so you

could get out of this rat's nest. Enough cash, you and me, we'd never have to do a dishonest day's work again.''

"Yeah?"

"And, Hollings. For some reason, don't ask me why, I'm of a mind to share the wealth with you.'' Giving him a lewd smile, flexing her left breast, then her right.

Martina opened the refrigerator door, leaned into it, humming as she moved things around in there. Hollings pulled up one of the stools at the Formica breakfast bar and sat. He still held on to the pistol, but he wasn't aiming the thing anymore.

In a minute Martina turned around from the refrigerator, holding up a cup of Dannon. She had a crimped-up smile.

"Christ, would you look at this. Blackberry, blueberry, mixed fruit, apple, Dutch apple. You're a goddamn yogurt freak, Hollings. I'm embarrassed for you, man.''

She pried off the lid, peered inside.

"Ex-gyrene like you, it should be bloody steaks, and hot grease, suck the juice out of the bones. But no, you're into candy-ass pudding.''

Martina put the yogurt back, shaking her head. When she turned back around to face Hollings, she stood for a moment, then shimmied her tits at him, sending some kind of message, but Hollings had no idea what it was. Hollings squinted. Another shimmy.

"Whatta you, blind? Look. Here.''

Martina flicked the military medal pinned to her bra.

"You goddamn bitch.''

"I can't help it, man," she said. "When I find a footlocker with a big-ass padlock on it, I just can't resist picking it open. That's how I am. A naturally curious Afro-American. So while you were having your wet dreams last night, I wandered around out here, and found out who the hell you really are, Hollings. A goddamn decorated war hero.

"I mean, I'm down there rooting around in all this Vietnam shit, uniforms, boots, socks, cute little silk kimonos. Hell, man, don't you throw anything away? And there you go, down on the ass-bottom of everything there's this little felt-covered box, and I'm going, yeah, I knew it. Keeps his diamonds hidden here, his Rolex. And what do you know? The whole damn thing written up in the *New York Times,* Corporal Glenn Philpot Hollings here, he pulls a John Wayne in some place I can't pronounce."

"Chu Lai."

"Chu Lai," said Martina. "Yeah, so he's out there in Chu Lai, up to his ass in a rice paddy ambush, and there's six VC machine guns crisscrossing the field, cutting everything down that moves out there, and this guy is running back and forth carrying wounded guys over to the forest. I mean, if I was to carry one guy on my back a hundred yards, I got to rest in bed for a week. But our hero, he carries eight guys to the medic over in the woods.

"But that isn't enough for Glenn Philpot. No, sir, now he's got to wipe out those rice eaters been shooting at him. So he goes back out there, armloads of grenades, crawls across that field. Lobbing those pineapples, he knocks out all six machine gun nests. Jesus Christ, Hollings, it's like Arnold what's-his-name with the muscles, or that other guy, Rocky."

Martina shaking her head, a weird smile on her lips. Torn between smartass and respect.

"Who is that dead woman, Martina?"

"Hey, I'm telling a story I read in the paper. In the *New York Times,* all right."

"Who's the woman, Martina?"

She huffed at him, went back to the refrigerator, took out one of the cups of yogurt, opened it, swiped her finger through it, then licked her finger clean.

"I told you, Deshawna Barkley. Recently deceased of gunshot wounds to the abdomen. See, I got a second cousin works the city morgue. I called him up, asked him what they had in stock at the moment, something in a five foot ten voluptuous African queen. A fresh corpse nobody was taking much interest in. And he came up with Deshawna Barkley, though I got to say, she don't have nothing like my knockers.

"Now you tell me something, Hollings. You saved eight guys, killed ten of theirs, the American president pins the goddamn Silver Star on you, the marine band is playing. Tell me, man, what in fuck's name are you doing living like this, this falling-down piece of shit house, you got pimps and whores on the sidewalk out front. How'd you get from there to here?"

"Why'd you kill that woman, Martina? What's the deal?"

"I didn't kill anybody. I told you, man. You not listening to me or what? I got that body from the morgue. She was ten hours dead."

"Why?"

"Be free."

"What?"

"Be free," she said. "Be free of Alvarez. You always hear how you don't quit the Mafia. I believe we got us the same situation with Alvarez. I seen it before, that look he has. The man's trip-wired. Set to blow. Guys like that don't lay off their help, man. They extinguish them. I was to walk up to him, say, hey, Ray, I'm giving you my week's notice, man. I got other things going down. That's the last you ever be hearing of this bitch. So I said to myself, hell, put my clothes on Deshawna, hacksaw her head off, arrange it so old Hollings sees the body, I know first thing that chickenshit's going to do is run tell Alvarez. I'll be a free woman. An independent operator again."

"Hell, you didn't need to do all that," said Hollings. "Last night, I told him I was through. I just walked out the door, he didn't do nothing. He just stood there, watched me go."

"Well, give him time," she said. "Give the man a couple of days, I bet he'll come calling."

Hollings watched Martina pace around the kitchen in her bra and panties. Washboard stomach, muscled arms. Had a kind of weird attraction, if you could get over how ugly her face was. And he was even becoming a little used to that.

"I wouldn't feel a hundred percent safe," she said. "I was you, I'd keep a mirror in my hand at all times, see who was creeping up behind me. Just might turn out it was Alvarez."

Martina touched the barrel of the pistol with a long finger, put a dab of blackberry yogurt on it. The traffic noise rising outside, horns, buses roaring past, some palm fronds fluttering across the street.

"The cops'll fingerprint the body," Hollings said, "find out who it was. It'll be in the papers, a thing like that. Then Alvarez's gonna know it wasn't you."

"Not right away, he won't. That's all this is, Hollings, a head fake. Just a little stutter step to keep the man off balance for a day or so. After that, it won't matter he knows I'm still alive. He won't be able to find me."

"I don't believe it," Hollings said. "I don't believe I got anything to worry about."

"You were cannon fodder, Hollings. That's what you were. He was going to get you to wade out into some deep shit, then give you up, and disappear himself. That's how it was."

Christ. Hollings knew it was true. Just like he'd said last night. Alvarez suckered him along to be the trigger man, be the one holding exhibit A when the sirens started.

'Cause hell, what good was Hollings beyond that? When they found the *Carmelita*, what was he going to contribute anyway? He couldn't read navigation charts, couldn't scuba dive. He got seasick on boats. Shit. Right from the beginning, the bastard must've been conning him, using the fact that Hollings was a needy person, an easy mark.

Martina said, "What I want to know is, Hollings, what was in your head, running around in that rice paddy that day?"

Hollings said nothing. Held his face still.

"See, what I think is, guys like you, doing things like that, it wasn't for any love of country. All that official horseshit. How I think it is, it's one of two things."

Hollings wiped the barrel on his pajamas. Getting a lift now from holding the pistol. Listening to Martina, but thinking about Alvarez, feeling more pissed the more he thought of him.

"Most times if a guy's a hero, it just means he's some kind of swinging dick," Martina said. "All full of chemicals telling him what to do. Guy's got a hard-on from the time he's little, all he wants is to punch and shoot, ram his thing into a woman. But you, Hollings, your dick chemicals didn't make you do what you did. Shit no, you're the second category, aren't you?''

Martina smiled at him, let him have a chance to say something, but Hollings just sat there, holding his .45, getting his pulse back into double digits. Listening to this totally insane black woman psychoanalyze him.

"The way I picture it, you're over there in Vietnam, been out in the jungle thinking too much, just like your type of people are prone to do, and lo and behold, you figured it out. The war thing, it's a shit sandwich, and now it's come round your turn to take a bite.

"You want to run, but you're too much of a Sunday school white boy to desert, and anyway where the fuck're you gonna run, you're in Chu Lai, for christsakes. So you snap. Old Hollings can't take it anymore and he goes into a quantum episode, steps across into the alternate universe."

Hollings stared at her, this black woman in her underwear, parading in front of the refrigerator. Thinking about the human head lying in the laundry room, a head inside the wet T-shirt. This woman, Martina, sawing it off, but Hollings having trouble picturing that part.

"Quantum episode?" said Hollings. "The fuck is that?"

Martina looked off, like she was trying to get the words right.

"Okay," she said at last. "In the goddamn parallel universe, your other self can't be hurt by bullets or any shit from this universe. Long as you stay over there, you can run around, nothing can fucking touch you. It's like you're transparent."

She said, "Thing's called quantum mechanics. I'm surprised you never come across it, 'cause they study it now in school. I saw a TV show on it. What you did, you took a quantum leap."

"Quantum leap."

"Myself, I been over into the parallel universe, that time at the Jockey Club, I was scoring all the diamonds. I was walking around, nothing could touch me. You could've put me in a minefield, wouldn't matter. I was over the line, the other plane."

"A quantum episode," Hollings said again, trying to get used to the feel of it in his mouth.

"Yeah," she said, smiling. The gold shining on her teeth. "Now you learned a goddamn word from me for a change."

# CHAPTER 23

THE SILVER STAR TINKLED AS MARTINA SWUNG AROUND TO the refrigerator, opened it, took out the yogurt. Using two fingers, she scooped out some more.

"The blackberry isn't half bad." She sucked her fingers off. "Though now I gotta floss all over again."

Hollings picked up the .45, raised it, and aimed. Not angry but feeling a need to get things back under control in his own damn house. Thinking it'd be good to scare her a little, let her look into the barrel of the .45. Though Hollings wasn't one of those guys who had to shoot a gun just because he picked it up and aimed it.

Martina looked up, saw the pistol aiming at her, and lifted her gaze to Hollings's eyes. The woman didn't flinch, seemed to start counting off the seconds, see how long it would take Hollings to back down. Without ever deciding to do it in his head, Hollings squeezed off a round.

And goddamn! He'd forgotten what recoil that sucker had, how noisy it was. The yogurt spattered out of Martina's hand. Winged the refrigerator. Hollings's gut shook from the impulsiveness of it, but all in all he felt good, his shooting eye still there after all this time.

As the racket died off, Hollings lowered the pistol and looking straight at her said, "Don't be eating my food, woman. Not without asking me first. You either start being polite, or get outta my fucking house.''

A smile worked its way to Martina's lips.

''Lock and load, soldier,'' she said. ''Lock and load.''

Hollings slapped the pistol down on the breakfast bar. Maybe the woman was right. Quantum mechanics. He guessed it could be something weird like that. That would explain why he felt guilty getting the medal. Feeling like it wasn't him that had actually done all the shit they were describing. It wasn't like anything else he'd ever done in his life. Hell, he hadn't even liked the guys he saved that day. Bastards were always getting on him for this and that. And after that afternoon, the other guys in his outfit didn't exactly warm to him either. Somebody called him Showboat, and it stuck. *Hey, Showboat, you trying to make us look bad, or what?*

Hollings didn't ever let himself think about that afternoon, 'cause when he did he got nauseated. All the noise and dirt coming back to him, the gut-shaking fear. The guys screaming and crying, the stink. And at the ceremony in Washington, they'd given out around fifty medals for bravery, gallantry, all that official horseshit. Hollings and a couple of other guys were the only living soldiers on the platform. All the families of the dead soldiers gripped their kids' medals and kept looking over at Hollings.

''So, Hollings.'' Martina was grinning. ''Maybe it's time you and me started exploring some of the *lower* purposes. Whatta you say to that?''

''What's that supposed to mean?''

''You know,'' she said. ''You put a beautiful part of you into a beautiful part of me. Sort of seal our deal. I always did have a soft spot for a man in uniform. A big hero.''

Hollings sat there and stared at her. No woman had ever said anything like that to him before. Add to that the fact it'd been almost a year since he'd been laid, many a day coming home horny from the beach, having to lie on the bed and do himself, that could explain why right then he was getting such a quiver in his dick.

Man, oh man. There was something wrong with Hollings. He knew it. First Brenda, the crossing guard, now this one, getting hot over Martina. Goddamn, Hollings's taste in women was totally screwed. But what could he do about it? Stuff like that, you were born with it. A blood thing. It got settled before you had a chance to decide.

Hollings said, "You got any diseases I should know about? I got to wear a double rubber with you?"

"Now you're talking," she said. "Now you're whistling my tune." Reaching into her bra and coming out with something and holding it up. Something shiny.

"And afterwards, remind me to tell you about this thing."

It was a flat piece of gold, size of a wallet. Hollings leaned forward. Like some kind of mask or something, the mouth all twisted around like somebody was torturing it.

Martina said, "I figure we can melt this little honey down, hell, it's probably worth a thousand bucks anyway. Enough we can move out of this apartment. Start practicing a more opulent lifestyle."

Marguerite ladled out a third helping of grits for Wills. Hap swallowed the last of his eggs, wiped his plate with a piece of buttered toast. The cop carved a chunk of butter off the stick with his spoon. He swirled it around in the steaming white mound.

"I didn't mention yet," he said, "I found your brother's car across the street from the river, at 2678 South River Drive, just east of Twenty-seventh Avenue. You know the place?"

Hap shook his head.

"I do," Marguerite said.

Wills said, "There's a 7-Eleven couple of blocks away, they sell chorizos, have them hanging up over the checkout." Looking at them expectantly, like oh, yeah, *that* place.

Hap said, "I'd forgotten about his car."

"What we did," said Wills, "is we looked all around the Sonesta parking lot for it. A gray Dodge, Metro-Dade car. It wasn't at the hotel. So I went by his office, woman there told me he usually worked weekends at this South River Drive address. There all day, digging by himself."

"I could've told you that," Marguerite said.

"But you didn't."

Wills wiped his mouth, looked outside at the gang of lawn men. The Happy Haitian Take Care of Your Yard Company. Five mowers going at once, two guys swinging machetes at the Commodore's bushes. Hap watched, fiddling with his fork, and tasting the warm bile that gurgled at the back of his throat. A couple of the uniformed patrolmen were still outside, lounging around on the porch. Hap assumed Wills had told them to stay.

Wills said, "People at Daniel's office tell me it was some kind of mill there, where the river rapids used to be. They said it was like his pet project, place he went off and on to dig around, just to piddle. His therapy place."

"That mill," Marguerite said, "is where my great grandmother lived, where she ground coontie. Down off Twenty-seventh Avenue."

"Coontie?" Wills said.

"It was a root," she said. "The pioneers ground it like flour. It's extinct now, far as I know."

"It's your land?" he said. "Where Daniel was that day?"

"My family's land, yes. We're going to rebuild the mill. You know, an exact replica of the original one. Use it for a pioneer museum. Daniel was looking for Ramona's remains. To give her a decent burial before the construction started."

"Like the female equivalent of this place," Wills said. "The Mangrove House."

Hap set his coffee cup down.

A couple of the Happy Haitians were just outside the kitchen, their Weed Eaters roaring, kicking up dust, the Haitians having a conversation in their fast, slap-happy voices. Marguerite got up, closed the kitchen window.

Wills cleared his throat. He drew a design with his fingertip against the tabletop.

He said, "Now, finding his car there, it could indicate he and the hooker went out to the hotel together in the hooker's car. They were planning for her to bring him back later to pick it up. Or, on the other hand, it's consistent with an out-and-out abduction. On the face of it, it's hard to say."

Marguerite came back to the table. This morning she'd put on a pair of Hap's bright yellow surfing shorts and one of his T-shirts, both of them very baggy on her. She sat down, and saw that she had their attention. The gray eyes, the slash of her cheekbones, the scuffed and raw places on her face, her long white neck, black hair with reddish highlights in it from the morning sun. She smiled politely, and when Wills looked away, she glanced at Hap, sent him some mildly erotic telepathy.

"My great-grandmother," Marguerite said, shifting her eyes to Wills, "the one that ground the coontie, she was Miami's first murder victim."

Wills held a spoonful of grits at his mouth, and stared at Marguerite for a couple of moments. He lowered the grits, tapped them off his spoon. Set the spoon beside his plate.

"Don't tell me," she said, "you never heard of Ramona Rawlings, the notorious fire at the coontie mill?"

"I may have," Wills said. "I'm getting a faint recollection."

"She came down here from Lexington, Mass, after her husband died. Started the mill, raised her son, made a small fortune with the mill. But she was a troublemaker. She wouldn't sell her land to Flagler or any of the others. She was antirailroad, antigrowth, and she was organizing the rest of the town to resist too. Very persuasive lady. So they killed her. Burned down her house and the mill. Her body was in the rubble, bullet through her skull. The culprit never caught."

"Has a nineties ring to it," said Wills. "Could be one of my cases right now."

One of the Haitian men was at the back door, big toothy smile, his face spattered with grass cuttings. Payment time.

Hap went over to the sugar jar where Daniel kept the petty cash. Paid the smiling boss. He glanced out the window at the rest of the crew already in the back of the pickup. A couple of the uniformed guys on the porch giving them a serious once-over.

When Hap sat back down Wills said, "So I guess we should take a closer look at the mill site. Last place he was."

"I'd like to go with you," Marguerite said. "If it's okay."

"Sure," he said. "I just want to walk around, see the place. I never been on an archaeological site before. If it looks promising, I'll have the tech guys come over, let them fine-tooth comb it."

"Wills," said Hap, standing at the door. "I need to talk to you a minute. Outside."

He gave Marguerite a reassuring look, and she nodded back.

"What's wrong with you?" Hollings said.

"Whatta you mean, what's wrong with me?"

"The way you are down there. It's not normal."

Hollings was sitting on the john, trying to finish his dump while he talked to her in the shower. Martina cut the water off, pulled the red shower curtain aside and stuck her soapy head out and stared at Hollings.

"Use the right words," she said. "Whatta you mean, down there?"

"You know what I mean."

"Use the words you mean."

"I don't know the goddamn word for it. Your thing. Your cooze. It's weird."

"My cooze!"

"Whatever the hell you call it then."

"You didn't like it, Glenn? You didn't come twice? Maybe that was somebody else I was with, 'cause I thought whoever it was, they were coming."

"Hey, I'm not complaining," Hollings said. "I'm trying to have a conversation with you, and you're getting all defensive about it. Christ."

"You said I wasn't normal. You were insulting to my body, to my sexual parts. My cooze."

"It's just different."

"You had so many women, Glenn? You had so much experience, now they come to you, the doctors and the scientists and they say, Glenn, look at this, tell us, is this normal? How about this one, is it normal? You had that many women, Glenn? Huh?"

Soap dripping down from all her little pigtails onto the floor. Hollings wanting to hurry up and finish taking his dump so he could get out of there, get some clothes on, get at a safe distance from this, and think what the hell he was doing.

"No, I haven't had that much experience," he said. "I'm just saying—"

"How many, Glenn? How many women you had? Fifty, five hundred? A thousand? More?"

"Three," he said. Knowing it was a low number and she was going to laugh, but saying it anyway, even though it was an exaggeration by one.

She didn't laugh.

"Three?"

"Three," he said.

"That include me, or without me?"

"Including you."

"Well, that explains it," she said. She took her head away, turned the water on again.

"Explains what?"

Hollings finished up on the john all of a sudden, standing up, flushing. Martina jerked away from the shower water.

"Explains what?" he said through the shower curtain.

"How you are in bed. Like a guy, he's heard the A-bomb is falling on his house, he wants to do just this one last thing, screw his woman, before he runs for his life."

"I do it the way I do it," Hollings said. "I never had any complaints before."

"From the other two?" she said.

"Not one complaint."

All there was really was Brenda, the crossing guard. And she was always too preoccupied with whatever batshit thing was fluttering around in her brain at the moment to make any observations about Hollings, pro or con.

"Reason you never had any complaints," she said, turning the water off, pulling the shower curtain aside. "Is 'cause you came and went so fast, they weren't sure it happened. You're gone before they had a chance to complain."

"Screw you."

"Yeah?" she said. "I wish."

"And how many guys you had, Martina? A thousand? They come to you, the scientists, and ask you what's normal?"

She was out of the shower now, drying her body with the towel. Hollings stared again at it, the way it was. Strong-assed woman, hell of a stomach on her, and big thick legs, and that thing between her legs. That pocket. Tight, yeah, but not deep enough for him. And he was no jumbo, he had to admit that.

"Let's just drop it," Martina said.

"Yeah, now you want to drop it. The spotlight's on you, so we drop it. It's on me, that's okay."

"So far I only had a few guys," she said. "Five, to be completely on-the-head exact."

"Including me or without me?"

"Before those five guys, I specialized in girls."

Hollings's mouth went a little loose.

"Girls."

"I was pretty successful with women," Martina said. "I don't have an exact number to give you. But I was successful."

Girls? Hollings staring at her as she dried her legs, putting her foot up on the sink so she could get between the toes. Girls? Oh, no. He knew something was peculiar about her, and now here it was, the woman was a converted lesbian.

"Does that make you sick, Hollings? Me with girls?"

"I don't know."

"It does, doesn't it?"

"It's okay," he said. "I guess."

"How you mean, okay?"

Hollings thought about it a little more. Tried to picture Martina with a girl.

"A girl with a girl," Hollings said. "It doesn't matter to me if you like girls. Shit, I like girls too."

"It doesn't matter?"

Standing there, both feet on the floor, looking at Hollings with the towel in front of her big heavy breasts.

"Naw," Hollings said. "The truth is I may even like it a little." He felt himself stirring inside his pajama bottoms. Just the thought of it getting him riled up again.

Hollings said, "I could go slower, I guess. If that'd be better, I got nothing against going slow. I just never had anybody request it before, is all that is."

She dropped the towel. Came over to him.

"You know, Hollings, you're the only Silver Heart I ever had. You're my very first of those. Male or female."

Hollings said, "Jesus, I don't know if I can do it again so soon. Twice is the most I ever did it in one day before."

"Relax, sugar. You can just lie back this time and let old Martina do the work. How'd that be?"

Hollings said that'd be just fine, and he followed her naked ass back toward the bedroom. Wondering to himself what in the hell they were going to do with that damn head. Wrap it up good and put it out in the trash or what?

CHAPTER 24

O N THE LAWN, HAP AND WILLS WALKED SIDE BY SIDE
toward the water. Hap led him down near the shoreline. Today the
surf was spilling past the rocky beach and into the grass. Full moon,
high tide, a hard wind from the south. All of that was piling up the
water on this side of Biscayne Bay, pushing it onto land, bringing
with it mats of seaweed, lengths of hawsers, plastic oil cans, a couple
of belly-up fish, boat trash. When the wind died later today or tomorrow, the muck would begin to rot in the sun, and the air down
there would turn to sewer gas. It'd be almost impossible to stand
within thirty yards of the shore.

"Okay, so what's up?" Wills said.

They halted beside the boathouse, the breeze beating around
them, tearing at the season's last pink frangipani blooms, hurling a
couple of them through the air.

"I've found something."

"Yeah."

"A piece of evidence in Daniel's murder."

Wills watched a bloom twirl into the grass nearby. He touched
it with the toe of his black shoe. The man wore dark trousers, white
shirt, boxy black shoes. Probably had to shop at the Tall and Big
Man's store. Not a lot of fashion choices.

Hap said, "But I want to know something in return."

"What would that be?"

"I want you to tell me the results of your tests. What you find out about this evidence."

Wills chuckled. Then he took a longer look at Hap, and stopped.

"You're not kidding."

"I'm not kidding."

"Well, that's simple enough," Will said. "I can't do it." He squinted at Hap like he was straining to see him through a smoky room. Not sure he had the right guy.

"Then forget the evidence."

"I'd have to arrest you," said Wills. "If I thought you're withholding."

Hap said, "I want to know what you know. If I'm in danger, it's only right I should have straight information."

"Who said you were in danger?"

"What're those uniforms still doing here?"

Wills shrugged.

"Hey, you live in a historical house. Oldest dwelling in Dade County. I can't just let some bunch of creeps have their way with that place, now, can I? Wouldn't reflect well on the department."

"Those cops aren't guarding the house, Wills. Come on."

"If you want, I can tell them to go."

"I can defend myself."

Hap looked out at the water. Some live-aboard houseboats and ketches anchored just to the north off Dinner Key. Bobbing in the rough wind. Maybe that's what he should do, cash out of the Mangrove House, sell it to somebody wanting to build the next condo theme park, move himself onto a boat, take Marguerite sailing around the islands. Hell, if Senator Rawlings sued to get her eighty-six five back, he wouldn't have a lot of choice. He had no way of paying his taxes this year, next year, any year. The county would take the place from him in a blink.

Wills stooped and picked up the frangipani bloom. He sniffed it, then held it out for Hap to have a sniff. Hap shook his head. Not in the flower-sniffing mood this morning.

"One thing I always wondered," Wills said. "Is it just a coincidence all the beautiful things have short lives, or is it because something has a short life we think it's beautiful?"

"I want the truth, Wills, whatever you turn up. It's either that, or I don't cooperate."

"All right," said Wills, "so let's say I'm considering your offer. As ridiculous as it is. Let's say I'm still entertaining it. Seems to me I'd need to know what the evidence is that you're illegally withholding, and now attempting to use as a bribe, before I could agree."

"You'll do it?"

"The evidence first."

Hap took out the packet of syringes and the blue vial, held them out to Wills.

Wills hesitated, tucked the bloom in his shirt pocket, then dug a handkerchief out of his pants and took the bottle and the packet. He raised an eyebrow. Snorted in surprise.

"Where'd you get these goddamn things?"

"You've got to promise me, Wills. I want to know whose fingerprints are on these, anything about them."

Wills tucked the vial and syringes into his pants. He took the frangipani bloom out of his pocket, twirled it with thumb and first finger.

"You know, I think maybe what it is," he said, staring at the flower. "The beautiful things just can't stand it. It wears them out being beautiful, so they die quicker. That's my new theory on that subject."

"You're not going to tell me anything, are you?"

"Of course not."

Hap burned him with a look, but Wills just shrugged.

"All right." Hap sighed. "The syringe and the vial came from Senator Rawlings's apartment. I found them in a medicine cabinet."

Wills peered at Hap, his head tipped to the side, and said, "Don't be confessing things to me that might land you in jail."

They drifted down closer to the shoreline, Wills stooping to pick up another frangipani blossom.

"Flowers," Wills said, "I don't know why, but they always seem to have a philosophical effect on me."

Hap glanced back up at the house. Marguerite and the cops were out on the front porch. She stood at the railing gazing down at Wills and him, the cops behind her.

"How 'bout you?"

"How 'bout me what?"

"Flowers," Wills said. "They make you think? Stimulate philosophical inquiry?"

"Jesus Christ, Wills. My brother was murdered. I find a headless woman on my lawn. I'm not gonna stand around and shoot the shit about flowers."

"Okay," Wills said. "How's this? When a living thing dies, maybe it gives off something. Call it its soul, call it electrical current, anything you want. But something that used to be there isn't there anymore once the thing's dead. So maybe how it goes with flowers and the other ephemeral things, they're giving off this current at such a fast rate, that's the thing we see. They're dying before our eyes, and it's like they're electrified. And that's what makes a flower beautiful. Or a butterfly. Or even this town."

He studied Hap for a moment and said, "How's that sound?"

"You should stick to police work, Wills. That's about all the intellectual challenge you can handle."

"Yeah? So you got a better theory?"

Wills turned and they began to stroll back up to the house.

"It's all sex," Hap said. "Flowers are sex. Beauty's sex. Everything's the way it is so it has a better chance to reproduce itself. If you're looking for the grand unifying theory, well, there it is. Sex, sex, sex."

"Now that," Wills said, "is spoken like a man who just got laid."

"That was slower, right?"

"Better," Martina said. "It was better."

"I could go even slower," said Hollings, "but I don't know, I might fall asleep."

Hollings lay there next to her, grinning, joking around with his woman. Feeling a little hungry, ready for something substantial, and not yogurt. Like Martina said, something with salt and grease, something he'd have to have a couple of beers to wash down.

"I lied once to you," Martina said.

"You did?"

"You know, at Alvarez's house that time. I said how when I was burglarizing Tyler's place, the guy never saw me. Well, he did. He got a long, good look at me. We had a conversation and everything."

"Yeah?"

Hollings didn't usually hang around in bed after. But here he was in the sheets next to this Amazon woman, touching her navel, feeling the prickly hairs around it, thinking, damn, if this didn't last with Martina, at least he was getting a sexual education. Something he could use later in life.

Martina said, "I'm sure Tyler reported me to the goddamn police. And they probably came out, checked for fingerprints. And if they got a good set, then they know who I am."

"You didn't wear gloves? I thought you were a pro."

"Pros don't wear gloves."

"So big deal, you're a wanted woman."

"Yeah."

"Whatta you so worried about all of a sudden? Sounds like to me, you been wanted all your life. They still got to catch your ass. Way I see it, you do something illegal, run a red light say, long as a cop isn't around, it isn't illegal. Like that tree in the woods, it falls and nobody's there to hear it. Same thing as that."

"What tree?"

"That fucking tree falls in the woods and no one hears it."

"We're talking about me, Hollings. Not about some fucking tree in some goddamn woods."

"I'm just trying to explain something to you."

Martina said, "Hapfield Tyler saw me."

"All right. All right, don't get all pissed off."

"He could put me there. In his house."

"So? I'm trying to tell you, that's no threat. Nothing to worry about there. Just a little burglary is all that is. Nobody's going to come looking for anybody in this town for a little breaking and entering. Shit, Miami, you got to kill yourself upwards of five, six people get them looking seriously for you. That or a cop.

"I mean, I knew a guy once, he lived out in Hialeah, and he comes home one night after a long night of drinking, couldn't find his house keys, he stands on his own front porch, houses close by on both sides, across the street, this quiet little neighborhood, the guy takes out his gun, shoots the lock out of his own door. Loud fucking .357 he had, too, bang, bang, like that after midnight. And nobody did nothing. Nobody called the cops. His neighbors must've woke up, sat there in the dark listening to him firing away, and it was like oh, go back to sleep, honey, it's just somebody forgot their door keys, they're having to blast their way in. I mean, that's how it is in this fucking town. Nobody cares you broke into some guy's house, Christ."

Martina stared thoughtfully at Hollings. She took a long breath and said, "What I don't like is, the fingerprints telling the cops to be looking for one person, and this Hap Tyler is describing somebody else."

"How's that? I don't get it."

"Nothing."

"I'm not following you here."

"I don't like it," she said. "I don't like it, that someone could blow everything."

Martina looked down at Hollings's hand circling her navel.

"Okay," Hollings said. "We'll shoot him. If it'll make you feel better, we'll just drive over there and kill Tyler's ass."

Martina put her hand on Hollings's hand, pressed it to her navel, then nudged it lower.

She said, "The guy's probably already given the cops my description. The damage is done."

"He can identify you, yeah, but he can't testify against you unless he's alive. That's one of the cornerstones of the American judicial system. You got to be alive to testify against somebody."

"You'd do that?"

Hollings thought about it. Things weren't like they had been. Nights working part-time at the 7-Eleven. Days digging up lost change at the beach, taking these small steps forward. Now he was taking giant steps. One after the other. Getting away from Alvarez was a giant step. Being in bed with Martina was another. Moving ahead, leaps and bounds.

"Sure," he said. "I'd kill Tyler for you. Remember those guys in Chu Lai? It'd be like that. Go in there, wipe him out, practice some quantum mechanics on him."

"Hell, I don't know, Hollings," she said. "You'd probably fuck it up."

"What does that mean?"

"Means, I better help you do the deed if it's going to get done right."

"All right," Hollings said. "We'll do it together. You hold the gun, I pull the trigger, or vice versa. It'll be like a date, going out on a date."

Martina put her head back against the pillow, lifted one of her big breasts up and picked a speck of lint out of her nipple. He'd never seen a woman do that before.

She caught him staring, and frowned.

"I don't know about you, Hollings."

"What don't you know?"

"How you could be so dumb and not be in jail by this time in life."

"Way you keep out of jail," Hollings said, "is you either stay indoors and don't get in any trouble, or you pick a time to chop that tree down in the forest when there isn't anybody around to hear it."

Hollings didn't like the idea of aggressive women, women who pushed your hand where they wanted it to go. Women's lib or not, when it came to sex, it was the woman's job to lie there and try to enjoy it. Least that's what he'd thought. But here he was in bed with this big woman, the lady stronger than Hollings, and he was getting off on the way she was running things, pushing Hollings's finger down into her pubic patch now, showing him where to touch. Giving him a reward for agreeing to kill Tyler. Didn't matter it was a reward. Nookie was nookie, however you got it.

It wasn't easy letting go of a lifetime of macho training, becoming a liberated man. It wasn't a thing he'd set out on purpose to do. But he felt it happening. Becoming more relaxed with her, as she guided his hand, mumbling in his ear what he should do. Go slow, speed up, harder, softer.

Hollings looked over to where he'd set the GTA 1000 in the corner of his room. Seeing it there usually brought him down. But now, fingering Martina, looking at the GTA, he felt okay, even a little hopeful. Feeling like he was mastering a few things now, getting some control in his life. Feeling for the first time maybe what it felt like to be completely grown-up.

And all of that from going to the barbershop one day, seeing the Max Hunter sign in the window. Weird how just that little thing could lead him to this woman. In a way, it was the same as with beach prospecting. You went out every day not expecting a fortune or anything, just put yourself in the right place. You got a beep on your detector, you bent down, dug around in the sand. You just never knew. You just never fucking knew.

Martina had her eyes closed, a dreamy look. She'd let go of Hollings's hand, was letting him roam around down there on his own. Hollings believed he was getting the hang of it.

Martina squeezed her eyes shut, groaned, then pushed her head back into the pillow, and reached down to drag Hollings's hand away.

"What?"

"Not so hard," she said. "That was too goddamn hard again."

He started to reach back down there, but she fended his hand away.

"I had enough for the moment," she said. "I'm getting raw."

"All right."

"Anyway, there was something else I wanted to show you."

"Yeah?"

"Something I found that day I was over at Tyler's."

"Another thing you held out on Alvarez and me."

"That's right. I was planning on keeping it for myself, but now, you know with us getting along, I'm having second thoughts."

She got up out of bed, went over to where she'd dumped her clothes in a chair, and dug around in her pockets. She turned around and held up a piece of white paper. Naked black woman standing in his bedroom, full frontal, big breasts, going to share something with him. Man, even if she was ugly, at least she was his. Hollings lay back, enjoying this moment. Man, it was about time.

"So what is it? You gonna show me or what?"

"It's a map," Martina said, holding it out so he could see.

Hollings sat up.

"I believe what it is is a treasure map," she said. "And I think I just figured out how to read it."

"Just figured it out? When was that?"

"A minute ago."

"When I was feeling you up, you mean?"

"All right, yeah. When you were feeling me up, it came to me. A bolt from the blue, how to read this thing."

"Shit," he said. "You're in bed with somebody, doing sex, you shouldn't be thinking about a hundred other things. You should keep your mind on what's happening."

"How about four hundred million other things, Glenn? Four hundred million gold things? Would that be all right to think about?"

Hollings considered it. He felt a grin start to come to his lips.

He said, "Yeah, all right. I guess that's okay. Long as you're being distracted by gold, that's fine. Yeah, shit, that's probably even healthy."

CHAPTER 25

H AP TOLD WILLS HE'D MEET THEM AT THE RAWLINGS
Mill site later. He had a couple of errands first. Wills said fine. He'd
give the syringes and the vial to one of the patrolmen to take down
to the lab. Probably have some results later today.

Hap found Marguerite upstairs in Daniel's bedroom looking
out his window toward the bay. He kissed her good-bye, told her
he'd see her at the mill later, then another couple of kisses, drawing
them out, one of them lasting, starting to become something more,
moving them sideways toward the bed, then both of them fighting it
off, pulling away, breathless. They stepped back, still holding
hands.

Hap looked at her for a long moment, then told her if she
wanted, she could stay at the Mangrove House till further notice,
and she frowned mildly and said she had her own place, but thanks,
and he kissed her on the forehead and told her to be careful and
she told him to do the same, giving him a complicated look that
seemed about equal portions bewilderment and desire. He let go of
her hand and left.

At nine o'clock Hap was the second one through the door at
the Coconut Grove Bank. He didn't bother looking up Romero,
just went straight for the safety-deposit boxes, sat in the privacy
room and made another very careful tracing of the map, and replaced the original.

Then he went around the corner to the Grove library to check out their collection of maps. A man with hunched shoulders and red-tinted glasses listened to Hap, kept his head bowed, staring at Hap's sneakers. He wore a red-and-green checked shirt, tan pants stained with ink and food. His name tag said Harry.

"You have anything like that? Early navigational charts."

Without a word, the man turned and went behind the counter and through a door, slogging along like he was wearing an airtank and flippers. Hap didn't know if he was supposed to follow or what. He wasn't even sure Harry had heard him.

Hap hung around in front of the counter for a minute watching a couple of old guys reading newspapers, then he pushed through the swinging gate, went behind the counter and through the same door. In a glassed-in office at the back of the large room, he found Harry standing over several maps spread out on a long conference table.

"The best collection of antique maps in Dade County," Harry said. "1876, 1881, 1803, 1766. Which do you want?"

"I want photocopies of all of them. Just the coastline, say, from Palm Beach down to Miami."

Harry lifted his arm, brought his watch close to his face.

Hap said, "I'll pay whatever it costs."

Harry lowered his arm.

"I'll have them at one-thirty," he said.

"Okay, that's fine."

"And it'll cost you fourteen dollars and thirty-eight cents."

"Wow," said Hap. "You know the exact price?"

"I already added it up once today."

Hap reached out and gripped Harry's arm. The man shivered once, and jerked it from his grasp. Strong for a pudgy little guy. Harry bowed his head even lower.

"Who did you add it up for, Harry?"

"She didn't tell me her name."

"It was a woman?"

Harry nodded sadly as if he'd been caught in a shameful act.

Hap said, "And she wanted these same maps?"

"These same maps," he said. "Just the coastline."

"Was she black or white?"

"I couldn't tell."

"You couldn't tell?"

Harry lifted his head, seemed to have conquered his shyness enough to look at Hap for the first time.

"She called on the phone," he said. "I don't usually ask people their race on the phone."

"What time's she coming for it?" said Hap.

"One-thirty," he said. "Same as I told you."

"I'll give you ten bucks extra if you can get mine done earlier."

"Sixteen dollars extra," said Harry, "and you can have it at twelve-thirty. Before I go to lunch."

"Why sixteen?"

"Not a penny less," Harry said.

The guy probably had his eye on a new CD, something by the Talking Heads. Maybe he was one of those. A nerd at noon, a midnight jiver.

"Okay, sixteen bucks, twelve-thirty," said Hap.

"Plus the fourteen dollars and thirty-eight cents for the photocopies."

"Right."

Hap had to fight the last of the morning rush hour north on Twenty-seventh Avenue. Killed time by running a couple of different scenarios for this afternoon. Pick up his maps, hang around across the street in Peacock Park to watch who went into the library at one-thirty. Follow her when she came out. Or confront her right there on the sidewalk, take along his .45 just in case. Force her into his car, take her back to the Mangrove House, scare the shit out of her, maybe get a little truth in the process. Or else share all of this with Wills, throw him the surveillance, let him shape the plan. He couldn't decide. Preferred the lone wolf plan, but there were a lot of ways it could go sour.

Stopped at a light at Twenty-seventh and Flagler, Hap listened for the voice. Even its advice would've been some solace. But there was nothing. He tried to prod it, calling it a cowardly turd. A cheap, worthless asshole. Come on, speak up, you prick. What, you don't have a thought on the issue?

Nothing. Just a symphony of horns behind him at the light.

At the Rawlings Mill site, Wills's white Ford was parked under a couple of oaks next to the rocky drive. An acre of weeds and a couple of Florida hollies grown huge. Across South River Drive to the north was the Miami River. All along its banks were warehouses, loading platforms and cranes. The desolate industrial edge of the city. The Miami airport ten blocks to the west. Gray vapors in the air, jet exhaust, diesel fumes, benzine.

Sometimes on the tours of the Mangrove House, Hap used the opaque projector to show photographs the Commodore had taken of the Miami River a hundred years before. Back then it was a shadowy, twisting creek overhung with mangroves and live oaks, long gray tangles of moss. Just wide enough in some places for two canoes abreast. The egrets and spoonbills perched in the cross-hatching of limbs, their necks cocked to strike. It always looked cool in the photos, and even in the primitive black and white, the foliage appeared jade green and unbearably lush.

The modern river had been straightened, its banks stripped of all vegetation. They'd poured so much kerosene and diesel oil into it that there was a constant iridescent rainbow on its surface. Now the sad, sluggish river moved only when the locks were opened far inland, from a need to purge the wetlands of built-up phosphate runoffs or dangerously high levels of mercury.

Every once in a while someone, motivated by a pang of guilt or greed, started a campaign to clean up the river. A healthy river might attract hotels, condos, pricier restaurants. But the job was always found to be too dangerous. To dredge up the acid sludge that coated the river bottom might stir so many toxins into the water it could poison all of Biscayne Bay. Better to leave it be. Let the freighters continue to flush their bilges, the fuel tanks continue to seep, let the bullet-shredded corpses bloat and rot and float downstream, let the long death-dance proceed.

Hap found Marguerite and Wills standing in an exploratory trench, bent over a hole scooped in the rectangle of dirt.

Marguerite was holding a sheet of blueprint paper in her left hand, a trowel in her right. Widening the hole, she scraped a handful of dirt onto the blade of the trowel and dropped it onto the dustpan Wills was holding. He looked over his shoulder and nodded to Hap.

"No wonder this archaeology stuff takes so long," he said. "Been at this for half an hour, and we looked through exactly a half pint of dirt so far. She's just showing me how it works."

Marguerite turned and gave Hap a quick secret smile.

Maybe if he'd been to college and had specialized in psychology, gone on for his Ph.D., written books, done a lifetime of polls and studies and round-table discussions, interviewed every woman in North America, maybe then he'd be able to make some minor sense of love. How the hostility they'd felt toward each other could have actually been some kind of yearning, and how the two things could have tangled into an impossible ball of knots, and then all at once, with a tug on each end, a parlor trick, easy magic, it had all disappeared, become a simple strand again, become this smile of hers, this warm flood in his gut.

"We're standing just above the basement of Ramona's house," she said, holding up the blueprint. "It was beneath the kitchen."

"Like at the Mangrove House," Wills said. "The root cellar."

"From what I can gather," she said, shifting the blueprint in her hands. "This is the spot where Ramona's body was found. In the kitchen, approximately here."

"Well, this has all been very interesting," Wills said. "But as far as the current murder investigation is concerned, I'm afraid I don't see any reason to order an inch-by-inch on this particular location. Been so long since we had any rain, the ground's too hard to hold a decent footprint. That is, if he was abducted in the first place, and didn't just leave off working here to join somebody at the Sonesta. All we've found is a couple of pieces of glass, some metal objects, a nail or two that he must've dug up on that last occasion. But beyond that, there's nothing unusual here I can see. Nothing to warrant the man-hours necessary."

"Except for the shovel," she said.

"What shovel?" Hap stepped down into the trench.

"Ah, yes," Wills said as he reached behind the trench to a stump where a shovel was leaning. "I guess we'll have to run it for fingerprints too."

Wills held it out by the throat. For Hap to see, but not to touch. The Sears adhesive sticker still on the shiny blade.

"What's the big deal about a shovel? This is a dig site. You use shovels on the rubble till you get down to the pay dirt."

Wills said, "Well, it seems odd because there's a perfectly good shovel over there by the panning station. Marguerite says Daniel was the only one who worked this site, so it might suggest someone else came out here at some point, brought along a shovel because he wasn't sure there'd be one here. And this person used it and left it."

"Used it for what?"

Wills waved his hand at half a dozen holes that had been gouged in the smooth surface of the site.

Wills said, "She says they aren't the kind of holes you'd find on a site like this. You work with a trowel. Take teensy-weensy bites. But somebody was out here taking big bites. Somebody was tramping around, doing some heavy-duty digging."

"Somebody who didn't give a shit," she said, "what they destroyed. They were in such a hurry to find something."

Hap sat down on the edge of the trench. Some chilly sweat coating his back. He rubbed his eyes, and looked at both of them.

"What's wrong, man?"

"I just had a thought," he said.

"Must've been a doozy," said Wills.

"How long has Daniel been digging here?" he asked Marguerite. "How many months?"

"Less than a year," she said.

"What is it, Hap?"

"But it's possible, he could've come out here before that and nobody would've known, isn't that right? I mean, the place is so isolated."

Wills asked him what the hell he was driving at.

"I mean," Hap said, "if he came out here, fifteen years ago, twenty, to dig around here, nobody would object. Nobody would have even known, would they?"

"Probably not," she said.

"Is there a point here, Hap?"

He reached back, pulled the map from his pocket, unfolded it and held it out for both of them to see.

"And what do we have here?"

"I don't know for sure," Hap said. "But it might be a drawing of the river. The course it used to take, a hundred years ago."

"What?"

Marguerite set aside her blueprint and moved to Hap's side.

"And this star," said Hap. "That might be where we're standing now. A spot as far upstream as a ship could navigate."

"You don't look so good," Wills said. "Maybe you should put your head down between your legs."

Hap looked up at them.

"Either of you ever hear of the *Carmelita?*" he said. "A Spanish vessel? It was the kind of ship they called an *aviso.*"

"You left the shovel out there?"

"It doesn't matter."

"Goddamn you, Ray! You're such an idiot sometimes."

"I had on my work gloves," he said. "No fingerprints."

"Jesus Christ. That's not the point at all."

"Look, I was excited. I found the necklace, I wasn't thinking straight. Okay?"

"No, it's not okay. It's not the least little bit okay."

Garnetta sat back in her seat and looked at her fingernails. She hated the color. A sickly red, too much green in it. Made them almost brown, like she'd been scratching in the dirt. God. She should cut Alvarez's throat, dip her nails in the blood. That would fix two problems.

Nonchalant, he was driving up South River Drive, away from

the mill site. Just a few seconds ago, as they'd approached, she'd spotted the white Ford parked out near the road, and she'd almost died. Then there was Marguerite, the Tyler boy. The policeman standing between them. She'd slapped Alvarez on the shoulder. "Drive! Drive on by, you imbecile."

No one had looked over. No one had seen them.

Now she pointed out a parking lot behind a motel, a nice private place where they could discuss Alvarez's stupidity. He pulled the Rolls off, slid it into a spot and stopped.

"Turn the motor off, Ray. I want your full attention."

He didn't turn around. Just sat there, cool. He didn't even reach up to touch his hair. She sent the panel back down.

"Ray, tell me something."

"I'm at your disposal."

"*Now* what are you planning to do?"

"Same as I was."

"You can't go there tonight. That's out of the question."

"Why not?"

"Because you left the damn shovel there, Ray. Now the police, or the Tyler boy, or my own daughter may have figured it out. Somebody else is after what's buried there. They'll be watching the place."

"Doesn't matter," he said. "I'll take care of whoever's there. None of these buttfaces are a match for me."

Years ago, after Garnetta Rawlings had been mugged outside a Georgetown restaurant, she'd started carrying a pistol. A little chrome Smith & Wesson .22 with a ten-round magazine. Once a month she went out to the police range to fire it. Her pop-pops among all those booms. The media sometimes made a story out of it. Senator Rawlings gets four bull's-eyes. Deadeye Garnetta. Ray knew she carried it, so maybe he wasn't all that surprised when she took it out of her purse.

But she bet it made his heart stutter just a little when he felt it pressed against the back of his head.

"Hey," he said. "You don't need to do that."

"Ray, did you ever ask yourself why a United States senator might hire an ex-police sergeant, a policeman who was thrown off the force for misconduct? Did you, Ray? Did that ever occur to you?"

"You wanted to satisfy your cop-fucking urges," he said. "You get off on street stink. Makes you think you're tough. Or else it reminds you of the gutter you crawled out of, I don't know."

She used the barrel to muss his hair a little. Knowing how much it would irritate him.

"Oh, there's another reason I could offer. A more devious one."

She met his eyes in the rearview mirror. Took the pistol away from his head. She had his attention now.

"Ray, all my advisors urged me against it. Said it was a terrible idea. If the six o'clock news people ever got hold of it, they'd chew me up. Make me look like I had no respect for the law."

"But they haven't got hold of it, have they?"

"Oh, that's not the point, Ray. The point is, the reason I over-ruled their excellent advice is that I saw a potential payoff in hiring you."

He was quiet, looking at her in the rearview mirror. Sitting there, cold-eyed, like nothing had happened last night, like he hadn't whispered all those things in her ear.

She said, "The fact is, Ray, our relationship has been built on a foundation much like yours with Hollings."

"Bullshit. I won't jump off any fucking buildings for you."

"But think about it, Ray. Imagine how the media would react. I have to do that, you know. In my position, I can't look at things like normal people do. I have to picture everything I do as it might be portrayed on a television screen. Because, you see, Ray, if the media discovered your background, I could make it appear that you were a project of mine, this very bad boy I was trying to give a second chance. A reclamation exercise. And, Ray, try to picture if you will, whether anyone would question it, given your ugly history, if one day you were caught in the middle of some illegal act."

"You could step back," Alvarez said, "get out of the shit storm. Keep yourself clean."

"That's right, Ray."

"Don't think that hasn't crossed my mind."

"Or think about this," she said. "What if one day, God forbid, I was forced to shoot you dead."

"Yeah," he said. "And why would you shoot me?"

A black kid came around the corner of the motel. Fifteen, sixteen, bouncing to a beat. He stopped and stared at the Rolls. Looked over his shoulder, then right and left. He squinted at the darkened windows.

"Ray," Garnetta said. "Do you remember about the Mayans? Their religion. Anything at all that I told you?"

The black kid edged cautiously to the car, brought his face close to the driver's window. Pressed his nose against it.

"The fucking Mayans again?" Alvarez said. "Oh, brother."

"You remember about the ball game?"

Alvarez ran his window down, and the black kid stepped back.

"You Jimenez?" the kid said.

"No."

"I supposed to meet Jimenez."

"In the backseat," Alvarez said.

The kid leaned over, tried the handle on the rear door. Locked. He tapped his big ring on the glass next to Senator Rawlings. She sent the window down, lowered the pistol out of view.

"Hey, you ain't Jimenez."

"That's true," she said. "I certainly ain't."

He shot a bird at Alvarez's darkened window, then pointed himself back toward the corner of the motel and be-bopped in that direction. She raised her window.

"You were saying?"

"I was saying that the Maya used their very best athletes in the ball game. Their bravest, swiftest warriors. And these men tried extremely hard to score a goal. Their priests were looking on. Leaders from nearby cities. But it was most difficult to accomplish. The ball was only a fraction smaller than the hole it had to fit through. Not impossible to score a goal, but very difficult. That's the point. It wasn't impossible. They might play continuously for days sometimes before the ball fit through the small stone circle, but it would fit. Eventually it would fit.''

"Like you and me," Alvarez said. "Eventually I always fit.''

She took a long breath, looked down at the pistol.

"It is a beautiful culture, Ray. Full of complexity and intelligence. But what you have to ask yourself is, How did it get to be so magnificent? Do you know, Ray? What made the Maya so great? What was their secret?"

"Why don't you tell me."

"It was because their leaders had absolute, life-and-death control over the people. That's why. There was no first amendment, second amendment. There were no guarantees, personal liberty, all men created equal. It was either do right, or die. It was either excel, or be killed.

"In that ball game, Ray, the winners were greatly honored. Given special rights, access to the temples, and to knowledge no one else in their community enjoyed. But the losers, Ray, you remember what happened to the losers, don't you?"

"They got their heads cut off."

"That's right. The priests cut off their heads. The head of every one of the losers."

"How I know that is," he said, "you told me that stupid story already. And it didn't scare me the first time either."

"It's not meant to scare you, Ray. I remind you of it now to inform you. Merely to let you know how things stand with me. On the one hand, if you succeed, I can open the doors of the innermost sanctum for you, Ray. Take you places you could never go otherwise. But on the other hand, if you screw up, if you lose the game, Ray . . . Well, you can see what I'm saying, I'm sure."

"Don't worry about me, Senator. I'm a good shot. I'll get that ball through, no problem."

"Yes, Ray," she said. "And if you don't, at least we're all very clear about the consequences."

He was silent, keeping his eyes from her.

She said, "Now, Ray, you're going to take me to the Brickell Bay Club. I have a speech to make. A war chest to fill."

"Yes, ma'am," he said. "Right away, Senator."

CHAPTER 26

I T TOOK HOLLINGS TWICE AS LONG AS NORMAL TO GET
dressed. He kept putting shirts on, taking them off, until he decided, hell, okay, he'd wear the one he really wanted to wear. The
shiny green rayon with red Indy cars on it. Also STP stickers, Holly
Full Race Cams logos. He'd bought it last Christmas. A present to
himself, wanting to buy a shirt that would be fun to wear. Something he could put on to celebrate, if anything worth celebrating
ever came along. But this was the first time he'd taken it off the
hanger. For the last eight months, it'd just hung there, back of the
closet, depressing him every time he saw it.

Except for that one shirt, clothes had never been an issue for
him. He usually walked into a K mart store, ran his eyes down the
nearest shirt rack he came to and picked up the first shirt that
didn't make him want to throw up, and carried it over to the regis-
ter. That was shopping.

But today, going out with Martina to pick up their maps at the
library, Hollings decided yeah, today was finally the day. The red
race car shirt was how he felt. Fast and hot. Heart going like it was
turbocharged.

"That what you're wearing?" Martina said.

Hollings was putting on a pair of Levi's jeans. His newest ones
with the leather label still on them.

"You got something against jeans?"

"No, but I got something against little red toy cars," she said. "Don't you have something more grown-up?"

Hollings went back to his closet, stripped off the shirt and wadded it. Pitching it back into the corner.

He took out a solid yellow and a blue-and-white striped, and held them both up.

"How about one of these?"

"The striped one."

"Jesus," he said. "I liked the race cars. What's wrong with it, that's what I want to know?"

"It stands out."

"So? Maybe I want to stand out today."

"This isn't the day for it, Glenn. We're going treasure hunting, remember? We're going out in public. You want to be dressed so you can go up to somebody, spend five minutes dealing with them, and then walk away and the guy can't give a decent description of you."

"So whatta *you* going to do then? Put a garbage bag over your head?"

Martina was wearing the clothes she'd had on before. Taken a shower and put back on those dirty clothes. Hard for Hollings to imagine. Stone-washed gray jeans, a long-sleeved blue blouse, more of a T-shirt, with a little fox or some kind of animal over her left tit.

"The thing about you, Martina, people don't ever notice what you're wearing, 'cause they're too busy trying to figure out what it is makes you so ugly."

"Wear your shirttail out," she said.

He'd already tucked it in. He was standing in front of the mirror in his bedroom, looking at Martina behind him there, sitting on the bed, lacing up her silver running shoes.

"Wear it out so it'll hide the pistol in your belt. We're gonna be strapped from this point on till we got the treasure and are off somewhere else."

"What's that mean, off somewhere?"

"Costa Rica, Guatemala, Ontario. Somewhere like that. Once

we get a couple thousand miles away, we'll start looking for a place we like."

"Well, shit, that's the first word I heard about that."

"You don't think we're going to stay around here, do you? All the heat there'll be."

"What heat? We go out into the ocean, swim down and get the gold, and we're done. Where's any heat?"

"You forget what you're going to do then?"

"Oh, yeah. Tyler."

"Tyler is one, Alvarez is two. And anybody else pops up, and gets in the way."

Hollings said, "Why we gotta stick Alvarez? I don't see any point fucking around with him again in any fashion whatsoever."

"Christ, Hollings. The man's got our names in his Rolodex. Knows details about us. Once he finds out we got the gold, he'll be after us sure as shit. Either sic the police on us or hire some bounty hunter, that or try to track us down himself. No, sir. We gotta do Alvarez too. No way around it."

"Christ. That guy, I hate messing with him again."

Martina got her laces done, and stood up and came over to stand beside Hollings. She smiled at him in the mirror. Those gold teeth. Hollings still wasn't used to them.

"So we do Alvarez, we do Tyler. Shit, there anybody we aren't going to kill?"

"We're not going to kill each other," she said. Giving him a wink. "Unless one of us acts up."

There it was again. Somebody saying something that made sense but didn't make sense. He thought for a minute about asking her what the hell she'd meant, but she was standing back from him now, looking him over, and he was afraid if he said anything else, challenged her in some way, she'd go quiet, and that was even worse.

Hollings said, "When we get the four hundred million in gold and shit, then I'll wear the race car shirt. Then there'll be something to celebrate."

She smiled again, this time not showing any teeth. A sad smile, covering up something else she was thinking. The kind of smile Hollings's mother used to give him. She'd be drinking in her bedroom, sitting up against the pillows, Ronrico bottles on the floor, the shades down, Hollings home from school, and he'd ask her, Ma, you doing okay? I get you anything? Some more rum? And she smiled that way. No, nothing, Glenn, she'd say. Just be a good boy. Be my good sweet simple boy. That's what she'd say, just about every afternoon. And it was how she smiled, covering up how she really felt. That same smile every afternoon till she ran off with the guy who came to check the electric meter. Hollings was fourteen. Never heard a word from her again.

Alvarez took the senator to the Brickell Bay Club, then instead of waiting around with the other jerkface chauffeurs, bunch of fags, half of them wore perfume and had fake British accents, he left the Rolls there, caught a cab back to his place in Kendall. From now on he'd use his white Ford Fairlaine. Black walls, just like the plain-clothes guys drove. Alvarez liked the hell out of that car. Everywhere he went, people looked at him when he got out of it, thinking he was the law. Standing back, giving Alvarez room.

He'd been considering it for some time. Dump the senator, go off on his own. Now, her pressing the pistol to his head like that, giving him her little speech about the fucking Maya again, how easy it would be for her to shoot him and walk away, he decided it was time, maybe even a little past time.

Not that he was scared of the old lady. Hell no. He could handle her easy. But there was just no good reason to hang out with her anymore. It was clear now, she wasn't going to move Alvarez into the penthouse, or even the floor below. He was her junkyard dog, her low-rent diddle, and it was all he was ever going to be. Her and her Maya phony baloney. All that high priestess bullshit had gotten into her bloodstream, made her hungry for more power than she could have just being a senator. What she wanted was to be a fucking dictator, walk around, wear her five-hundred-year-old necklace, decide every day who lived, who died. No sir. That was the end of it for the two of them. He was jumping down from that speeding train.

It was eleven-forty by the time he got home. His boy, Ricky, would be getting out of summer school in another hour and would go over to Alvarez's sister's in Hialeah. If Alvarez didn't come to pick him up, the sister would just keep him indefinitely. And that was what was going to happen this time. She'd do a better job of raising the kid anyway. Make him softer than Alvarez would like, but still, all in all, it was probably better for the kid, let him live longer.

Alvarez went into the den. Looked at himself in the mirror. Got out his comb and took a couple of strokes to get everything going the same way again. Then he went into the bathroom off the den, opened the linen closet, and pulled out the three or four towels and washrags in there. He jimmied the shelves out, set them on the floor. He craned in, found the swivel lock he'd put up in the right-hand corner, twisted it, pried open the compartment, and pulled that out too.

Alvarez had met some gun nuts in his time. Guys that collected every kind of heavy artillery ever manufactured. Most of them, when it came right down to it, were pussies. Guys who had pecker troubles of one kind or another and this was the way they were working it out for themselves. Uzis, antitank guns. Christ, he even knew of a guy up in Opa Locka who was just pawing at the ground, waiting till he got a message over the shortwave receiver he had inside his head that it was time to take his collection of Sidewinder missles out to the perimeter road next to Miami International and start bringing down jumbo jets.

But Alvarez was no gun nut. He had only one. And no more Remingtons for him either, the weapon he'd taken down to Jamaica. He'd switched to a Franchi SPAS 12-gauge dual action with the two and three-quarter inch chamber, pistol grip, folding metal butt. Front blade sight and rear peep. It was a recoil-operated semi-automatic with slide-action backup. A seven-shot magazine that he'd expanded to twelve.

A man didn't need a dozen different kinds of weapons. It made more sense to have just the one. To be an expert with it. The

Franchi SPAS was his. Ray Alvarez took it out of the gun rack behind the linen closet's false wall. He might be able to get by with less firepower. When you got right down to it, there wasn't anybody he'd run across lately he couldn't handle bare-handed. But why risk it? This was the job of a lifetime. The four-hundred-million-dollar job. Yeah. Shoot the works on this one. The Franchi SPAS and four boxes of three-inch steel Magnum shells. You could bring down a lot of geese with four boxes of Magnum load.

Man, he'd like to be there about now at the Brickell Bay Club. The senator finishes her chicken cordon bleu, she goes up to the podium, looks out at this bunch of bankers and lawyers and other assorted rich fucks, and then starts in giving them her full load of free-enterprise horseshit for fifteen minutes. They're out there drinking their coffee, clinking their spoons, eating the last of their Key lime pie, and she's jerking them off, telling them what a good job they're doing ripping off the poor and hungry. That was her job, near as Alvarez could tell. Twice a month another of these fat cat clubs would invite her to lecture after the cordon bleu lunch, just so she could tell 'em it was all right what they were doing. It was good for the country, good for the world that these fat fucks were getting as rich as possible, stealing every loose dollar in sight.

Near the end of her speech she'd tell a joke or two, something downhome she'd heard in one of the projects, or in a day-care center, or abortion clinic, or one of those places she liked to criticize. And then right at the end she'd tell them just like she always did, that it was up to them. They had the key to all the problems. All they had to do was keep on humping for more cash flow, keep on sticking it to the lower classes, everybody was going to be better for it, sharper, faster, more competitive. She'd wave her hand at whatever applause she got. Sometimes standing ovations, sometimes just polite patting, depending on how the stock market was doing that week.

And then she'd shake a few hands, pat a few good old boys on the back, and she'd work her way to the back of the room, start looking around for old Alvarez, keep edging toward the door, not seeing him anywhere, and she'd wind up outside on the sidewalk at valet parking, starting to get the idea finally.

That was when the guy Alvarez had paid twenty bucks to, Francis, the guy with the bad teeth and the jittery eyes, would come up to her wearing Alvarez's white captain's hat with the gold braid. And he'd tell the senator what Alvarez had paid him the twenty to say.

Senator Rawlings, Ray Alvarez said to tell you something's come up and he's not working for your shriveled-up old ass anymore. He's awful sorry, but he got himself a better offer. Then Alvarez hoped Francis remembered the best part. The part about how if the senator wanted him to, Francis could take her over to his place now, and her and him could split a bottle of Thunderbird wine and then get it on. 'Cause he'd heard how even though the senator was kind of sluggish in bed, a little dried out, a good strong hit of street stink could really get her going.

Alvarez was sorry he had to miss that. He truly was.

Marguerite said, "I don't care if there's a hundred treasure ships buried on this land, the most important thing to me is Ramona's remains. And I'm not going to have anybody endangering them just to look for some Spanish ship they think might be here."

They were in the shade of an oak tree, Wills leaning against the panning table. A small creek glimmered in the woods nearby. Seemed to have gone stagnant. A fog of insects around it.

"Your great-grandmother's remains?" said Wills, looking out at the acre.

"I want this place protected, Wills, do you hear me?"

"I hear you, I hear you."

"You've got to post a guard here, Wills," Marguerite said. "I mean, you don't have to explain what it's for, just get somebody out here to watch the place."

"What? I don't need to explain what the guard's for?" Wills chuckled. "That's what you think? I just go in and say, hey, Captain, I need a thirty-thousand-dollar-a-year guy in uniform to stand around on an acre off South River Drive. Don't ask me why. Just trust me. He won't be wasting his time.

"Oh, okay, Captain, if you must know, it's because of this treasure ship we think is buried on the land there. Yeah, about five miles inland, yeah. I know it sounds crazy, but Hap Tyler, you remember him, well, yeah, old Hap has a map, actually just a jagged line running down the center of a page, and he thinks that line might be the shape of the river a few hundred years ago. And there's a star next to the line, and Hap Tyler, yeah, *that* Hap Tyler. Well, Hap thinks this star is the X that marks the spot, you know. And oh, yeah. There's a shovel. It's new, and it's just sitting there. So that obviously proves something, don't you think, Captain? Don't you think it'd be a good idea to take a guy out of Liberty City, say, or out of downtown mugger patrol, let him stand around on this big old empty lot and make sure nobody digs anything up there? Whatta you think, Captain?"

Wills looked at the two of them, and said, "That sound like a good idea to you, huh? Good use of your tax dollars?"

Hap watched a man pushing a shopping cart down South River Drive. In the ninety-degree heat, he was wearing a blue pea jacket and a watch cap, fighting off some inner freeze.

"And by the way," Wills said, "just so you two know what kind of people we're dealing with here, that wasn't Martin Phelps's body you found on your lawn last night."

"It wasn't?"

Wills pulled out his handkerchief, patted his neck dry. With a finger he combed a strand of hair back in place.

"Dispatcher called me a few minutes ago, just before you got here, Hap. Put me through to Bachay's office. That corpse was a lady by the name of Deshawna Barkley. A pretty good arrest record in her own right."

"I don't get it."

"Well, let me put it this way. Deshawna's main claim to fame other than being a thief and a hooker was she was Martin Phelps's girlfriend. At least she was couple of years ago when he was still a man."

Wills glanced up at a helicopter flying over.

When it was out of earshot he said, "Of the five murders Martin Phelps is wanted for, all of them are former girlfriends. All murdered in the two years since Phelps escaped from prison."

"Jesus," Marguerite said.

"So what I'm saying to you two is, we got us a serious problem here. A real problem. This isn't just some treasure hunt. We're talking about a very dangerous guy who seems to be taking an interest in your welfare. Maybe he wants to adjust your life span, I don't know. But in my book, that's worth an extra policeman or two, not posting a man out here to guard somebody's hundred-year-old grave."

"Okay," Marguerite said. "You put it that way."

"Well, good."

"But I don't understand it," she said. "A man becomes a woman, then starts killing his old girlfriends. Why?"

"Maybe it's his way of starting over," Wills said. "Wipe the slate clean. Kill everybody reminds you of the old life. Or maybe, I don't know, maybe down deep he hates himself so much, if anybody gets affectionate with him, he gets crazy, turns on them."

"In any case," Hap said. "Those estrogen shots he's getting, apparently they aren't working."

"Guys like this make my job so much easier," Wills said. "They find something they like, man, it becomes a compulsion. They couldn't stop if you cut off their arms and legs. They'd find a way, get themselves a new girlfriend, kill her. Get another one, kill her."

"Only you'd think, the way he is now," said Hap, "he'd have a boyfriend."

"Well, maybe he does," said Wills. "And he just hasn't gotten around to making the poor sucker into a corpse yet."

CHAPTER 27

"THAT LIBRARIAN GUY, HE TOLD US ONE-THIRTY,"
Hollings said. "Wouldn't be ready till then." Fast-walking along
behind Martina. They'd parked the Bel Aire in the covered lot at
CocoWalk, a new pink and neon shopping place a couple of blocks
away, and now Martina was striding along so fast, Hollings had to
take a skip step every few feet to keep up. "Christ, it isn't even noon
yet. Whatta you want to go in there so early for?"

"I like to get places ahead of time. Settle in, check the vibes.
It's the way I always been. There a vocabulary word for that? Somebody's always early?"

"Yeah," Hollings said. "Premature ejaculator."

She glanced sideways at him.

Hollings said, "Let's stop, have a beer, wash down those
McMuffins."

"We're going in the library, Glenn. Maybe I'll browse, find a
book to read. Get as smart as you are."

"It'd take a lot more than one fucking book."

They passed a red-haired woman in a tube top and white
shorts, going the same direction. Hollings turned around to check
her out and she smiled at him, and he smiled back.

Man, the world was different when you were getting laid. Like
some kind of sex musk was collecting in his body hair, and women
could smell it and it made them smile. Got their nectar flowing. It

reminded him a little of foraging for coins with the GTA. Out walking and winking, winking and walking. You never knew what you'd come across out here.

Tagging along behind Martina right then, Hollings could swear the air was sweeter, the light had a buttery color. The palms and oaks over in the park across Main Highway appeared shadier than he'd ever seen trees. All the cars driving by had just been washed and polished, all the people were fresh from the shower, dusted with talcum and sprinkled with lime scent. There was jazzy music coming from down the street, from a car or out the front door of a restaurant, and it was just right, everybody walking in time to it, the sparrows hopping on the bird feeder out in front of the library, one hop for every beat. Hollings was hungry and satisfied at once, ready for whatever was coming. Breathing deep and clean. Man, all that from a little sex.

"You ever read a book, Martina, one wasn't all pictures?"

"Just keep insulting me, Hollings. That's what women like."

"I'm joking around with you. Can't you tell the difference? What's wrong, you got no ear for humor?"

Martina stopped abruptly at the front of the Grove Library. Two old women were helping each other down the last couple of steps. One of them had a little white poodle in her arms and the goddamn dog snarled at Martina as the old ladies passed by.

"You're starting to piss me off, Glenn. That's not a good development."

Hollings said, "Hey, I joke around. Sometimes it turns out, it's not that funny. All right. I'm sorry. I was joking is all. It's the way I am." He brought his voice down to a whisper. "Like you and that goddamn head in the washer. Now, that wasn't funny. And believe me, it isn't ever going to be either."

"So far," Martina said, "I haven't heard one thing come out of your mouth was anything but stupid. So why don't you just give it a rest, man. A complete rest. Know what I'm saying?"

"Yeah, yeah, yeah."

The redhead in the tube top had caught up to them and came walking past, and Hollings gave her a wink this time. She winked back. The sex musk still working. Or, wait. Maybe it was something deeper than that, something that wouldn't wash off, like it had seeped down into his bloodstream. God, wouldn't that be something. A whole different thing happening between him and women. Hot damn.

"Now we're going in here," Martina said, "one at a time. And we're not going to sit together or look at each other or act like we know who the other one is. You got that?"

"I heard you, but I don't know what the big deal is."

"Hollings," she said, getting a hiss in her voice. She bared her gold teeth at him, cheeks stretched so tight her skin looked like that film on top of chocolate pudding, like it might crack any second. She took him by the biceps and dragged him over behind a mailbox, glanced up and down the street. "Look, you moron, until I've got that gold and I'm two thousand miles from here, we're on alert. Full-scale alert. We're taking precautions. Okay?"

Hollings said, "Whatta you mean, "*I've* got the gold, *I'm* two thousand miles from here. That's what you said, I. Not we."

She sighed, shook her head. Kept scanning the surroundings till she was starting to make Hollings a little nervous too.

"It's a way of talking," she said. "That's all. Till you and me're two thousand miles from here. Okay, is that better?"

"You're planning on dumping me, aren't you?"

"Fuck, Hollings. Let's just get in there, in the goddamn library. See if the map's ready, and don't act like you know me, all right. Now come off this shit. I'm not dumping you. I like you, boy. We got a thing going. We're hot, we're cooking."

Hollings smiled warily.

"Yeah, we are, aren't we? Cooking."

As they were going up the stairs, another good-looking woman with short blond hair came out the door. She was carrying a stack of books, pressing them up against her tight T-shirt. Hollings gave her a regulation, factor-five smile, a wink too.

The woman saw him, went on down a couple of steps, then stopped, came back up so she was standing on the step just below

Hollings. She had big lips, five or six earrings in one ear. She moved her books a little and he saw her shirt said SO MANY MEN, SO FEW BRAINS.

"Excuse me," she said. "Did you speak to me?"

"No," Hollings said. "But if I had, I would've said you were awful cute." Then he winked at her again.

"Fuck off," she said. "Or I'll break you in two."

Hollings kept smiling at her.

"If you did that, young lady," he said, "then I guess there'd be two of me thought you was awful cute."

The woman shifted the books in her arms like she was getting ready to shoot a karate kick at him. He kept smiling and finally she made an exasperated snort and walked off. Hollings stood there and watched her go. Martina had already disappeared into the library.

He guessed what it was, his sex musk must've been evaporating a little, standing out in that August heat, the sun sucking it right off him. Probably all he needed was another hour or two in the sack with Martina, he'd get it back. Another couple of hours learning to take his time.

The voice, the goddamn voice, came to Hap out of nowhere just as he sped through the last second of the yellow light at Twenty-seventh and Dixie, going south into the Grove. Like a high frequency whistle, something only sharp-eared dogs and the deeply insane could hear. Followed by the stab of an icepick into an overinflated tire, a violent sizzle of air. He nearly wrenched the car into a bicyclist.

The goddamn voice shivered up his backbone, fizzing against his neck. Sounding like a tea kettle shuddering on the reddened coils, hissing, ready to scream. He saw a parking space just before Tigertail Avenue and swerved the MG into it, reached up and cranked the rearview mirror around to see his face, how red it was, or white. But nothing showed.

Now it was silent. And for a moment Hap thought what he'd heard might not have been the voice after all, but some biological failure inside his body, some small aneurysm erupting, a vessel trickling blood into cavities where it didn't belong. Or a spew of stomach gas from the huge breakfast Marguerite had made them this morning.

The daylight had dimmed, and his chest was tight. He rested his hand on the shifter knob and watched a skinny Latin kid poke through a Dumpster up ahead. It was probably just stress. Pressure building up inside him, probing for fissures until it found light, then spurted through.

That seemed to be the source of all the troubles these days, the great culprit, stress. Everybody suspended in the same quivering jelly of tension. Packed tight, too many rats in the cage, the tread-mills going nonstop, the lights never off. No dark, no quiet, no real sleep. Everyone revving, revving. Jaws clamped, teeth grinding, all the teapots at full boil.

He had to stop this shit. He had to break its hold. He'd been believing in the voice whenever it reappeared, trusting in it since that night in Nha Trang, the night it saved his life. But now, sitting there, watching the kid lean into the Dumpster, he thought maybe he'd been wrong. Wrong then, wrong ever since. Maybe if he'd jumped down that night, gone with his platoon, he could have made the difference, an extra pair of ears, an extra M-16. One extra guy swinging the whole thing the other direction, beating back the VC ambush. Why not?

And the Grande Biscayne episode, burning the trailer that night. Had that changed anything? Hell, no. Shorty Busser had gone right ahead with it. The building got built. Nothing good whatsoever had come from the voice. Ever. It had just been fucking him up. Wasting his time, isolating him from everybody.

People found a way to live with worse things. There were people who heard ringing in their ears every minute of their lives. There were people who picked up rock stations on their braces. There were the truly insane. Everybody had voices. Daniel told him so. His shrink at Radisson had said so too. Everybody had them. Good voices, bad, impish, evil, nightmarish, goofy. Everyone heard them. But only the weak and foolish obeyed them. Only the easily hypnotized, the mush-headed.

Hap took a passable breath, massaged his neck for a minute, then started the car and pulled back out into the traffic on Twenty-seventh. A block, another block. No noise inside his head or gut. A right onto Bayshore, past the Grande Biscayne, around the big curve, and he swung into a space twenty feet from the library. Quarter after twelve. Fifteen minutes early.

He found Harry in the large back room. Head down, sealing magazines into leather binders, working at a heat press.

"I got your money, Harry."

Harry lifted his eyes an inch or two from the stack of *Modern Photography* until he was staring at Hap's knees. Hap raised a shoe and waggled it in his line of sight.

"Remember me? Guy in the Keds. One that wanted the maps?"

"Thirty dollars and thirty-eight cents," said Harry, still fixed on Hap's knees.

"I got it right here."

"The money first, then the maps."

Harry the hardass bargainer, been in Miami long enough to know if you didn't get it upfront, you probably weren't going to get it at all.

Hap took out his wallet. Counted out thirty-one dollars and handed them to him.

"They came out pretty good," he said. "The photocopies did."

The librarian led him into a small office. Stenciled on the door was HARRY WELBORN, REFERENCE LIBRARIAN. The room was so neat it might have been vacant, waiting for its first occupant.

Harry opened a drawer and laid the stack of paper on the desk in front of him. Hap spread them out, side by side, and made a quick check to see if the Miami River was marked on each map. It was. On all of them, the river went west off the bay and just a few hundred yards from its mouth, it cut a sharp dogleg to the north. The rapids were marked on all four.

"Great, Harry. Thanks."

"No problem," he said. Harry the conversationalist. Couldn't

shut this guy up. Probably went home at night, got drunk and yak-
ked to his parakeet till dawn.

"You can keep the change."

Harry nodded like he'd planned on it anyway.

Harry said, "Your friends were by already."

"My friends?"

Harry ducked his head and was mute.

Hap said, "The ones who ordered the maps?"

Harry made two quick nods.

"Shit," Hap said. "I missed them."

"No," said Harry. "They're still out there. I told them about
you and they said they've been dying to meet you."

"They said that?"

"Yeah. The exact words. Dying." Harry made a sour face.
"Those two are no good. You got lousy friends."

"Not my friends, Harry. Quite the contrary."

Hap folded the pages, tucked them in his back pocket and
walked out through the large work area. A couple of older women
sat in front of computers, one was talking on the phone. A youngish
black kid in a singlet and shorts was standing on a stepladder fiddling with the smoke alarm.

The voice, loud and forceful, told him to go. Escape out the
back way. Hurry!

Hap halted by the double swinging doors out to the main
stacks. Go. Fast. Out the back, go. A wave of gooseflesh flowed up
his back. Go. Go. Go. Rising in volume. Its wordless message piercing straight to Hap's nerve centers. Run for your life. Run. Run.

Hap hesitated at the door, peered out the eye-level window slit
in one of the swinging doors. He sucked down a breath, blew it out,
sucked down another. Readying himself, as if he were about to take
a deep dive, had only this one chance before what was sinking
slowly to the dark ocean floor was gone forever from his grasp.
Another breath, then he pushed open the door. The voice was
there, telling him to break into a run, raise it to a sprint, dodge the
young couple with their child, go faster toward the front door, cut
around a table and out into the street.

Hap walked across the room. He took his sweet damn time. The hair on his neck stiffening. He smiled, nodded to the young couple. Nodded to the librarian helping them. Nodded to the guy coming into his path from the left, a guy with brown hair cut in a flattop, a button-down shirt with the shirttail out. The guy didn't nod back, but blocked Hap's way just beside the globe stand. A kid, five or six in a green T-shirt, was spinning the globe, trailing his finger across it till it came to a stop.

The guy with the flattop lifted the tail of his shirt and showed Hap a .45 wedged in his belt. And even then, even as he saw the man's small eyes shift over Hap's shoulder toward the footsteps that were coming up quickly behind him, even then Hap was certain he'd done right to finally ignore the voice. Better or worse, at least he couldn't blame this or anything else on the voice, on the Commodore, on anybody. This was it, by god. For the first time since that night in Nha Trang, he was on his own.

The man gripped Hap's shirt, brought him close.

"Let's don't have any fuss now, you hear," he whispered in Hap's face. "It's a fucking library. Got to keep our voices down, know what I mean."

"Fuss?" Hap said. "Me make a fuss?"

The man let Hap go and moved behind his shoulder, nudged him toward the front door. Hap glanced to his right and the black woman with the cornrows smiled at him from a couple of feet away near the encyclopedias. Martin Phelps. She looked at the flattop guy and swept her hand toward the door.

"Move it," the guy said, and nudged him again.

Hap threw an elbow into the guy's chest, lunged to his left, gripped the base of the globe, swiveled and swung it into the guy's face. He staggered back and Hap hammered him again, dropped the globe, and seized the man's shirt. Got his gun from under his shirt, and pivoted quickly toward where the black woman had been. Not there.

The kid who'd been spinning the globe was edging away. A couple of middle-aged ladies had halted at the front door of the library and were watching the tussle from the steps. Irritated expressions. Another mugging had clogged up the traffic.

Hap was vaguely aware of chairs scraping. He heard a door slam, people rushing to other exits. With the flattop guy groaning at his feet, Hap turned his back to the front door, and panned the .45 around the room.

"Come on, now," he called out. "Let's step outside, Martin. Talk this whole thing over. You want to talk to me, I want to talk to you. No reason for any civilians to get hurt now."

Hap caught a flash in the stacks to his right. He glanced down at the flattop guy, still groggy. Or maybe playing possum. Hap bent down, and with the butt of the .45 gave him a modest thunk on the back of his head. Sominex with a lump.

He hustled over to the stacks. Listened. But over the crying of a baby in the back, he could make out nothing. The shelves were gray metal, about a dozen rows of them filling this wing, narrow aisles on either side. Stooping, he tried to peer through the open slots between the books, but it was no use. She was crouched down back there somewhere, her pistol cocked.

He could work down one of the aisles, row by row till he'd flushed her. Risk her getting behind him somehow, reverse the roles of the hunt. He glanced back at the flattop guy still on the floor. A few feet away the kid in the T-shirt approached, a half smile on his face.

"Is this a movie?" the kid said. He was standing out in the middle aisle, studying Hap like he was trying to place him, which video he'd seen him in lately.

Hap heard a flutter of movement back in the stacks. He waved the kid off, but the boy just smiled.

In a harsh whisper, Hap said, "Yeah, it's a movie. Get the hell back or we'll have to shoot this scene again."

There was another scrape a few feet into the stacks.

"Anybody back there?" Hap shouted. "Anybody innocent? Let me hear you if you are. Call out now, 'cause I'm about to start shooting."

No response.

Hap crouched and put his right shoulder against the first shelf and rocked his weight into it. He tipped it an inch or two off the ground, but it came back down. Like trying to budge a bulldozer.

"Need help?"

Harry stood a few feet away. Eyes bright.

"How much will it cost me, Harry?"

"On the house," he said. "I don't like that woman. She stiffed me for the photocopies."

The librarian stepped in beside Hap, and they planted their shoulders against the same shelf. Hap one-two-threed and they groaned in unison, and that goddamn Harry must've ripped up fireplugs in his spare time, because the shelf rocked up easily, leaning over. A few books falling to the floor, and then it crashed against the next one and the dominoes began to fall. One after the other, a tidal wave of books and metal.

When it was done, Hap winked his thanks and Harry hurried over to the kid in green, picked him up like a sack of groceries and hustled him away.

Hap found the black woman pinned in the next to last row. Under an avalanche of Hardy and Brontë.

"Martin Phelps?"

The woman looked up at him, a scowl twisting her face.

"Martina," she said.

"Well, get up, Martina. There's somebody dying to meet *you*."

With the pistol in his left hand, Hap used his right to budge the shelf off Martina's legs. She dragged herself backward a couple of feet, books tumbling all around her.

A half second before the blow came, Hap saw Martina's eyes change, her lips pull into a smile. It was a vase, a glass vase. The narrow kind that holds a single rose, thick and heavy, and with a pebbled surface, the sort you buy in the hospital drugstore. He saw the vase through a yellow haze as he swung around to face the flattop guy, the light wavering, his eyelids drawing down. He heard the .45 he'd been holding clatter to the floor.

"Wait a minute," Martina said, her voice distant. A bad connection getting worse. "I owe him one too."

Hap sagged, starting to drown in the yellow haze. He reached a hand out toward the flattop guy, grasping for a lifebuoy, anything to keep his chin above water. The guy stepped back.

"Be my guest," the guy said to Martina.

And Hap heard the sickening crunch of another blow against his skull and he began a long, numb slide into black.

# CHAPTER 28

"**B**OOKMOBILE?" WILLS SAID. "WHATTA YOU CALLING ME about a goddamn stolen bookmobile?"

He looked over at Marguerite, shook his head at the outrageousness of it all. She was standing at her desk in the newsroom, out there in the wide open pandemonium. Middle of the afternoon, the phones ringing, people at their screens, mail carts, a couple of groups gathered here and there, messengers bustling in and out. Nobody paying any attention to her and Wills.

After Wills dropped her off at the Grande Biscayne to pick up her car, they'd gone their separate ways. She drove home, showered, put on a pair of beige slacks and a blue-and-white-striped blouse. Her skin still with a faint whiff of skunk. Then drove to work.

Wills appeared beside her desk about five-thirty, smiled, and said he'd thought of a couple more questions, things about the senator, but before he got around to them his beeper went off. And now he was using her phone, standing there, his eyes on her the whole time, giving her looks like she could hear the whole story and was just as bowled over as he was.

"Did anybody get a look at these people?"

Wills shrugged at her and put his hand over the mouthpiece and whispered at her, "Hap. Kidnapped."

Wills said into the phone, "Yes, that's the description. Yeah, close enough, the gold teeth, right. Martin Phelps. Yeah. Do it all-points. Dade County Bookmobile, now that shouldn't be so hard to spot, huh? Right, armed and dangerous. Right, right.'' Wills shooting her looks she couldn't read. "Yeah, yeah. Talk to you later, then. Right."

He set the phone down, and fanned himself with his notebook.

She said, "Hap was kidnapped in a bookmobile?"

"Dragged out of the back of the Coconut Grove Library, a librarian injured. Place in a shambles. Black female and white male abducted him, stole a bookmobile parked in the alley behind the library and made their getaway."

"Jesus Christ!"

"My thoughts exactly," Wills said.

Marguerite reached out and put her hands on her keyboard. "What're you going to do?"

"Nothing I can do. Up to the guys on the street to find 'em."

"And what if they don't?"

Wills thought about it for a second, fanning himself some more, and said, "Mind if I ask you something? You know, a fairly intimate question."

She looked up at him, this big man, doughy complexion, greasy hair that looked like a couple of swipes of black paint over his bald head. But the guy grew on you. His bull-ahead impudence.

She said, "You want to know if I'm sleeping with Hap. If maybe I had a thing going with both brothers at once? In other words, a motive to kill Daniel. Or maybe Hap had one."

He smiled.

"Well, now that you bring it up, it's an interesting line of speculation."

She said, "The answer is no. I had a thing with Daniel." She glanced up at him, frowned. He was giving her a very suspicious look now, tipping his head to the side, squinting through one eye. "Okay. And then yesterday, last night, Hap and I . . . Well, you know, because of the stress. It just happened."

"Stress can be magical that way," he said. "Opens up glands you'd never know were there otherwise."

"Why is this important, Wills?"

"I don't know. I guess I just saw something different today. Looked at the two of you and there was something, a shine in the air. I thought it might be relevant. That's the way I work, like if I know the emotions in operation, I have a better feel for things."

Marguerite, taking a quick glance around, said, "The fact is, Wills, for as long as I've known Hap I've considered him a superficial, self-indulgent, lazy sack of shit who sponged off his brother and preyed on women who should've known better."

"And today? Still feel like that?"

She tapped the space bar on her keyboard. Five, six, seven.

She said, "I don't know why going to bed with someone should change how you feel about them."

"I never understood that either," he said. "But that seems to be how it works, isn't it?"

She looked around the newsroom, up at Wills.

"Yeah," she said. "It's true."

"So I guess you'll want to come along. I mean, on a strictly professional basis. As a reporter."

Marguerite pushed back, came to her feet. She'd been trying to keep her voice down, but something about her posture, some hitch in the way she was moving was attracting attention all around the newsroom. People hushing, trying to overhear.

She said, "You have an address on Phelps? Where he might be headed?"

"Nothing recent."

"So what do we do? You have any ideas?"

He smiled at her, but there was tension in his forehead, the lines around his eyes.

"Oh, I've always got ideas," Wills said. "Ideas are my strong suit."

"Well?"

"The mill site," he said. "That seems to be the current destination of choice. I say we go there, make ourselves comfortable, commune with the mosquitoes. How 'bout you?"

"Let's go," she said. "Whatta you waiting for?"

\* \* \*

Keeping to the speed limit, Martina drove the bookmobile west on Flagler while Hollings leaned against a rack of books, trying to keep his balance and watch Tyler at the same time. They'd laid the guy out on the floor, his wrists and ankles bound tight in the clear wrapping tape Hollings had ripped off as they were going out the back door of the library.

Tyler had struggled a little going into the van and Hollings had clipped him a third time on the back of the head with his .45. Payback. Now the guy was awake, staring up at Hollings, but the five or six turns of plastic tape they'd taken around his head was keeping his mouth good and shut.

Hollings said, "We gotta ditch this bus quick. They'll be looking for us."

"Relax, Glenn. Just relax. We're almost where we're going."

"Oh, yeah, I'm really going to relax. We fucking kidnap a guy right in front of about a hundred people. Sure, I'm peaceful and untroubled. I like being on every cop computer in the city about now. In the number one slot on the evening news."

"How I see it is, it's a little bit of luck this truck was sitting out there. We needed a larger vehicle anyway, something to haul the gold in."

Hollings looked down at Tyler. The guy was rolling his shoulders, fighting against the tape, but not getting anywhere.

"Goddamn it, Martina," he said, "We gotta dump this thing. It stands out like a nigger in a snowstorm."

"Glenn," she said. "Why don't you just shut up your bigoted mouth for a while, huh?"

"I'm telling you. We can park this thing somewhere, steal a truck if that's what you think we need."

Martina pulled onto a side street. Hollings didn't catch the street number, small concrete houses, small lots with one or another Catholic saint or Jesus himself in glass cases out front. Lots of cars parked in the driveways. Typical Cuban area, sixteen family members in the same house, each of them with a big car.

Martina went down a block, turned and turned again and they

were in the driveway of a little yellow wood house, and she climbed down out of the bookmobile and opened the double doors of the attached garage. Not saying a word, she got back behind the wheel and drove the big van inside. A tight fit.

"So, Hollings, now you get to see how the other half lives."

"Last time we went someplace you said was your house, we wound up killing a guy."

"*We*, huh?"

"Okay, *you* killed him. I was the accessory. Same difference. Both of them get the chair."

She turned the key off, shot him a look, smug.

"So whatta we doing here?"

"I thought maybe it'd make you happy, calm you down, we put a gallon or two of paint on this thing, cover up the letters. Then we can rest awhile, maybe have a couple of glasses of something cold. And in a little while, it gets dark, we go out and dig up that gold and cart it off."

"How you so sure you know where it is, anyway?"

Martina leaned forward in the seat, took out her wallet, and pulled out a piece of white paper from one of the pockets. She handed it to him.

"What's that look like to you?"

Hollings unfolded it, held it up, turned the paper different ways. Glanced at Martina sitting sideways on the driver's seat, her knees almost touching his leg.

He said, "Like, I don't know. A graph?"

"A graph? What the fuck're you talking about a graph?"

"Like the stock market, up and down, you know how they show it on the TV. A zigzag, just like that."

"Turn it the other way, doofus," she said. "Up and down."

"Oh."

"Now what do you see?"

"It's not a graph," he said. "Wait, I know. Somebody traced something. They ran a pencil along the edge of their house key."

Martina snorted.

"Now, why the hell would somebody draw a picture of their fucking house key, Hollings? Can you tell me that?"

"You asked me what it looked like, I told you."

"It's a river, you idiot. The drawing of a river."

"Just 'cause I look at something, I see a different thing in it than you do, that doesn't make me an idiot. Okay? Can we get that straight?"

Hollings glared at her. He'd always heard how hard relationships were, but he'd never had an appreciation for it. Brenda, the crossing guard, except for her talking, she hadn't been so hard to live with. But this, this was hard. Even the sex was a kind of work. With Martina it looked like he'd have to be fighting all the time just to stay even, to get his 50 percent. He had the feeling, if he started slipping a little, backing down here and there, before long, Martina would be sprawled out over the entire bed, and Hollings would be sleeping on the goddamn floor.

It wasn't his training to be tough with women. He'd always thought you let them pretty much do what they wanted. Unless they were fucking around on you or something. But now he guessed that was another thing he'd have to take a long second look at soon as he had a free minute.

"Somebody might draw his house key," Hollings said. "I don't know why, maybe in case they lost it and wanted to make another one, instead of having to call a locksmith out."

"Jesus Mother of Christ, Hollings. It's the river. The Miami River. And that star, it marks the place where the ship sank, upriver somewhere. Not out in the ocean at all."

She climbed down from the bookmobile, squeezing around the front of it, working her way around to Hollings's side.

He looked back at Tyler. Guy had given up fighting against the tape and was staring up at Hollings, his eyes set, not blinking. Hollings recognized that look. He'd seen it plenty of times in Nam, guys getting ready to make a run across an open field, they don't know what's out there. Could be mines, could be VC with Vladimirov heavy machine guns, could be nothing at all. He'd seen it there on the edges of those fields, guys with everything in their eyes turned off, all the lights, all the thinking. Eyes just blank, staring, not angry, not scared, not anything.

Martina leaned in the passenger door.

"Okay," Hollings said, "so how you figure that's a river from some fucking doodle on a piece of paper?"

"How I know is, I've done my homework."

"Yeah?"

"It isn't my nature to trust nobody," she said.

"What the hell're you saying?"

"With Alvarez, you know, something isn't right about him and I saw it the first goddamn minute he came up to me. So when he asked me to go in with him, I said I'd think about it. And from then on, I started following him around town, checking him out, see how the man spent his time."

"You tailed Alvarez?"

"Yeah, and he didn't see me once."

"Man, you got balls. I'll say that."

Martina gave him a peculiar look and said, "So, last weekend, Saturday afternoon, I followed him over to some vacant lot along the river. There's some white guy digging in the dirt. Alvarez went over to the guy, pulled out his piece, aimed it at this guy, and dragged him off."

"Along the river?"

"Yeah, along the river," said Martina. "I didn't think much about it at the time, I mean the place where it happened. But now I get it. That white guy digging was Tyler. This one's brother."

"Whereabouts on the river?"

Hollings picked up the maps they'd gotten from the library. Unrolled one of them.

Martina said, "I don't know the goddamn address, but I think I could find it again."

"For four hundred million bucks, I sure as shit hope so."

Hollings held up the squiggly line next to the map. Martina, standing on the step-up, leaned over to see.

"It isn't the same," said Hollings. "The squiggles don't match up. Not even close."

Martina ripped the maps from Hollings's hand, went around to the front of the van and flattened them out on the hood. Hollings got down, walked up and stood behind her, looking over her shoulder.

"See," he said. "Not the same."

Martina unrolled each map and flattened the squiggly line next to the river.

"Doesn't have to be perfect," she said. "I never seen a map yet was exactly perfect."

"Okay, then," said Hollings. "If we could figure this out, what's to keep that goddamn Alvarez from figuring it out, and being there trying to dig it up himself?"

"Nothing," Martina said. "Nothing at all."

"Aw, shit, I knew that was coming. I fucking knew it."

"So you gonna punch Tyler's ticket like you said?"

"Right now?"

"Didn't I hear you say it this morning, lying in bed, all big and brave, how you were going to keep this guy from identifying me? Or was that some other guy I was in bed with?"

"Let's paint this goddamn van first," he said. "All right? Paint it, catch our breath for a few minutes, have a beer or two, then I'll get it done, okay? Just don't keep ragging me, okay? I'll do it, I'll fucking do it."

# CHAPTER 29

WHILE THE TWO OF THEM PAINTED THE VAN, HAP SAT UP and did as thorough a check of his surroundings as he could manage. After a minute or two, he made up his mind. He scooted backward a yard and pressed the strapping tape that bound his wrists against the rough edge of the metal bookshelf and began to scrape. Though it was duller than he'd thought, still it was the sharpest angle he could locate on this kind of notice.

Five minutes, ten, while the two of them talked just a few feet away, he sawed and sawed. The ache in his shoulder began to build toward a cramp, but there was no loosening at his wrists. It was like trying to slice a steel cable with a butter knife.

Useless. He should probably just quit now, take these last couple of minutes to make his peace, buckle up for the long last flight out. But then, shit, he didn't believe in anything powerful enough to pray to, and there was no one alive he needed to make peace with. Even the voice that had bullied him for so long seemed to have turned to smoke and blown away. He expected no afterlife, no choirs, no angels. Far as he was concerned, the only god there was was the god of sharp edges, the god of sawing. The god of getting the hell out of there.

When Martina opened the passenger door and climbed back into the van, Hap had made no progress on the tape, at least none that he could tell. She came in so quick, he barely had time enough to lie back down on his hands. In a moment he was staring up into the sour, smiling face of Martina Phelps.

She gripped his shoulder and rolled him roughly onto his stomach, wrapped a few more turns of the strapping tape around his wrists, gave his arms a savage upward jerk, like a roper tying off his steer, then lifted him a few inches off the floor and dropped him back facedown. She kneeled beside him on the metal floor and put her finger against the wound at the back of his head. Dug her nail into the open flesh. Hap bit down hard, and tried to twist his head away.

"Hapfield, you been a baaad boy." She held her finger in front of his eyes, speckled with white paint and his own blood. "You tried to bury me under about a thousand pounds of books, son. That any way for a gentleman to treat a lady?"

The other one said, "Guy almost broke my fucking nose with that globe too. Trying to mess up my handsome face."

Martina bent lower so her mouth was only inches from Hap's.

"You oughta see somebody about this cut, Hapfield, know what I mean? We wouldn't want you to bleed to death out here before we had a chance to shoot you through your brain. I mean, boy, this thing looks serious, like maybe somebody's been executing quantum mechanics on you."

He heard the flattop man laugh, and then out of the edge of his vision, he saw the .45 float from the man's hand to Martina's, saw her take a grip on it, and move behind him, and then he heard the crunch again, felt the jolt against his skull, and he was once again on the long, slippery ramp that led nowhere.

But this time he fought it. Holding still for their benefit, his eyes closed, while inside his head he swam against the dark, churning current as if he were one of those fish, salmon, or whichever one it was, he couldn't remember at the moment, but the one that fought its way back every year, salmon, yes, it was salmon, struggling against those tons of frigid water, the gravity, the steep rapids, everything in its narrow universe pitted against it. Bears along the stream swatting at the silver prizes. But those fish fought, they swam and swam, one obsessive need compelling them on against the rush, one thought, one small hard thought. Keep fighting. Keep fighting. Don't pass out.

He heard Martina talking as a door closed behind them. He heard them laugh, their voices growing distant. Half blind with pain, swallowing back the nausea, Hap turned his head to his right shoulder and he could see a shelf of children's books. *The Turnip and the Shoe, Six Cats and Three Green Mice, Rotten Ralph*. He blinked. Tried to read a fourth title to keep himself awake, but his eyes were blurred and burning. He needed to close them, sleep this one off. But no. If he did that, if he lost his focus even for a second or two, he knew he would be carried, like that fish, that salmon, backward out to sea, out to the cold midnight waters.

Groaning, he rocked onto his side and tried an experimental wriggle forward. An inch, maybe less. He took a breath and began to squirm toward the driver's compartment. His shoulders ached, and blood was seeping down his neck. From all that straining against the wrapping tape, his hands had turned to ice. He could picture his fingers, blued and puffy.

Writhing forward a foot, he hooked his elbow over a shelf and pulled himself to a sitting position. Before they'd gone they'd slid the panel closed, separating the back of the van from the driver's compartment. He raised himself to his knees and pressed his chin against the lever and pushed down. Locked.

He dropped back onto his side, gathered himself, then rolled over onto his back. He pictured for a moment the move he was going to try, then lifted his feet, drew his knees to his chest, bent his head forward and rocked. On three, he blew a breath out his nose and pumped himself up to his feet. Tottered briefly, bumped a shelf, then found his balance. The gouge in his head roared.

Huffing hard, he stared out the windows of the van. It was parked inside a garage, not more than a foot or two of room on each side. From the fading light through a high, grimy garage window, he estimated it was close to five o'clock. Happy hour. Time the afternoon wind quickened, the sky curdled and darkened out over the 'Glades. The huge cumulus clouds jostled against each other, and long rumblings began to roll across the sky and shake windows through the western edge of the city. Then the gator gushers would set in, the palmetto pounders.

On his feet like that, Hap found there was some play in the strapping tape at his ankles. Enough so he could do a tight shuffle down the aisle of books. The handle on the back doors was a chrome lever, grip-and-twist. It was installed chest-high, out of reach of his hands.

So he bent forward, tipped his head at different angles till he wedged the nib of the lever under the edge of the wrapping tape. He twisted and pulled his head against the lever, digging it hard into his cheek. And the tape moved, dragged down an inch from his mouth. He sucked a breath past it, then another, and he straightened up, pushed all his force at the tape, wriggling and straining upward against the pain.

The lever moved, the door unlatched.

He shouldered it open, squatted, and jumped down to the floor of the garage. There was rock music coming from inside the house, a song he'd danced to once or twice, but couldn't name. Cars grumbled past outside. Next door a dog barked listlessly.

With his ankles aching, Hap hopped down the narrow passage beside the van. There was a small wooden tool closet hung from the wall at the front of the garage, but it was padlocked. Probably where she stored her shrunken heads. He saw no sharp objects anywhere. No rough metal edges, no glass to break, no nail heads showing.

The motor of the bookmobile ticked as it cooled, and Hap heard what sounded like voices in the room just off the garage. The neighbor's dog continued its monotonous baying. The dog that would bark forever. Hap's cheek throbbed where he had mauled it against the lever. He touched his tongue to a loosened molar. His legs were going watery.

He hopped to the back of the van, and pressing his back to the rear door, he bent his knees and lowered himself to a crouch. With a finger, he reached below the bumper and touched the mouth of the tail pipe. Hot, but not hot enough. He let himself down to the greasy concrete, dropped to his side, rolled onto his stomach. The salmon. The salmon.

On his belly he snaked backward beneath the van, feeling the heat prickly through the back of his shirt. When his head was beneath the bumper, he stopped. Drew his hands up from the small of his back, feeling for the exhaust pipe. A double-jointed man would've had no problem. Or a yogi. But Hap had earned his muscles on the water, hauling up the sail, spinning it, leaning against the brawn of the wind. Pinned under this broiling truck, he felt hopelessly bulky and tight.

He pressed his left cheek against the slick concrete, arched his back up, and offered his wrists to the greatest heat he could feel radiating from some pipe or manifold he couldn't see. When the sting came he flinched, but jammed his butt up higher, bit back the bellow he wanted to make. And some cool jelly began to trickle down his wrist, perhaps the rupturing blisters or blood. He smelled the putrid char, the sweet scorch of his own flesh.

Hap groaned and crushed his wrists into the teeth of the pain, and smelled this other thing, a wisp of chemical, the toxic stink of liquifying plastic. He rubbed his wrists back and forth against the heated metal, felt the tape begin to give, shoved it harder, moaning, and with every fiber of his fading strength, he held it there. Until the tape broke apart.

He dropped flat on his stomach. Pulled down the adhesive covering his mouth till it was loose around his neck, a wrapping tape noose. He lay there trying to get his breath. Thinking again of the salmon, that even for them, even in the midst of their horrendous journeys, there must be pools along the way, small eddies off to the side of the river where a fish could bask for a minute or two in the still waters, consider its progress. Regain its strength.

The door to the house opened and shut, and the two of them came out into the garage.

"But say it isn't," the flattop man was saying. "Say we dig and dig and there's not a goddamn thing. You know, like it was a trick, or we read the map wrong, or some fucking thing."

"Map isn't wrong, Hollings."

Their voices with the soft slur of a couple of belts of whiskey.

"But say, just for hypothetical, we dig, it's not there."

Hap could see their legs in front of the truck, facing the pad-locked storage cabinet. The heavy metal clank and rasp of hardware being handled roughly.

"You want the Heckler and Koch, or the Grendel?"

"Jesus, Martina, where the fuck you get shit like that?"

"I'm a thief, remember?"

"Christ, man. I haven't seen an armory like that since Parris Island."

"The Grendel's just a .22, but it holds thirty rounds." Hap heard the harsh snap of a magazine locked into place. "That's maybe more your speed, Hollings. Hero like you wants to spray the lead around I suspect, huh?"

"So say we keep the guy alive," Hollings said. "If something goes wrong out there, we still got him. We can put his dick in a flashlight, like you said, see what he knows. Or we got him to bargain with if something goes real wrong."

"Isn't nothing going real wrong. Isn't nothing going any wrong at all."

"I know, I know."

"We aren't gonna need to fucking bargain with anybody, Hollings, not after tonight. We gonna have the gold in a few hours. Won't be no need to bargain ever again."

"I'm telling you, in case something doesn't turn out like we thought."

"You're a gutless wonder, Hollings. Simple as that. Trying to find some way to keep from getting shit on your hands."

"I'll take the Heckler," Hollings said.

"I don't give a limp dick which one you use."

Hap heard the snick of the padlock shutting, watched the feet shuffle around at the front of the van, like they might be trying out the sights on the garage door. Hap hadn't been able to pull the tape from his ankles. No way he was going to make a run for it like this. Couple of guys with autoloaders, nuh-uh. With guys like this, his only hope was to keep it hand-to-hand.

"Look, if you want Tyler dead so bad, why don't you kill him, Martina?"

"That's not the point, Hollings. The point is, right now at this moment, I done all the bad shit, and your fucking hands are still lily-white clean. Till you're dirty as I am, I don't trust your ass one little bit. Nothing to keep you from sneaking off, getting on the phone, calling the cops, and put them on to me."

"Now, why would I do that?"

" 'Cause you're chickenshit, Hollings, that's why. You're so scared right now, it's all you can do to keep from pissing yourself. Only way I'm gonna trust you, boy, is you get down into the shit deep as me."

Hollings said, "Look here, it doesn't bother me shooting the guy. I'll do it, no problem when the time's right. I'm just saying we should wait, see what happens out there with the gold. If we find it, I'll pop him right then, do some major quantum mechanics on him, okay, leave the body out there in the dirt. Then on the other hand, we don't find the gold, Tyler's our plan B. Get us a flashlight, put his dick in it."

"All right, all right," she said. "I hate hearing you whine, man. Makes me want to puke right here. You're such a pussy, Hollings."

While the two of them fiddled with their weapons, Hap squirmed out from under the van, climbed quietly into the back, eased the door shut, twisted the lock, crawled back to the spot where they'd left him. He pulled the tape back across his mouth, put his hands behind his back and lay on them.

A moment or two later Martina and Hollings got back into the bookmobile. Hollings slid the panel aside, looked back at Hap and said, "How we doing back there? All comfy?"

Hap said nothing. But the truth was, he couldn't remember the last time he'd felt so good.

# CHAPTER 30

I N THE *HERALD* PARKING LOT WILLS'S WHITE FORD TURNED over but wouldn't catch. She followed him back into the lobby, where he called the Metro motor pool. Nothing available for the rest of the evening? Get outa here. You gotta be kidding me. Wills told the guy he needed a fucking car right now. But apparently there weren't any cars. You're telling me, Wills said, there's not a goddamn available police car in all of Dade County? Wills getting a little color in his face. Yeah, Dade County, Wills shouted. Ever hear of it? Yeah, and what's your name, asshole? Then he said, Jordan Wills, Homicide. No, I'm not giving you my fucking badge number. It's Jordan Wills, Homicide. Don't worry about it, he told the guy, yeah, I'll be there, yeah, tomorrow, nine sharp. Better do some push-ups tonight, tough guy. He slammed the receiver down. That's when Marguerite volunteered her 'Vette.

Wills crammed into the bucket seat, she put the top down, and drove them west on the surface streets for a few blocks, debating it. She glanced over at him once or twice. He was quiet, watching the streetlights coming on. A minute or two more went by and he said, "Nice car" as she accelerated from a light.

"Would you read something for me?" she said. "Give me your honest opinion."

"I don't have any other kind."

With one hand on the wheel, she reached into the glove compartment, hit the map light. She dug around under her cassettes, where the article was wedged. Printed out a copy yesterday after Bernie ripped up the other one.

She handed it to him and he glanced at it, read the first line or two maybe. He looked across at her, an eyebrow arched, then leaned forward and held the pages to the light.

The farther west they went, the more the traffic thickened. At Sixth Avenue she almost hit a guy selling lemons from a plastic sack. She wasn't paying attention to the road, glancing over at Wills, listening for any sign. He was quiet. Going through the pages fairly fast. Giving nothing away.

When he was done, he folded the article in half and slid it back into the glove compartment, switched off the light, closed the door. He looked out his side of the car, into the Little Havana storefronts.

"Well?"

He showed her his blank face.

"Well, say something."

"You think they'll print this?"

She groaned, downshifted for another light.

"My boss's already refused," she said. "But I think I can wear him down. If not, I'll go the TV route."

"Man," he said. "For blowing your own mother out of the water like this, you seem awful calm."

"Only regret I have is I didn't do it sooner."

It was well after seven now, losing the last of the light. They were stopped on Northwest Twentieth, ten cars back from the red light. Working their way west with the last of the commuters, the ones that stayed late at the office or had a couple of belts at Cye's or Fort Dallas.

The avenues in this part of town had been renamed for Cuban generals, Maximo this, Luis Gonzalo that. Her hometown was being taken over by another country's heroes.

"You got proof for all this?"

"I was an eyewitness to a lot of it. I know the names of his holding companies, which variances she swung his way, special considerations, bid rigging. Inside information she provided him on road construction from her post on the transportation committee."

"I mean documentation. Court of law stuff."

"I'm working on that."

"Well, if you could prove all this, the senator could be looking at some jail time, depending on what DOJ wants to do. You aware of that?"

"Of course I am."

"It comes as a surprise," said Wills. "I mean, I liked her, what I've seen of her on the news, you know. A straight shooter. Doesn't mince words. I can't say I much care for her social views, but the lady has rooted out some pretty worthless shitheads over the years. I thought she was basically okay."

"Crooks come in all denominations."

"Yeah, tell me about it."

A middle-aged gentleman in a dark suit was moving down the row of stalled traffic, selling roses. Marguerite waved him off and he said God bless you and went on down the row.

"This Mayan stuff she collects," Wills said. "You don't mention it in the article."

"Collecting artifacts isn't illegal."

"Maybe not," he said. "But far as the homicide I'm looking at here, it seems to be more in the center of things than the fact she and Shorty Busser have been in bed for years."

Marguerite's eyes were on the line of cars in front of them.

He said, "So I'm now assuming the stuff the senator collects, all of that's been coming from this ship, this *Carmelita*."

"Apparently."

"And we're also assuming at this point, the ship is there buried on her land."

"Seems that way."

"So that would mean Daniel Tyler was out there digging on that land for years, on the sly. And all that time he was selling the senator stuff that was hers anyway. Now, if that's true, you gotta hand it to him, that was ballsy."

"Or desperate."

"Desperate? How?"

"He sold my mother those things to keep the Mangrove House. He used the money every year to pay his real estate taxes."

"How do you know that?"

She tapped her horn at the BMW ahead of her. A car phone dawdler.

"Hap figured it out. He told me this morning. He talked to a friend of his at the bank, and the guy said Daniel brought in cash every year and used it to pay his tax bill. And apparently it was always the exact same amount he charged Mother for the Mayan stuff that year."

"Well, well, well."

"Daniel wasn't a bad man," she said. "He was doing what he felt he had to do to save his home. I would've done the same. Even if I had to compromise my values a little, bend them, I'd do it. Whatever it took to save my family home."

Wills said, "But think about this from another point of view. Imagine if you discovered somebody was conning you like that, basically stealing what was already yours and selling it back to you. Wouldn't you be a little pissed?"

Marguerite glanced over at Wills. The breeze had torn loose a couple of greasy strands of his hair, so they hung like limp wings off the back of his head.

As she edged ahead, Wills said, "We had another interesting development this afternoon. Another corpse. Another notable."

"Yeah?"

"You heard of Max Hunter?"

"The treasure guy."

"Yeah, right. Wife was away a couple of days, comes home, there he is, decomposing on the shag rug. Four gunshots to the head and body. Some files stolen. And it so happens the material was about the *Carmelita*. Some coincidence, huh?"

"Somebody's on a tear," she said, and accelerated through the last millisecond of the yellow light. Two cars followed her across the intersection. At this rate, they were ten, fifteen minutes from the mill site.

Wills let out a long sigh that was part groan, pressed back into his bucket seat. Not used to major horsepower.

When she slowed down, he said, "Hap tell you about the blue bottle and packet of syringes he found?"

"Yeah."

She turned off Twentieth, north onto Seventeenth Avenue, also known as Alonso Herrera something. Who *were* all these guys! She cut over a block, a shortcut she knew. Kept her eyes ahead.

Wills said, "Well, the fact the stuff came from Hap, I didn't have much hope it would amount to anything. But sure enough, trumpets and drumroll, the vial, it still had a trace of *Papaver somniferum* and scopolamine inside it. They ran some lab work on it, and whatta you know, it's an identical match to the concoction that gave Daniel Tyler his heart attack."

She missed a four-way stop, almost got sideswiped by a van.

"Maybe I should drive."

"I'm all right."

She felt him watching her for a minute as she struggled to keep the car in her lane, oversteering like a late-night drunk.

Wills said, "You know, the senator, being a federal employee, she's in the computer, her fingerprints, everything."

Marguerite watched her headlights burrow through the gathering dark.

"Most of the prints on that vial were smudged," said Wills. "Like it got passed around a little. But there was one beautiful print, very clear. Your mother's thumb."

Marguerite swerved onto the gravel shoulder, braked hard. Coming to a stop a few feet in front of a group of kids playing under a streetlamp. They stopped and stared at the car, at the dust rising like steam in its headlights.

She sat there a moment, looking at the kids, then switched the ignition off.

"Then it's true," she said. "She killed him."

Feeling something happening behind her eyes, a sting. Her vision hazing. But she fought it. Not now. Not here.

"Well, this is pretty strong physical evidence," Wills said. "But I'm still a man in search of a clear and certain motive."

"That's what you came to talk to me about?"

"I got one or two questions," he said. "You up to it now?"

She nodded.

"I think so."

"I need to have a few things real straight in my mind before I could push this forward. I mean, with Senator Rawlings, the publicity factor and all, I don't want to click the handcuffs on, then turn around and find out it was some kind of sleeping prescription in that bottle, or cancer drug she was taking, something like that. I mean, that would pretty much be the conclusion of a distinguished law enforcement career."

Marguerite blew out a breath. Leaned back. The kids had stopped playing and were staring curiously at the Corvette.

Wills said, "So, like for one thing, I'm curious where this all started, your mother's Mayan obsession. You know about that? The origin?"

"Royalty," she said.

"Do that again?"

"Kings, queens, viceroys, dukes, duchesses, high priests. She used to read about them. Books everywhere when I was growing up. I didn't think anything of it. Biographies of famous leaders, monarchs, rulers, Henry the Eighth, Caesar, you name it. She was on a Napoleon kick for a while. Seven, eight books on him. If they wore a crown, sat on a throne, she read about them."

"Studying up on how to be one herself? That what you're suggesting?"

She nodded.

"But where's the Mayan thing come in?"

"Oh, she read Egyptian things, books about some Zulu king, Shaka Zulu I think it was. American Indian chiefs. Tsali, Sitting Bull. Everything she could find. I remember Genghis Khan, Mary, Queen of Scots. Toltecs, the Aztecs, Incas. And Maya too."

"But listen to me, Marguerite. What I'm asking you is why the fixation with that one in particular? The Maya."

She looked down at her lap.

"I was twelve, thirteen, I don't remember exactly, but I was young. Eighth grade maybe."

"Yeah?"

"Well, Mother used to take me with her sometimes, to lectures and art shows, things like that. Daddy would be in Washington, and she'd drag me along with her. And I remember that's where I saw Daniel the first time. At the public library downtown. He was giving a lecture about recent developments in Mexican archaeology. Slides and everything. It was just one of the things he did back then. Fresh out of school, full of energy.

"He was very handsome, articulate. I had an instant crush. And after the talk, Mother went down and spoke to him, introduced herself and they chatted for a few minutes. And I don't know, maybe a month or two later, one afternoon when I came home from school, came in the door and just stood there stunned. Because there he was, Daniel Tyler, in my living room talking to Mother."

"Aha."

"I went over, said hello, and there on the table, sitting in front of them both was this little gold frog, a pendant. Turned out that frog became the first piece in her collection."

"So he sold her one," Wills said. "Then another. Got her hooked. One every year after that."

"Yeah," she said. "And little by little, the royalty thing turned into the Mayan thing."

"All right, good. That's better. I'm starting to get a feel for this."

"Then maybe what happened," Marguerite said, "she got tired of Daniel dribbling them out. She's getting impatient maybe. Her delusions of grandeur growing bigger every year. Or maybe money's the issue. Daniel ups the price every year as taxes keep rising. I don't know, Wills. I don't know that much about my mother anymore, really. But for some reason she might've decided she had to have it all. The mother lode."

"So she gives him a drug," Wills said, "to get him to tell her where he's been getting them all these years, but he dies instead."

They watched an EMS van pass by on the cross street in front of them. Lights on, sirens.

"The Maya," said Marguerite. "Mother couldn't have picked a more brutal culture to obsess over."

"Yeah, I know," said Wills. "I read a *National Geographic* piece on them yesterday. Doing my homework on this thing. Those people were very fond of blood. Lots of sacrifices."

"Off with their heads," she said quietly.

Wills said, "That's probably every politician's secret wish. Keep a nice sharp ax around for the protestors, the malcontents."

"Daniel," she said. "He must've known what was happening."

"Known?"

"How screwed up she was getting. How twisted. And that he was part of the cause. I think he was feeling guilty, scared even. He thought he saw somebody following him. But he was trapped. He'd gotten so he depended on her by then."

"Why couldn't he find some other place to sell this stuff? Someplace reputable. Sotheby's or something like that?"

"Yeah, I thought about that," she said. "But you know, places like those might draw too much attention. A piece from the *Carmelita* could've set off alarms all over the place. Maybe get all the treasure hunters in an uproar, out there sniffing around. Mother at least had the advantage of being discreet. And anyway he had a good thing going with her, why change it? He wasn't money hungry. He just wanted enough for the yearly bill."

Marguerite watched a couple of the kids in the street, a boy ten or so and what looked like his sister. They separated from the others and began to edge toward the car. The boy held a bat. Poised. Going to defend his territory if necessary.

"Another thing I'm curious about," said Wills. "Why's that vial just sitting there in her medicine chest? The bottle of opium and scopolamine. I don't see that. The woman's world-class smart. She isn't the type to screw up like that, murder some guy, leave some major loose end hanging around."

The boy with the bat moved defiantly in front of the car, his sister a foot behind him.

"You're wrong."

"Yeah? Well, enlighten me."

"You ever been up to the penthouse of the Grande Biscayne?"

"I been in the lobby once or twice."

"Forgive me, Wills, but you're not likely to get invited up either. The senator maintains a very rarified guest list."

"Okay, I can accept that."

"See, the air's thinner. You breathe it long enough, it changes you. Day after day, you take that long ride upstairs, it's cotton candy up there, but it starts to seem real. From there the streets look tiny. All the terrible crap going on down below, it's just some tasteless movie you can draw the curtains on anytime you want."

Wills looked out his window for a minute, then back at her.

"So whatta you saying? One night she comes home," he said, "rides up her elevator, this time there's blood on her hands?"

Marguerite said, "Yeah, and she's gotten so secluded up in her clouds, it's like it didn't happen. Maybe she's a little dazed. She's smart enough to throw away the syringe she used, after all, that's a murder weapon. Then she washes her hands, and then puts the vial back in the cabinet. And like that, the whole awful mess is gone from her mind. Never even a second thought. That's the idea, Wills. That's why they make thirty-nine floors. To cut down on second thoughts."

He thought about that a moment, then said, "It occur to you, she might want to hang on to a little of the drug, maybe use it on you, or maybe Hap, see what you know?"

Marguerite massaged her temples. It had occurred to her. Her own goddamn mother, flesh of her flesh, blood of her blood.

The boy with the bat was moving in on the headlights, lifting the bat as he came. Maybe Marguerite had him all wrong. Not a defender of his turf, but a mugger trainee. Preyed on tourists who'd taken one wrong turn too many. Sitting there reading their road maps.

Marguerite started the car, and he jumped away. She revved it, and he leaped back off the street.

As she drove, Wills was quiet, watching the neighborhoods change from houses to shacks, from shacks to weeds.

Finally, with the river coming into view, he said, "That bottle is fairly hard evidence. But it'd still be a tricky case. It's got her fingerprints, but hell, it was illegally obtained. Makes it next to worthless."

"What do you need, a confession?"

"I do have one other small piece of the riddle."

"Yeah?"

"Ever hear of a place name of Sheer Heaven?"

"Sheer Heaven?"

"A lingerie shop on Key Biscayne, a mile from the Sonesta. I thought maybe a woman like you, your taste in fashions, you might've run across it."

"I haven't, no."

"Well, the fishnet stockings stuck in my mind. So I went out to the Key, drove around, visited some women's dress shops out there. Jesus, the things I wind up doing. But it was a no-luck situation. Five dress shops, zip. I was about to give up, go on home, when I saw this little place in a strip shopping center, next to a pet store. Shop was going out of business. Sheer Heaven. Another day or two, I would've missed it entirely. I went in, showed her the stockings, asked her if she carried them. She did. Then I asked her if she happened to remember anybody buying a pair of them in the last few days. And right off she said, oh yes, she remembered it very clearly."

"Mother?"

"No, not your mother," Wills said. "A big guy, dark hair, kind of good-looking in a brutish way. The woman said she remembered him because of the car he drove, parked it right outside the shop. Big beautiful Rolls-Royce."

Marguerite was quiet, winding past the boat yards, the stacks of cargo containers, rusty tankers up on blocks, old broken ships.

Wills pointed out a 7-Eleven on Twenty-seventh Avenue, told her to pull in there. Walking distance to the mill.

She shut off the motor. Put her hands on the wheel.

"It occur to you," Wills said, "that with the murder scene set up to look like a sex thing gone wrong, you become the number one suspect? The girlfriend of the victim."

Marguerite glanced over at Wills, then back out the windshield. She felt light-headed, in zero gravity land.

"Yeah, it occurred to me."

"Now, why would she do something like that? Go after her own daughter."

Marguerite watched an old man shuffle out of the 7-Eleven with a heavy sack. A little girl at his side licking a Popsicle.

"Maybe because I stole Daniel from her."

Marguerite watched the little girl reach up and offer the old man a lick of her Popsicle. He just smiled and waded on into the dark with his heavy sack.

"Wait a minute," Wills said. "You're saying they had something going? The senator and Daniel Tyler?"

"No, no," she said. "But god, I know Mother wanted it to happen. I saw it in her eyes that very first time. She had a crush too. Something more serious than a crush. I didn't even understand what it was back then, but I saw it, the way she lit up. The way she looked at him. Here was a man, a real leader, a man with genuine power. Charisma, like I said. Power she could only wish for. She wanted him. She wanted to eat him up. Just like she ate up my father."

"But you got him instead."

"Yes. Eventually I did."

"To spite your mother."

"I guess that's part of it," she said. "I think I believed I was saving Daniel from her. Keeping him out of her clutches. I'm not sure anymore what I thought at first."

Marguerite couldn't take her hands off the wheel. Her head sagged, a couple of tears had formed and were about to break loose down her cheek.

A jet passed overhead, coming in for a landing at Miami International. Its thunder vibrated through the car. Marguerite watched a bearded guy slouch against the wall of the 7-Eleven, drinking a can of beer in a paper sack.

She licked her lips and looked over at Wills. Everything about the cop was soft except his eyes. They seemed to be rooted to some intense, gristly man who lived inside him.

"Go on," he said. "You got something else. Say it."

She took another breath, reset her hands on the wheel. Across from them the derelict finished his beer, dropped it on the sidewalk, and ground it with his heel like a cigarette butt.

"I didn't kill Daniel."

"I know you didn't."

"Then why do I feel like I did, Wills? Tell me that."

"I don't know," he said. "It just works that way sometimes. There's always a lot of loose guilt floating around. Some people are just more susceptible to it than others."

"When I was growing up," she said, "I felt like I didn't have a mother. She was never there for me emotionally. No warmth at all. She didn't love me. So I found another mother."

Wills reached out, took one of her hands off the wheel and held it.

"Ramona," she said. "I looked a little like her photographs, so I invented this relationship with her. I talked to her. It was even like I was praying to her sometimes. Baring my soul to this woman who'd been dead a hundred years. But she got me through. She still does. Does that make me crazy, Wills? Am I nuts?"

"No," he said. "That makes you complicated. Complicated is good. Complicated is what it's all about."

"All this makes my article about her, all her little political schemes with Shorty Busser, it makes that all seem pretty shabby, huh, compared to this. Compared to murder."

"Compared to murder, everything seems shabby. It should. It's supposed to."

Wills gave her hand a squeeze and let go. He pried himself out of the car. Stood beside the door and told her he was going to call in, see if there was anything new about the bookmobile.

When he came back to the car, she could see it in his eyes.

"Neither hide nor hair," he said. "But something tells me he's okay. Hap's a resourceful guy. A little bent, but he's got imagination. I don't think you need to worry, he'll be okay."

Marguerite wanted to say something flip, a snappy comeback, something a tough broad would say at a moment like that. But she couldn't think of anything, and the second or two passed by when it would've worked. So she said nothing.

# CHAPTER 31

ALVAREZ SAT ON A MOUND OF DIRT, NOT EVEN SWATTING the mosquitoes anymore. He spoke out loud to himself, weighing the best way to commit suicide. The easy choice was to use the Franchi SPAS, press it to the bottom of his chin, brace the butt against the ground and fire it with his thumb, spatter his brains up into the oak tree he was sitting under there at the Rawlings Mill.

But then that was too easy. Not painful enough.

What he should probably do, he should walk across the street, over to the docks along the river, climb one of those fences, slice himself good on the razor loops, then jump down on the other side, whistle and stomp his feet, and let the Dobermans finish the job. That's how he felt. It should hurt. Dying should be a binge of pain and blood and broken bones.

He didn't particularly want to die. He had things still to live for and all that bullshit. What he wanted was punishment. To pay some heavy penalty for what he'd done. Because Ray Alvarez had fucked up again. Another in a long string of fuck-ups.

The gold wasn't here. He'd been wrong. He'd been wrong, and wrong and wrong. One way or another for over thirty years he'd been wrong. Sitting there in the dark, he couldn't think of a right thing he'd done in all that time. His quick-draw mentality, his goddamn Cuban temper, and then lately his greed pushing him into one bad choice after another. Marrying that Puerto Rican woman was a bad choice, going down to Jamaica after her was another one, getting involved with the senator was wrong, and then breaking off with her like he'd done just at the exact moment when she might be about to let him into the good life, that was wrong again. Picking that moron Hollings had been a bad choice, and Martina, that was totally fucked up.

The gold wasn't there. He'd looked. Looked good. And it wasn't there. And goddamn him if he could figure what he should do next. Whatever it was, he was certain it would turn out to be wrong. He knew it. Look at him. Look at him sitting out there in the dark. Big stupid guy, he'd had a chance at four hundred million dollars in gold. Had a chance to make a permanent connection with a United States senator, one of the couple hundred most powerful people in the world. But what had he done? He'd blown it. Walked away, gone off free-lancing, thinking he was so much smarter than everybody. Now look at him. Sitting on a hill of dirt, his hair all wild and messed up, the mosquitoes coating his arms, his neck. And he didn't give a shit. It felt good to hurt. He wished he hurt more.

That's what he was thinking when the Rolls-Royce crunched down the gravel drive, and right away, Ray Alvarez was glad he hadn't shot himself or done one of those other things. Maybe there was still a chance.

He picked up the Franchi SPAS and angled over through the darkness toward where the Rolls had come to a stop. He crouched down, and moved along the edge of the bushes. The Rolls's lights went out, but the doors stayed shut. Yeah, maybe there was a chance this was all coming out okay. At least, this time if Ray Alvarez fucked up, he was going to keep his finger on the trigger, make a hell of a lot more noise doing it.

Thirty yards, twenty-five. He was behind some kind of flowering bush maybe twenty feet away when the front door opened, and the tall, skinny guy with the hunched shoulders and the jittery eyes who Alvarez had hired to play a joke on the senator, this guy named Francis, got out of the car, and called out into the darkness Alvarez's name.

Ray Alvarez stood there a minute, watching the guy pace back and forth beside the car. The guy called out his name again a little louder this time, and then Alvarez could hear some whispering. The senator and this guy talking. After only a couple of hours together, they were chummy already, whispering, plotting.

Ray came out of the bushes, carrying the Franchi in one hand down by his leg. Maybe she had her peashooter aimed at him, maybe when she saw him, she'd open fire, maybe the driver had a gun, too, and both of them would start shooting at once. But the thing about considering suicide was, once you'd done it, once you'd gone down there into all that blackness and gloom, and said yeah, fuck it, who cares, it made walking out of the bushes easier. Walking across that ten feet of dark ground, walking into one gun, two guns, a hundred guns, it made all that a piece of fucking cake.

"Hey, how you doing?" Ray said.

Francis grunted. Startled, glancing back in the car.

"You like driving that car, do you? Think you might make a career of it?"

"I might," Francis said, turning back toward Alvarez.

The skinny guy had recovered quick and was talking brave, so there *must* be at least one pistol pointing at Alvarez. Though he couldn't see anything in the guy's hands. Alvarez stopped about seven, eight feet away. Nowhere to hide out there. The Franchi SPAS down by his leg. Everybody squaring off like some kind of cowboy gunfight, another quick-draw contest. Problem was, he wasn't sure which person he was dueling with, Francis or the senator. He wasn't sure which one to blow away first.

The window slid down and there she was. He could see her hair like a halo in the darkness.

"Well, Ray," she said. "I see you've been busy."

"I'm a worker," he said. "I got a strong back."

"You have any luck? Find what you were looking for?"

"No. I didn't find nothing. Some old bottles is all."

"Then I suppose you made a mistake."

"I'd say I made more than one."

Ray Alvarez was straining to see, but hell, he must've not been eating enough carrots lately or something, 'cause he couldn't make out anything in that light. Francis seemed to be staying put. And he could see her hair, and the glint of her gold necklace. But that was about all. The lights of the docks and warehouses across the street were behind her, so that was no help to him. Though it did mean that she could probably see him a lot better than he could see her, see the dark shine of the Franchi.

"You want to be my driver again, Ray? You want to come back to work for me? I think Francis here is a little uncomfortable with the Rolls. It might be too much car for him."

"You want me back?"

"I would consider it."

"Yeah, and what would I have to do?"

"You'd have to behave, Ray. You'd have to be obedient."

Francis was staring at the senator. Alvarez moved a step to his left, into a slab of shadow coming from an oak tree.

"He's got a gun, Miss Rawlings," Francis said. "He's got a shotgun."

"I see it, Francis."

"I think I'll be getting on back to my room now," Francis said. "I got a couple of things to tend to."

"Stay the fuck where you are, dead man," Alvarez told him.

"You were going to steal it from me," the senator said. "Weren't you, Ray? You were going to take all that gold, and all those artworks, all those things that meant so much to me. Those things I'd devoted my life to. Those things that you don't care about at all, Ray, except how much money they're worth. And then you were going to run off."

"Yeah," he said. "That's right. I was."

"Does that mean there's somebody else, Ray? Another little Puerto Rican, maybe? Somebody who'll slap you, run around on you, humiliate you, disgrace you, all the things you like so well. Is there, Ray? Is there one of those?"

"No."

"You see, Francis," the senator said, her gray-white hair moving a little in the dark. "Ray Alvarez, big tough street smart Ray

Alvarez, is a sucker for women who abuse him. That's what he likes. He likes to be slapped and punched, dishonored. He likes his women to talk mean to him, dominate him."

"I heard about shit like that," Francis said. "Though I never met one before."

"The man wanted me to treat him like that. To kick him, disparage him. To humiliate him like a dog. And I tried. But it wasn't enough. He wanted degradations that even I couldn't manage."

Ray Alvarez could see Francis smiling. He saw his yellow teeth, his twisted yellow teeth.

"But, Ray, you must have forgotten our discussion about the Maya, about the ball game, how it works."

"I haven't forgotten."

"I think you just lost, Ray. I think you just failed to put the ball through the small hoop. And you know what that means, don't you?"

Alvarez saw headlights coming from the east along South River Drive. The first headlights he'd seen all night. And they were coming very slow this way.

Although he'd been pleased with himself for how he'd stayed under control in this tense situation, how he'd not just lifted the Franchi SPAS and whacked these two right off, now with the headlights coming, and with Francis smiling at him, and the old woman berating him, he had all the reasons a sensible man could want. It wasn't temper. It wasn't quick-draw mentality. Whatever he did now would be a hundred percent justified.

So he waited another few seconds, got his balance right, then lunged to his left, diving for the ground. And man, who would've thought it? But she'd given Francis a pistol. And from the sound of it, a .357 or something just as big. But one thing about caliber was, it didn't matter how big the bore, how powerful the load, if it was wide of the mark, all it did was blow a bigger hole in the dirt.

Ray Alvarez rolled onto his back, aimed, and blew the tall, skinny man with the jittery eyes onto the hood of the Rolls.

Alvarez rolled and rolled, until he was at the front of the car, by its grille. That winged angel hood ornament shining just above him. A sign maybe, though normally he didn't believe in shit like that. But there it was, a silver angel in the moonlight, looking down on him, giving him whatever blessing a hood ornament could.

"Ray," she whispered into the dark. "Ray?"

He didn't say anything. The headlights were coming closer now. Just a few hundred yards up the street.

"Ray, listen. Ray?"

"I hear you," he said, then moved to his left a couple of feet.

"Maybe I was wrong." Her voice hoarse all of a sudden. She said, "Maybe the ball game isn't over after all. I can be wrong sometimes. It happens. I make mistakes like everyone. Maybe we can work it all out. You could come back, be my driver. Would you like that, Ray? Be my lover again, Ray. We can put this night behind us, forget it happened. Do you hear me?"

He heard the door unlatch, watched the headlights approaching very cautiously out on the street.

"Ray, listen. Listen to me. It hasn't gone so far that we can't recover the way it was. Really. Trust me. Trust me, Ray."

Saying it now in that tone of voice she used with her campaign speeches. He'd heard her use that tone before, after the chicken cordon bleu, after the Key lime pie. Talking to the men in their suits, drinking their coffee. Selling herself to them, the political whore, appealing to them in this same sincere-sounding voice. All those men staring down at their plates, deciding just how much to make out their tax-deductible checks for. That same tone. Trust me. Trust me.

Ray Alvarez stood up. He came around the front of the Rolls.

And there she was, sitting on the edge of the backseat, her legs out the open door of the car. Her head bent over like she was showing him the part in her hair, the yellow roots. Just sitting there, deserted, without her speechwriter, probably trying to remember one of them, one of those speeches that had worked so well on those men with their Key lime pies.

He waited till she raised her head. He waited till she looked at him. He waited till she figured it out, what was going to happen. But he didn't wait so long he had to hear another goddamn word come out of her mouth.

"Oh, shit," said Hollings.

"Maybe somebody's dynamiting," Martina said, giving Hollings a smile.

"Oh, shit," Hollings said again.

"I'm going on in there," Martina said. "You keep that thing pointing out the window, you hear? Finger on the trigger. You hear me, Hollings? You listening to me?"

"Oh, shit."

"Christ," Martina said. "Listen to you. Listen to your chickenshit self, would you? I'm going ahead, parking this thing. There's two of us, Hollings. We're loaded for bear. You're an ex-marine. What the fuck you worried about?"

Martina pulled off South River Drive, drove the bookmobile over the bumpy ground a few yards into this vacant lot where she'd seen Alvarez kidnap Daniel Tyler that day. Hollings sat there, his finger inside the trigger guard of the Heckler and Koch.

There was a wad of something in the back of Hollings's throat. It'd been there ever since they heard the first blast. And he'd been trying to swallow it down. A big slippery gob that was keeping him from breathing properly.

Martina pulled the bookmobile into the center of the lot, and the headlights shined on a Rolls-Royce about fifty yards off, the driver's window sparkling with broken glass.

"Holy shit, look at that," Hollings said.

"Alvarez is already here," she said.

"Aw, shit. Come on, Martina. Now we lost the element of surprise. We got nothing going for us now."

"We got the element of bravery. We got a Silver Star soldier on our side. Hey, isn't that right, Hollings?"

"Listen, how 'bout this? We go back to my place. Go on back, get drunk maybe, split a bottle of Mateus, you know, get back in bed. Just forget about all this bullshit. How'd that be? We don't need all this goddamn gold to be happy. You and me, we got each other."

"Hollings, you moron. You earthworm."

"Come on, Martina. We don't need this shit."

"We knew, didn't we, sooner or later, we'd have to fuck with Alvarez. So it's sooner. Hell, let's get it over with."

"How you so sure it's Alvarez, anyway?"

"That's what he uses," she said. "What we heard. I listened to him brag about it a couple of times. A shotgun."

"Aw shit."

"Just shut up with that, Hollings. Keep your ears open, let me just sit here half a second, think how to approach this."

"Martina's a man," Hap Tyler said from the back of the book-mobile. "You knew that, didn't you, Hollings?"

Hollings swiveled around and looked back there. The guy had gotten the tape off his mouth some way and was sitting up, hands behind his back. He had a little smile.

"What?"

"She had a sex change operation. Go on, ask her."

Martina was looking back at him too. Her rifle on the floor between the two front seats.

Staring at Martina now, Hollings said, "What sex change?"

Martina kept watching Tyler.

"You didn't tell him, did you, Martin? You had Hollings thinking he was screwing a woman."

"We'll fucking talk about this later," Martina said. "Now, Hollings, you going to put this asshole out of his misery like you said or you gonna make me do it?"

"You're a man?" Hollings said. "I been screwing a man?"

"Do I look like a man to you? Huh? Is this what a man looks like?"

"Something was funny about you. I knew it all along. How you looked, how you are down there."

"Hollings, now isn't the time for this shit."

She made a move for the Grendel, but Hollings raised the

Heckler and Koch and brought it into her face, and said no, hold it right there. And she did.

"Tell me, Martina. Just tell me straight out. Are you a man or a woman?"

She stared at Hollings, back at the Heckler. Christ, now Hollings was glad he'd shot the yogurt out of her hand that day. Showed her how rash he could be.

"Jesus Christ."

"Tell me, Martina. Say it."

"Okay, goddamn it. I used to be a man. Now I'm a woman. I transgendered myself."

"You what?"

"It's a word. A vocabulary word for what I did."

"Holy shit. I don't fucking believe this." Hollings sat there, thinking about it, sliding his finger across the trigger. "You fucking made me into a homosexual. That's what you did. I'm a homosexual now."

"Hey, Hollings," Martina said. She passed her hand through the air between them, like she was checking if he was awake. "You forget what's going on? You forget about Alvarez? He's out there somewhere, Hollings, in the dark. He could be creeping up on us right now. And the fucking guy isn't going to be real happy seeing us here either, you can bet your ass on that. You see what I'm saying? This isn't the time for a personal conversation. This is the time we should be out there on our goddamn bellies staying out of sight."

"She murders her lovers too," Hap said. "She's murdered five of them. And she's probably planning on doing you next, Hollings."

Martina was breathing through her mouth, moving her eyes back and forth between Hollings and the Grendel that lay on the floor between them.

"How you know all this, Tyler?" Hollings asked him, without looking away from Martina.

"I know it, the cops know it, the newspaper and TV people.

Everybody knows it but you, Hollings. You're the last one to find out.''

"This true?" Hollings said very quietly to Martina. "Is what he's saying true? Take a minute. Make sure you get it right. 'Cause I can tell if you're lying to me, Martina. I can tell how you say it, it's true or not.''

"All right, Glenn. I have a troubled past. I never tried to hide that from you. I had some clashes with people.''

"She cut the head off her last girlfriend. Left the body at my house last night.''

"Shut up, you asshole.'' Martina glared back at Tyler, then turned to Glenn and tried to make her face softer.

"Woman by the name of Deshawna Barkley,'' Tyler said. "Martin Phelps's old girlfriend.''

"Is that right?'' Hollings said. "That head in my washer, that was somebody you screwed?''

Martina didn't say anything. But from just the way she was sitting there, silent and looking square at him, he knew it was true.

He didn't pick his target, at least not in his conscious mind he didn't. It was like with the yogurt, he just reacted, going with the signals his unconscious mind was sending up, like that quantum thing, just going ahead with it, not thinking. He squeezed off a round into her foot. Then he shot her in the other foot. She screamed, and it sounded to Hollings like a man screaming. She writhed around in her seat, fell forward against the steering wheel. Her eyes tight. Moaning, trying to bite it back, but not succeeding.

Hollings was no damn murderer. He was basically a good man. Something of a loser, all right, he'd admit it, but that didn't rule out being a good man all the same. He'd only killed that one time in Vietnam, and he'd had official encouragement from the U.S. government to do that. That was nothing to feel guilty about. But if he killed Martina, shot her right there, that would be something else. He wouldn't be able to live with that. Even though this person, this deviant, had turned him, without his even knowing it, into a homosexual, even then, he still couldn't kill her. So he shot her those two times in the feet, and saw that she was disabled. Crying and moaning, twitching as she pressed her face against the steering wheel. The woman wasn't going anywhere now, except maybe if she crawled there real slow.

Hollings turned around and looked at Tyler there in the back of the bookmobile. The guy had told Hollings the truth. Set him straight. But of course, he'd done it to throw a monkey wrench into how things were going, to save his own ass. Still, the guy had been honest, so maybe he should let him go. On the other hand, the truth the guy had told was the worst news of Hollings's life. He was debating it like that, going back and forth, shoot him, not shoot him, wound him, kill him, let him be. His eyes on Tyler, the Heckler and Koch pointed at him. Tyler sneaking looks down at Martina's Grendel, so Hollings leaned over to pick it up, get it out of his reach. Leaned down just at the exact lucky moment when the blast came, and the windshield glass exploded all around them.

# CHAPTER 32

Marguerite and Wills were a hundred yards from the mill site when the blasts came. Wills took hold of her arm and turned around and together they ran back to the 7-Eleven. From the pay phone, he called for backup, shots fired. When he hung up, he led Marguerite over to the car and settled her into the driver's seat. She protested. But he told her she had to stay there, no two ways about it, he'd just trot on down the street, see what all the noise was about. Saying it in a slow, bored voice like this was an every night thing for him, then started away into the dark, pulling out his pistol as he went.

When he was a good fifty yards away, Marguerite got out of the car and followed, tacking off into the darker shadows at the edge of the street, having to race to stay up with him. Down the street she heard shouts, then nothing, no gunshots, nothing.

A hundred yards, another hundred, Marguerite out of breath, slipped in the loose gravel, fell, cut her knees and the palms of her hands, but scrambled back to her feet and ran after Wills. He was almost out of sight, going down the road into the middle of the mill site. And in another thirty yards, heaving loud, Marguerite was there, on the path into the vacant lot, seeing Garnetta's Rolls off to the east, and a big white van near the dig site.

She staggered to a halt and stared. Felt her knees begin to weaken. In the moonlight, and the yellow security lights from the docks across the street, she saw what had happened. The acre of ground was completely plowed up. A front end loader on the western perimeter, its big scoop cocked up in the air. The land criss-crossed with trenches, piles of dirt, mounds, the earth scarred and broken.

She groped ahead between the hills of dirt, heard Wills call her name, shout at her to go back, but she couldn't, she had to see this. She walked ahead between the pits and trenches. The place looked like a bombing range. She heard scrambling in the woods, sticks breaking, dry brush rattling, but she didn't care.

Then there was another blast, a shotgun perhaps, something very loud with a bright flash. And several fast shots, automatic fire. A voice yelled her name. More shots. Men grunting in the dark.

Numb, she walked toward where the stream had been, the rapids, where her great-grandmother's big paddle wheel had turned and driven the heavy stone roller that ground the coontie. And there she saw what all along she had known was there, and what tonight had drawn her ahead through all those heaps of earth, as if she'd been towed by the call of it, unconcerned by the gunfire.

Her eyes fixed on the white rubble at her feet. Bones, luminous in the darkness. An arm, perhaps. A leg. The skeleton broken apart. A rotten plank of pine or some kind of wood lay nearby. Marguerite stared at the remains, thinking there should have been a bony hand reaching up through the dirt, reaching up for her. That would have been the right thing, the grim, awful, perfect thing. For a moment, her imagination working so hard, she thought maybe that's what it was. But no, as she closed in on it, bent forward, she saw it clearly. A foot, the heel toward the sky, as if the bones of Ramona Rawlings had heard the giant machine coming to tumble her from her last and final grave, and those bones had tried frantically to swim back into the soft ground, and had been caught that way, transfixed, one foot still showing as she dove for cover.

Just behind her, a voice spoke. But she didn't turn. There were more shots nearby, an explosion of dirt in a mound just to her left. In her ear Detective Wills said something, quiet, soothing words she couldn't make out, then he took hold of her, apologized, and heaved her up onto his shoulder and carried her. He carried her off the property, back out to the street, and she heard more shots, and then more answered them. Loud blasts, but she wasn't frightened. She didn't think she'd ever be frightened again.

Wills stumbled along with her, jogging awkwardly, carrying her all the way, a half mile, maybe more, back to the 7-Eleven. And he put her into the passenger seat of her Corvette. He went inside the store, came right back out with the young clerk. Then he raised the top, rolled up the windows, locked her door, and he climbed in behind the wheel and started the car, squealed the tires as he drove her Corvette behind the grocery store and parked it in the security area where the clerk's car was. The clerk watching all this, a young man with a baseball hat worn backward.

And Wills told her again to stay right there. Police were on their way, he had to go back to the mill site. Stay right there. Did she hear him? Of course she did. Really, Wills, come on. She was a big girl, a newspaper woman. Street smart. She knew about the world. Don't worry about her. In a way, she told him, this was the best night of her life. She'd met Ramona. Her body was there, just as she'd known it would be. Everything was going to be all right. Sure, it's gonna be fine, he said, his voice no longer bored, no longer trying to pretend. Absolutely, he said. Now you stay right here. You'll be safe. Okay? Okay, she said.

Where's Hap? she said, before he could go. And Wills said, don't worry, he'd go get Hap now. He was down the street. Yes, go get Hap, she said. He should know about what she'd found. She wanted to talk to him. She wanted to talk to Hap. Wills took her keys from the ignition, put them in his pocket, and left, running. He was a big man, and looked silly running. A lumbering Kodiak bear. But he was, he was running, his gun drawn. Running back to the mill where Ramona's bones lay basking in the moonlight.

In the dark, bracing his back against an oak tree, his finger on the trigger of the Heckler and Koch, Hollings was thinking that maybe what it was, a guy like him only had one heroic chance a lifetime. And he'd already used his up. Like that hundred-yard-dash kid he remembered from years ago. Sixteen-year-old kid from the ghetto, never done anything in his life, not read, not watch TV, nothing. Didn't know the world existed outside his tarpaper house. Then in some state track meet the kid sets the world record. Fastest human alive. Everybody takes his picture, asks him what he thinks about this and that. Microphones in his face. A week later somebody beats his record and bang, you never hear of the kid again. His big moment happening when he was too young and dumb to enjoy it. Like Hollings.

Because here he was, fairly heavily armed for peacetime in a friendly country, and just a couple of enemy shooters so far as he could tell, Alvarez and some other big guy running around out in the dark, but still he couldn't get his body to cooperate. Couldn't get his legs to carry him away from the safety of that tree. He just wanted to wait there, wait till the gunfire died out altogether, stay behind that oak, keep his eyes and ears sharp, and hope the fucking sun would pick today to come up a few hours early.

After the windshield exploded, Hollings dove out the door of the bookmobile and wriggled over to the oak, and that's where he'd been for the last five minutes. Or it could be an hour, Christ, who could tell?

He'd fired a few rounds up at the sky just out of sheer fucking terror, but now he just sat quiet, trying to figure out where all this started going rotten. How in less than two weeks he'd gone from a quiet, ordinary life to a guy with a girlfriend who was a man. From a guy who was happy finding twenty bucks in loose change, to a guy about to die over four hundred million.

Maybe it started at the beach that day with the Hispanic girls. After Alvarez walked up to him, he should've shot him right there, seeing that look he had in his eyes. Or no, even before that, that afternoon in the parking lot at the Holiday Inn. Alvarez acting all buddy buddy, inviting him in on something without even knowing him. Hollings should've gotten in his car, and hauled ass back to his house, got out his GTA and right away gone hunting for loose change.

But maybe more than anything, what did him in was that

higher purpose bullshit. Thinking he was due something better than the miserable fate he had. Because the truth was, guys like him didn't get the brass ring. They didn't win the lottery, or find sunken ships. He'd been happy enough on a hundred bucks a week. Happy driving around in his beat-to-shit Datsun B-210. Complaining, sure. But still happy. Nothing wrong in his life. Everything ahead of him. Even the hunger he felt, the higher purpose hunger, that was good, that made him sharper, more alert. But as soon as he actually started getting close, started thinking the brass ring was coming around and this time he had a good shot at it, he lost it all. He wasn't free anymore. Always thinking about that ship. About the gold, about being rich, being in the paper, in *Newsweek,* on TV. More than being rich, being famous, having people come up to him, say hello, know who he was, wanting to shake his hand. He got eaten up by it. And it kept him from seeing straight, seeing what Alvarez was up to.

And now here he was. One week he's happy-go-lucky, next week he's being stalked by a maniac with a semiauto shotgun in a dark vacant lot, he didn't know where the fuck it was located, and the feeling he had was, this was it. He was out of hero miracles. He was out of quantum mechanics. He was just scared. And he was pretty sure he was about to turn around any second and look right into the double-dark eyes of the devil himself.

It was about twenty yards back to the bookmobile. And Hollings started to think maybe he could just squirm back over there, get in it, drive off, head somewhere else. With a truck full of books, he could pull off, have a beer, read for a while, then get back in front and drive some more. Now, that was something. That was a plan. There was sure as shit nothing holding him in Miami. This town where he'd been born had been trying to squeeze him out for the last thirty-something years. Cubans squeezing him, Haitians, rich people, retirees, tourists. All of them coming to Miami and buying up every goddamn square inch of it, till there wasn't a decent place left for a guy like Hollings, a guy who'd been born there, a fucking native, lived there all his life. Not a decent place left for guys like him.

And as soon as he started thinking about leaving Miami, looking at those twenty dark yards, his stomach twisted even more. And the hot wad deep in his throat got bigger. Only twenty yards. A straight line. Get back in there, turn the key, haul ass. Yeah, like *Route 66*, he'd watched as a kid. The two of them in their Corvette going across America, washing dishes or tending bar when they ran out of money. Getting into trouble here and there with redneck sheriffs, sleeping with pretty girls, fighting with the locals now and then, but always moving.

Yeah, that suited Hollings. Especially now he was on more solid ground with women, was beginning to see what he'd been doing wrong in the past with them. Not smiling enough, not winking. Not going slow enough with them. Even if he'd learned all he knew from a man, still it seemed to work so far with the women he'd bumped into on the street. He couldn't hold that part against Martina.

Yeah, things could work out. He could save his money, maybe sell some library books along the way, and use the profits to buy another GTA. Then he'd be set. Books, loose change. A van big enough he could sleep in it at rest stops along the highway.

'Cause look, it was just twenty yards. Christ, in Chu Lai that day he'd run around in the middle of machine gun fire for most of an hour and not even got nicked. He could do that again. Why couldn't he? Look at how close it was, how fucking close.

"Going somewhere?"

Hollings didn't even need to turn around. He knew what he'd see. The look that would be on Alvarez's face, the shit-eating grin. The guy might even be combing his hair with one hand while he aimed with the other. No, there was no point in turning around, messing up the front of his face with the blast. No, he'd just go ahead with his plan. It was a good plan. It was something he should've done about ten years ago when he had a little more energy. See the USA, drive coast to coast. Meet people, learn something about geography, learn whatever he could pick up out there. He should've done that a long time ago. That's probably how it always went, people on their deathbed, they realize where they went wrong, what they'd do if they had it over, which of course they wouldn't. Like some kind of fantasy game they had to play out right at the end. What if I'd gone down that street in 1956 instead of that other street?

Yeah, so Hollings stood up, dropped the Heckler on the ground, and just moseyed on over toward the bookmobile. Feeling good and relaxed. Probably confused Alvarez a little, too, the guy not saying anything as he walked off, got halfway to the bookmobile, and still Alvarez hadn't said a word. Got a few more steps and started thinking, shit, this was easy. You just did what you wanted to do, and people didn't know what to make of it. The world stepped aside for a man who knew where he was headed. He'd just get in the bookmobile and start off up the highway. Have to get himself a good map, find exactly where route 66 was. Hell, it might not even exist anymore. But by god, if it didn't exist, he'd find another road as good as that one. Better.

Glenn Hollings had pictured dying many times. A game he played at night, falling asleep. Lately he'd decided how it would feel was, at the exact second you died, it'd be like everybody in the world was dying too. All the people, all the animals and trees, the mountains, the clouds, all of it withering up. Like all it had ever been was a movie for his benefit. A movie coming out of his own goddamn head. His eyes projecting it into the air in front of him, and then his body walking toward it. That's what he thought. You died, all it was was, the film got stuck inside the projector in your head and you watched the last frame you'd been watching go a little cockeyed, freeze, then a hole in the middle of it starts to turn dark and it melts and then it catches fire and then everything goes black. That's how he'd always imagined it.

Hap clawed at the wrapping tape on his ankles, fumbling, searching for the tail end of it. Finally he got his thumbnail under it, peeled it up, and the damn thing started to split apart down the middle. He was suddenly unwrapping half a width of tape, leaving the other half on. The gunfire had been quiet for a few minutes while Hap struggled frantically to strip it off. He listened, tried to keep his breathing quiet, tried not to bump the noisy metal floor.

Martina had been passing in and out of consciousness the whole while. Groaning, then passing out. Waking up and groaning some more. Finally she mumbled something, lurched sideways and tumbled out the door. He thought he could hear her outside now, scrabbling through the brush.

Finally, maybe five minutes after the windshield was blown out, Hap unwrapped the last of the tape and stood up. But before he had a chance to take a step toward the back door, the flattop guy, Hollings, appeared in the driver's door. He glanced back at Hap for half a second, the man's face very composed, almost a smile. He looked like he was about to say something to Hap, something pleasant, when the blast came, and Hollings's head jerked backward, as if someone had yanked a noose around his throat, and in the same instant his body blew across the front compartment, flattened against the passenger door and stayed wedged there. When the echo faded Hap heard the unmistakable rack of another shell into the chamber of a shotgun.

His instinct was to dive out the back doors, hit and roll and make a run for it. Take his chances. Anything but cower back there. But he caught himself, and forced himself down into a crouch behind the driver's seat. If it was Alvarez, the man had no way of knowing Hap was in the van. Everything in Hap's body said to take flight. But his mind said, wait, see what happens. Try not to sneeze, keep his stomach from growling.

For a moment he thought he heard the voice starting to speak again. A whisper from his gut. Out of old habit, he strained to hear. And slowly, slowly, it rose in volume, suffusing him with its glow. A different tone, a new cadence. But eerily familiar.

It took him a moment more to absorb it. Spanish. A long string of Spanish curses. The names of the holy trinity, the names of sexual acts, the names of some select bodily fluids.

Yeah, it was Alvarez. Standing in the doorway of the van, looking across at Hollings's body. Hap could see the gleam of the shotgun barrel, the man's thick hair bedraggled now. He drew his head back behind the seat, huddled lower.

Hap felt the springs give as Alvarez stepped into the van. He bowed his head, drew his legs in. A fetal curl behind the seat. The big man sat down at the wheel of the van.

Hap watched the barrel showing at the edge of the seat. Watched it bob in time with Alvarez's breathing. Hap could reach out six inches, seize it from his grip. So tempting.

He took a long, slow breath, poised, waiting for more of the barrel to show itself, just enough to get some leverage. But Alvarez moved it away, speaking to himself, cursing at Hollings. Blowing his nose once into a handkerchief. The barrel jiggled into view, then twitched away.

Then he went quiet. He stood up. Hap could feel the van shift. The squeak of his leather soles. He could smell the sour sweat on the man. The van shifted again. Hap tightened his crouch, tilted his eyes up to catch the first glimpse of Alvarez coming around the driver's seat. He readied himself to lunge.

He heard nothing for a moment, then some kind of quiet scratching. He brought his head to the edge of the seat, took a one-eyed peek around it. The man was combing his hair in the rearview mirror. A silver comb, brushing the thick black hair with a hypnotic absorption.

It would have been easy to stand up now, tackle Alvarez from behind, drive him forward into the dashboard. After all these years, it would make up for the night in Nha Trang, the night he stayed put. This time he could uncoil, scream the war cry, match his flesh against another man's flesh. It would have a purifying rightness to it. Risking his life to balance things out. Erase an old debt. The ghosts of his platoon cheering him on. Finally, Hap, finally you have jumped down to join us, to tilt the balance.

But he did the harder thing and stayed huddled back of the seat and waited till Alvarez was finished with his hair and stepped down from the van. Hap waited there a few minutes more until he heard Martina's voice, pleading to Alvarez like he was the almighty god. Then another blast of the shotgun.

A minute later, Hap heard a motor roar to life, a diesel engine, the headlights passing for a moment through the windows of the van. Hap peered around the edge of the seat. A front end loader, bouncing away toward the street.

Hap waited till the motor chugged away a hundred yards or so, then he stood up, stepped over Hollings's legs, jumped down to the ground. A few yards away, Martina was on her back, her head hanging backward into one of the trenches. She wasn't moving.

Hap ran for the street, away from the diesel motor, then saw the Rolls parked off to his left, and veered in its direction. The diesel flared up behind him, but Hap didn't look back, just sprinted to the Rolls. He ripped the door open, and dropped into a pile of broken glass in the front seat. He fumbled with the ignition key, got the car started, heard a man's voice shout his name, heard the roar of the shotgun.

He jammed the shifter into drive, pressed the pedal to the floor and the car heaved forward toward the street, and the body of a tall, skinny man rolled up the hood of the car and pressed itself against the windshield. Bellowing a wordless curse, Hap braked hard, then accelerated, yanked the wheel to the right, and the body slid away.

Then there was another blast from the shotgun and the rear window of the Rolls shattered and Hap felt a hot sting, and a sudden numbness in his left shoulder. The car lumbered out to South River Drive. His foot was pressed to the floor, but the car picked up speed at only a polite, leisurely rate.

He swung the car west, taking a quick look in the rearview mirror, the dark shadow of a man raising a shotgun and taking aim, and Hap swerved the big car right, ran over the curb, then left, and then he believed he was out of range, rolling fast, fifty, fifty-five down the narrow, darkened street, the headlights washing over a man running, he only caught a glimpse, a big man in a white shirt, Hap driving on, past a 7-Eleven, tires screaming as he slewed out onto Twenty-seventh Avenue, still picking up speed, because he could not raise his foot from the pedal, he could not slow down.

# CHAPTER 33

MARGUERITE WAS STANDING AT THE FENCE OF THE security parking lot, exchanging looks with the clerk in the baseball cap, when she heard the car coming, recognized its plush rumble. She dashed over to the side fence to see it. And yes, it was her mother's Rolls rolling past. Forty-five, fifty miles an hour, too fast for that narrow, darkened street, swerving recklessly.

"Hey, wait," the clerk said as she headed for the Corvette. "You gotta stay here. Cop said." The kid tried to cut her off.

She stiff-armed him in the chest, ran to the car, patted under the front bumper, found the Hide-a-key, turned and climbed inside, started it. And the clerk, just eighteen, nineteen, the shadow of a goatee on his chin, his cap still on backward, a flunkie doing what the cop told him, stood in the path of her headlights. She jammed it in reverse and flattened the accelerator, screeched backward through the chain link fence, gouging her candy apple paint job, spinning and fishtailing through loose gravel into the street.

The taillights of the Rolls were gone. She shifted into first, hammered it. In a few seconds she was out on Twenty-seventh, the long brightly lit avenue stretching before her, and there, a half mile away, she saw her mother's car speeding down the middle of the street.

She followed, hanging back a block or two. Running stoplights when she had to, but keeping the Rolls in sight south through the

Gables and into the Grove. As she followed the car, a glow began to spread inside her like the warmth of brandy after a full meal.

With absolute clarity, she saw what she had to do. Confront her mother, tell her everything. Tell her what she had only explained to Wills, what she had gushed out at Bernie Saterfield, what was in her article, what was in her heart. Tell Garnetta everything. Not to punish her or forgive her, and not to bring them closer. Christ, no. She'd long ago given up hope for that. But because it was overdue, because it was right. She had been telling the truth to the wrong people for too long.

She needed to have this conversation. She had not had one with her father because he had died before she knew how important it was to say these things out loud. She would never have that talk with him, the one where she asked him, Daddy, how did I do? How did I turn out? The one where she told him, Daddy, you were wonderful, just exactly what I needed. Even loving me more than I could bear, more than I could possibly return. It was fine. It was all right. Marguerite Rawlings could never have that conversation, but she could have the other one, the one where she told Garnetta how it felt to be a Rawlings. How it felt to be linked by blood to a woman dead a hundred years, a woman she understood, respected, a woman she had always loved more than her own living mother.

As Marguerite drove her Corvette across town, the calmness spread through her, driving through the Grove, down to Bayshore, seeing where her mother was headed. Not sure why she was going there, but still, it seemed right that Marguerite should confront Garnetta at the Commodore's house, the place the Tyler children had managed to preserve. A house that had survived a hundred years of Shorty Bussers knocking on the front door, inquiring whether finally the Tylers were ready to cash in, sell this choice piece of real estate. A house that had defeated Shorty Busser, defeated Miami's compulsive desire to scrape the ground clean every five years and cram in a fresh set of flimsy cement-block cubicles with all the trendiest amenities. The Tylers had managed to do what the Rawlingses had not. They had managed to hold on to who they were.

\*   \*   \*

Hap parked the Rolls off in the trees to the east of Mangrove House. He sat there a moment watching the dark bay silvered with moonlight. A fifteen- to twenty-knot wind drove an armada of shredded clouds past the moon. It was a perfect night to be out there sailing. Not here, hopelessly land-bound, trapped in that maze of man-made things, walking the hallways others had designed, driving their paths. Going only where the roads led, planting his feet inside the footprints painted there. On land there was no choice. You conformed to the rigid structures others had left behind. But out there on the bay, it was different. Everything was fluid. Go here, go there. No signs, no narrow lanes, no walls, no paths worn into the water. Out there you were restricted only by the draft of your boat, your energy and will. Your imagination.

Hap opened the door and got out. His left hand was partially numb, and even marginal movements of his head sent bolts of raw current through his belly. But no arteries were cut, and the throb in his left shoulder had subsided to a vague howl.

He went into the house. Cooler than the night, the perpetual breeze filtering through. He washed himself at the kitchen sink, touched his shoulder, found three or four buckshot puckers. He avoided the mirrors as he toweled off, patted the blood from his neck. There would be shrapnel to pick out tomorrow. There would be punctures to sew shut. There would be antibiotics and a tetanus shot and pain killers. There would be clean bandages. But for now there was another kind of work.

Marguerite parked the Corvette a few hundred yards from the house. She walked down the path of pine needles and sand to where the Rolls was parked. There was nothing in her head. No speech, no curses. She felt as empty as if she had wept for a week.

Seeing Ramona's bones, seeing them scattered, this woman who had been so real to her, a living presence, and now was only those bones, only those white fragments in the dirt, that finished it for Marguerite. No more conversations, no more prayers. It would be true madness to pray to bones. She was finally and thoroughly released from that.

She approached the Rolls. A side window and the back window were blown out. She came close, looked into the front seat. Nothing. There was a smear of blood on the hood of the car.

She craned forward, looked through the broken window into the back seat. A woman's shoe lay on the floorboard on the passenger side. A black low heel. Her mother's shoe. Marguerite opened the door.

Her mother's body was slumped on the floor of the backseat. Her face serene in the moonlight. She looked as if she might be asleep. Dreaming about some utopia where the rich and powerful could climb together to the summit of a great pyramid, be free forever from the wretched lower classes. And there she and the rest of the select few would put on their golden robes, their crowns, their amulets, and make their holy bargains with the stars.

Garnetta Rawlings had made her last bargain, sailed out beyond pyramids and pain. Out beyond golden frogs and golden masks and gold of any kind. All she was now was spatter and gore, just bloody hash. Her dress torn open, shredded. It seemed that only her face had been spared.

At her throat a necklace of jaguar heads shone in the moonlight. Some Mayan bauble. It hadn't saved her. It had given her no power over the dangers of this world. Maybe it would work better in the next. Marguerite hoped so.

She leaned forward, reached out and touched her mother's face. Cool, soft. She smoothed the backs of her fingers across her cheek. Combed a single strand of hair out of her left eye.

Marguerite gathered herself for a moment, took a breath, then she leaned forward, pressed her cheek against her mother's cheek. Her mouth near Garnetta's ear. She breathed in the mild scent of the Camay, that familiar clean aroma, and the thousand occasions when Marguerite had been close enough to her mother to smell that Camay before, all of them flooded through her at once.

Somewhere she'd heard that even when all the other senses died, when the brain was no longer functioning, the heart quiet, even then, the dead could still hear a few last sounds. So when she spoke into her mother's ear, she imagined it as calling down a bottomless well, her mother dropping away from her, falling endlessly into that dark pit, with Marguerite's words echoing after her. And of the many things she had long wanted to say, she could think of only one. For the first time, and the last, Marguerite spoke those words. She whispered to her mother, yes, she loved her. Yes, yes, despite everything, she had always loved her. Always.

After Hap washed up, he went into the dining room. Switched on the Beseler opaque projector. A photograph was still inside it from the last tour he'd given. That afternoon of the schoolmarm who, by god, knew her Florida history. And as the machine's thousand watts warmed up, Commodore Randolph Tyler came to life against the dark wall.

Hap stared at him for a moment, the Commodore standing next to the Devil's Punchbowl, water flowing from a slot in the limestone. He had his hat on, a long-sleeved, brilliant white shirt, a stern gaze. In that photograph, he was a man of fifty, a man who'd lost his wife, and had seen the death of many friends, but there was not a trace of any of that in his eyes.

This was a man who was going to live forever. He was going to be the first of those. The first immortal. Floating on the wall, his eyes on Hap, eyes without a trace of compromise or fear or hesitation. What in the world could challenge this man? What in the world could nick him, hurt him in any way, draw him down into the grave? Nothing could. His eyes said that. Nothing could bring him down. Just try. Just damn well try.

Using his good right hand, Hap lowered the lever for the feeding shelf, slid the photograph out. He reached into his back pocket, took out the maps, unfolded them and flattened them on the dining room table. With a book from a nearby shelf, he ironed out what wrinkles he could, then placed the 1881 map into the feeding shelf and cranked it closed.

The coastline from Palm Beach to Miami appeared on the wall. He looked at it for a moment, then went back into the kitchen, found a roll of Scotch tape, came back into the dining room and fastened the map he'd found in Daniel's safe-deposit box in the center of the white wall.

He went back to the projector, focused it. But the scale was considerably off. The Commodore's map much smaller than the library's. So he scooted the Beseler forward toward the wall. He moved it inch by inch, watching the image shrink and sharpen. Until the maps were approximately in scale. The squiggles on Daniel's map about equal to those that shined against it.

First he tried to align the Miami River from the ancient map against the wavering line on the wall. Not even close. The line on the treasure map was ragged, but held a steady course. While the original Miami River took several hard turns north and south, then a series of lazy S curves wandering west toward the Everglades.

He nudged the machine an inch or two to the right, so the Florida coastline moved over the jagged hand-drawn map. With the elevation screw he raised the machine tick by tick, watching the wall for any mesh of image, coastline against coastline. He went up and down, very slowly, from Palm Beach to Miami, trying to find the place where ripple fit to ripple. In this scale, the five-pointed star was roughly a hundred yards offshore. But the ripples didn't coincide.

After completing the whole length of coastline, he tried edging the machine a fraction inch closer to the wall, repeated the process, but still no congruency. Three bays in a row, a peninsula, lay over two bays and a node of land. Nothing matched.

Now what the hell did he have here? Perhaps this was no map at all. Nothing more than a single random jigsaw piece that didn't fit the puzzle he was playing. He had pinned so much on this and now it seemed like nothing.

"Turn it over."

Hap whirled around. The pain in his shoulder flashed, and he staggered to his left, caught himself against the table.

"Turn it around. You've got it upside down."

Marguerite stood in the doorway. Striped blouse, white pants torn at the knees, clothes marked with smears of blood and dirt.

"What?"

"The thing on the wall. It's upside down."

"Marguerite." He started toward her, but she raised both open hands, and he halted.

Her eyes were stunned but still focused, looking at the wall, at the map.

Her cheeks were damp, but there was a shy, almost rueful smile on her lips. When she brought her eyes to his, they cleared and deepened.

"We're going to be all right," he said. "You, me. We're going to get through this. We're tough, we're pioneer stock."

"Yes," she said. "We are."

He started toward her again, and this time she didn't resist. The smile still there, a faint heat in her eyes. She opened her arms and he stepped inside them and they embraced. He breathed in her hair, the dusky scent, her sweat, her human oils. She turned her head and pressed the side of her face to his chest, and he felt something, a deep tangling of molecules and atoms, all those complex electrical currents rearranging themselves to accommodate this fusion, like two halves of an equation finally brought together.

When it was over, they stepped out of each other's grasp, hands lingering against hands.

"I'm a good map reader," she said. "I've always tested out very high in visual relationships. You know those tests, drawings of perforated boxes, you predict what shapes they'd become if they were folded up. I'm always good at that."

"Who would've thought?"

"You're hurt," she said, and reached a hand out to his neck. Ran her fingertips lightly over bruised and broken places.

"I'm all right."

"What happened to you?"

"I'll tell you later. There's lots of time for that."

She went slowly to the bright wall, took down the map, turned it over, and retaped it.

"Try this, I think I see a match."

"But that puts the star east of the shore, on land."

"Of course," she said. "That's possible. Hurricane comes out of the east. Storm surge. Flooding. The ship runs way up onto shore, cracks up. Storm passes, waters retreat, boat stays there. Time comes, time goes. What's left of the ship rots, gold gets covered over. That's how it could go. A lot can happen in a few hundred years."

Hap looked at her for a long moment, then turned back to the machine. He used the elevator knob, cranked the map up and down until finally, yes, he saw it coming, yes, then there it was. The grooves nestled together, merged into one solid wavy line.

"Good god," he said.

"And women are supposed to have lousy spatial skills."

"You see where it is," he said, "where the star is?"

"There's the Miami River," she said softly, "then south of that there's Brickell Point, then Dinner Key. And a little south of that, it's here. Right here."

For several moments they looked at the wall, listening to the hum of the cooling fan inside the Beseler.

He said, "Maybe it's not a treasure map at all."

"I was thinking the same thing."

"Just a diagram marking the land he was going to buy, where he wanted to settle. A note to himself."

"Yeah," she said. "Just what it looks like. A doodle."

"Then why did Daniel save it?"

"Maybe because it was old. Maybe that's all."

He looked at the bright wall another moment, then told her he'd be right back and turned and walked into the kitchen. He snapped up the phone, dialed information, got the home number for Michael Overbeck from Crandon's Jewelers.

"Hap Tyler," he said when Overbeck answered. "Yeah, I know, it's past my bedtime too."

Overbeck must've remembered the possibility of a lawsuit, because he calmed down almost instantly, and very politely asked how he could possibly be of help.

"When you cleaned the jewelry that Daniel brought to you

every year, I'm curious, what was it you cleaned off? Rust? Mineral deposits? Like had it been underwater, or what?"

Hap watched Marguerite standing in the bright pathway of the opaque projector. She stared at the maps, reached a finger out to touch the wall.

"You're sure?"

Overbeck said, yes, he was quite sure. He'd unfortunately been forced to make an extensive study of the subject, living in an old roach-infested house as he did.

"Thanks," Hap said. "Yes, that's very helpful. Very."

"Well?" Marguerite said when he came back to the dining room.

"Roach shit," said Hap. "The gold pieces always had an outer crust of roach shit."

"So?"

"You have any problem with roaches?" he said. "You know, wading through a certain number of palmetto bugs."

She followed him into the kitchen. He scooted the table aside, and stooped to pull up the trap door, but a jerk of pain threw him sideways. Marguerite stepped beside him, put her arm around his shoulder and steadied him.

"You need a doctor, Hap."

He told her no, and shrugged off her arm.

"So bullheaded."

"Hey, how did you know I'd be here, anyway?"

"I followed you. I was at the mill tonight."

"You were?"

"Wills is there now. Lots of cops were on their way when I left. It's all over now."

She smiled vaguely, then glanced around the kitchen. She seemed in a trance, a peaceful waking sleep. There was a dazed brilliance in her eyes, her movements composed, but at the same time her flesh seemed to vibrate like some gong that had been struck an enormous blow.

Hap went to the pantry, found a flashlight and the roach spray, brought them back and held them out to her.

"I guess you should be the one to do this," he said. "I seem to be a little groggy."

She took the flashlight and spray can and opened the door to the root cellar. She flashed the beam down into the dark. The light faltered, and Marguerite gave the flashlight a hard tap against her leg. It came back on.

"What am I looking for?"

"I don't know," he said. "Maybe a door. Something that leads under the foundation. I've only been in the root cellar once or twice. Never to stay very long."

"I can see why."

She gave the roach spray a couple of hard shakes, then eased down into the root cellar, and dropped out of sight. Hap went again to the pantry, found a tack hammer and brought it back.

"Tap the wood," he said as he kneeled and handed it down to her. "See what you can find."

She began rapping at the walls, working her way around the small room. The cellar wasn't more than six feet square, its walls made of the same Pensacola pine as the rest of the house.

In a minute, he heard the echo of a hollow wall.

"What do you see?" Hap bent to look, but another hot stab behind his eyes took his breath away. He drew back.

"A clasp," she said. And he heard her groan as she struggled to open it. After a couple of moments, she tried tapping it with the hammer. Then he heard the long screech of rusty hinges.

"What is it? What do you see?"

She said nothing.

"Marguerite?"

"Hap," she said. Her voice sober. "You have any other batteries? These are starting to go."

"What do you see, Marguerite? What is it?"

"I'm not sure. Just a minute. Hold on."

Then behind him, he thought he heard the creak of the front door, and he stiffened, caught his breath, listened. Nothing more. He walked quietly over to the knife rack next to the sink, slid out the heaviest one. Tiptoed out the kitchen door, across the dining room. Pressing himself flat against the wall next to the doorway, he lifted the knife, took an underhand grip. With absolute attention, he monitored the snaps and cricks of that old house. Just the natural sounds. Wind straining against wood.

He exhaled. Stepped out into the hall. Looked up the stairs, in the parlor. He went slowly to the top of the stairway, surveyed the landing, but nothing was there.

He came back down. Stood in the foyer and listened again. Still nothing. He blew out a sigh and turned and headed back through the dining room. He was a step or two inside the room when he halted. Standing a few feet away, Ray Alvarez was combing his hair in the octagonal mirror that hung above the oak side table. Combing with one hand, holding a shotgun in the other.

"Hey there, Tyler. Am I on time for the tour?"

"As a matter of fact," Hap said. "We were just about to begin."

CHAPTER 34

"Brought you a present," Alvarez said, still looking at himself in the mirror, reshaping a ducktail. "Think of it like an early Christmas. I'll give you mine, then you can give me yours."

Alvarez patted the side of his head, just above the ear. Didn't seem that interested in getting the hair right, more like a theatrical effect, doing something casual while he made his audience fidget. Working like a charm with Hap.

"Okay, then, so let me show you what I got for you." His blue eyes were as lightless and inert as scars.

He broke away from his image, stooped, and picked up a small cardboard box, and set it in on the dining table.

"How 'bout you let me borrow that knife for a minute?" Alvarez gestured toward Hap with the shotgun, and Hap stepped forward, put the knife down on the table and slid it to him.

Alvarez bent over the box and sliced it along the seams, glancing up at Hap.

When he had the box open, he set the knife on the table in front of him, slid his hands inside the box, and in a white shower of Styrofoam pellets, he drew out a large silver toaster.

"This is *my* present." He held it up on the palm of his right hand. "Black and Decker. Naturally, they had cheaper ones, but I thought, what the hell, I had this in mind for a long time, I wouldn't want to fuck it up using a cheap toaster."

While Hap stood across the dining table, staring at him, Alvarez placed the toaster on the end table, and squatted down to plug it in. Then he stood up and surveyed the room.

Everything about the man was thick. Though he wasn't any taller than Hap, he displaced twice as much air. But for a man so chunky, when he had stooped to plug in the toaster and risen again, he did it with surprising suppleness, like a matador who had simply overpowered a few too many meals.

Alvarez pushed down the lever on the toaster and peered into one of the slots.

"You're out of luck, Alvarez."

"Yeah, and why's that?"

"I don't believe in Christmas. I'm a pagan."

Slowly, all the amusement seeped from Alvarez's eyes, and with it went what meager human shine had been there. It became the face of a man who knew excruciating secrets about the human anatomy, which vessel to pinch off, where to grind a stubby thumb. The G-spots of torture.

Staring at Hap, Alvarez held his hand over the toaster, brought it close to the slots. He held it there for a half minute until it began to waver. He strained to survive a second or two more, then blew out a puff of breath, and jerked it away and rubbed the scalded palm against his thigh.

"I don't think you got it into your mind yet, Tyler, what I'm willing to do to find out where it is." Alvarez fiddled with the settings on the side of the toaster, moving the slide up and down to pick the level of browning. "Okay," he said, looking at Hap. "Come on, baby, let's do the dance."

"You could toast my cock, I wouldn't tell you shit."

"Your cock," Alvarez said. He studied the slots of the toaster. "Now, there's an idea."

"So you killed Hollings, Martina, the guy on the hood of the Rolls. You're having quite a night, Alvarez."

"You left one out," he said. "I bagged myself a U.S. senator tonight. Yes sir, brought her right back down to earth."

Alvarez cocked his head to one side, giving Hap a long look as if he were about to paint his portrait and was sampling different angles of light.

"Whatta you, about one seventy-five?"

Hap didn't reply.

"A guy your size, I think four cc's is about right. You know, 'cause with your brother, six cc's turned out to be too many. Six drove him right over the top. But I went back to my guy at Jackson Memorial, I checked with him. He agrees, six might've been pushing it. See, my guy's made a study of shit like this. Worked for Fidel for a while, experimental medical research in Cambinado del Este prison. How much of this or that chemical it takes to make a hard-case start to yammer."

Alvarez groped in his shirt pocket and came out with a syringe. He held it up toward the light, shook it once, squirted a small shot, then started moving around the table toward Hap.

He said, "In a way, I'm helping this guy out, carrying on a little field testing. So what we thought was, we'd lowball it this time. Four cc's of this, and add in the bagel toaster, that might be sufficient."

He was on Hap's side of the table now, a couple of yards away, blocking his route to the front door or the kitchen. The syringe was in his left hand. He lifted his right hand as if he were going to offer to shake and make up, then took another step forward.

He said, "See, I believed that ship was buried down there by the river. I had good reason to believe it. I went to a whole lot of trouble too. Rented a little bulldozer and everything. Put myself in some considerable jeopardy. And I had to take some human lives as a result. Now, I kind of blame that on you, Tyler. If you'd been a little more cooperative from the start, there's some people would still be alive right now."

He came a step closer. With his head he feinted right. When Hap didn't respond, Alvarez smiled.

"You know, when you drove off like that in the Rolls, I didn't know who the fuck you were at first. I thought I'd accounted for everybody, then there goes this car. Man, if I'd known it was you, I wouldn't have fired. 'Cause you're my goose, man, my golden egg maker. I don't want you dead, at least not yet. So anyway, I took a chance, decided to pay a visit over here, give you one last opportunity to make amends, you know, get a load off your chest.''

He flipped the syringe to his right hand, and waved his left at Hap. When Hap didn't respond, Alvarez came another step, smiling more boldly.

Hap wasn't sure how much fight he was capable of. The pain in his left shoulder had died to a leaden heat. And his arm felt like it had been detached, and replaced with a sack of stones.

As he watched Alvarez move in and felt the current of air moving through the house, Hap wondered absently how Daniel had faced his death. Had he struggled, or been an easy kill? So absorbed by history, the bygone things, perhaps it was simpler for him, an effortless stepping across.

Hap took a slow breath, kept his eyes on Alvarez, shifted his feet slightly. As the big man crossed the final yard between them, Hap feinted right, then dove left across the dining room table. He came up scrambling for the kitchen doorway.

But Alvarez made it around the table before he could get fully to his feet. The big man grabbed Hap's throat one-handed, raised the needle. With his good arm, Hap chopped at his hand, but Alvarez tightened his grip on Hap's throat and stabbed the needle through his cotton shirt, deep into Hap's chest. Hap hammered at Alvarez's hands, but couldn't move them as the big man thumbed the plunger down.

"Now," Alvarez said. "Maybe we can have ourselves a meaningful conversation."

Marguerite crouched on her hands and knees, aiming the weak flashlight beam out across the two trenches. About five feet apart, they ran parallel from the south to the north end of the house. Very neat and orderly. Apparently, the Tyler men had been taking their jolly good time. Going only as fast as was absolutely necessary, taking only a gold frog here, a gold mask there.

Marguerite was no engineer, but it looked to her that if they'd gotten too greedy, they might've undermined the foundation of the house, the coral boulders that held the structure three feet off the earth. Perhaps they could've had the house lifted, moved it, and then mined all the gold that was there. But probably the structure was too old and fragile for that. And that would mean they were forced to choose between their dwelling and the gold. From the size and length of the trenches, it was clear that the Commodore and Daniel had chosen to spare the house, for they had removed only the smallest fraction of what was there.

On the west side, propped against the coral, she saw a wide dark plank covered with intricate carvings. She crawled closer and played the light over it. Mermaids, stacks of cannonballs, dolphins playing in the choppy sea. A match to the chunk of transom that hung out in the breezeway. The piece she had passed by dozens of times going into the house, on her way up to Daniel's bedroom.

She let herself down into one of the trenches, and overhead she heard the dry scuttle of palmetto bugs along the floorboards. She passed her light over the side walls of the exploratory furrow, and everywhere she saw the glint of gold. The soil was littered with coins, the edges of gold bars, some delicate strands of woven gold. In five minutes she could have scratched out hundreds of thousands of dollars' worth of precious metal. It was as if someone had stirred so many chocolate chips into the recipe, there was hardly any room for the batter at all.

Her heart wild, she wriggled back toward the root cellar, the flashlight dying and reviving. Every foot of the way, her hands brushed across the chill gleam of silver and gold and jewels. Roaches swarmed in dark waves above her, and she heard the papery tick of their passing.

This was too many graves for one night. Though she had not seen a skeleton down here, or any fragment of bone, they must be here somewhere, the sailors, driven hard aground into this final landing. Flung overboard in the crash, or sunk with the ship. Or if they had somehow managed to escape, surely the fierce Calusas had made quick work of them somewhere nearby.

Her heart was churning. She wanted out of here, out of this dark claustrophobic space. This catacomb filled with the moist exhalations of the dead, the damp, rotten smell of opened earth.

As the feeble light passed over the two-by-fours that framed the entrance to the root cellar, she caught the glitter of more metal. She leaned to her right, craned to see into a small nook between the cellar wall and the coral foundation. Someone had wedged a wooden shelf in there, and on it sat a metal box.

It was not an antique, but shone like polished steel, no rust, no sign of decay. A fireproof case, just large enough to hold a pair of shoes. She'd seen ones like it at office supply stores. Something of very recent vintage. So in all probability it was Daniel who had thoughtfully left the key in its lock.

She reached for it, had to dust a large black roach away. She held the flashlight in her armpit as she pried open the lid. And inside the box was a stack of folded papers bound by a red ribbon. She set the case to her left on the flattened dirt, and pulled the ribbon off, and shook open the first brittle page.

After just a line or two, she knew what she held in her hands. Down there below the kitchen floor, trembling, she read each letter all the way through, and was about to begin them again when she heard Hap's voice coming from upstairs. A wild warbling of words. She bent to the trap door, tipped her head and listened. It didn't sound like him at all. But it was him.

She pulled herself up into the root cellar and lifted her head to the trap door. He was talking in a loud, off-key voice. He was speaking about windsurfing, about sailing. He was babbling about the water and the wind, about leaving footprints on the surface of the bay. Wearing paths into the ocean. About weight ratios and buoyancy factors. His voice was high and broken, straining against some pain she could almost feel herself.

Hap knew she would come. It was simply a matter of which of many unlucky moments she would choose. He listened to himself speak, a gibberish that seemed to flow through him, coming from the lowest cavity in his body, up through his chest, into his throat and mouth, spilling from him without his control.

Hap could see that Alvarez was growing more and more impatient. Twice already he had pressed Hap's hand into the scorching coils, and each time Hap had stifled a scream, trying in the only way he could to delay the inevitable. The moment when Marguerite stumbled into the room, put herself in the line of fire.

The drug that was cruising his body had put a sparkle in the air. Confetti of light fell in long spirals from the ceiling. He felt dreamy and wise and numbly terrified. Alvarez was speaking to him, but Hap couldn't make out what he said, and could no longer tell what he was saying in reply.

Marguerite stood in the doorway of the kitchen, dirty and disheveled. Stood in that doorway much as Louise, his mother, must have, as Rebecca before her had stood, bringing the evening meal into the narrow eating room. The table set, flowers in a vase, the fish and corn and greens filling the house with their hearty scent. And these women would come, following the requirements of their era. Entering the room as Marguerite was now, something in their hands to set before their men, the fruits of their labors, their contribution to this primitive life on the edge of the bay. Food for the family, to be praised, relished.

Marguerite carried a bundle of papers. As Alvarez pressed Hap's right hand into the coils, she crept closer. Alvarez kept glancing into Hap's eyes as he muscled the hand deeper, and though Hap could feel no exertion, he must have been resisting, for Alvarez sweated, the veins rising at his temples as he pushed Hap's hand down. He was in some kind of soundless vacuum. The words coming from him, and Alvarez answering, but none of it registering in Hap's ears. All he could hear was the quiet hum of his own charged blood.

Hap was certain that if he let his eyes wander to Marguerite again, Alvarez would see, turn in time to retrieve his shotgun and do the unthinkable. So he endured the pain, made it into somebody else's agony, somebody a long way down that foggy corridor in his head, a man who sweated and struggled, and moaned.

Hap didn't look at her when she set the papers carefully on the dining table. Only at the edge of his peripheral vision did he see when she reached out and picked up the heavy butcher knife that Alvarez had laid there. He didn't watch her as she moved down the side of the table, raising the knife as she came closer, until she was just a yard behind Alvarez, the big man speaking to him again, his mouth moving noiselessly, and though Hap did not look at Marguerite, somehow he saw her wince as she slashed the heavy knife down between the big man's shoulders.

Alvarez bellowed in Hap's face. He heard that. And the big man fell forward onto the dining table, then tumbled to the side, the knife planted deep in his back. While Marguerite screamed, Hap drew his bleeding hand from the toaster, came to his feet. The room was wobbling, the ceiling rising up and falling. Marguerite swayed a few feet away, looking helplessly at Hap.

With a fierce growl Alvarez pushed himself upright and twisted his arm behind him vainly to pull the knife free. Down the long, misty tunnel in his head, Hap watched Ray Alvarez in frantic slow-mo begin to search for his shotgun. Time scrambled. The seconds slowed and stretched without reason or connection. Hap reached out for Alvarez as the man extended his hand for the shotgun, which leaned against the end table, Hap saw his own hand draw back, become a fist, and fall like a mallet against the handle of the knife, and with another faraway roar Alvarez rose up, gripping the shotgun now, lifting it, aiming it. Hap struck the knife and struck it till it sunk to the hilt, he struck it again and another time. The seconds out of order.

And Marguerite staggered back, seemed to be thrown sideways, or she dove. He heard her scream. And then Hap heard the blast of the shotgun, coming from the end of that long, empty hallway, a remote echo of the blast, and he hammered the handle of the knife again, and hammered it another time, and he watched Alvarez fall forward onto his face, onto the wood floor.

The room whirled and squealed like some cheap carnival ride.

Steadying himself against the table for a moment, Hap found a breath, then another, and started the long, impossible walk across the room to locate Marguerite Rawlings. To hold her body, or what was left of it, against his own.

# CHAPTER 35

H AP CLEARED HIS THROAT, AND WAITED TILL THE GROUP
was quiet.

"Welcome," he said. "To the home of Miami's first and most
famous murderer."

The group mumbled among themselves. Fifteen of them this
afternoon. The ghoul train, he'd begun to call it. The second tour
today. Saturday, breezy. This morning he'd had to turn away about
a dozen. Sorry, folks, but these days you have to make an appoint-
ment a week ahead. This afternoon it was more venerable citizens,
another condo field trip.

Now with Thanksgiving approaching, the first cool fronts rolling through, people were getting out more. Seventy-eight degrees
and about the same humidity. It was what passed for autumn in this
town. And suddenly with the cooler weather, it seemed that everybody in Miami wanted a look at the scene of the crime.

Hap led the group into the dining room. They grew quiet,
respectful, old ladies in front, four or five men straggling at the
rear. This excursion clearly wasn't their idea. They looked more
like the dog-track set.

Hap closed the venetian blinds, switched on the Beseler and
the Commodore flickered onto the wall.

"That's him?" one of the women said softly.

"Yes," said Hap. "Commodore Randolph Tyler."

Hap let them have their fill of his image, then lowered the feeding tray, slid out the Commodore, and slid in Ramona Rawlings's photograph. The one of her he'd found in Daniel's safe-deposit box. She stood proud and smiling, her arm around her son Anthony. The rapids roaring behind them.

"And that was his victim," one of the ladies whispered loudly to her friends. "His lover."

"His would-be lover," Hap said. And he told them almost all he knew about Ramona, her ten-minute life story.

"Coontie?" one of the men said, when he'd finished. "Sounds dirty to me."

"Everything's dirty to you, Philip," one of the women said.

Hap removed Ramona's photograph, replaced it with the next item. He levered the Beseler closed and one of Romana's letters flashed onto the wall. As the old folks began to fish for their glasses, Hap read it for them. Saying the words that he'd repeated now a hundred, two hundred times. Little by little killing their hold on him.

" 'Dear Randolph,' " he read. " 'The necklace is exquisite. But I can not accept such an extravagant gift. Please come and retrieve it at once. For as I have told you on repeated occasions, as much as I am full of respect and admiration for you, sir, and feel everlasting gratitude for your vigorous support on behalf of our common cause, I simply do not have the emotional feelings that are required for the union you propose. And I assure you, no amount of jewelry will alter this fact. Sincerely, Ramona Rawlings.' "

"What necklace?" Philip asked.

Hap stepped into the brilliant light of the opaque projector and held up the jaguar necklace, displayed handsomely inside a glass case, compliments of Michael Overbeck at Crandon's Jewelry.

"As near as the police can reconstruct it," Hap said, "Ramona was murdered before she was able to return this necklace to the Commodore. It was discovered, we believe, in the rubble of the Rawlings house."

"These days," Philip said, "if the lady rejected him, she would've kept the necklace anyway." His women friends tried to shush him. Dear old Philip, white shoes, black knee socks running halfway up his bony legs, plaid Bermudas, a shirt that looked suspiciously like Ban-Lon.

Hap said, "Ramona Rawlings died the night of January fourteenth, 1898. As you'll see, Ramona sent another letter earlier the very day she was murdered."

Hap slid it into the feeding tray.

His audience shuffled their feet, muttered to each other. Even the men getting into it now.

Hap focused the Beseler and began to read.

" 'Randolph, I am shocked and horrified by your display of violent temper last night. Your actions are beyond apology. You say that if you can not have me, no one will. I am aghast. To believe you could woo me, win my hand with threats of murder and suicide, this is unforgivable. Please know, sir, that any future private meetings between us after this night are out of the question. If I must, I will protect myself and my son from you in any way I can. Do not come around the mill again.

" 'I considered telling Sheriff Parkingson what transpired between us on yesterday. But I decided I would spare you the public notoriety. For you to be disgraced in such a way would only do damage to our overriding concern, to save our paradise from further encroachment. However, be absolutely aware that I am fully prepared to go to Parkingson if any sort of similar threats of violence reach my ears. I have no doubt he will arrest you. So I ask you with all my heart, spare us both any future agony, and abandon your deranged quest for my affections. In the morning I will have Savannah bring over to you the jaguar necklace and one or two other tokens you have given me in the past few months. Ramona.' "

He let the group digest the letter and talk among themselves for a few moments.

"So," he said. "If you'll follow me upstairs."

"Those letters," one of Philip's friends said. "That's all the proof there is? I mean, son, I hate to rain on your parade, but once upon a time I was a lawyer, and believe me, those letters are not exactly evidence that would hang the old guy."

"It's enough proof for me," one of the women said. "The lady scorned him, and he was full of jealous rage."

"If I was on the jury, I'd vote to hang him," a man said. "He obviously threatened her."

"Where'd the murder happen?" Philip asked.

"At the mill," said Hap. "Across town. Mrs. Rawlings was shot through the head while standing in her kitchen."

"No, I mean the murder here."

Hap Tyler opened the blinds. He swallowed and brushed some dust off the edge of the dining table. He hated this. It was hell, but it was working. The same questions, the same answers, his own brutal brand of therapy. Better than the dulling drugs, the croquet at Radisson. Better than simply trying to dodge it all, spending his time out on the water.

No, this was working. Hellish, but working.

"On the night of August the twelfth, last August, the violent episode you're referring to occurred right over there, next to the fireplace."

Everyone craned for a look.

"What happened?"

"The newspaper clippings," said Hap, "are in a scrapbook by the front door. You can read them when the tour is finished."

Philip made a joke only a couple of his cronies could hear.

"What kind of wood is this?" one of the men asked, tapping his tennis shoe against the planks at the doorway.

"That," said Hap. "That's Pensacola pine."

"It's so red," he said, lifting his eyebrows.

Hap smiled vacantly at the man.

"The reddish hue comes from the chemicals the Commodore used to treat it. A mixture of diesel fuel and creosote. To make it impervious to rot and termites."

"It's not bloodstains?" Philip said.

"Philip, please. Be good." One of the women angled back through the group, and took the man's arm, and tugged it.

"Doesn't it cost a lot to keep up an old house like this?" one of the women asked. Deeply tanned, she was wearing shorts and a golf shirt.

"Yeah," Hap said, "it costs a bundle."

"You make enough from just the tours?" the grandmother said.

"The tours help. But I have a sort of private trust fund."

Hap raised his arms to herd them out of the dining room. He said, "Though I don't like to dig into that fund unless it's absolutely necessary."

"I can identify with that," Philip said.

"You know," the retired lawyer said, "I realize there're those who say we should study the past, learn from our mistakes and all that. The doomed-to-repeat school of thinking. But it seems to me, with a history like this house has, it'd be better to forget it. Tear it down, build something cheerful here. People don't come to Florida to hear about murder and mayhem. They come here to get away from all that stuff."

The lawyer looked around at his friends for approval. He got a majority vote of nods and murmurs.

"I like gloomy things," Philip said. "They cheer me up."

Hap Tyler led them upstairs, giving them the Commodore's history as they went. On the second floor landing, he pointed out the transom the Commodore had designed, showed them Daniel's bedroom. His collection of arrowheads, and flecks of pottery.

"What about that room?"

Hap stood in front of the closed door of his own bedroom.

"That's private," he said. "No admittance."

He was just winding up the tour when Jackie Wills came up the stairs. Jackie was fifteen, Jordan's kid. Hap had put him to work out in the boathouse, three afternoons a week. Together they'd already turned out a couple of dozen boards.

Hap was making them sleek again, painting them with the jazzy colors that most of the windsurfers liked. The design wasn't as fast as his old one had been, but fast, as he had come to believe, wasn't everything.

Jackie stood there waiting. Cut-off jeans, a long-sleeved white

T-shirt, orange lenses in his sunglasses. A thin kid with lots of blond hair. Took after his mother, Wills liked to say.

"Feel free to wander the grounds if you like," said Hap. "Take a look at the Devil's Punchbowl, the boathouse. And don't forget, if you're looking for something else to do, the Rawlings Mill museum will be open the first of next month. On South River Drive, just east of Twenty-seventh Avenue."

As they were going down the stairs, Philip told another joke. Hap heard something more about coontie. It got a good laugh, even a couple of the women joining in.

"Dad's here," Jackie said. "He came early again. So you think I could knock off now, go sail with him for a while? Wind's picking up pretty good."

"Sure," said Hap. "Go ahead."

"Okay, then, see you later."

He watched Jackie jog loose-legged down the stairs and out the front door. Having the kid around was giving the house a new set of vibrations. Made it feel lived in, vital, not just some gallery of horrors. Hap stood at the top of the stairs for a few moments, listening to the condo group scatter across the lawn.

Jackie was right, the wind was rising. It was pushing against the house, making the old timbers creak. In a minute or two it would find its way inside, swirl around downstairs, gather up the musty air, then bring it in a rush up the stairway, washing over Hap, and then it would rise up obediently and flow out those huge transoms, up into the Miami sky where it could begin its long recirculation.

When he heard the rumble of her Corvette, Hap went out on the balcony and watched her pull in next to his MG. She climbed out of the car, pushed her rich black hair out of her face, said hello to a couple of the condo crowd who were headed back to their van. He watched Philip take a long look at Marguerite's backside as she walked across the lawn to the house.

She stopped to talk to Wills and his son. Wills wearing a pair of pink surfer shorts and a yellow T-shirt, looking like a hot air balloon ready to lift off. The two adults laughed about something while Jordan's kid kept making motions toward the water.

Lately, Wills and Marguerite had been getting friendly, having private conversations sometimes, talking about things they wouldn't discuss with Hap. He didn't mind that. Kind of liked it really that Wills and Marguerite had secrets. It was good to have friends. And it was good to see that your friends had friends. Nothing wrong with a few secrets between friends.

Millicent Benitez presented the Commodore's letters and the Dade County medical examiner's report on Ramona's remains to Judge Merrie Beth O'Connor. And a week before Thanksgiving, Judge O'Connor called a special pretrial hearing. The five attorneys representing the various corporations owning businesses on the disputed land argued for over an hour that such a technicality as the one Miss Benitez was bringing forth, while legally having some small merit, would in practical terms cause such serious confusion and turmoil in the city of Miami were it to be substantiated, that the court could not possibly grant in favor of the litigants. The ninety-nine-year leases should simply be allowed to roll over, and the status quo maintained.

When they were finished, Judge O'Connor asked Hap if he had a position on this matter. He said as far as he was concerned, the goddamn land belonged to the Rawlings family, not his. And certainly not to these guys in blue pin-striped suits and eighty-dollar manicures. He was a hundred percent behind Miss Rawlings's suit.

Then Judge O'Connor listened silently to Millicent make her case, and to the five lawyers make their counterarguments. Then the judge stood up and came around to the front of her desk and sat on the edge of it. She told Marguerite that while clearly it seemed that her great-grandmother's murder was the means by which the land was taken from the Rawlings family, and that her suit did in fact have considerable merit, she nevertheless had to agree with the opposing attorneys, that the chaos Marguerite's action could cause within the city would be enormous and potentially quite damaging to the economic structure of Miami.

So, to spare everyone the ordeal of a public trial, perhaps Miss Rawlings would accept a financial settlement from the parties. The opposing attorneys mumbled that yes, they supposed their clients were willing to discuss a cash settlement of some kind.

"No," Marguerite said. "I'm not interested in money."

"Miss Rawlings, please," said Judge O'Connor. "Help me with this. I don't want to dismiss your action without some kind of due compensation."

"All right," she said, "then here's the deal."

Marguerite stood up, Millie staring at her. This wasn't part of the plan. Hap watched her pace silently in front of the manicured lawyers, her eyes down.

"I want three full-time attorneys of my choice who would represent the Miami Preservation League from this time on."

She came to a halt in front of Merrie Beth O'Connor.

"What?" the judge said.

The pin-striped guys looked at each other. Millicent simply stared. Hap was smiling, admiring her posture, the cut of her gray suit, the deep shine in her hair. That look she had in her eyes, a quiet self-assurance. She had these guys by the short and curlies, and everyone knew it.

"At present," said Marguerite, "Millie here is our only attorney. As good as she is, because of her own substantial practice, she's unable to do more than donate her energies on a part-time basis. What I want is for the affected businesses downtown to put aside funds sufficient to pay three attorneys of my choosing, full-time salaries for the next ninety-nine years. The term of their new leases on my land."

One of the young lawyers rose and stepped forward.

"Your Honor, Miss Rawlings expects us to pay the salaries of people who will have as their top priority to make our lives difficult? To fight every new construction project we might propose?"

"Exactly, Your Honor," said Marguerite. "They pay for our gunslingers to go up against their gunslingers. Simple as that. That's my deal. If they don't like it, we'll all go to court, and win or lose, a case like this is going to get a lot of press, and none of it is going to reflect well on your corporate clients or on your law firms."

The attorneys huddled. They made phone calls. They consulted privately with Judge O'Connor. The judge asked Millicent, Hap, and Marguerite to wait in the marble hallway outside the judge's office. So they went out into the hallway and listened to the voices inside the office, arguing, someone pounding on a desk. Hap was smiling like a simpleton the whole time. Millie shook her head a lot but said nothing.

When finally Judge O'Connor invited them back inside, she announced that Marguerite's proposal was acceptable. Details would be worked out under the judge's personal supervision.

"There's one other thing I want," Marguerite said.

"Oh, no, you don't," one of the attorneys said. "This is extortion. This is outrageous."

"I want to own my land," Marguerite said. "For just a day, I want what's mine, what I'm entitled to. One day, that's all."

The room was still for a moment, then one of the attorneys said quietly, "The woman's nuts."

"Maybe I am," Marguerite said, and smiled at Hap. "But that's what I want. Three full-time attorneys. And for one day before the ninety-nine-year leases roll over for another ninety-nine years, I want to legally own that land. My great-grandmother's land. My land."

"Well?" Merrie O'Connor said, looking at the five exhausted lawyers. Even the judge was starting to smile.

Hap said, "So how does it feel?"

It was late afternoon, the last day of November, the light beginning to thin. Marguerite's day to own the city. They'd finished their picnic beside the Miami River, they'd thrown rocks into the water for a while, watched the dark ripples die out before they reached the shore, and they'd watched a kid on the opposite bank fishing stubbornly in the acid sludge.

In the shade of an oak that had probably been a sapling during Ramona's lifetime, a checkered red-and-white tablecloth was spread out on the rocky ground before them. Burgundy wine, some Brie, grapes, an apple. Temperature in the seventies. Both of them watching the freighters pass by loaded with bicycles, mattresses, old cars. The kid across the way wore jeans and a white T-shirt. He looked about fourteen. And didn't seem to be disheartened that he'd caught nothing in the last few hours.

"So come on, tell me," he said. "How does it feel?"

"Not like I'd thought."

"How?"

"I know I own it." She patted the earth beside the tablecloth. "But it feels the same, maybe even a little less. It's better the other way."

"The other way?"

"Wishing for it, but not having it."

She tossed another pebble into the dark water.

"Maybe you just can't own anything," she said. "Not really. Not anything that matters."

"Maybe not," Hap said. Then a moment later, "My god, look."

The kid was hauling up a grouper. It splashed at the surface, but the kid had it hooked well and brought it in. When he had it up on shore, he held it up for Hap and Marguerite to see. Maybe ten pounds. Marguerite clapped for the kid's benefit.

"He did that fish a favor," Hap said. "Got him out of all that muck."

"You ready to go?" she said.

"Where to now? Want to go ride up and down inside one of your skyscrapers?"

"No," she said. "I want to go home."

They folded up the tablecloth, put the wine bottle back in the straw basket. They took a minute to scout the area, see if they'd left anything behind. Nothing. Just as they'd found it.

"My home or your home?" he said.

She looked at him for a moment, shifted the picnic basket to her other hand.

"Just home," she said.

"Yeah," said Hap. "That sounds good. Home."